"You wanted a business arrangement, Rafe.

"And that's what I'm offering. You help me save Sean. I help you save Zoe."

What about the fact that every time we come within kissing range, sparks fly? Rafe wanted to say. He was half tempted to reach for her and prove his point. But let him stroke her once and she might fly to pieces. Still, he couldn't let it go. "Zoe's requirement for her baby is a two-parent loving family. I don't see how I can sell her on a make-believe marriage."

"You seemed to think you could before," Dana observed.

Putting a finger to her chin, he brought her head around. "I meant to wed you and bed you and make the best of the deal while we were together," he said fiercely. "I don't call that a sham."

She jerked her chin away. "Whatever you care to call it, I don't want it! I'm offering a merger of interests—not a marriage of hearts."

Marriage. To Dana. Rings and lace and driving off with tin cans clattering, hands clasped. *With my body I thee worship.* He wasn't alone in this feeling, whatever she said. *Patience*, he reminded himself.

"Well?" she demanded. "Take it or leave it."

He shifted uncomfortably in his seat. "You've got yourself a deal," he said huskily. "When?"

Dear Reader,

The nicest thing about being an author is that I get to "fix" things. Doesn't work that way in the real world. But, on paper, Readers, I can make the world so...sweet.

Better yet, I can take the best of the dozen best men I've ever met and meld them into one great man. I can give him the postman's gorgeous eyes, the buns of that senior quarterback who never even knew I existed back when I was fourteen, my father's fierce "family man" instincts, my own man's deliciously arrogant, maddening, entrancing sense of macho—but maybe I'll insert a tidiness gene stolen from my accountant.

Well, I knew from the moment I created Dana Kershaw, in *Don't Mess with Texans*, that I'd have to get back to her. Her life needed fixing. No way could I leave her pregnant and grieving, fighting a gallantly losing battle to honor her promises, while she struggled to hang on to a tottering little dude ranch in southwestern Colorado. She needed help, and so did her confused and lonely stepson, Sean.

They needed a good man, a family man, a tall-in-the-saddle, blue-eyed, steadfast Solution to their problems. They needed...Rafe Montana.

So I sat down to my ancient computer, put the cat in my lap and started to write. ("This I can fix!")

Hope you enjoy their story, and thanks, as always, for reading it!

Peggy Nicholson

THE BABY BARGAIN
Peggy Nicholson

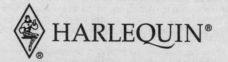

HARLEQUIN®

TORONTO · NEW YORK · LONDON
AMSTERDAM · PARIS · SYDNEY · HAMBURG
STOCKHOLM · ATHENS · TOKYO · MILAN · MADRID
PRAGUE · WARSAW · BUDAPEST · AUCKLAND

ISBN 0-373-70929-3

THE BABY BARGAIN

Copyright © 2000 by Peggy Nicholson.

This book is for my dad, Erwin Grimes of Kerrville, Texas, who gave me my wings.

And as always, Ron. Thank you.

CHAPTER ONE

A YEAR AGO TODAY, St. Patrick's Day, he and his dad had sat here in this booth, eating bacon cheeseburgers. Guys' Night Out, his dad had called it, and he'd ordered the jumbo basket of onion rings, then winked at Sean, both of them knowing that if they'd brought Dana along, she would have fussed about too much grease and cholesterol.

That was the last meal they'd ever shared. Sean had slept over in town that night with the Wilsons, though he'd protested that he was old enough to stay by himself out at the Ribbon R for a three-day weekend. "Or you could take me with you," he'd pleaded, not for the first time. "It's not like missing one crummy Friday is going to hurt my grades." He'd been a straight-A student last year in ninth grade, when things like that mattered. Seemed to matter.

If you'd taken me along... He'd never have let it happen. Somehow Sean felt that if he'd been with them, he'd have known not to cross that hillside. Or if it had happened— the avalanche—he'd never have quit—never, ever, *never*— till he found his dad and dug him free. Not like Dana, who hadn't dug deep enough, fast enough, long enough. Stupid, gutless Dana, who quit and skiied off for the help that came too late.

Quitter. Anger felt like a lump of smoldering charcoal in his stomach, gray-white dust over a ruby center. He picked up his glass of soda and took a tiny sip—had to make it last—then jumped as Judy, the night waitress at Moe's Truckstop, loomed up behind him.

"Here, you're done with that, kiddo." She reached for his plate, which still held a curl of limp lettuce and a slice of tomato.

"Am not!" He caught hold of it and glared up at her. He didn't have enough money to order anything else, but he was darned if he'd leave yet. The Ribbon R was nothing but an aching and an emptiness. Nobody but Dana and her loudmouth baby waiting there for him.

"Suit yourself." Judy shrugged and turned to welcome the group coming through the arch from the front room—the convenience store Moe ran—of the truck stop. "Sit anywhere you like," she called, and headed toward the counter where she kept the menus.

Kids from school, Sean realized, watching them as they chose the big circular booth on the far side of the café. Seniors. They didn't spare him a glance. The biggest guy, a football jock, maneuvered his date with a possessive hand at the small of her slender back.

The skin on Sean's palm tingled as if it slid across silk. He curled his fingers hard around the feeling, making a fist, as the jock's date smiled up at him and edged into the booth. She wore a long, slinky yellow dress, with a dyed green carnation pinned between her breasts. Sean swallowed with an audible gulp, wondering if she had let the jock pin it on her—the lucky stiff—then jumped as the three boys at the table swung their heads to fix him with cold, unblinking stares.

Caught me looking. Wishing. He turned back to his plate and hunched his shoulders. With the girls' giggles sounding like sleigh bells behind him, he felt his face grow hot, then hotter. Frantically he grabbed his drink and rubbed the misty glass across his cheek. Oh, no, was the back of his neck turning red?

"California," one of the guys jeered, not bothering to lower his voice.

Almost a curse word, Sean had learned since he'd moved here from San Diego two years ago. Coloradans thought Californians were buying up every last acre of their lousy state that the Texans hadn't already grabbed. Though who in his right mind would want it? *If I had my way, I'd go back to San Diego in a heartbeat.* He would, too, any day now, as soon as his mother felt well enough to take him. A wave of emotion swept through him, like a black hole yawning wide; greasy slopes led down into his own private darkness. He closed his eyes tight and waited for the feeling to pass.

"Sean?" Judy patted his shoulder. "Your mama's on the phone." She nodded toward the corridor that led to the rest rooms and the pay phone.

"My—" Hope flew up like a startled bird—then fell as he realized. "My stepmother, you mean."

"That nice, nice lady named Dana, who your daddy liked enough to marry—yep, that one. She wants you."

"Tell her I'm not here," he blurted desperately.

"Ha! I'm not your press secretary, Mr. President. Tell her yourself."

He kept his eyes on his sneakers as he casually crossed the room, but he stole a glance over his shoulder as he reached the hallway.

The three girls in the booth were all primped up, wearing fancy dresses in bright colors. The St. Patrick's Day dance was tonight, he remembered. Another reason he'd felt blue today. *I wonder if I'll ever have a date.* The few friends he'd made in his first year at the high school he'd lost, because he just couldn't make himself care. The only girl he really talked to was Zoe, but she was a senior and his boss on the yearbook. The head editor. Nobody a sophomore could ever date.

The receiver of the wall-mounted pay phone dangled at knee level. He sighed and picked it up. "'Lo."

"Sean?" Dana's low voice hummed with tension.

"Yeah." He should have just hung up on her. He sighed again and swung around to slouch against the rough plaster.

"You…didn't come home."

Yeah, no fooling, Sherlock. He didn't say anything.

"Did you miss your bus?"

I gave it a miss, right. If there was one day of the year he couldn't stand the sight of Dana…that he needed to spend by himself, this was it. Crappy St. Patrick's Day. "Looks like it, doesn't it."

He heard her sigh down the telephone line. "I can't pick you up, Sean. We have guests tonight—for the whole week—skiers. I'm just about to put supper on the table."

"Doesn't matter." In San Diego he could have taken a cab home, the way his mother always did when she'd partied too much. In Trueheart, Colorado, it'd be easier to catch a coyote and ride it home. Or hitch. "I'll manage."

"Judy gets off work at ten. She said she'd be happy to give you a ride."

No way. He'd rather walk ten miles in the snow and slush than listen to one of Judy's pull-up-your-socks pep talks. "Don't worry about it. I'll manage."

"Sean, honey, *please*. Come home. I know what you're—"

"No. You don't." He replaced the receiver on its hook with stony deliberation—it was that or smash it against the phone, then keep on smashing till he held nothing but splinters. *No, you don't.* He was standing, staring at his fingers curled around the black plastic, when an icy draft brushed his cheek.

Someone coming through the fire exit at the end of the hallway, he saw from the corner of his eye. She slammed the door behind her and stood panting, one hand pressed to her throat—long, tall Zoe Montana, reminding him of a

Christmas tree with her shiny green dress and her carrot-red hair. He felt better already, just looking at her.

"Oh, *rats!*" she said. Her fine, goldy-red eyebrows drew into a scowl. "You didn't see me."

"I didn't?" She was hard to miss. She was taller than his five foot six-and-a-half inches by several more, though he was all muscle while she was all freckly skin and bones—most of that leg, like one of those big wading birds. *A stork on fire,* the captain of the football team had called her once in the cafeteria, and everybody had laughed.

She let out a long-suffering sigh, the way she did when one of the airheads on the yearbook staff failed to meet a section deadline, and hooked a thumb at the door to the ladies'. "Is anybody in there?"

"Uh, don't think so."

"Thank *God.*" She slipped around the door and vanished.

Sean crossed his arms, leaned back against the wall and waited. Zoe Montana was maybe the only person in True-heart worth talking to.

She came out a few minutes later, looking less wild eyed. More like the yearbook editor about to give her most junior photographer a shooting assignment. But then, Zoe's assignments were always interesting. She was the smartest girl—the smartest *person*—in their whole regional high school, and that probably included the teachers.

"What are you doing here?" he asked. And in a long, silky dress. She always wore slacks or jeans to school, with bulky sweaters and funky lace-up knee boots. Or clunky Steve Maddens, which raised her height to over six feet, when she was in a mood to kick butt. Idly he lifted his fingers, shaping a square to frame her, and wished he had his camera. It was the first time he'd ever realized Zoe was more than funny looking. *Snckk.* He took a mental photograph.

"Is there anybody out there?" Zoe nodded toward the café. "Anybody from school, I mean?"

"Some jocks and jock-bunnies, eating supper before the dance." The dance that Zoe must be going to, also, Sean realized with quickening interest. He didn't know she had a boyfriend. Who would be sharp enough to keep up with her?

"Shoot. I'm dying for a cup of coffee." She sagged back against the opposite wall.

"Then come have one with me." He was astonished at his own daring—then his heart sank as he remembered. *Crap!* He had less than a dollar left.

"Thanks, but…" She shook her head. "I'm not in the mood for company." Her eyes sharpened on his face. "I mean the kind of company in there." She crossed her forefingers between them. "No clowns tonight. Not one more."

"Oh." He had clowning down to an art form, but he didn't think she meant him. Still, Sean felt like a bozo, with nothing more to say. "I guess you're going to the dance?" He threw out the question at random.

"I guess I'm *not.*"

"But you're all…" He waved his hand, taking in her finery. She even had boobs, he realized, stealing a peek at the gap between the long lapels of the coat that matched her party dress. Not honkers, but somehow right for Zoe. Her clothes had always disguised them before.

"The creep stood me up—okay?" she said between clenched teeth.

"Or maybe he had car trouble," Sean suggested, wanting to wipe that look of angry humiliation off her face. She didn't deserve to be stood up just because she was too tall and too smart for her own good.

"No, I finally called his house. His little brother told me he had a date with Amanda Clayton and that he'd already left.'' Zoe stared blankly down at the toes of her green high heels.

Amanda Clayton? A babe, if Sean had ever seen one. Little and brunette and cuddly. *And dumb as a post.* Her longtime steady had rolled his car after a party last weekend, Sean had heard, and was in the hospital down in Durango with both legs in casts. High school dances were like a game of musical chairs, he'd always thought, and this time poor Zoe was left standing. Stork ablaze. "So why didn't you just…" *Call me?* He'd have been happy to help her out.

"Stay home? Right, and tell my dad why? He'd have stomped down to the gym and dragged Bobbie out by his ear. Or maybe shot him. I have enough to live down without that, thank you. So I—" Zoe shrugged and turned toward the fire exit. "I've got to go." She spun back again, tottered on her heels, and braced one long arm out against the wall. "Oh, and Sean, do me a favor? You never saw me.''

She must be just riding around, he realized, killing time till it was safe to go home. "Then how about a favor for a favor?" Her embarrassment made him feel bolder. "Could you give me a ride out to the ranch? There's no hurry,'' he added, as she opened her mouth. "You could drop me at my turnoff out on the highway—any time tonight at all.''

She closed her soft pink lips and cocked her head, studying him. Being Zoe, he knew, she saw more than he wanted to show. He shrugged and held her blue-eyed gaze with an effort.

"Yeah, I could do that," she said thoughtfully, her eyes turning inward in that look that usually ended in another crazy assignment for him—like the time she'd hidden him in the ceiling above the teachers' lounge to take candid photos. "I'd be happy to.''

TWO HOURS OF CRUISING around in Zoe's baby-blue antique Mustang. Sean had held his breath when they drove past the small sign out on the highway that said Ribbon River Dude Ranch, 4 miles, Guests Welcome, but Zoe had given him a sideways smile and had kept on driving. All the way to Cortez, where they bought hamburgers and French fries—Zoe's treat—at the drive-through window in the McDonald's. They ate in the parking lot while they punched the buttons on her car radio, ceaselessly scanning the airwaves for anything but country music. Sean preferred hard rock, golden oldies, songs that reminded him of the West Coast; Zoe liked anything with a Latin sound. Her mother had been Hispanic, Sean remembered her telling him once while they developed film in the school darkroom. That was another thing they shared, besides their impatience with small-town life: they'd both lost a parent; though Zoe's mom had died ages ago, when she was six.

Driving back, they passed the Ribbon R again. "You don't want to go home yet," Zoe said, and it wasn't quite a question. She drove almost halfway to town, then flipped on her blinker as they neared the turnoff to the private airport that lay a few miles to the south. Sean felt his stomach jump, then swarm with butterflies. Surely she couldn't mean to—

But she did. Zoe chose the left-hand fork in the road, which wound around the back side of the airport, and stopped at the far end of the north-south runway, where the road skirted the edge of a bluff. She parked facing the drop-off, with the far-off lights of Trueheart twinkling in the thin mountain air like diamonds scattered in the snow. Two other cars were parked at discreet intervals along the overlook. Sean stole a glance at the one on his right, but its windows were too steamed up for him to see anything.

"I come here in summer to watch the planes take off," Zoe said, ignoring their neighbors. "Did you ever do that?

They zoom right overhead. It feels like they're going to snap off your antenna they fly so low—then *whoosh*—they're out there beyond you and gone.''

"Wow." His throat was too dry, and his mind a blank. What did she want from him?

"I'm going to fly away like that one of these days. Soon. I just got admitted to Harvard—early admission. Did I tell you that?''

She hadn't, but he'd heard. The whole school had been abuzz with the news last week. Nobody from their school had ever been admitted to Harvard. And Zoe Montana was the baby of her class, a year younger than the next youngest senior—not even seventeen yet, since she'd skipped a grade of school back in elementary.

"That'll be neat." For her. For him it meant he'd have zero friends next year, instead of one. "I wish I could fly away." His mother's last letter from the health spa had said he should be patient, finish the tenth grade in Colorado. But after that, surely she'd agree that he belonged with her. If he belonged anywhere.

"Yeah," Zoe murmured without conviction, then said it again, louder and brighter. "Yeah! Boston…Harvard… Everything's going to be different then. Better."

He glanced at her, surprised. What was wrong with her life now? She had an overdose of brains. A grudging respect in the school, if not popularity. A rich rancher daddy who loved her—he must love her to have given her this wonderful car. And she was escaping Southwest Colorado, going off to the real world where exciting things happened. She was practically grown up, practically free, while he—he was trapped here in Nowhere City. Trapped by his own age—couldn't drive, couldn't drink, couldn't vote, couldn't hold a real job. Couldn't choose with whom he wanted to live. His dad had appointed Dana his guardian, and had never once asked Sean what he thought about that.

"Oh, rats, rats, *rats!*" Zoe started the Mustang, reversed it hastily onto the road, then popped it into forward gear. The tires slipped on an icy rut, then caught, and they zoomed off around the perimeter road.

"Hey, your headlights!" Sean reached for the switch, and she batted his hand aside.

"Uh-uh! Look behind you."

Sean turned—to see that a car had stopped behind the first car back at the bluff. A spotlight switched on, illuminating the luckless couple twined together in the backseat. "The sheriff!"

"Nosy Noonan. And he's a friend of my dad's." Zoe passed the first hangar and hung a hard right, driving along the far side of the building toward the airfield, then tucked her Mustang in neatly ahead of a pickup truck set up as a snowplow.

The giant curved blade blocked Sean's view of the road entirely, provided perfect cover. "Whew!" She was clever.

"Get down, get *down!*" she cried in a giggling frenzy. "If he shines his light…!" She leaned sideways toward him over the gearshift, her frizzy hair brushing his knees. Sean laughed and hunched down over her, his chest pressed against her quivering shoulder. He stayed there that way, in a state of total bliss, long after the sheriff's car had cruised past. Her shampoo smelled of lemon and a spice Dana used sometimes in her cooking; rosemary, that was it. Something soft was touching his thigh, and he thought— hoped—prayed—it was her breast.

"Is it safe to come out?" she asked finally in a muffled voice.

"I think…" Except he wasn't. He was absorbed totally in feeling all the wonderful sensations of a warm girl sprawled across his lap. Zoe. Her giggles made her seem younger, more his own age than an impossible two years older.

She jabbed an elbow gently into his ribs, and he had to sit up. Curling one hand around his thigh just above his knee, she pushed herself upright—then slowly turned her head to look at him over her right shoulder. Their lips were only inches apart.

Every muscle in his legs tensed and hardened. Heat pooled in his lap. *Oh, Zoe!*

She pulled completely away from him and sat, clutching her steering wheel, staring out through the windshield.

He counted his own heartbeats, dizzy from the lack of blood in his head. *What do you want from me, Zoe Montana?* Anything, anything at all that she wanted, he'd give—and give gladly.

"Want to see a special place?" she said finally, not looking at him, her voice sounding funny. "My special place?"

TEN MINUTES LATER they sat in the cockpit of a wrecked Cessna, which was parked on the far side of the hangar. Zoe had claimed the pilot's seat, which to Sean seemed only fitting. She could take him anywhere she wanted tonight.

They even had supplies for their journey. Zoe had pulled two down sleeping bags, and a sack that contained water and granola bars, from the trunk of her car—part of a safety kit her father made her carry in winter, in case she ever was caught out in a blizzard.

"I found this last fall." Zoe stroked the Cessna's steering yoke. "Some elk hunter flipped it coming in for a landing. He walked away and swore he'd never fly again. Something's twisted in the frame. Luke, the mechanic here, bought it cheap from the insurance company. Said he's going to fix it one of these days. But meanwhile she just sits here, all lonely."

"Cool." In every sense of the word. Huddled in his ski

jacket, Sean was starting to shiver, partly from the cold, partly from excitement.

"I'm going to be a pilot someday," Zoe said dreamily. "Dad promised he'd pay for my flying lessons when I graduate from college."

And *his* dad had promised that when Sean graduated from high school, he'd give Sean a motorcycle, an old Harley he could fix up himself. That they'd ride together all the way up to Alaska, then back again, the summer after his senior year. Dreams…so fragile that a mound of moving snow could crush them. The snowbound runway beyond the windshield shimmered, then blurred, and Sean blinked frantically. "So tell me about college, what that'll be like."

"College…" She tipped back her head and stared up at the dented ceiling. "It's going to be…different. Very, *very*…different."

"Different how?"

She turned to fix him with her wide, light eyes, and was quiet so long that he wondered if he'd said something really stupid. "I'm freezing," she said at last. "Want to get into the bags?"

They zipped themselves into the puffy down bags and sat shoulder to shoulder in the wide, flat space in the rear that once must have held passenger seats.

"Much better," Zoe murmured, leaning against him. She sighed contentedly. "Mmm…how will college be different? Well, for starters, nobody's going to call me a brain, or a grind or a teacher's pet at Harvard. I won't be a freak. I'll be normal."

Just as he had been a normal kid, back in San Diego, before Dana married his dad and lured them off to Colorado. "That's good."

"Yeah…and maybe I'll throw all my clothes away and start over. No more thumbing my nose at the cowgirls and the cheerleaders. I want a whole new image—sleek, elegant, sophisticated. I'm going to scout the campus for a day or two when I get there. Before I check in. See what everybody's wearing…''

He was so used to Zoe's rebel tomboy looks that it was hard picturing her dressing to blend in, but Sean knew what she meant. You got tired of fighting, but what else could you do? Once they had you pigeonholed, they'd laugh at you even harder if you tried to change. If he broke down and bought a Stetson and boots like the cow-patty crowd wore, that wouldn't get him accepted now. They'd brand him as a phony—and a coward.

"And maybe I'll switch to using my middle name. Elena.'' She gave it the Spanish pronunciation, making it sound rich and exotic.

I'd miss "Zoe." But he nodded gravely. A fresh start; it was what he wanted, too. "Elena—it's pretty.''

"And…'' She tipped her head down to rest it against his shoulder. "Promise you won't tell anyone?''

"I swear.'' He drew a shaky breath and, holding it, put his arm around the soft, puffy expanse of her waist. When she didn't stiffen, didn't pull away—actually seemed to settle a little closer against him—he felt as if the Cessna had taken off. He was floating, flying… "I swear I won't.''

"I'm thinking of dyeing my hair. Black. Or maybe an auburn so dark it's practically black.''

He loved her crazy red hair, loved the fact that, in her own way, she was a freak like him, a fish in the wrong pond. Even holding her, he felt a wave of loneliness wash over him. She was soaring away, off to somewhere she'd fit in, while he—

"You think that's crazy?'' Zoe demanded in a tiny, dubious voice.

While he—he was her friend. Here to back her up, even when she was crazy—and dyeing her fire-engine-red curls was the worst kind of crazy crime. "No... No, I don't think so. I think you'd look wonderful with black hair," he lied. "Or maybe...um...auburn? That might be an even better idea." At least, less of a crime.

"Good!" she laughed delightedly. "I'm *so* glad you think so!" Somehow she'd slipped down to half-lie across his lap—the nylon bags were slippery. She squirmed around to rest her head across his thighs, smiling up at him. "And that brings me to one last little thing I mean to change."

He stared down at her, helplessly, hopelessly enthralled. "W-what?"

"I thought maybe you could help me with this..." She stared up at him, smiling no longer, then reached up to finger the collar of his jacket. "You see...the problem is...I'm still a virgin."

CHAPTER TWO

WHEN MITZY BARLOW invited him over for Saturday supper, the first week in June, Rafe Montana had gone gladly, anticipating an evening of hot, no-holds-barred sex.

Instead she'd served pot roast.

She'd served it up with such a hopeful, fluttery smile—fussing over the homey details like candles on the table, bran rolls she'd baked herself, glazed carrots just like the ones he'd enjoyed in the restaurant last week when he took her out on their first date—that Rafe realized immediately, with a sinking heart, that this wasn't to be a simple night of fun between two healthy, sensible adults who knew precisely what they wanted.

Oh, no, this was an audition. Along with the peas, pot roast and carrots, Mitzy was dishing out all the unspoken reasons she'd make a good—no, a perfect—wife. *His* perfect wife.

How could a man so misread a woman's intentions? Rafe wondered, scowling through the windshield as his headlights fled before him up the valley. He would have sworn from the way she talked last week—hell, from the way she came on to him—that they were in complete agreement. After dinner they'd danced, and you couldn't have wedged an ace of hearts between them, the way she'd melted into his arms. And later, when he'd walked her to her door, Mitzy had made it crystal clear what she wanted. While he kissed her good-night, she'd drawn the hand he'd placed lightly on her shoulder down to her breast—then held it there while she moaned and squirmed against him. He'd felt plain apologetic, when he came up for air, explaining that he couldn't stay. That since he hadn't presumed to make arrangements for someone to sleep over with his daughter out at Suntop Ranch, he had to go home to Zoe.

Mitzy had caught him off guard on their first date. But this Saturday, when she'd insisted in a husky voice that it was *her* turn to entertain *him,* he'd come prepared. At his pointed suggestion, Zoe was sleeping over in Trueheart tonight with her best friend, Lisa Harding. And yesterday he'd stopped by the barber's for a trim, a week before his usual cut. Plus he'd shaved for the second time today, just before setting out. And along with a thirty-dollar bottle of French wine, he'd brought a wallet full of condoms.

But then Mitzy served pot roast—her great-grandmother Barlow's recipe. Rafe had sat there at the table with his expectant grin fading on his face, wondering if he should tell her how he felt before the meal. Or after.

Like all men, he was a coward when it came to hurting a woman, so he'd opted for after, praying with each bite of overdone beef that he was wrong. That Mitzy just liked to cook. Or that maybe she was building up his strength for the evening's entertainment.

No such luck. Along with the strawberry shortcake, their limping conversation had taken a turn for the worse. Mitzy had started quizzing him on Zoe. How had he ever *managed,* raising a small daughter alone out on a ranch miles from anywhere, without even a neighbor's wife to give him advice?

She'd shaken her head and smiled knowingly when he'd insisted they'd managed just fine. Seeing that smirk, he'd felt his temper rise. No one had better hint to *him* that he hadn't done his best for Zoe. He'd shaped his whole life around her from the very start.

And he hadn't been fool enough to try to raise her alone,

though he owed Mitzy no explanation and so had given none. He'd recruited Mrs. Higgins to be their live-in housekeeper after Pilar's death, and that arrangement had worked out fine.

At least it had up until last year, when Mrs. Higgins had fallen head over heels for the new county agent and, after thirty years a widow, remarried. Since then, she could only come three days a week to cook and clean, but neither Zoe nor he would have dreamed of trying to replace her. After all these years, she was family. Besides, by this time Zoe hardly needed constant supervision.

"But if it wasn't so bad before," insisted Mitzy, "what about now, now that she's…um…a young lady?" Didn't Rafe find himself at a loss dealing with sex and the other issues a young woman faced?

"When it comes to the birds and the bees, ranch kids learn most of the answers before town kids think up the questions," Rafe had observed dryly. As to other issues— things a teenage daughter wouldn't care to discuss with her own father—she could take those to Mrs. Higgins.

Besides, though this was nothing he'd share with Mitzy, Zoe was maturing late. That date earlier this spring, for the St. Patrick's Day dance, had been her first real night out. And apparently nothing had come of it. The kid—what had his name been—Bobbie?—must not have measured up. Which hardly surprised Zoe's father. She had been chosen valedictorian of her class this spring, just as he'd predicted. He'd been so puffed up with pride, watching her give the graduation address last week, he'd thought he might burst. But where was a girl like that going to find someone to match her in a small town like Trueheart? It was one more reason he'd pushed her to apply to Harvard.

"But now that she's interested in boys, don't you think she needs advice on how to dress, how to behave…how to flirt?" Mitzy demanded.

"She's not interested. Not yet," he said to close off this line of inquisition. He felt his teeth come together with a *click* when Mitzy burst out laughing.

"At sixteen? Of course she is, Rafe! And if you think she isn't, that just shows how out of touch you really are."

He kept the edge out of his voice with an effort. "She's been pushing herself hard in school these past four years, Mitzy. Really hard. She has won national awards four years running in the science fairs. And then with her extracurricular work—the yearbook and choir. And volunteering down at the hospital in Durango—"

"But I suppose Zoe knows you'd disapprove of her choice," Mitzy mused, ignoring him entirely. "I imagine any young man who dared to date *your* daughter would have to pass a pretty fierce inspection at the door."

She had that double-damn right, at least. But that was beside the point. As yet, there were no randy young studs sniffing after Zoe for him to check out. Zoe was too busy being a tomboy and a scholar. "That doesn't leave much time for boys," he finished, and smacked down his coffee cup. End of subject.

"Oh, there's *always* time for boys," Mitzy purred, rising from the table. She came up behind him, and, resting one hand possessively on his shoulder, reached around him for the dessert he'd barely touched. Her forearm drew across his chest, and her breast brushed the back of his arm.

Rafe felt himself stiffen all over. He went too long between women. Managing a spread the size of Suntop Ranch, he had little time or energy left to go courting in town, where the available women were. And bringing a lover back to the ranch, with his daughter living there, had never been an acceptable solution. At least that would be changing soon, when Zoe went off to college.

"Let's have our brandy in front of the fire, shall we?" Mitzy said from the counter, lifting two balloon glasses.

Rafe sighed and followed her to her big couch in the living room, which he'd noted with approval only an hour ago when he first arrived. One reason he went a long time between lovers was that he refused to play the games that some men played. He couldn't stomach stringing a woman along, pretending to agree with her dreams when he was after something else entirely.

Still, though he believed in straight talk, he hesitated. Telling another person that you knew what she wanted, before she'd declared herself, felt downright rude. On the other hand, maybe these tippy-toe hints were as close to a declaration as Mitzy could come.

She handed him his brandy, then clinked her glass against his. *"To us,"* she said softly, and held his gaze over the rim as she drank. She licked her upper lip, then smiled a slow invitation.

But Rafe was stuck back on "us." There was no "us" yet, as far as he was concerned. "Us" sounded like a matched pair in harness trotting down the long, long road together. *No, thanks, Mitzy.* She was moving way too fast. "To good times," he said firmly.

"What about you?" Mitzy murmured, snuggling back into the hollow of his shoulder. "With your chick leaving the nest in September, won't you be terribly...lonely?"

"No." He finished half his glass in a gulp, and straightened the arm she was leaning against along the top of the sofa, making himself into a hard, unbending corner. "I won't be." At least, he thought not. "You've got to understand, Mitzy. I've been sitting on that...nest for almost seventeen years." Hatching his one fabulous, freckled egg for the past ten years all by himself, except for Mrs. Higgins. "I was nineteen when Zoe was born."

"That must have been *so* hard," she said softly. "But I suppose the good side of it is, now you're still a young man. Why, you even have time to start a second family, if you feel like it.''

"What I feel like, after all this time of being a responsible, hard-working daddy, is taking a break," he said bluntly. "Being footloose and fancy free. Free to come and go as I choose, when I choose." To chase one woman or twenty, or none at all.

She was right; he was still a young man. But he'd missed most of the good times that a young man enjoyed. Those wild and crazy times that made the best memories, that a man could look back on with rueful pleasure when he reached his settle-down years. So far, Rafe had had to live his life backward, and though he didn't regret it—look what he had to show for his hard work—still… If this wasn't his time now, when would it ever be?

"Oh," Mitzy said in a small voice.

Good, she was getting his message.

"Do you mean to…travel much?" She tipped her head to gaze up at him.

"Some," he allowed cautiously. As manager and part owner of one of the region's largest ranches, he'd never be able to travel far or long. But he'd finally found himself a good foreman, and he paid the man well enough to keep him. Anse could take up the slack if Rafe wanted a week or two away in the off-seasons.

Though it wasn't as if Rafe had any particular plans. He wasn't one of those middle-aged idiots desperately trying to recapture the lost years and live them now. At thirty-five, he was too old, too stiff, to hit the rodeo trail, although that had been his intention before he and Pilar had made a baby.

And he was too wise to chase the girls he'd missed out on seventeen years ago—the pretty rodeo queens, the spunky barrel racers, the sassy waitresses. Somewhere along the line his tastes had changed. To him, those girls all looked like slightly older sisters of Zoe, staying up way past their curfews. No, nowadays when he wanted company, he wanted a warm and knowing woman in his bed, not some giggling child.

The warm woman leaning against him stirred. "I've always wanted to travel, too. I've been thinking about flying down to Cancún, sometime this month. Laze around the beach, drink too many margaritas, take a lo-o-ong siesta every afternoon." She arched her back and smiled up at him then, and hooking an arm around his neck, leaned backward. "Want to come with me?"

If there hadn't been so many strings attached... Rafe had shaken his head regretfully, resisting the urge of both gravity and nature to follow her down on the cushions. "June is branding month, moving the cows up from the home pastures..." And he was a full-time father for one last summer, before he could cut loose.

She pouted prettily. "What if I waited till July?"

"I don't think you should wait for me," he'd said in all truth. Any woman who dreamed of starting a second family with *him* would have a long, long wait, indeed.

He'd made his excuses and left soon after that, though it had been a hard-won retreat. Sensing his cooling, Mitzy had redoubled her efforts to fan his flames. But knowing she wouldn't thank him tomorrow if he took what she was offering tonight, he'd politely declined—and gained no gratitude for his self-control. He winced, remembering her final tearful reply as he stood shuffling on her doorstep, hat in his hands.

"Thanks? Thanks for *nothing,* cowboy!"

"Well, damnation, what was I supposed to do?" he now asked the night and the mountains. His truck was mounting the last rise of the county road that twisted up the valley past Suntop.

He'd given nothing tonight, taken nothing. Felt nothing

now but shame and frustration and emptiness. A man felt nothing but small when he failed to give a woman what she needed, wanted. And as for his own wants— He thought of that handful of condoms in his wallet and groaned aloud with embarrassment. If he hadn't needed both hands for steering, he would have yanked them out and tossed them to the winds!

He reached the main gate to the ranch, and, as his truck turned under the big name board that arched overhead and rumbled across the cattle guard and onto his own land, Rafe heaved a sigh of relief. At least here on Suntop, everything was simple.

As he drove the last half-mile up to the manager's house, his eyes automatically swept the pastures to either side, his mind cataloguing the state of the grass—greening up nicely since they'd moved the yearlings last week. The condition of the fences—a post on the right looked wobbly, tell Anse tomorrow. He braked as a whitetail deer soared over the right fence, touched once, twice on the roadway, then flew away over the left into darkness. He brought the truck to a halt and waited, and sure enough here came a second, then a third, fourth and fifth. A fawn raced frantically along the barbed wire, calling, and one of the does leaped back the way she'd come to meet it.

Rafe drove on—then let out a grunt of surprise as he topped the last rise and saw Zoe's Mustang.

Must have just arrived, he realized as he parked beside it, outside the back door. She'd yet to shut off her headlights, and the passenger door swung wide. Great. Much as he loved his daughter, she wasn't the sort of company he'd had in mind tonight. And given his mood, he'd sooner get over his frustration alone, with a cold beer and a good book by the fire, than be forced to sit in the kitchen, eating a bowl of ice cream, while Zoe quizzed him in cheerful detail about his big night out.

"Daddy!" Zoe leaped down the porch steps to the yard, with the dogs, Woofie and Trey, bounding at her heels. "What are you doing back?"

"Called it an early night," he said, walking around to her door to close it. As he leaned in to turn off her lights, he saw the bags of groceries crowding the seat and the floorboards. He scooped up the nearest four and straightened. "You're supposed to be over at Lisa's," he noted.

"She, um...got sick. Flu, I guess. It seemed smarter to not stay over. So I swung by the grocery store, then came back." Zoe reached for one of his bags. "Here—give me that one."

"I've got it."

She tugged it out of his arms. "This one's got the eggs. There's a *really* heavy one with lots of cans. If you'd get that..."

"Sure." He followed her up the steps to the porch, the dogs surging delightedly around their feet, celebrating this reunion as if he and Zoe had been gone a month instead of hours. "Woof, sit."

The Airedale dropped on the stoop, stub tail wagging, while the jealous Border collie, hearing a command, spun on her furry length and shoved out the kitchen door for her own—just as Zoe stepped up over the threshold from the mudroom.

"*Watch* it!" Arms full, Rafe lunged helplessly toward her, then stopped short as she tripped over the dog and went sprawling headlong. "Zoe!" He set his bags down. "Baby, are you—"

"I'm fine." She pushed herself to her elbows, laughing, as the collie bathed her face with apologetic kisses. "Stop, Trey! Back off!" She curled her long legs under her and sat, as Rafe dropped on his boot heels beside her. Then her smile vanished, and her mouth rounded to an "Oh" of dismay.

"You're hurt! Where?" He ran his hands down her slender arms. She'd broken her wrist years before in just such a fall. Not yet grown into her legs, she was always tripping, still clumsy as a foal.

"N-no, I..." She was staring beyond him at the cans and boxes that had scattered across the floor. Her eyes switched to his face and she gave him a shaky smile. "I'm fine, Daddy, really. Perfectly fine." She started to rise. "If you'd go get the rest of the groceries, I'll—"

"You'll sit till you catch your breath." Rafe glanced around for a chair, stood to get it. He scanned the spilled groceries, seeking the carton of eggs she'd mentioned. A blue box had tumbled nearly to the stove. As the words on its label registered in the back of his mind, his gaze stopped. Swung back. And locked on.

"Um, Daddy?" she said in a tiny quaver as he crossed the room.

He could hear the blood thumping in his ears. Those words *couldn't* say what he thought they'd said.

What they really said.

Impossible. He straightened, holding a pregnancy test kit.

"What's this for?" he asked in a voice that didn't sound remotely like his own.

THE DUDES in Aspen Cabin and Cottonwood Cabin, who had driven over to the Indian cliff houses at Mesa Verde National Park for the day, had returned, tired, sunburned and happy—and an hour and a half later than they'd promised.

By that time Dana had assumed they'd stopped to eat in town. Recklessly switching her menu at the last minute, she'd decided that Sunday would be Barbecue Night, instead—you really needed a crowd out on the deck to make it a festive occasion. She'd told Sean to scatter the coals and let the fire die out in the outdoor grill, while she'd whipped up a tomato-and-onion quiche with a spinach salad for her remaining guests, the two sisters from Boston. They were perpetually fussing about calories, anyway, so let them eat light for once.

But no sooner had Dana pulled the quiche from the oven than the truants had trooped in, appetites raging, consciences shameless, innocently expecting a hot, home-cooked meal to materialize out of thin air.

"They're brats," she confided to Petra in the privacy of her kitchen. "Could even teach you a thing or two, sweetie, but don't you listen."

No fear there. Utterly absorbed in a game of Follow the Leader with Zorro, the cat, Petra scuttled across the linoleum, rump high, diaper askew. "Ca, ca, ca, *ca!*" she declared, reaching for Zorro's tail, as he leaped up to the safety of a chair tucked under the kitchen table. Zorro whisked the endangered prize out of sight, then stepped serenely onto the next chair and sat to lick a paw.

"*Cat,* that's right," Dana crooned absently while she sliced the quiche into cocktail-size bites and arranged them on a platter. This, two bottles of wine and a bowl full of cherries, should keep her guests amused for the next twenty minutes or so.

But what then? *Think, Dana.*

She was too tired to think, and the pressure of ten healthy appetites demanding satisfaction in her living room sent her thoughts whirling like clothes in the dryer. Oh, drat, she hadn't moved the load from the washer an hour ago, had she?

Focus, she commanded herself as she tucked the bottles of wine under her elbow, then hoisted the platter and bumped her hip against the swinging door that led into the dining room. As she passed the long mahogany table, she realized she'd told Sean to set it for four. She'd need another eight settings now.

But first food, she reminded herself. "Cocktail hour!" she announced with a smile and a flourish, handing the platter to Caroline Simmons and nodding at the coffee table. "And Leo, would you play bartender?" He was the one member of the latecomers who'd had the grace to look embarrassed. She placed the bottles of chardonnay on the sideboard, where he'd find glasses and a corkscrew.

"Could you use any help in the kitchen?" he asked, smiling down at her.

"Oh, thanks, not at all! Just sit down and put your feet up. You've had a long day." She threaded her way through the rest of her milling guests, with a smile and a word for each, then went up the front stairs, consciously imitating Zorro's unruffled serenity. Once she'd turned at the newel post on the landing and was out of sight, she took the last steps three at a time. *Help? Oh, no, not me!*

Arriving at Sean's door—closed as always—she paused and drew a breath, steeling herself. Then knocked. "Sean?"

No answer, though she could hear music turned down low, beyond his barricade. "Sean, please." He hated it if she opened his door without permission, but then, the other rule of his game was that he never seemed to hear her. "Sean!" She gritted her teeth and opened the door. "Sean, honey—"

"I *told* you, you're supposed to knock!" he growled, glaring back at her from over his shoulder. He lay sprawled on his stomach on the bed, a book propped on his pillow.

"I need help," she said, voice quivering with the effort to keep it level. She didn't sound far from tears, she realized. Wasn't. *Oh, do I need help.* This job had never been intended for one. That wasn't the way she and Peter had planned it.

But now all she had was Peter's son, glaring at her with Peter's brown eyes. And none of Peter's tenderness.

"Please, Sean? I need eight more places set at the table, then some help in the kitchen."

"Uh."

She resisted the urge to demand if that meant yes or no. *Hope for the best.* "Thank you." She shut the door gently.

Go ahead with the original barbecue? she asked herself as she hurried downstairs. No, the coals would take forever to reach grilling heat. But she couldn't see cooking tomorrow's steaks indoors tonight—what a waste. And Monday's chicken was still frozen solid. Pasta, she decided, topped with peas, bacon and roasted red peppers. Garlic bread and salad. She shoved through the kitchen door.

Petra sat on the floor, face screwed to a tiny red knot of woe, beating on the linoleum with a wooden spoon in time to her hiccuping sobs. "Oh, *sweetheart,* did you miss me?" Dana scooped the baby up, kissed the top of her downy head, then settled her onto one hip and set to cooking one-handed. *Peter, Peter, oh, Peter, if you could see us now...*

CHAPTER THREE

LATE AS IT WAS, supper had been a success, Dana told herself as she paraded a steaming apple tart straight from the oven to the table. Sean followed glumly, carrying a bowl piled high with round scoops of vanilla ice cream. "So who wants pie?" she asked gaily amid the groans of delight and "oohs" of admiration.

Beyond the kitchen door, the phone rang. Dana glanced over her shoulder, her brows drawing together. It was well past nine, late for anyone to be calling. The phone rang again, and she bit her lip—Petra was sleeping in there in her playpen!

"I'll get it," Sean muttered, thumping his bowl down beside her.

By the time she'd served out dessert, he'd still not returned. So either the call was some tourist inquiring about vacancies at the Ribbon R, and for once Sean was handling it, or the caller had wanted her stepson in the first place.

Much as they needed to fill all the gaps in their summer schedule, Dana found herself hoping the call had been for Sean. At fourteen, he didn't seem to get enough phone calls—didn't seem to have any friends to speak of. Although, he confided in her so little, she supposed she'd be the last to know if he did. Still, a schoolmate calling Sean nights—she pictured a giggling thirteen-year-old charmer with a terrible crush and twice Sean's social skills—now, that would be a welcome development. Dana ached for his loneliness, but so far she'd found no way to cure it. *Peter would have known how—*

Stop, she told herself firmly. After fourteen months, it was time she stopped calling on Peter.

Fourteen months or fourteen years or fourteen lifetimes, how could she not? She sat, smiling at her guests around the table, glad for the candlelight that turned tears in the eyes to sparkles.

WHEN ALL HER DUDES had left the table to wander sleepily from the main house and off up the hill to their cabins, Dana set to clearing away. A very long day, she mused as she entered the kitchen, arms loaded. "Sean?" she murmured to warn him, in case he was still engaged in conversation.

No Sean.

Dana frowned, staring at the phone on the wall beside the back door. Its receiver had been dropped on the counter. And— Her frown deepened. He'd left the door ajar.

Hand at her throat, she spun to the playpen—then breathed again at the sight of the small, blanket-draped lump in its center. At least the baby was still covered. The draft of cool mountain air would have done her no harm. Still... *Does he ever think?* She lifted the receiver to her ear, heard the dial tone, let out a *tckk* of irritation and hung it up.

What had caused him to bolt like that? The worst of it was, if she went after Sean and asked what was wrong, she knew exactly what he'd say. "Nothing," she murmured, and grimaced.

Okay. So leave him alone, then. He'd be up in the loft of the barn, one of his hideouts when he wanted to escape her. Or else mooching along the Ribbon River—the snow-melt stream that stairstepped down the mountain, chuckling past the cabins, then the house, to spread out into glistening trout pools when it reached the valley meadows.

Dana turned back to her daughter. *If I can't help Sean, at least your wants are simple, my love.* Gathering the sleeper into her arms, she buried her nose against Petra's warm neck and, with eyes closed, simply breathed in her scent for a moment. Then she carried the baby softly up to bed.

HALF AN HOUR LATER she was rinsing the last pots and pans. Sean had yet to make an appearance, though a few moments ago she'd half thought she heard him thump through the front door. Had he returned that way to avoid her? But if that wasn't him... Dana frowned out the window into the darkness. Go find him and coax him home? Or leave him be?

Something moved in the glass. She blinked, and then realized—a reflection from the room behind her; the dining room door swinging open. Sean stood in the doorway, one arm bracing the door wide, as silently he watched her.

The skin along her spine contracted in a rippling shudder. *Not Sean, but someone much taller, wider, darker.* Standing with the stillness of a predator.

Why didn't I lock the door?

She hadn't for the same reason she never did. Guests trooped in and out all day; Sean came and went; and this wasn't Vermont, where she'd been raised, where everyone locked up. Out here in the West, you depended on distance to protect you. The guest ranch was four miles down a private road from the highway. No one came here by chance.

Behind her, the stranger moved at last, letting the door go and striding on into the kitchen. The blood thrummed in her ears. Dana chose her longest carving knife from the drainage rack, examined it for imaginary food specks, rinsed it, then, still holding it, let her right hand casually droop below the rinse water. She shut off the faucet and half turned.

"*Oh!*" She'd meant the word to deceive, but her shock was real. He was closer than she'd expected. Bigger.

And angrier—black, level brows drawn down over deep-set eyes.

"Wh-wh-what do you—" She stuttered to a stop. Did she really want to know what he wanted?

"Sean Kershaw. Where is he?" A low, gravelly voice, its steadiness somehow more deadly than any shout. No drama to this rage, but pure, cold intention.

"Sean?" Whatever this invasion was, it wasn't what she'd thought. Still, it was bad—trouble. *Teacher?* she asked herself, and rejected the hope immediately. This was no indoor man. His face was tanned to the color of buckskin. The lines fanning out from the corners of his blue eyes spoke of years squinting in the harsh sun. "Wh-why do you want Sean?"

"That's between him and me."

The intruder turned a slow circle on his heels, scanning the kitchen as if Sean might be cowering in a corner. He wore boots, Dana realized, which was why he seemed so enormous. Though even in his socks he'd still top her five-three by nearly a foot.

Nevertheless, she let go of her weapon. She could no more imagine herself stopping this man with a knife than she could imagine stopping a train. "I'm afraid it isn't," she said coolly—to his back. He was striding back the way he'd come.

Hey! She goggled after him, then felt rage awaken as he retreated. "It's considered polite to knock, you know!" she cried, hurrying to catch up.

"I knocked. You didn't hear me." He was already past the dining room, heading for the front door.

Good riddance, whoever he was! But no—her mouth dropped as he turned toward the stairs.

"He's up there?"

"Don't you *dare*—"

"Good." He took the stairs two at a time without a backward glance.

Her baby! The hair bristled on her arms, at her nape. Dana flew up the steps, a primal humming sound in her throat. *You stay away from my baby!*

The door to Petra's room stood wide. Dana flung herself through it and slammed into his back—"Ooof!"

"Huh?" he muttered absently. He'd stopped short just inside the room to flick on the light. She grabbed his elbows from behind and, with a little growl of despair—might as well try to uproot the oak banister!—she attempted to wheel him around and out. He glanced over his shoulder with a startled frown, then simply shrugged, breaking her hold. "Who's this?" He nodded at the sleeping child.

"Mine," Dana said flatly. She caught a fistful of the back of his shirt and tugged, and, lucky for him, he allowed himself to be towed backward out of the room. He hit the light switch as he passed it, then pulled the door quietly shut.

Dana let him go and swung around to put herself between him and Petra's door. Chin up, she stared at him, breathing hard. "Get out of my house this...minute."

Startling white against the tan, a reluctant smile flickered across his hard face. "Good for you," he said simply, then turned away...

To open the next door down the hall—Sean's room! Dana pressed a hand to her throat, swallowed, then charged after him. But—*thank you, God*—Sean hadn't returned.

The stranger stood in the center of Sean's bedroom, surveying the posters pinned to the wall—surly rock groups and a surfer shooting a blue-green pipeline at Maui. The desk piled high with books and camera accessories. Discarded shirts and jeans draped over the chair and the top of the closet door.

"Get *out*." Dana bared her teeth. She supposed she could run uphill and ask her wrangler, Tim, for help, if by any miracle he was home on a Saturday night. Or run downstairs and phone the sheriff. But no way would she leave Petra to do either.

"You're his sister, I reckon?" the man murmured, without turning.

"His stepmother."

His dark head snapped around, and the blue eyes reassessed her, a quick head-to-toe appraisal. She crossed her arms over her breasts and glared back at him. *Why the surprise?* "And who the hell are you?"

"Rafe Montana." He brushed past her and stalked out the door, headed for her bedroom.

"He's not *here*," she hissed, bracing her hands against the doorjamb and leaning after him. "Can't you see?"

He stood there, looking down at the big brass bed that she'd shared with no man for fourteen months and thirteen days. The soft, rumpled down comforter that was no substitute for Peter's living warmth.

"So where is he?" Montana turned to take in the rest of her room.

She felt his eyes touch the books stacked on her bedside table, testimony to all the nights she could not sleep; the vase of blue columbines on the wide windowsill; the bottles of perfume on her dresser, which she hadn't uncapped for more than a year—and she felt as if he'd run his hands across her body. *You trespasser.* She stamped her foot to reclaim his attention. "I'm not *about* to tell you, when I don't know what you want. When you barge in here like a—a maniac!"

"That's about how I feel," he said, swinging to face her.

Two long strides and he towered above her. "I'm Zoe's father."

"Who's Zoe?"

"Who—" His eyes narrowed with rage. "You don't *know?*"

She shook her head wordlessly. His daughter. He was no longer a maniac, but an outraged...father. *And he wants Sean.* Her hand rose of its own accord to her lips. *My Sean?*

"Uh-huh," Montana said dryly, as if she'd spoken her thought aloud. "And where's *his* father?"

"He's...not here, either." Montana might seem somewhat more human, claiming a daughter, but still, no way was Dana admitting she didn't have a man to back her. "He should be home any minute."

"Sooner the better." Montana walked out of her bedroom, glanced through the open door to the empty bathroom, then headed back down the hall.

Hands clenched, Dana tagged at his heels. "If you would just tell me what this is about—"

"He's around here someplace, isn't he?" Montana growled, descending the stairs. "You thought he was in his room. So..." He walked through to the kitchen again, then out the back door.

She caught up with him on the deck. He stood with big hands on his lean hips, staring up the slope toward the corral and the barn. A light shone through the cottonwoods from one of the cabins along the creek. "Where is he, Mrs. Kershaw? In the barn? Or—what's that house beyond—the bunkhouse?"

"One of the guest cabins. But if you barge in on my dudes, I'll call the sheriff and have you arrested, so help me God. Now, *tell* me—" She stopped with a gulp as a thought hit her. *"Oh..."* She drifted past him, down the two steps to the gravel where her old pickup should have been parked. Turned a slow circle of bewilderment.

Montana joined her, glanced down at the ruts made by the tires, and swore. "Where's he gone?"

"I...don't know." At fourteen, Sean had no license yet. Peter had allowed him to drive the truck on their property, and though Dana didn't entirely approve, she hadn't dared revoke that privilege after Peter was gone. Sean had extended his range without asking, she'd noticed this last six months, to include the private road out as far as the highway. But he wouldn't dare— "Did you pass an old pickup on your way in from the public road?"

"I passed nobody."

Which meant, she supposed, that Sean had already departed. Or fled, she realized, staring up at Montana. *He knew you were coming!* That phone call during supper.

"Where would he be on a Saturday night, Mrs. Kershaw? Down in Trueheart at one of the bars?"

"Sean?" She laughed incredulously. "Of course not!"

He stepped closer, till they stood almost toe to toe. "You haven't a clue where your punk is, do you, lady? I guess I should have expected that. Running wild..."

Insults on top of invasion, and the truth in his charge only made it sting more. She tipped up her chin. "And I suppose you know *precisely* where your daughter is this minute, huh?" What was she supposed to do? Keep a fourteen-year-old boy who outweighed her by twenty pounds— who barely could stand the sight of her—on a leash? She was doing the best she could!

"You better believe I do," Montana said coolly. "Zoe's locked in her bedroom without even a phone for company. And that's where she'll stay till I thrash this out."

A tyrant, on top of all else! Dana paired two fingers and jabbed them directly into his second shirt button—it was like prodding warm stone. "Thrash *what* out?" *Please, not what I'm thinking.* This had to be some sort of ridiculous mistake. Perhaps he had the wrong Sean.

They both jumped as, inside the kitchen, the phone rang. Montana caught her arms and moved her aside with a gentleness that belied his temper. She stood for a moment, blinking, strangely undone by the sensation of a man's hands upon her—it had been so long—then spun and went after him. She saw him lift her phone to his ear. "Don't you *dare!*"

"She's right here," Montana said in response to the caller's question, then handed her the receiver with ironic courtesy.

"Mrs. Kershaw?" inquired a male voice. "This is Colorado State Trooper Michael Morris calling, ma'am. Do you have a son named Sean?"

"Oh, *God!*" Not Sean, too! Slowly she sagged against the counter. *No, no, oh, no.* She was dimly aware that Montana had set one broad hand on her shoulder, steadying her, and that he'd tipped his head down close enough to hear the trooper's voice. His temple brushed her hair.

"Oh, no, ma'am, nothing like that—not an accident! Sorry to scare you. But I've got a Sean Kershaw stopped here on Route 160, and it appears he isn't licensed to drive. We've checked the plates, and you're the owner of record of this vehicle. Did you give him permission to drive, ma'am?"

"I..." She drew in a shaking breath. Sean was all right! He wouldn't be once she got hold of him, but for now... *Thank you, thank you, oh, thank you!* "No, Officer, I did not." She straightened, and Montana's hand fell away from her shoulder, though he still hovered within hearing range. She met his eyes and smiled her relief, and, wonder of wonders, his mouth quirked with warmth and wry humor. A very nice mouth indeed, she noticed, when it wasn't hardened by temper.

"Well, that's good," said the trooper. "I'm afraid, though, we've got a situation here, ma'am. I ought to take him in and book him, but we've had a tractor trailer tip over, down by Durango. Took out a few cars with it. All the tow trucks are out on the job, and I should be over there, too. If you and another licensed driver could get down here in a hurry, I'd release the car and your son into your custody. Saves me a trip to the station.''

"Tell him yes," Montana said in a whispered growl, his eyes lighting.

No way was she taking *him* along. "I'll...yes. Of course." She'd ask Leo Simmons, the dude in Cottonwood Cabin, to help her out. "Tell me again where you're located?"

The trooper told her quickly, then added, "I've got a second kid here, too, ma'am, in case you could contact her parents for me. She won't be charged, since she wasn't driving, but..."

"Who?" Dana asked with a sinking heart. Somehow she knew already.

"She refuses to say, ma'am. A tall, redheaded, mouthy kid."

The shock dawning in Rafe Montana's eyes was almost laughable. He shook his head, shook it again as if he were slinging water out of his eyes, and snatched the phone from her grasp.

"Ask her if her name's Zoe Montana," he rasped. "Never mind who I am! *Ask* her."

There came a long pause. Montana stood as still as a rock, teeth clenched, as he glared into the distance, utterly oblivious of Dana's wide-eyed scrutiny. Then, as the trooper spoke again, Montana swore under his breath and said, "You tell her for me, Officer, that her father's on his way."

"Know *just* where your daughter is, do you?" Dana couldn't resist murmuring.

CHAPTER FOUR

STRAPPED INTO her car seat on the rear bench of Rafe Montana's long-cab pickup truck, Petra whined and fretted till they reached the smoother highway. As the big truck settled into a mile-eating drone, her long lashes drooped on her fat rosy cheeks and she slept.

"Never fails," Montana murmured, glancing in the rear-view mirror.

The voice of experience, Dana realized, studying his hard-edged profile. Perhaps he had other, younger children aside from Zoe. And for that matter— "Where's Zoe's mother?"

Five fence posts whipped into the headlights, then passed, their barbed wire swooping and falling, before he spoke. "She died in a car wreck when Zoe was six."

"Oh. I'm sorry." She watched his mouth curve wryly. Yes, she supposed it was a bit late to be offering sympathy. For that matter, he might well have replaced Zoe's mother years ago. With his darkly smoldering good looks, that intense vitality, he'd find plenty of volunteers for the job.

The taillights of a car appeared as the pickup topped a rise. The country was flattening out into sagebrush-covered slopes, the dryer land to the west falling away toward the state border. The truck closed on the car in a rush—slipped out, passed it by and roared on.

"What about your husband?" Montana asked without taking his eyes off the road. "You didn't leave him a message."

She didn't answer the question behind that statement. "No, I…didn't." To confess would be to admit he'd scared her. Scared her still in some way she could not fathom. But her instinct was to raise any and every barrier against him she could find.

At the same time, though, necessity demanded that she understand his outrage before they reached Sean, that she defuse it if she could. "Why did you want my stepson, Mr. Montana?"

"If I'm going to drive you halfway to Utah, Mrs. Kershaw, you can call me Rafe." A tractor trailer thundered past, shaking the truck, and he flicked on his high beams.

She would have preferred the formality of last names, but he'd maneuvered her neatly. Now she'd look ungracious not to reciprocate. "Then it's Dana." She straightened her shoulders. "But what about Sean?"

"My daughter's pregnant." He glanced at her, as she shook her head. "Oh, yes. I caught her sneaking a pregnancy test kit into the house this evening."

"Not Sean!" Dana said emphatically. "That's not possible."

"You're saying my Zoe's a liar?"

His voice grew softer and more level with rage, she was learning. "No, I…" Wouldn't dare, but still… She thought of three ways to ask the same essential question—*Is she sure Sean is the father?* But no matter how she phrased it, she might as well set a match to a stick of dynamite. "There must be some mistake," she said, instead. "Is she sure she's pregnant?"

"She told me she's missed two months, almost three. What do you think?"

The worst, quite likely. Dana bit her lip. But still… "Sean isn't even dating." How could he? She gave him an allowance, but it was woefully meager. Peter had cashed in his main life insurance policy to buy the ranch. His little term policy had paid off enough to create a trust fund that someday would cover Sean's and Petra's college tuitions. But the family's day-to-day finances were cut to the bone. Sean had no money for dating, and no transportation aside from his beloved mountain bike. "Where have they been, um, meeting?"

"Didn't get to the bottom of that. She clammed up on me, so I locked her in her room to think about it."

"For all the good that did you." Dana couldn't resist the jab, and noticed it made the muscles in his jaw jump and his knuckles tighten on the wheel. To her mind, a girl who was old enough to make a baby was too old to be locked up like a rebellious ten-year-old.

"You're doing a better job? Your kid's running wild and unsupervised, stealing your car when he wants it. Speeding...knocking up girls."

"*Girl.* If he did that at all. I still don't believe it."

"I'll ask him when I meet him, how's that?" Rafe suggested darkly. "Your sonny boy and I are going to have a *long,* earnest talk, believe me."

Withdrawn, unconfident Sean pitted against this full-grown, outraged male in his prime? "No, I don't think so. Not tonight. Not till I talk to him myself." Peter would never have allowed his son to be bullied, and now she stood in Peter's place. "Tomorrow..." Once she'd gotten Sean's version. Once Rafe Montana had cooled down. Perhaps after she'd consulted a lawyer. *God, where would I find the money?*

"We'll see about that," Rafe said with dangerous calm.

Indeed they would. Dana clenched her hands. Sean's refusal to forgive her might wound her daily, but still, she was all he had. No way would she throw him to this wolf. She changed the subject. "How much farther?"

"Another twenty miles. Almost to Four Corners."

"Where could they have been going?" California? Sean

missed San Diego, somehow seemed to believe that if he could go back there, life would be as it was. As if Peter waited there on the front lawn of the suburban house that he and Sean had shared when Dana first met them. If only it were that easy.

"They were headed for Arizona, I imagine. Zoe's great-aunt lives in Phoenix. She's Catholic, like all Pilar's folks. I suppose Zoe figured she'd take her side."

"Side on what?"

"Zoe is all set to go away to college in three months," Rafe said obliquely.

"College?" Dana had been picturing a ninth or tenth grader! Sean with a senior? Sean, who had all the social sophistication of a golden retriever pup? Now she *knew* there was some mistake!

"Harvard, just like her—" Rafe paused. "Harvard. She's…bright."

As in *very bright,* Dana interpreted the pride echoing behind that western understatement.

"She's been working all her life for this. Aims to be a doctor, a surgeon—though the school counselor tells me she could shoot higher than that if she wants. Sky's the limit. But Harvard's the start…the door she has to walk through to get where she's going. Where she deserves to go. Her life's just blossoming, just starting to happen—" He slammed the wheel with a fist. "And now this? I don't think so. Now that your kid has messed her up, there's only one way out."

"Abortion, you mean," Dana murmured. She suppressed a sudden urge to look back at Petra. To grab the baby and pull her over the seat and into her arms. "Does Zoe agree?" Zoe, who'd broken out of her room somehow and tried to flee the state?

"She… Neither of us was making much sense back

there," Rafe growled. "We're not used to banging heads. But once she's calmed down and thought it through…"

I wonder. "There's always adoption," Dana observed, her voice carefully neutral.

"Zoe starts college in *three months.*" Montana's words might have been carved from Rocky Mountain granite.

THEY DROVE THE REST of the way in silence. But angry as he was, Rafe found he couldn't focus all his thoughts on the coming confrontation. Sitting only two feet to his right, she tugged at his awareness. *Dana Kershaw.* Small and dark, she should have looked boyish with her short, silky brown hair falling into her big slate-green eyes, yet she was anything but. She had a softness and a warmth about her that were feminine to the core. Reminded him of the little half-Siamese cat Zoe had owned for years, all silky fur to the touch, daintily elegant—and absolute hell on dogs five times her size, if they looked sideways at her kittens. His lips twitched as he remembered the way she'd faced him down at her baby's door. Not a woman to be crossed.

Kershaw's a lucky man, he found himself thinking. You could tell the good 'uns at a glance, just like he could size up a corral full of horses and choose the best mount. He grimaced, realizing where this thought was heading—it was just a leftover from his earlier frustration. God, was it only three hours ago that he'd been sitting across a table from Mitzy Barlow? It seemed another lifetime.

What he'd learned about Zoe—like a knife stroke cutting that happy life from this strange present, him speeding through the night with a gentle, fierce woman, her eyes reflecting like fathomless pools in the windshield whenever a car passed them by. And Zoe, turned from his loving, loyal daughter into a defiant stranger! One stumble across the kitchen floor and he'd picked up someone he'd never met before—a young woman who'd loved a man, made a baby by him, cast her father's wisdom aside to fly to her mate. To flee as if he were some kind of ogre, not the father who'd turned his own world upside down to make a good life for his own baby... How could everything change this fast?

Nothing's changed, he told himself savagely, and wished he could believe it. *Not really.* There'd be a week or two of hurt feelings and ugly necessities, a week or two of sorrow after that, then they'd get back on track. *She's worked too hard. I won't let this ruin her life.*

His headlights picked out a creek bending in from the darkness to edge the highway, then a state police car parked on the shoulder above it; ahead of that, a pickup. Two pale faces stared back through the truck's rear window, as Rafe swung in behind the patrol car and parked. "We settle with the Statie first, Dana. He'll want to hear that we're taking this seriously."

"Believe me, I am." She checked her child, who was still sleeping, then hurried after Rafe as he strode to meet the state trooper, now unfolding from his car.

She handled it well, Rafe had to admit, as Officer Morris assured them that he could arrest Sean for everything from car theft to speeding. Dana didn't try to excuse or defend her son, but simply promised that he would be punished, that such a grievous misjudgment would never be repeated. Clearly of a mind to be satisfied, the trooper finally nodded, marched off to his car, got in and carved a swift U-turn, then headed off toward the truck crash near Durango.

"You were lucky," Rafe observed, hearing the distant engine shift into overdrive. He turned. And now, for someone who'd run flat out of luck...

Both doors of the shabby pickup opened as he stalked toward it. "Daddy?" Zoe called fearfully from the far side.

But Rafe had another target in his sights. The greedy, undisciplined spoiler who'd led them all to this disaster. "I want a word with you, punk," he said quietly, barely aware that Dana Kershaw plucked at his elbow. He shrugged her off.

Head high, the boy paused beside his open door and let him come. Rafe's strides slowed and he drew in a harsh breath. This was his enemy? Half a head shorter than him, with the gangly limbs, the too-big feet and hands of a boy? He'd pictured an eighteen-year-old, at least! "*You're* Sean Kershaw?" He glanced toward the cab in spite of himself, as if the kid's older brother might burst forth.

"My stepson," Dana declared, swinging around to stand shoulder to shoulder with the kid.

Rage and frustration had been building inside Rafe all night. He'd contained himself—barely—but had promised himself a full and glorious venting when he found its deserving target. But now? You could stomp a man, but this—this unshaved brat? He caught the kid's collar between thumb and forefinger. "How the hell old *are* you?" he demanded, ignoring both Dana's and Zoe's yelps of protest.

"Old enough and get your hands off me!" The boy chopped up a forearm, breaking his grip.

"Old enough for what, you little runt? To wreck my daughter's life?"

"He's fourteen, and you leave him alone," Dana cried, stepping between them. "I said we'd talk *tomorrow*," she added in an urgent undertone.

"Fourteen!" Rafe shook his head. What the hell?

"Daddy!" Zoe pleaded.

Zoe had betrayed him for this—this puppy? "Get in the truck," he snapped without glancing aside.

"Don't," countered the kid. "He can't make you do anything you don't want."

"Oh, can't I?" He prodded the boy's shoulder. "Mind your own business, sonny."

The boy batted his hand aside. "This *is* my business."

"Sean, be quiet! Rafe, *please.*" Dana caught his upper arm with both her hands.

Even through the mists of rage, he could feel each separate small fingertip digging into his muscles. *She's married,* he reminded himself, and felt his rage kick up a notch. He swung his arm back, pushing her away from the fray. "Yeah, you've made it your business, big shot. You've made a baby nobody wants or needs. A baby the grown-ups will have to deal with now. Good going!"

"Nobody's asking you to deal with anything—" The boy's voice cracked on the last word and jumped half a squeaking octave.

Rafe threw back his head and laughed. The situation was so absurd, it was that or weep.

Sean shoved him hard with both hands. "Zoe doesn't *want* an abortion, and if she doesn't want one, I don't want one!"

Rafe rocked back on his heels, then rocked forward, looming over the kid. *How do you like that?* Sixty pounds lighter, yet the kid was going toe to toe with him. Guts. Still, "Easy for you to say, twerp. You won't be around to pick up the pieces."

"I will! If Zoe needs me, I'll be there. I'll get a job and take care of her. I'll— I'll—"

"At fourteen?" Rafe jeered incredulously, shaking his head—and saw the blow coming from the corner of his eye, a roundhouse swing. His head tipped reflexively to the right, and the blow whistled past his ear. *"Hey!"*

Sean growled wordlessly and took another shot. Rafe caught it on his palm and swept it aside. "Back off!"

They circled, Rafe with open hands up and out, dimly aware of the women shrieking from outside the whirlwind of Sean's flailing fists. *Duck in and put a shoulder into his stomach,* Rafe told himself. He could toss the kid up over his shoulder, trundle him down to the stream that gurgled beyond the truck. Dump him in to cool off.

Another blow sailed in, and he took it on his raised forearm as he stepped to one side. Somebody should have taught this kid to hit. Anyone really wanting to hurt him could have done so with ease.

"Rafe, *please*, he's just a child!" Dana cried, and that decided him. Sean was a child—acting as a man. And standing by his woman, as foolishly touching as that might seem to an adult. And though apparently Dana didn't understand, the masculine code required that you honor your opponent's courage, no matter how incompetently displayed. *So don't demean him. Treat him as I would a man.* Sean had earned that courtesy with his spunk. The kid came in grunting and slugging. Rafe sighed inwardly, chose his shot and, pulling his punch to the limit of credibility, hit the kid as lightly as he could.

Sean wobbled two steps backward and sat—and Rafe found himself nose to nose with Dana Kershaw. "You…big…*bully!*" She smacked her hands against his chest. "*Stop* it!"

Just what he'd been trying to do.

She smacked him again. "What kind of a man picks on a child?"

"Be quiet, Dana." He'd been showing his respect, man to man. Now she was ruining his gesture—would humiliate the kid, if she didn't hush up. "He'll be fine." Learning to take his knocks—that was how a boy became a man. And the kid wasn't sniveling, Rafe noted with approval, glancing over her head. He was staggering to his feet with Zoe's help…brushing her aside. Crap, was he coming for more?

Fearful the kid might wade in all over again, Rafe allowed Dana to back him down the road. "Take it easy," he warned her, as she shoved him again. He caught her slender wrists and pinned her hands against his heart, scowling down at her. "Ea-sy!" Her pulse leaped beneath his fingertips, and he felt his own surge to meet it. He threw her hands hastily aside and retreated.

"*Me*, easy?" she cried, and turned up her palms in an appeal to the heavens.

Behind her, Zoe had caught the kid in a bear hug and was holding him back. Tears streaming, she glared over his shoulder. "I'm so ashamed of you, Daddy!"

Ashamed of me?! Now that punch landed—knocked him speechless. All those years of being his daughter's hero, to be shattered like this? Rafe felt the first stab of pain, then rage overwhelmed it like a breaking black wave. Rage felt *much* better. "Get in the truck! *Now!*"

If he'd lost her affection, still she had a sixteen-year habit of obedience. She murmured something in Sean's ear, then let him go.

"Zoe!" he called hoarsely after her. But head down, she marched off to Rafe's truck, scrambled in and slammed the door mightily.

A moment later, a baby's startled wail split the night.

"Petra!" Dana homed in on the sound, then brushed past Rafe without a glance.

The sobs gained volume and heartache, mixed with the crooning cries of two sympathetic women.

Damn it all to hell and back again! All he'd wanted to-night was to get laid. Rafe turned heavily to glare at Sean Kershaw. "Nice sound, huh? They do that for the first twelve months without a break to draw breath, except when they're puking or pooping. Think about it."

Halfway to his truck, he met Dana returning, arms full of the child and her bulky car seat. He opened his mouth to offer help, then shut it, knowing her answer already. Their eyes locked, held as they neared. She tipped up her chin and swept proudly past him, her baby's hiccuping sobs trailing back on the cold night air.

Rafe sighed, then stood beside his truck till she'd started hers, completed her turn and headed for home. He followed at a wary distance.

CHAPTER FIVE

DANA WOULD HAVE LOVED to pull a pillow over her head and sleep in the next morning—she'd tossed and turned most of the night, worrying about Sean. But the demands of a dude ranch, on top of the more strident demands of a baby who rose with the sun, had her stumbling from her bed at the usual hour.

In spite of her worries, morning flew by in a rush—diapering, nursing and dressing Petra, then rushing downstairs to cook a hearty breakfast for Tim, the dude wrangler. His customary Sunday hangover had rendered him even surlier and more silent than usual, she noted with despair. This time he hadn't bothered to shave. And he was scheduled to take all her dudes into the high country for an all-day trail ride, leaving at ten. So much for the cheerful, dashing trail boss of her guests' fantasies—a Disneyland cowpoke on a rearing steed, who'd spin thrilling yarns, dispense homespun cowboy wisdom, whisk them off on the Wild West adventure of a lifetime. Dana supposed the larger, sleeker, full-service guest ranches could afford to employ such entertainers, but the Ribbon R was a minimalist outfit, at minimalist prices. Her dudes would have to make do with a shambling, groaning, tobacco-chewing misanthrope, who at least wouldn't lose them in the back hills. She hoped.

Packing box lunches for the ride, at last she had a moment to think about Sean. When she'd come downstairs, a dirty plate on the counter and a tumbler with a puddle of milk in its bottom told her he'd preceded her.

He'd yet to return.

Gone off on his mountain bike? She hoped not. She hadn't had the heart, last night, to mete out a punishment for his driving escapade. It would have seemed one blow too many, after Zoe's announcement and Rafe Montana's brutality. So she'd told him they would discuss his behavior—discuss everything—this morning.

Sean-fashion, he'd given her his silent answer. *Oh, yeah? Catch me first.*

Sean, Sean, what am I going to do with you? He had been so unhappy before—and now this? Every time she thought things were as hard as they could be, they got a little harder. She bit down on her lip and finished wrapping the sandwiches, while Petra pulled at her pants leg and whined.

Once she'd seen Tim and his dudes on their way up through the home pasture, she prepped for the evening barbecue—got the steaks marinating, the baked beans simmering, the potato salad made. While Petra dragged out the contents of her special kitchen cabinet—the only one without a baby-proof latch—and sat fitting lids onto aluminum pots with scowling concentration, then lifting them off again with shrieks of glee, Dana made bread. Enough dough for this week's evening meals, plus enough to freeze for the next. Kneading it, she leaned into each stroke, her head drooping tiredly.

Sean still had not returned. Hanging out in the barn, or perhaps gone hiking up into the mountains? He rarely rode, though Peter had given him a surefooted, spunky little paint named Guapo when they'd first arrived. They'd all ridden that first fall, the three of them, laughing and awed by the beauty of their new home. Sean had liked her back then.

They'd been able to talk about anything and everything. But now...

We'll have to. This couldn't be shoved under the rug, as Sean preferred to do. This had to be faced. Responsibility acknowledged.

And then?

That depended on what Zoe decided to do, she supposed. *What Rafe Montana decides,* she corrected herself, grimacing. The bully. But there was no way to deny that he was the dominant personality here, the one who would call the shots. He would shape his daughter's future, and therefore Sean's. *Should I find a lawyer?* Someone to advise her stepson on his paternal rights and responsibilities? The money made her hesitate. She'd decided this morning that she'd wait to see what Montana did next, but she wasn't certain this was the wise approach.

Petra dropped a pot lid with a *clang* that made Dana jump. "Petra, what a noisy girl! You're going to be a drummer someday?" Please, anything but!

"Ga," the baby chortled, then smile gave way to frown. She rolled over onto all fours and crawled purposefully toward her mother.

"About that time, is it?" Dana wiped a forearm over her brow, brushing back her hair. "Can you wait a minute, sweetheart?" She patted the dough into balls, placed them in greased ceramic bowls. "Yes, sweetie, I know. Just a minute more. Be patient." After covering each bowl with a clean cloth, she set the dough to rise on the warming shelf above the stove. "There." She scooped up her tearful daughter and blew into her neck till Petra giggled. "See, silly girl? I didn't forget you."

She checked her diaper, then carried her out to the back deck and their favorite spot: a porch swing that hung under an arbor of climbing pink roses and honeysuckle. Sinking into one cushioned corner, she kicked off her shoes, dragged a pillow onto her lap, propped one arm and her baby against one bent knee while she left the other foot on the ground to rock them. "Lunchtime," she agreed, as Petra patted her blouse. And no one around for miles, she assured herself, looking uphill as she unbuttoned. Just birdsong, the fragrance of sun-warmed roses, a precious moment of peace...the delicious tingle as the milk let down in her breasts...the rhythmic suck of warm lips drawing her down into sleepy pleasure.

Sometime later, a ripple of consciousness disturbed her waking dream. Dana's eyes drifted half open, focused drowsily on a long pair of jeans-clad legs. Idly she rode them upward, up past lean hips, a flat stomach, a wide chest in a snap-front western shirt that flared to wider shoulders...up a strong brown throat to the startled face of Rafe Montana. His lips had parted in surprise; his eyes were narrowed slits of sapphire in his suntanned face. She felt her own face turning a color to rival the roses.

"Pardon me, ma'am!" He wheeled and walked back down the steps to the ground, then stopped there, facing away. "Didn't meant to intrude like that. I..."

The liquid pleasure of the moment seemed to flow over his form like honey, taking him in, making him a part of the mountains, the sunshine, the fragrance, her love for her daughter. He had all the power and grace of a bull elk who had suddenly walked into her world. It took an effort to remember that she disliked him—that he'd hit Sean last night, something she'd never forgive. "Of course." She supposed he'd tried the front door, and receiving no answer to his knock, this time hadn't barged through, but had walked around to the back.

"If you could wait a minute?" Gently she detached Petra and moved her to her other breast.

"Sure." He glanced awkwardly down at his boots, then

he stepped backward and sat on the top step of the deck, careful not to look behind.

She felt oddly powerful and more than a little smug at being able to abash a man like this with a simple, earthy act. Women's magic.

Sleepy, swirling magic, which bound all it touched, enchantress as well as enchanted. Petra's lips suckled at her nipple and the enchantment spread—a golden wire drawn from her breasts to her womb, then drawn tighter in soft, rhythmic tugs that her hips yearned to answer. The sensation spooled out to include the man, as if he were the cause, the one who held the gilded wire, the one who tugged, instead of an unknowing bystander. Dana closed her eyes and shuddered. She'd been dead to her own body for so long—just a mother, a widow. How odd for it to awaken just now.

Means nothing, she told herself. *I don't even like him. He hurt Sean.*

He was overwhelmingly male and perhaps "like" had nothing to do with instinct. Simply by being, he reminded her she was female. A woman without a mate—not a reminder for which she was grateful.

Montana spoke without turning. "I asked Zoe about Sean's father."

As if he could read her mind! Dana tipped back her head to stare at a pendant blossom. Blown, its vibrant rosiness fading to drab violet, the first petals fallen. "Yes?"

"I...meant to talk with him. But Zoe tells me I can't."

I talk to him all the time. But he never answers, not in words. "That's right," she said bleakly. She reached to pluck a petal, rubbed it across her lips.

"I'm...sorry. If you'd told me..."

"Mmm," she hummed wordlessly. *Who owed you an explanation?*

"I reckon I scared you, stomping in like that. And I wanted to say I'm sorry."

"Oh." It was handsomely done, no self-justifications, no excuses. But Dana wasn't in a forgiving mood. Not because of the intrusion, but because of Sean. "Thank you," she said coldly.

"Hmmph." He pulled his Stetson off, inspected it, whacked a denim-clad calf with it.

Clearly he had more to say. She waited, and when it didn't come, she asked, "How's Zoe?"

"She threw up this morning." He whacked his leg again. "Not the first time, she tells me."

"She needs to see a doctor. Forget that test kit. Let a gynecologist examine her. She should be on vitamins, eating right—"

He let out a huff of bitter amusement. "I'm known around these parts, Dana, for being a devil on nutrition. Pound for pound, my cattle are the best fed in the state. You think I'd neglect my daughter? But she'll be eating for one, not two."

A rancher. She should have known it, with his boots and his outdoor tan. A man used to giving orders, not taking them. King of his own small kingdom. "That's what Zoe wants?"

"What she will want, once she sees sense."

So he'd yet to bully her into submission. In spite of the complications Zoe's stand might mean for the Kershaws, Dana felt a flash of admiration. It would take courage to cross this man.

"In the meantime, she should see a doctor."

He grunted assent. "Another reason I wanted to see you. She has a pediatrician, of course, but now... Is there anybody you'd recommend?"

Had he no other female in his life to advise him? A sister, a lover, a friend? Despite his high-handed arrogance, his explosive temper, Rafe Montana was one of the most attractive men she'd ever laid eyes on, so surely he had a woman. Petra had fallen asleep while they spoke, and now her mouth slipped away from the breast. Dana buttoned her blouse one handed while she considered. Ought to stay out of this. The fewer ties between the Kershaws and the Montanas, the better, to her mind. But a good doctor was essential. "Yes, I go to a woman obstetrician in Durango. Cassandra Hancock. She's gentle and extremely competent."

"Does she do abortions?" he asked bluntly.

Dana winced, worked the top button through its hole, and reached for the hand towel she'd brought from the kitchen. "I wouldn't know. But I'm sure if she doesn't, she could advise *Zoe*. Tell her the best place to go." She laid the towel over her shoulder, moved Petra to burping position and stood. Patting the baby's back, she walked slowly back and forth. Rafe shifted to watch, and she felt herself drawn irresistibly closer with each turn, till she stood above him, staring out over her land. She glanced down, and their eyes linked. His were the dark, high-altitude blue of the mountaintop skies, direct as a bolt of summer lightning. Her heart bumped in her breast half a dozen times before his eyes released her and shifted to her baby.

The straight line of his mouth softened. "But I suppose you don't believe in abortions."

"I believe in choice, Mr. Montana."

"Rafe."

"But choice cuts both ways, doesn't it...Rafe? What does Zoe choose? It's her life, her body, her baby."

All restless energy, he surged to his feet. "She's in no emotional shape to choose wisely!" He took all the steps in a stride and stopped on the last one, which put them on a level—too close. So close Dana could see the pale line of a scar drawn across the carved fullness of his bottom lip.

She rocked back on her heels, but held her ground. ''Whether she is or not, you can't take that choice from her.'' *Or can you?* He was so clearly used to having his way.

The muscles along his angular jaw fluttered and stilled. ''Someone should have taken that choice from Zoe's mother.''

Dana blinked. Blunt words, indeed. ''Oh?''

''Pilar was eighteen when we…found out. And—'' His jaw clenched again and his gaze swung off to the east, to the mountain that walled off that side of the valley. ''And it ruined her life.''

But she got you. He had a profile like the head on a Roman coin—harsh, emphatic, all jutting lines and angles, with not a softening curve except for that bottom lip. Zoe's mother had gotten herself a harsh and beautiful man. *Was that the choice that wrecked her life?* Eyes wide, Dana rested her cheek against Petra's dark curls and waited.

''It's like…'' His shoulders jerked, then squared and went taut. ''Like history repeating itself. Some kind of enormous, ugly joke. Pilar had already been accepted into Harvard when we… Full scholarship—she was from a poor family. Would have been the first of her family ever to go to college. She was brilliant—that's where Zoe gets her brains. Meant to be a doctor, too. Instead she—'' He shook his head. ''It was a criminal waste.''

''Or maybe she…chose what she wanted.''

One bark of savage laughter—it was instantly stifled. ''You think so? No, it was a waste of her talents, her hard work, her dreams, her family's hopes. Just when Pilar's life was about to open out, to expand—she'd never even been out of Colorado before—we made one stupid mistake. I made one. And her life contracted to a crummy one-room trailer, a baby with colic, a nineteen-year-old husband who could barely keep himself in boot leather, much less support a family. Yeah, she made one hell of a choice.''

''I see…''

''I hope to God you do.'' Rafe shrugged, setting aside any personal connection to the picture he'd just painted. ''So, a wise man learns from his mistakes. And if he loves his daughter, he damn sure stops her from making the same mistakes.''

Do we ever get to shield the ones we love from their mistakes? She'd tried to stop Peter from crossing that south-facing slope, nervously citing what she'd read about alpine snow conditions, but he'd teased her about learning cross-country skiing from a book and had pushed on. They'd both been cold and tired at the end of the day, eager to reach their lodge… *Wouldn't have needed to cross that hill at all if I hadn't read the map wrong, taken us down the wrong fork in the trail.* She hadn't even been able to shield Peter from *her* mistakes, much less his own.

''Hey.'' A warm, rough hand cupped her cheek. ''Are you okay?''

''I…'' She blinked back the tears, took a step backward. Slipped a hand down to Petra's bottom. ''Oops!'' She managed a trembly smile. ''Flood tide. If you'd excuse us a minute?''

SHE TOOK CLOSER TO TWENTY, stopping to wash her face after she'd put Petra down in her crib. *What's gotten into you?* she scolded the damp face with its shadowy eyes, which gazed back at her from her mirror. After months of gray, steely calm, suddenly she felt raw and ragged, her emotions swinging wildly from elation to despair. Like a compass needle following a prowling magnet.

Not enough sleep, she answered herself, heading downstairs. *Forgot lunch.* She pushed through the dining room door—and stopped short. *Rafe Montana in my kitchen.*

Peeking under the towel that covered a bowl of her rising dough. He whipped around, as guilty as a boy caught scooping a fingerful of icing off a cake. "You were so long, I wondered if something was wrong."

I'm fine. Dana didn't want to acknowledge his concern. "She took a while falling back to sleep."

He grimaced. "At least she sleeps. Zoe worked a double shift from the word go. Started climbing out of her crib at nine months. I'd wake up at 3:00 a.m. and she'd be bumping around the trailer like a raccoon on the hunt, turning out cupboards. Pulled the phone down on her head one night—Lord, what a racket."

"A handful." She could imagine him at nineteen, working a man's job all day, still needing the sleep of a boy at night. *It must have been desperately hard for you and Pilar, both.* But watching his face, she could see his memories of Zoe's baby years were rueful, not grudging.

His expression hardened. "A handful still. Which brings me back to my problem…"

"Yes?" But problems or not, she had an evening meal to prepare. She dusted flour over her marble pastry slab and turned out the first ball of risen dough. Dug the heel of her right hand into its spongy softness, folded its far edge back toward the center, turned the dough, then shoved again, settling into her rhythm—knead, fold, rotate a quarter turn. Knead again…

Rafe drifted closer and stared down at her hands. "You've got to help me, Dana."

An order, not a request, she noted wryly. Knead, fold, turn, knead… She sprinkled more flour on the marble. "Help you how?"

"Zoe got her brains from Pilar, but she got her stubbornness from me." He gripped the edge of the table and leaned closer. "I'm not getting through to her, what a disaster this baby would be. I thought maybe a woman... somebody who's gone through it recently and who's going it alone..."

She looked up at him with something like hatred. "You'd use me—me and my baby—as an object lesson? How handy that my husband died. It makes us seem more pathetic!"

He jerked upright. "I didn't mean it like—"

"Oh, I'm sure you didn't think at all." She brushed the hair away from her eyes with the back of her hand.

"I didn't think of it like that, dammit. You're anything but pathetic." His scowl softened. The corner of his mouth slowly tilted. "Though, with flour all over your face..."

I look like a clown? So much for indignation. She swiped the back of a hand across her nose, and he burst into laughter.

"Here—" He tucked three fingers under her chin to support it.

If her hands hadn't been full of dough, she would have edged out of reach. Instead, she stood paralyzed, her lashes falling to shut him out—to shut out this fragile, disturbing moment—while he cleaned her off, his fingers brushing across the bridge of her nose, the tops of her cheeks, her shivering lashes.

"Better," he observed huskily.

Was it? Was it really? A wave of black dismay—of echoing loss—washed over her. "Thanks," she whispered, staring down at her dough. After a moment her hands moved again—knead, fold, turn...

"*Will* you help me persuade her, Dana?"

Give a little to get what you wanted, she thought, loss turning to disgust. He thought he could buy her cooperation that easily, with one gesture of tossed-off tenderness? "No, Rafe, I won't. Zoe doesn't need some stranger telling her what to do.'' Nor, for that matter, a parent trying to shape her life according to his own lights. ''What about getting her some professional counseling? I'm sure that Dr. Hancock—''

''*I'm* the only counselor Zoe needs, dammit! A baby will wreck her life!''

''Then if you're all she needs,'' Dana said coolly, ''she doesn't need me.''

''But, dammit—'' He saw her chin tip up in warning and he shut his mouth with an effort, locked his jaw over his words. Stood rocking on his boot heels and scowling, while she patted the first ball of dough into a loaf, settled it into its greased pan and placed it on the warming shelf. She turned out another ball of risen dough, pressed out the yeasty gas, commenced kneading.

''All right,'' he said grimly, ''then look at it this way. You owe me this help.''

Her hands paused as she looked up. ''Excuse me?''

''Your son knocked up my daughter. If you'd ridden herd on him, hadn't let him run wild, had taught him a proper respect for girls—''

Dana threw up a floury hand. ''Now, wait a minute. Your daughter is—what—two years older than Sean? And everyone knows girls are *years* more mature than boys. So just who seduced *whom?* And *who* should have known better?''

''At fourteen, he's old enough to know right from wrong! Or at least, old enough to know how not to get caught. Didn't you tell him about condoms?''

''Didn't you tell your brilliant daughter?'' she shot back.

''She knew,'' he said with dangerous calm.

''Then—''

''Condoms do fail.'' His gaze turned distant and bleak.

''Is that what—''

He shrugged and spun on his heel, surveyed her kitchen, swung back again. ''She's not giving me any of the gory details, and frankly—'' His shrug was more of a shudder. ''Frankly, I don't want to know. Every time I think about it, I get this urge to hammer your kid into the ground like a cedar fence post.''

Dana dusted her hands and came carefully around the table. ''If you ever lay so much as a *finger* on Sean again—'' She prodded his chest with a fingertip ''—I'll have you in jail for assault, Rafe Montana. See if I don't!''

''Assault?'' He caught her wrist, trapping her hand in that gesture of threat, forefinger touching his breast. ''Last night, he swung on *me*.''

''Yes, but who finished it?'' She yanked backward, but he held her easily.

''That was a lesson he needed to learn. You don't take on someone you can't handle.''

''I'll thank you not to give my son lessons!''

''Then who will?'' He brought her hand down to his side, then drew it slightly behind him, a subtle tug that swayed her closer. She flattened her other hand on his chest to catch her balance—could feel his heart thudding against her palm. ''*You'll* teach him how to grow up a man? Not your strong point, I'd say.'' His eyes roved down her face to her mouth. He smiled slowly and shook his head. ''Not your strong point at all, thank God.''

She shoved his chest hard, and he let her go. ''Nobody asked you for lessons, and I'm telling you again, don't you *dare*—'' She cut herself short as the screen door to the deck creaked.

Sean stood there, gaping at them both.

CHAPTER SIX

THE BOY'S LOOK OF SHOCK turned to a thunderous scowl and he stepped backward—spun away. Rafe Montana lunged after him before the door banged shut. "You! Come here!"

So much for her warning! Dana yelped a protest and followed. She flung out onto the deck to find them faced off like a couple of dogs, hackles risen and weight on the balls of their feet. She caught Montana's collar and gave a warning tug. "I said don't!"

"And I heard you," he told her evenly, his eyes locked on Sean.

Which was hardly a promise to obey, she realized. Retaining her grip, Dana glared at Sean. "Sean, if you'd please go in the—" The bruise on his jaw registered—blue-green and glorious. "Oh, Sean!" She let go of Montana and flew to her stepson, caught his chin in her hand.

Sean jerked out of her grasp and edged away. "It's nothing."

"Oh, no, it isn't!" She touched his shoulder, but he stepped aside. "Sean, please…"

"Shut up, Dana." Sean didn't spare her a glance.

"*What* did you say?" Rafe demanded in a voice of quiet thunder.

"I—I s-said…" The boy stopped as Rafe shook his head.

"Don't," he said with ominous calm. "Not ever. Not around me."

"Rafe, I can handle this, thank you," Dana insisted.

"Some job you're doing." His eyes switched to Sean. "You and I have to talk."

Sean clenched his hands. "I've only got one thing to say to you, Mr. Montana. Where's Zoe?"

Montana seemed to grow a foot. "You went looking for my daughter? You went on my *land?*"

Sean gulped and shook his head, but he didn't back down. "Uh-uh. Zoe was supposed to meet me where—" His hand flew toward his mouth—a touchingly childish gesture—and stopped midair. Fisted again. "She didn't meet me," he finished sullenly. "What'd you do to her?"

"Zoe is grounded. She doesn't set foot off Suntop till I give the word, and when she does, believe me, it won't be to meet you."

"No!" Sean shook his head wildly as his voice cracked. "I've got to see her!"

"Get this straight," Rafe said softly. "You won't be seeing my daughter again—ever. You've done your damage, and now you're finished. It's over."

"It isn't!" Sean cried raggedly. "Dana?"

"Oh, Sean…" He never asked her for anything, and now that he had, she'd give all she held precious to help. But he might as well ask her to move a mountain.

"You come sneaking on my land, and I'll have you arrested for trespassing," Rafe continued. "And I promise you, sonny boy, this charge will stick. You got that?"

"Try and stop me, asshole!" Sean spun, jumped three steps to ground level and took off running.

Rafe took two strides after him, but Dana blocked his path. "Don't."

"So help me God, Dana, if he comes sniffing after her onto my land, I'll hog-tie the brat and haul him home to you in my truck!"

"I've heard enough threats for one day." Dana swiped the hair from her eyes, retreated to her swing and sat.

"How long have you been raising him alone? He's out of control."

"And I've had enough criticism about my child-rearing techniques, thank you. Want me to start in on yours?" Crossing her arms to wall him out, she closed her eyes, tipped her head back. Willed him to disappear in a puff of smoke.

No such luck. He growled something wordless, and the swing tilted as he sat down beside her. Their thighs brushed, and she shied away. After a moment, the swing rocked backward on its chains, glided forward. Dana heaved a sigh up from around her toes, lifted her heels up to the cushion, clasped her ankles. The swing arced gently through her self-imposed darkness, through the fragrance of roses. How odd to be rocked; she'd grown so used to doing for herself.

"Well, what now?" he asked finally.

"Now? I suppose I take the steaks out to warm up. I start the coals, bake the bread, make cookies for dessert tonight..." A distant, sleepy wail drifted through an upstairs window. "I comfort my daughter..."

"And what do I do about mine?"

"Try listening instead of ranting?" she suggested.

Warm fingers closed around her arm, just above her elbow. "Help me persuade her. Please?"

She bet he didn't beg for help often. Still, she sighed and shook her head. "Can't do it, Rafe. Zoe needs to find *her* way, not be shoved into somebody else's plan for her life."

"It's the best plan," he insisted. "The only plan right for her."

"Then maybe she'll come to see that in time. But it's not for me to say." *Nor you.*

The swing lurched as he stood. She squeezed her eyes

tighter shut, then waited, willing him gone. At least her life had been peaceful before he stormed into it. If he left now… Was it too late to go back to that?

"Thanks," he said bitterly.

"You're welcome, Rafe." Eyes closed, Dana waited till the crunch of his steps across the gravel had faded. Till she could hear nothing but the Ribbon River, chuckling down the mountainside. She sighed again, opened her eyes and went into her kitchen.

Who was she kidding? From now on, nothing would be the same.

"HERE COMES YOUR DADDY," drawled Anse Kirby from his higher vantage point. He'd been lounging sideways, one arm braced back on the rump of his red roan, Tiger, watching Zoe wrestle with the top wire of the fence. Now he straightened in the saddle and gathered his reins.

"Oh?" Zoe levered her pliers around the curve of the cedar post, tightening the wire, then hammered the loosened staple home. She pulled a second staple from the carpenter's apron she wore over her jeans and whacked that in, downstream of the first. "What should I do? Turn cartwheels?"

"Smile might go a long ways." Anse apparently addressed the lowering sun.

"Yeah, go ahead. Take his side." As her father's top hand, he could hardly do else, Zoe supposed, but she was in no mood to be fair.

"Just a general observation. Woofle's outgrinned you 'bout twelve to one, today."

"Well, he had a banner day—found something dead to roll in. Me, I've done nothing but ride fence." A chore she usually loved in the summertime. But not today. Not when she'd been given into Anse's care like a five-year-old pest, with the implicit order, *Keep her occupied.* "I'm sorry, I know I've been a grump."

"We all get a mood on, from time to time." He made no visible move, but, responsive to a tensing of Anse's thighs, Tiger swung to face the oncoming rider and set off at a lazy jog. Ignoring the horsemen, Zoe slogged off to the next post. Out on her flank, Woofle rose from the grass and trotted on a parallel course, careful to preserve the twenty-foot margin she'd ordained.

She'd completed that post, when the shadow of a horse and rider blocked the sun. "Anse will finish up here, Zoe. Let's go."

She shrugged and hung her hammer over the wire, untied her apron and draped it over the post. Anse had already dismounted and collected Miel, her little palomino, who'd been standing ground-hitched, placidly grazing. He passed her the reins with a wink. "Thanks for the help, Zoe."

Like he needed it. She gave him a reluctant smile. "Sure. Anytime." Probably every day this summer, if her father had his way. *But he won't.* She cast Rafe a mutinous glance as her leg swung over the saddle and she found her stirrups.

Under the brim of his Stetson, his eyes were expressionless. He jerked his chin uphill. "Suntop?"

It was their favorite ride. A rift in the mountains to the west allowed the setting sun to shine through, gilding that hilltop long after the rest of their valley was plunged in to purple shadows. The ranch took its name from the peak. But today? She shrugged, and when he turned Tobasco, his big half Arab, half quarterhorse gelding up the slope, she went with him. But not knee to knee as they usually rode, with her on his left so that his roping hand was unobstructed. Tensing her inside leg, she forced Miel five feet to the left of their normal position. The palomino lashed her silver tail, but accepted the command, ears disapproving. Zoe pulled her Stetson low over her forehead, giving her father nothing but the top of her hat.

They rode in silence, just the *jingle* of a bit, the soft *swish* as the horses breasted the waist-high wildflowers, the lush grass. June was always her favorite month, but this year? Everything had changed—such a stupid jerk, *she'd* changed everything. *And now I get to live with it.*

Her eyes lit on a blue columbine, robin's egg blue, with a central streak of white in its throat. A keeper. "Don't wait," she called, twisting around in her saddle. She chose one of the whippy bamboo poles from the bundle she always carried behind her, reached for the orange surveyor's ribbon in her saddlebag. Dismounted and set up her flag so she could find the plant tomorrow. She'd been hybridizing wild columbine since she was twelve, combining colors and petal markings in search of bluer blues, bigger blossoms, odd new patterns. She had some stunners by now.

He waited for her, of course, and this time their eyes met as she mounted. "That's just what I mean, Zoe. You won't have time to think about things like that if you keep your baby. You know a lot, but there'll be professors at Harvard who could take you to the next level, then the next, and the next. Show you things you've never dreamed about."

Or that I have. But she couldn't let it matter. "Do you remember that time back in ninth grade when Mrs. Pollock tried to make me dissect that frog?"

His lips curved up, then abruptly down. "That's different."

"Sure is. That was just a poor dorky frog." A frog she'd ransomed, with a month of detentions and a twenty-page essay for her refusal. "But this is a baby."

Tobasco danced sideways to some inner turmoil of his rider, then snorted and swerved back into line. "I brought you up to face the hard choices. Do you remember the time I shot Nacho?"

She would never forget it. They'd been up in the high country, moving the cattle to their summer range, a day's ride from the nearest vet, and a vet couldn't have healed that break, anyhow. Nacho had been Rafe's friend, his partner, the smartest, funniest horse she'd ever known. If her father could have cut off his arm to save that old gelding, he'd have done so. "I remember. But you had no choice, Daddy. I have."

"It's the wrong choice. It'll wreck your life. Wreck everything you've worked for."

"It'll *change* my life."

"For the worst!"

"Is that what it did to yours—what I did?"

His eyes swerved away. "I was thinking about your mother."

"I wrecked *her* life," Zoe said flatly. But she'd known that from the time she could toddle. For the first three years after her mother's death, there had been no one to keep her, while her father cowboyed from ranch to ranch, except her mother's parents—Zoe's *abuelo* and *abuelita,* Paco and Inéz Cavazos. She'd understood their language long before she spoke it, and the house had been filled with it, her presence constantly invoking words of regretful, soft Spanish. Long, meandering tales recounting Pilar's scholastic triumphs, her shining talents, her grace, her beauty, her ultimate tragedy. Nobody's fault, *niña,* but *¡qué lástima!*— what a pity and what a waste! A waste that she'd been ransoming all her life, just as she'd paid for the frog, report card after dazzling report card.

But now that obligation collided with this. Couldn't he see?

"You didn't wreck anybody's life. You were Pilar's pride and joy."

Was I? But then, where was Pilar going the day she slammed out of the house, weeping and raging, and drove off—never to return? Zoe couldn't recall the words of that last fight; it merged into too many before it. But she could remember the bitterness, the rifle-crack retorts flying back and forth, while she peeked through her bedroom door. *If I was her pride and joy, then why did she leave me? Why wasn't I in the car with her when it hit the abutment?*

She'd never dared ask. Without Pilar, she and her dad had simply closed ranks and soldiered on.

"You're *my* pride and joy," her father continued huskily. "I want only the very, very best for you. And a baby at seventeen, sweetheart. That isn't it."

"You always taught me to make the best of things."

"The best of this is to own up to your mistake. To look an ugly but necessary choice in the eye and to take it, like I did with Nacho."

"But this time I'm not deciding just for me, Daddy. What's best for my—"

"No!" he cried harshly. "Don't think like that. It's a possibility, not a person. Just a fork in your road. You take one fork and your life will be a trap—a cage with you looking out through the bars, wishing for what might have been. You take the other fork, Zoe, and you—" He turned up his free hand to the blue above. "You fly…you fly as high and far as your wings will take you. *Trust* me on this. I'm right. I know I'm right."

There was a lump in her throat the size of an ice cube. His love was so much harder to resist than his rage. But still… "It's not just a fork. It's a teeny bit of Sean and me, dividing and growing by the hour."

"Sean!" Tobasco threw up his blood-bay head, then snapped it down and pranced in place, a drumbeat of frustration; speed denied. "If I was choosing a sire for my grandchild—"

"Daddy!" He was hopeless—a hundred years out of date—and she knew she was turning as red as a stoplight.

"Nothing but an insolent little—"

"He's a good kid!" *An absolute hunk in the making,* but she knew better than to say that.

"That's all you were shooting for—good? You deserve the best—in another five years or so."

"He is the best. You're underestimating him."

"Whatever he is, he's out of this. This is between you and me. Someday you'll know I was right."

She shook her head. *Don't say it, don't say it!* Once he'd said something he never backed down.

"You're getting an abortion as fast as I can arrange it," he said. "Tomorrow I'll—"

"No!" she yelled, yanking off her hat and slamming it to the ground. Miel shied violently, and Zoe spun her back around, half rearing. "No, I am *not,* and you can't make me!" They were back to where they'd deadlocked last night.

"Zoe…"

She'd heard that tone before, like gravel sliding down a chute—that time he'd fired a hand for beating a horse, the time he'd thrown that party of drunken hunters off the ranch. Heard it only once or twice in her life aimed *her* way. She shook her head, helpless to stop him or back down.

"You take my advice on this one…or you get out of my house. Off my land."

"F-f-fine," she cried through trembling lips. "Then I'll do that!" She touched her spurs to Miel's flanks and shot off down the mountain.

"Zoe!" he yelled after her. But even had it been safe to take her eyes off the slope ahead, the grass blurring with the horse's speed and her tears, she wouldn't have looked back. She swerved Miel to the right, choosing a gentler grade before they fell head over heels. Woofle shot off to the left, ears flying, tongue flapping, taking the direct down-hill line, racing her home.

Her home no longer. *You want me, you come stop me,* she thought, gritting her teeth against the threatening sobs. *Please, take it back.* Tobasco could catch her mare any day. But she heard no thundering hoofbeats behind—only Miel, huffing like a little steam engine through the high grass.

She'd thrown half a dozen shirts, a few pairs of jeans into the open suitcase on her bed, when he filled her door-way. She yanked open her lingerie drawer and seized a handful of underthings. Dumped those on the growing pile. "You'll have to keep Miel for me," she muttered without turning her head. "Till I can…" Her eyes filled with tears. There was no way she could afford to keep a horse on her own. She'd be lucky to keep herself. *And my baby.*

He stalked across to the bed, lifted her stacks of clothes out and set them on the spread, closed the suitcase and tucked it under one arm. "Forget what I said, Zoe. I didn't mean it."

"Oh." She spun away, hugging herself to contain the sobs. "Oh, Daddy, I…"

He came up behind her, hovering, unable to touch her. "You're my daughter, right or wrong, baby. But this is *wrong.*"

"I can't do it. I won't!"

"Whoa! *Hush.* Don't be so quick to decide. We've both been shooting our mouths off way too much. I'd like you to consider it, just for a day or two. Would you do that for me? Please?"

She stood, face averted, tears dripping, torn between pleasing him and speaking her heart. "If I—" She stopped and knuckled her nose. "If I do that, Daddy, will you do something for me?"

"Whatever you need, sweetheart."

"I need to see Sean."

CHAPTER SEVEN

"THEY'RE COMING!" Sean yelled as he loped up from the meadows, waving his fishing rod. For the past hour he'd kept vigil on the low concrete bridge that spanned the Ribbon River, a quarter mile below the house.

Ever since Dana had informed him of the Montanas' request for a Monday-afternoon interview with the Kershaws, Sean had affected a sullen nonchalance, but the details betrayed his true emotion. He'd taken a second shower after lunch—an unheard-of event—then changed from his father's old Grateful Dead T-shirt to a blue cotton dress shirt, tucked into a fresh pair of jeans.

"It's them!" he panted, stumbling to a halt where she knelt at the foot of the stairs to the front porch.

In the distance, Rafe Montana's shiny black pickup raised a trail of dust as it approached the bridge. Dana glanced down at the window boxes she'd been planting—her own form of nervous make-work. "Sean, would you run grab the pitcher of lemonade from the fridge and that platter of cookies on the counter?"

Might as well do the thing handsomely, she'd decided. High tea and civilized conversation on the porch. Petra had done her own small part to make the affair a success by nursing earlier than usual, then allowing herself to be put down for an afternoon nap. "Sleep on, sweetie," Dana murmured as she pulled off her gardening gloves and brushed her bangs from her eyes. She glanced down at her jeans, swept them free of peat moss, then tucked the tails of her red sleeveless shirt. She'd had a strange impulse to wear a sundress for this occasion and had rejected the notion. Who was she trying to impress—Zoe? Though she *had* clipped on a pair of opal ear studs that she hadn't worn in more than a year.

She touched one lobe nervously, then turned as Sean banged out the front door. "On the table, thank you." The view from the front porch out over the lower valley was one of the ranch's finest—soothing, serene, conducive to calm discussion. *Now, if Rafe and Sean will just keep their tempers...*

"Welcome," Sean muttered, rattling down the stairs. He clutched half a dozen of her shortbread cookies bundled in a paper napkin.

"I thought we'd eat those here on the porch," she called after him, but if he heard, he didn't respond. He brought up short beside Rafe's pickup and yanked open Zoe's door.

For one dreadful moment Dana feared he'd lift her down from the truck and kiss her. She could see Rafe scowling already through the windshield. Then Zoe tumbled out, all impossibly long legs, raucous red hair and brilliant smile. She turned to wave up at Dana. "Good afternoon, Mrs. Kershaw!"

"Hello, Zoe." So finally, she'd formally meet the girl. There had been no time, the other night. Or no, apparently not. Because Zoe had already spun away to grab Sean's arm and drag him toward the river.

"Half an hour and not a minute more," Rafe called after them. "And stay in sight." He crossed his arms. *"Zo-e?"*

This time she glanced back impatiently. *"Yes,* Daddy, we will!"

Rafe sauntered up the lawn to Dana, shaking his head. "Not quite what I'd planned. I meant to introduce you two."

"Bound to happen one of these days." She stood irresolute before him for a moment. Shake his hand? No, that didn't feel right, but some gesture seemed necessary....

She tipped her head toward the porch. "Well, there's lemonade for the chaperones. Come on up."

Rafe accepted a glass and a cookie, then prowled her porch, staring down toward the river. Finally he settled on a chair that gave him a clear view of the proceedings. Dana followed his gaze and saw Zoe perched on a water-smoothed boulder on the far side of the creek; Sean sat cross-legged before her, leaning forward intently, courtier at the feet of his queen.

"I told her if they so much as held hands, I'd call a halt," Rafe growled. "So far, so good."

"What exactly did you have in mind?" Dana pulled up a chair beside him. She'd assumed some sort of family council, perhaps a discussion of Sean's, and therefore her, responsibilities.

Eyes fixed on the distant pair, he heaved a sigh. "Being the hard guy has gotten me nowhere. So now I'm trying the soft approach. I asked her not to knee-jerk rule out abortion—to consider it for a day or two. And in return, she asked to see your boy. I'm praying that maybe what she has in the back of her mind is asking his approval to terminate." He turned to skewer her with his gaze, twin spears of blue. "Do you think he'd give it, if that's what she's asking?"

"I think Sean wants only one thing in the world—whatever's best for Zoe."

"If that were true, he'd never have gotten her in trouble."

"You never made a mistake?"

He growled something wordless and gulped lemonade. "What burns me up," he muttered after a moment, "is how unfair it is! His life will roll merrily on, exactly as before. While Zoe? Her whole life has been derailed."

"Only if she chooses for that to be so." And it was Zoe who had messed with the track switch, Dana was sure, watching the girl's animated gestures.

Rafe grimaced. "She may not feel she has a choice, at this point. Zoe has her principles. Always has. She's been a vegetarian since she was eight, when it hit her what happens to the cattle after we ship 'em out."

One more reason to get her to a doctor—and soon, Dana worried. She'd need to take extra care with her diet if she ate no meat.

"One more reason she has to go away to college, find a career," Rafe said, echoing her thoughts grimly. "She loves the outdoors, but she'll never make a rancher or a rancher's wife."

"She's your only child?" Dana already knew his answer. He looked like an eagle, guarding his one fledgling from the top of a pine tree.

Eyes fixed on the girl, he nodded.

Which meant he'd carved himself a kingdom—and what a struggle that must have been, the way land prices were rising in Colorado—and now he had no one to cherish and inherit his achievement. *Does that hurt, I wonder?* How could it not? And it showed the man's basic generosity— Rafe was looking to his daughter's good at the cost of his own. *He'll never force her into an abortion,* Dana realized with a rush of relief. If he wouldn't demand that Zoe follow in his footsteps with the ranch, then he wouldn't insist on this, despite how deeply he felt it.

He turned the full weight of his gaze upon her. "What about Sean? You're his stepmother. I suppose that means his mother's dead, too?"

"No. His mother's in San Diego." She found that it was easier to speculate about Rafe's past than to reveal her own, but his eyes dragged the story from her. "When she and Peter divorced—a year before I ever met Peter..." Though

Margot still saw her as the thief, the home wrecker. Somehow she must have thought that someday, someway, she'd win Peter back. "She gave him full custody."

"That's odd."

"Not, apparently, if you knew her. She has…problems."

Rafe dropped a hand on the back of her chair and leaned closer. "The sort of problems that Sean might pass on to his child?"

"N-no." This had never occurred to her. She bit her lip and turned to look down at Peter's son. He'd been depressed this past year, but that was entirely understandable, normal…

Two fingertips hooked around her chin and reclaimed her gaze. "What are we talking, here, Dana? Mental illness?"

"Oh, no. Not unless you want to call extreme self-involvement an illness. She just sees the world as circling around her own problems."

"*What* problems?"

"She…drinks too much. And takes pills—downers, uppers, whatever her mood requires. Not illegal drugs, just too many drugs from too many obliging doctors."

"Wonderful!" His hand dropped away. "My grandchild's likely to be an alcoholic—or an addict. Well, that settles it!"

"Don't think that way!" she pleaded. "It's just a rotten upbringing, that's all. Her mother was an actress—B movies and such. And apparently the father bailed out early—sent money, but no love or attention when she needed it. Margot was dragged up, a typical Hollywood child, alternately spoiled and neglected. How can you blame her?"

"Hey, that's the beauty of it nowadays. Nobody's ever to blame. So she gave her kid away like a pair of worn-out shoes?"

"Maybe it was the one truly unselfish thing she's ever done. She was going into a clinic to dry out at that point.

Peter was a rock, obviously the one who could best care for Sean. So she gave him up.''

''But after his father died? How long had you two been married?''

''Only a year.'' The skiing weekend had been their anniversary gift to each other.

''She didn't want to change her mind after that?''

Dana shrugged. ''She toyed with the idea, I think. But Peter had appointed me guardian. He made me promise that I'd never let Margot have Sean. He was convinced she'd ruin him, just as she'd been ruined. So if she'd insisted, I would have fought her.''

''Though you'd only had the kid for a year?''

She met his eyes point-blank. ''Sean was the person Peter loved most in all the world. And I promised.''

She felt as if no one had looked at her—really *seen* her—for fourteen long months. Now his blue eyes moved through her like sunshine through clear water. As his gaze roved down to her lips, she turned away, but saw nothing, felt only the drumming of her heart, the play of his gaze upon her stirring flesh.

''So she didn't insist,'' he murmured finally.

''What? Oh, no, she didn't. At the time Peter died, she'd just entered another clinic, her third or fourth attempt to dry out. Some sort of health–exercise–clean-living community. No room for children, apparently. She wrote Sean once or twice, maybe made some promises she didn't keep—that's precisely her style. And that's the last we've heard of her, thank God.''

''Wish to God she'd taken him!'' he muttered.

So much for their moment of connection. ''Well, she didn't.''

Restless, he stood and paced behind her, looking down at their children. Sean and Zoe had taken off their shoes and were now wading downstream toward the bridge, arms outstretched for balance, still talking nonstop. "Whatever else they are, they're friends," she murmured, as he paused behind her.

"So?"

"So I'm glad. To my mind, at the very least, babies should be made in friendship."

He snorted. "Babies shouldn't be made by accident—period!"

But now that they've made one, what do we do? And Sean—she'd worried that he had no friends, while all along—for the past few months, anyway—he'd had Zoe. However they solved this problem, Rafe wouldn't allow their friendship to continue, she was sure. *Sean, I'm so sorry....*

Rafe stopped to lean out over the balustrade, and she went to join him.

"Nice land," he murmured, peering out over her valley. "Great water, wonderful grazing—and you're wasting it on dudes."

"I'm afraid I know a lot more about people and cooking than I do about cows."

He made a wry sort of sound, something between a grunt and a laugh. "I tried to buy this spread, 'bout three years back. A nice old girl owned it then, a widow lady. She was running it as a dude ranch, too, though it seemed like she had more cats around the place than tourists."

"Peter's Aunt Harriet. She decided that she and the cats had had enough of snow country, that they were moving to Florida. So she offered the place to Peter—she wanted it to stay in the family. We bought it summer before last." Dana swallowed painfully, and turned her empty glass round and round on the railing. "I was the one who really wanted it. Who pushed Peter into buying. He was happy enough teaching high school in San Diego. If..." *If I'd let well enough alone...* The vista below blurred to a rainy watercolor.

"Ifs will break your heart if you let them, Dana."

He was right. She'd made a resolution, months ago, that it was time to stop grieving, for Petra's sake if not her own. Above all else, Peter would have wanted her to raise his daughter in happiness. A child's first perceptions were crucial and they should be of a joyful world—a world of butterflies and skyrockets and laughter—not a world of sorrow. *But sometimes it's so hard, Peter!*

"So it's just you running this outfit?" he asked after a moment. Moving them back to a safe topic.

"No, there's also Tim, my dude wrangler, such as he is."

"Meaning?"

"Meaning he wrangles with the dudes, he wrangles with me, he'd kick the dog if we had one. I guess you'd call him a cowboy curmudgeon." And a lazy, hard-drinking bum. But for the money she could pay, Tim was probably as good as she could get. At least he showed up for work most days, since his cabin was part of his salary.

Rafe frowned. "That can't be good for business, can it?"

"It's not the best." One of her guest families last week had demanded a discount at the end of their stay. Tim was supposed to have given them daily riding lessons, but he'd failed to appear for three of the seven days. If they'd complained earlier, she might have corrected the situation, but they hadn't. After their refund, she'd barely recouped her expenses on that one. "I try to sell him as local color."

He opened his mouth to disagree, and she hurried on. "And Sean helps out." When he felt like it. "He owns a fourth of the ranch, by Peter's will."

"Does he," Rafe muttered, turning around to study the clapboards with which the house was sheathed. "So how come he isn't painting his inheritance? If he lets this go another year... And I noticed your corral around back, when I was here yesterday. Some of those rails need replacing. Then there's your truck. If he owns a piece of that, too—''

"Rafe, he's not even fifteen."

"If he's old enough to make a baby, he's damn sure old enough to take care of what he owns. Old enough not to be dogging it, while you're working yourself to a frazzle."

"Thank you, but I'm on top of the situation."

"Are you?"

High-handed. She'd had him pegged right the first time he barged into her kitchen. "You could mind your own business, you know." Maybe he could.

"That's just what I'm doing. You think I wouldn't look into the character of a young man who seduced my daughter?"

"Rafe." She jabbed him with a forefinger and leaned into it. "Your precious Zoe is a *cradle robber!* She's the one who should have known better. A fourteen-year-old boy is a slave to his—"

"Hush!" He shoved her fingers aside. "Here they come."

She glanced aside guiltily, to see Zoe and Sean walking up the lawn with their arms wrapped around each other's waists, presenting a united front, Sean's face glowing with a pride of possession that made Dana blink. Her stepson's feelings ran deeper than friendship, she was beginning to fear.

"Daddy?" Coming to a halt on the lawn below, Zoe tipped back her head.

She wasn't a pretty child, but someday she would be a striking woman, Dana thought, when she grew into her body. Right now, Zoe was too thin, too awkward and too pale—her clouds of freckles stood out against her pallor.

Her eyes were Rafe's own—dark blue, direct and, at the moment, very anxious. "We've decided," she announced.

Beside her, Sean squared his shoulders and nodded.

"What?" Rafe said tensely, moving to lean out over the railing.

"You brought me up to make the hard choices..." Zoe gulped and continued, her eyes suddenly sparkling with tears. "So I— So we're—making it."

"Good girl," Rafe murmured.

"We're keeping our baby," she blurted defiantly.

CHAPTER EIGHT

"THE HELL YOU SAY!" Rafe started for the stairs. "You spent half an hour deciding that? Playing patty-cakes with Romeo there? Right. We're out of here."

"Rafe!" Dana caught at the back of his shirt, then let go and scurried after. "Rafe, wait!" As Rafe stalked toward his daughter, Sean pulled away from Zoe and moved to block him, chin up, hands fisting.

"No!" Dana cried, dashing between them, arms raised. "Now everybody…just…calm *down!*" She flattened either hand on a heaving male chest. "Zoe, dear, it looks like you want what's good for your baby," she said, speaking very fast. "And of course, your father—" she patted his chest— exhibit A "—only wants what's best for you." Her audience was nodding reluctantly. She caught a breath and forged on. "So, in that case, since we're all agreed on that, perhaps there's another possibility you ought to consider. Have you thought about adoption?"

"Um, not really," Zoe admitted. "I—"

"I think you should, then—we should be exploring *every* option. So if you and Sean would sit down and drink a glass of lemonade, and think *very* carefully about that, consider the pros and the cons, your father and I are going to take a walk." She clamped onto his forearm and swept him downhill.

"Wait a minute!" he protested, though she'd gotten him moving. "Adoption? I don't think—"

"*Don't* think, please, not yet. Just walk with me, Rafe."

She transferred her clasp to his inner elbow, and reluctantly he came along. "The first rule of negotiations is to keep talking, right? If you grab Zoe and stomp off now, you're ending any chance that we can work this out."

"Adoption isn't a satisfactory ending, dammit! She's off to Harvard in September."

"You know, you might have to compromise." The slope steepened to a rocky path as they neared the river.

"Compromise, hell!"

"She isn't one of your silly cows you can just shove down a chute. She's your—*oops!*" The rock she'd stepped on rolled out from under her.

He spun around, his free arm whipping around her waist to clamp her against him. "Easy!"

She dangled for a startled moment in his arms, then he lowered her toes to the ground. "Easy there." His voice had dropped to an intimate growl. They stood molded together from breast to thigh. "You've got to watch where you're going."

In this electric moment, all she could watch was the pulse hammering in the hollow of his throat…his smiling mouth when she made herself look higher. Blue eyes to drown in. She could drown in this sensation of infinite strength, hers for the asking.

She couldn't ask. She squirmed, then he let her go, except for her hand. "Take it slow," he advised, following her down the path.

Resentment flared as she heard the amusement in his voice—an insufferably masculine smugness that he could make her aware of him, make her body respond to his. *I suppose he thinks I'm the starved little widow.* But if she hungered, it was for something much deeper and more essential than a superb male body.

"As I was saying," she said determinedly, "you may have to compromise. You probably could bully Zoe into having an abortion, but at what cost?'' Reaching the river, she stopped on a boulder and kicked off her huaraches. ''Do you think she'd ever forgive you if you did that?''

''Maybe not right away, but eventually.'' Rafe watched as she rolled up her jeans. Sitting on a nearby rock, he pulled off his boots. ''But maybe that's my role here, Dana. I'm the guy who has to make the tough decisions. The ones nobody thanks you for, but that are right in the end.''

''Maybe.'' Arms outstretched, she stepped delicately into the ankle-deep, icy water and grimaced. ''Or maybe you're the tough guy whose daughter never speaks to him again. What if, ten years from now, Zoe decides to start a family and finds out, for some reason, that she can't? That you'd forced her to abort her one chance ever.''

''That's not likely to happen,'' he protested, joining her as she waded downstream.

''No,'' Dana admitted. ''But if it did?''

He scowled unhappily.

''Or maybe Zoe never forgives you for stealing a choice away that should have been hers to make. A choice that would have shaped her growing up.''

''It's too early for her to grow up! Too rough a way to grow up. I wanted something better for her than Pilar—'' He shook his head helplessly. ''Dammit!''

He was so frustrated that she wanted to laugh aloud. He probably hadn't met a problem in years that he couldn't fix, handle or demolish—and now this, presented to him by the person he loved most in the world. Not an enemy to be overwhelmed by superior force or wit, but his own fragile daughter.

''If you let *Zoe* make the choice, whatever choice she makes, I think you stand the best chance that she won't regret it one day. That she won't blame you. Won't blame herself.'' They'd reached the midpoint of the river, and Dana halted, with water the color and clarity of aquamarines rushing around her calves. "That's worth a compromise, surely?"

They waded on till the chill in the water drove them out, then she led him to the smoother boulders on the far bank. Stretching out and closing her eyes, she let the delicious heat of the rocks soak through her body. Rafe sat beside her, looking moodily back at the porch, where Zoe and Sean talked intently on the top step.

BAD ENOUGH TO BE WORRIED about Zoe, without this distraction. Rafe glanced down at the woman beside him, wishing she were teasing him, reluctantly certain she was not. He'd seen the tears in her big gray-green eyes whenever she spoke of her husband. *She's not ready for a lover yet.* But tell that to his hormones, which stood to attention and saluted every time he laid eyes on her.

With her off in a daydream, he could feast his eyes, and he did so now, turning to rest one hand on the rock beside her head. That motion had its own momentum—he could see himself turning all the way over and settling down upon her...lacing his fingers into her shiny hair...tasting those ripe-berry lips for the first time, while she sighed and molded her softness to his urgent hardness.

Down, boy. He glanced toward the house, hauling his thoughts back to reality with a major effort of will. Zoe and Sean paced the lawn, talking, talking, talking. Nothing resolved there yet.

Rafe's head swung back to Dana the way a sunflower follows the sun. His attraction was much more than physical. She had warmth, wit, a sense of humour. And she was a keeper of promises. *If I'd found you any other time...*

But not now. This was a woman in no mood to be chased, and even if she were, bedding her should be the last thing on his mind, what with Zoe's disaster.

She stirred beside him, and guiltily he turned toward the

house, where the kids were—surprise, surprise—still talking.

"What's wrong with adoption?" she murmured drowsily.

"Turns my stomach." He glanced down and found she hadn't opened her eyes. "To think of my own blood out in the world where I can't protect it? Blown off to God knows where like a bit of dandelion fluff? Always wondering if it lit on hard rock or fertile ground? That isn't right. If you make a child, then you care for it—all the way through. Better her child was never born than that."

"The child might not agree."

"You're thinking of a happy, well-cared-for baby like your Petra. But once she's out of your hands, who knows what happens to her?"

Dana opened her eyes and gave him a gentle smile. "A lot of good people out there are desperate for a baby. An adoption agency—"

He scowled and shook his head. "Even assuming that, good people divorce, grow ill, go bankrupt...die. So there's your baby, given off to fate, and you not knowing. Not ever able to step in and fix things if they need fixing. Doesn't strike me as much of a solution."

She turned over abruptly and sat up, facing away from him. "But it may be the best solution you can hope for, in this case."

"Maybe." He could feel a muscle ticking in his jaw. "But I don't feel it. It's not right for the child, and it's damn sure not right for Zoe. I want her to walk away from this with no damage, no regrets, no looking back. If she gives away her child, she'll always be wondering where her baby is. Is the kid happy, healthy, loved? It would be an anchor she'd drag behind her all her life, when I want her to fly."

"Rafe, no matter what she decides, there's going to be some heartache in this one."

"I'm here to minimize it."

"If you can." Dana drew up her knees, crossed her forearms on top to support her chin. "It's not as if I'm thrilled with the idea, either. That's Peter's grandchild she'd be giving up. He told me once that grandchildren are the payoff for all the grief your children give you. He wanted lots of grandkids. Imagined them coming here, summering with us, riding, playing in this river... So to give away his first grandchild—who knows?—possibly the only one there'll ever be—"

"If Sean keeps scoring like this, believe me, there'll be more."

Her back stiffened. Regretting the dig, he yearned to rub a knuckle up her spine, apology and exploration all in one—but he didn't.

His eyes shifted to a movement on the lawn. Zoe waving at them. "Uh-oh, here we go."

WHEN THEY REACHED the house, Dana tried to persuade everyone to sit up on the porch, but Zoe wasn't having it. She stood, arms crossed low over her flat middle, her chin tucked, Sean at her side. "We've thought about it," she said dully, "and I guess we could do that—give our baby up for adoption." She clamped her teeth onto her lip and stared at the ground. Sean rubbed her shoulder blades, and Rafe shot him a warning glare, which the kid blandly ignored. "But we have some conditions," Zoe continued with soft determination.

Rafe opened his mouth to state that she and Sean were in no position to make conditions, but Dana nudged him and spoke. "Like what, Zoe?"

"We couldn't just give her—him?—away and never know what happened. If our baby was happy. Treated right.

So first, if we give her up, whoever adopts her has to be somebody we like and trust. And it's got to be somebody local, so we can keep an eye on her. And I want visitation rights.''

Dana blew out an audible breath. ''I can see why you'd want that, Zoe. But a lot of people who adopt wouldn't—''

''Most wouldn't,'' Rafe amended, gripping her arm to stop her. ''But wait—what about this?'' The answer had come to him all at once, fully formed, almost laughable in its simplicity and its rightness. ''Let Dana adopt your baby.'' He felt her body jolt, and she swung to stare at him, but he kept his gaze fixed on Zoe, *willing* her to see the rightness of this. Why hadn't he thought of this sooner?

''Dana would make a wonderful mother—you can see that, the way she is with her own. She raises your child, and I pay for it—schooling, medical, college, whatever—I handle every penny of the cost. And, of course, since I live just the other side of the mountain, I can drop in from time to time, see how your kid is doing and let you know. And then Sean will be right here to keep an eye on things.'' And change the diapers. He shot the kid a malicious grin. *Thought you'd play and not pay, sonny?* ''How about that?''

''Umm…'' Zoe's narrowed eyes moved from his face to Dana's. She pursed her lips and frowned. ''I don't know if—''

''It would work—work beautifully. What do you think, Dana?'' Rafe turned to meet her eyes—and flinched. The sensation was akin to staring down the bore of a double-barreled shotgun, with a shaky finger on its trigger. Her pupils had expanded to two black circles of shock, her brows were arched in disbelief, her face had gone greeny-white.

From a second-floor window, a plaintive wail sounded—

Dana's own baby. Dana blinked rapidly, as if coming awake from a trance, then murmured with brittle calm, "If everyone will excuse me?" She backed away a step. "Come with me, Rafe."

Once they'd passed through the front door, she closed it—and flew at him. "How *dare* you?"

"Whoa! It's a good idea." She'd caught a fistful of his shirt, but clearly her intentions weren't to undress him.

"It's a rotten, stupid, *despicable* idea! You dump your troubles in my lap and go your merry way? And how could you toss it out like that, without asking me first?"

"I just thought it that minute." He peeled her fingers from his collar and held them.

"Well, *un*think it!" She glanced toward the ceiling. Petra's wails were gaining in volume and conviction. "I'm almost overwhelmed as it is! I can barely take care of my own. And you want to double my load?"

"No, I don't. You weren't listening. If you needed child care, a nanny or whatever they call 'em, I'd—"

"You need your head examined, Rafe Montana. That's what you need!" She snatched her hand from his grasp and turned toward the stairs.

"Think about it," he urged her, as she started up. "It's the perfect solution."

"For you, maybe!"

THAT NIGHT AT SUNTOP, they had a fire burning in the den. Rafe sat watching the evening news, while Zoe was curled in an easy chair across the room, tapping away on her laptop computer. When the phone rang, they glanced at each other warily. Rafe used the telephone for business, rarely for pleasure. Zoe normally kept in touch with a couple of girlfriends, but not this week, not since Rafe had grounded her. Car and phone privileges had been revoked till further notice.

"Shall I—" Zoe began, then stopped as Rafe shook his head.

She sat, glowering, while Rafe punched mute on the TV control and went to his adjoining office to answer. "Hello?"

"Rafe, it's Dana Kershaw."

An odd little jolt of pleasure shot through him. "Dana." He shut the door to the den, meeting Zoe's inquiring gaze as he did so. "What can I do for you?" He glanced toward the door that led to the kitchen—his office had been a pantry before he remodeled the house—but decided against closing that one.

"Actually, it's what I can do for you," she said briskly.

Still hadn't forgiven him for dropping his brainstorm on her like that. He'd thought to give her a little time to consider it, then push it again. "Oh?"

"I called my obstetrician, Dr. Hancock in Durango, and made an appointment for Zoe, this Friday at four p.m."

His smile faded. A doctor made the baby less of an abstraction, more a bitter reality. "You shouldn't have."

"Yes, but *you* should have, Rafe, and since you haven't..." She went on to request that if he and Zoe decided on some other doctor, would he please be sure to cancel this appointment. "And that's all I called about," she added, sounding less sure of herself in the face of his icy silence. "Oh, except I meant to ask, is Zoe taking a good multivitamin every day?"

"I set out mineral blocks in the pastures for my cattle to lick. You think I'd forget my daughter?"

"I'm sorry. It's just that..." She sighed, a soft sound that tautened the muscles in his thighs, as if she'd breathed upon him. "I'm sorry. But as long as I'm minding your business for you, here's one more thought. If you'd like me to, or if Zoe would be more comfortable, I'd be happy to drive her to the doctor. Accompany her into the office if she liked, or wait outside in the parking lot or whatever.''

Rafe didn't know about Zoe, but it certainly eased his discomfort. Women's business was best left to women. ''I'll ask her and get back to you.''

''Well, good. Then…''

Suddenly he didn't want her to cut their connection. ''You see that you're proving me right, don't you?''

''About?'' she asked on a note of caution.

''You've got just what it takes. You're organized, caring…'' Her house smelled of baking cookies. ''If I was choosing a mother for Zoe's baby—'' *My grandchild,* he realized with a grimace. He was too young for this nonsense!

''Rafe, you can forget it. Now, if that's all you—''

''But why?'' he blurted. ''I promise you, we could make this work. I've got more than enough money to smooth your way.''

''It's not a matter of money. I just—no! No, absolutely not. Forget it.''

''Hard to, when it's the obvious answer staring us in the face. And since you won't back me on arguing for an abortion, don't you think you should put your money where your mouth is?''

''No, actually I was thinking what a splendid father *you* are, Rafe. You've clearly done a fabulous job on Zoe. Me, I'm a rank beginner—Petra's less than a year old. But you've got sixteen-plus years of on-the-job training. I think *you* should adopt.''

Sixteen years was enough for a lifetime. *It's my turn to play, dammit! My turn to be free.* ''Thanks, but as I've made plain from the start, I'm not in favor of perpetuating the problem, much less diapering it.''

''Ah, but you could leave that to your nanny,'' Dana

observed with wicked innocence. "With all that money to smooth your way..."

When it came to verbal encounters, women were cutting horses, men were calves. Whichever way he turned, she was there ahead of him, blocking his path. "Besides," he said, giving up and going for a knock-out punch. "I'm seriously seeing a woman right now—" He'd dated Mitzy Barlow only last Saturday, though that seemed a lifetime ago, and she, at least, had been way too serious. "And I doubt that she'd want to adopt someone else's child."

"Oh," Dana said blankly.

There was an odd resonating silence between them, which Rafe suddenly wanted to fill with retractions or, at least, qualifications. But elaborating on a lie was the last thing he should do. *Quit while you're ahead.* And now, at least, they were even. She had a ghost for a husband, and he had an imaginary lover.

"Oh," said Dana again. Then her voice gained confidence. "Well, in that case, you'd better start working on Zoe. Convince her that insisting on visitation rights, once she gives up her baby for adoption, may not be practical."

"Right," he said gruffly. Though if he worked on anyone, it would be Dana. He still thought she was the perfect solution. But he needed a lever to move her, some argument she couldn't counter or ignore.

"So will you and Zoe decide about Dr. Hancock, and whether you want me to chauffeur?"

He'd ask his daughter, Rafe assured her. As Dana said goodbye, some instinct made him turn—in time to see Zoe fading back from the kitchen door. He hung up and sauntered after her.

She was neck deep inside the freezer, rummaging through its contents. "Pizza or chicken potpies?" she muttered.

"Eavesdropper," he said mildly.

"Well, you were talking about *me*." She yanked out a pizza, then slammed the door and turned to glare at him, unrepentant.

"Among other things."

"Yeah—like who are you seeing seriously? You mean that woman, Mitzy What's-her-name? You've only been out with her twice, Daddy!"

Swearing to himself, he did his best to look like the cat that has been into the cream. "Sometimes it happens that way." Her eyes glinted, and as she opened her mouth with the obvious retort, he aimed a finger. "But *not* to minors."

From: RedColumbine@Westbest.com
To: SanDiegan@Pipeline.net
9:30 P.M. Me again. Dad thinks I'm updating my journal. Wonder how long till he catches on that I'm plugging into the phone jack, not the electrical socket? But meantime, I just found out—he has a serious babe-friend!!! Mitzy Barlow, a real estate agent down in Durango. And I wanted to know: have you had a chance to ask Dana yet? I thought she looked pretty weirded out when Daddy popped his suggestion. But if she did like the idea…and you did. (Do you?) Tell me soon as you find out? 'Night, now, and I kiss you in the place that always gives you goose bumps.
Zzzzoe

P.S. Dana didn't seem at all like I imagined she'd be. Seemed sort of nice. Is it all an act or what?

CHAPTER NINE

THE FEINSTEINS had checked out of Aspen Cabin that morning. So after lunch Dana and Petra went up to ready it for the next set of guests, due sometime that evening. Dana spread a blanket on the bedroom floor and left the baby there, while she cleaned the bathroom and kitchenette.

Before starting on the living room, she checked and found that Petra had discovered the lowest drawer on the bureau and was working it open with fierce determination. Dana admired her discovery, drew the drawer out another inch to be sure nothing temptingly mouth-size awaited within, then hurried off to sweep the living room and plump the couch pillows.

Shrieks of glee from the bedroom announced that the drawer had been conquered, and Dana went to applaud. "You got it open, you clever girl!" She presented the tennis ball she'd brought along in her cleaning kit by dropping it into the drawer. "There. See? It's a place to put treasures."

Petra giggled uproariously, snatched up the toy and did her best to cram it into her mouth. When that didn't work, she offered it to her mother with a brow-crinkling frown.

"Thank you, sweetie. It's a beautiful ball. Why don't we put it in here and *close* the drawer." Dana left it open a crack so the baby could see the prize, and went to the bed. She whipped off the sheets, bundled them and turned—to find Sean slouched in the bedroom doorway. "Why, hello," she said. "Did you need something?"

"Nope. Just wondered what you and the monster were doing." He sauntered over to the dresser and squatted beside it. "What ya got, cupcake?"

His latest nickname for his sister, from an epic encounter she'd had with a chocolate cupcake last month. Sometimes Dana wished she hadn't named Petra after her father. The tribute apparently pained his firstborn. *One more time I blew it.* And Sean had been keeping score ever since the avalanche. *I wish you'd been there, too, Sean. To see how hard I tried.*

"Whoa—a ball!" he exclaimed, suitably impressed by Petra's revelation. "Check this out." He sent it careering off the inner walls of the drawer, while Petra stared in stupefaction. She flapped her hands with excitement and reached for it, eager to try the new trick.

Sean stood, as Dana snapped the first sheet out over the mattress. "Here." He crossed to the far side of the bed and pulled the fitted corner into place.

"Thanks," Dana said casually, careful to hide her shock. They finished that sheet, and she wafted the top one into position.

"What Mr. Montana said yesterday," Sean mumbled, tucking in the bottom corner. "About you adopting the— Zoe's— Um, our…"

She'd thought it was too good to be true. Not spontaneous forgiveness, but need. "Your baby, yes." She smoothed out the sheet and reached for the blanket. Still, she shouldn't knock it. They were talking; that was something. "What of it?"

His face was very pink. "I just wondered if you'd— What you thought about…that."

"Well…" *Is this where I fail you again, Sean? I'm doomed forever to be the wicked stepmother who won't come through for you?* But even to win his forgiveness, she couldn't see it. *There's only so much of me to go around.* "Well, I thought it was...interesting. What did you think?"

She shouldn't jump to the conclusion that he'd necessarily second Rafe's motion. At fourteen, Sean was more likely to be wishing this dilemma would simply go away, leaving him a footloose teenager with no more than a normal teenager's worries or burdens. *Never mind me. For Sean's sake, I shouldn't do it.* It would mean the end of his childhood. She tossed him a pillowcase, and shook her own pillow into its cotton sleeve. *Oh, Peter, should I give up your grandchild to save your son?*

"I, uh...guess it could work. Petra would have somebody to play with." He went to his half sister, who was emitting little grunts and whimpers of frustration—the drawer had jammed halfway out. "That better?" He eased it open a trifle.

So he did want her to adopt. She couldn't win with him. "We could make it work, if we had to," she agreed, sitting down on the bed. "But you and Zoe want what's best for your baby." He nodded solemnly, and she saw for the first time the resemblance between him and Petra—something about the eyebrows, the shape of their foreheads. "And what a baby needs most of all, Sean, is *two* loving parents."

"Petra doesn't have that," he muttered, reaching for her ball. He sent it flying up toward the cabin ceiling and caught it, then challenged Dana with a look.

"That's right," she agreed, willing the tears not to come, but they came anyway, blurring his face. "And I would do anything in the world for that not to be so, Sean. But it is so."

Petra let out a yelp and patted Sean's arm, reaching for her toy. He handed it over, but held on, so they grasped it together.

"Petra's fine right now," Dana continued, "but her life would be so much richer if she had a daddy to tickle and cuddle her.'' To show her the safety and strength of a man's arms. The wonderful comfort of a man's deep, loving voice. *I miss it, but she doesn't even know what she's missing. And do you ever find it in a lover if you never knew it first in a father?* ''I try to be her world, but I'm only half a world.''

The baby started to complain, and Sean released the ball. ''I play with her. Sometimes.''

They both knew it wasn't often. He seemed to shun his sister, though when he was trapped into interacting, he did it with sensitivity and humor. He was Peter's son; she would have expected no less.

''Yes, you give her a glimpse of what a daddy could be,'' Dana agreed.

''So I could do that for Zoe's and my baby, too. I can tickle and hug, can't I, cupcake?'' He caught the baby around her fat middle and lifted her overhead. ''Huh, how's that? You like that, huh? Huh?'' He brought the chortling child down to his lap, wrapped his arms around her and blew into her hair. ''That's not so hard.'' He looked up at her mother expectantly.

''Yes. You do a good job. But in four years, you'll probably be going away—off to college or some such.''

His gaze dropped to the baby's downy head. ''If not before.''

So he still dreamed of escaping Colorado—her—the heartache life had handed him. *But escaping to where, Sean?* A mother who never grew up? Who seemed to want a parent more than she did a son? Dana wasn't going to argue that one now. ''Yes, well… So, about the time your baby really started needing a father, you'd be gone.'' *Leaving me holding the bag.* Rafe and he both were thinking like men. *I should be surprised?*

''Um, yeah, I guess so.''

''And what if your baby turns out to be a son? A little

girl learns to be a woman by watching her mother, copying what she does—dolls, dress-up, makeup. But it's best for a boy if he has a man to tag along after, to show him how to walk like a man, think like a man.''

"Yeah..." Sean whispered. "I had that once."

And if I could give that back to you—give it back to me...

He sat there, thinking, while she smoothed the bedspread, then abruptly he set Petra aside and stood. "Well, thanks."

A retort born of guilt leaped to her lips, but she smothered it stillborn. That hadn't really sounded like sarcasm. "You're welcome," she said quietly, as he walked out the door.

From: SanDiegan@Pipeline.net
To: RedColumbine@Westbest.com
Hiya, Gorgeous! I asked Dana about adopting, and she said NO WAY. But I'm not sure she was being selfish (this time). Her reasons why not sort of seemed to make sense. I never thought about a baby needing two parents before, but— Oops, here she comes! HATE this computer in the kitchen. I'll write you tonight, after she goes upstairs. MegaKISS, your Sean

On Wednesday, Rafe gave Zoe two assignments. One, start halter-breaking the foals born this spring, and, two, make up her mind about adoption, if she still wouldn't take his advice. "We'll talk this evening," he warned her, as he set off with two of the hands to inspect the irrigation ditches.

He rode in again an hour before supper, as she was working with the third foal of the day—a fine husky colt that was as stubborn as he was intelligent. Willy, the oldest hand at Suntop, had helped her halter the fuzzy black baby, then shackle him by a short lead to the fence post planted in the center of the training corral. Zoe stood before the post with one hand on the lead, so the foal thought that she held him, while Willy led his dam to the far side of the corral and tied her there.

After an hour of plunging and squealing and fighting the lead, the exhausted foal was about to give in. Rafe reined Tobasco to a halt outside the pen and sat, watching. Ignoring him, Zoe kept up her nonstop flow of soothing words. "*Ah, caballito, no seas tonto.* Some things you gotta accept, you muleheaded little fuzzy black beauty. It's okay, 'sokay, *guapacito,* there's nothing to fear. *Ninguna cosita…*"

The colt reared one last time—and surrendered, plunging toward her, clearly feeling the wonderful slackening of the hateful pressure behind his ears as his resistance to the halter ended. "*Good* baby. Yes, that's the way. You see, there's *ninguna cosita* to fear." Zoe reeled him in, and he came haltingly, to stand at last trembling before her. She praised him with her hands and her words, then unclipped him from the post. "And now I lead you to mama. That's not so bad, is it?" The colt walked by her side, his eyes fixed on his dam, who nickered a placid welcome.

Zoe stopped him halfway there, and he snorted, but obeyed the halter's pull. "*Such* a smart one." She brought the foal up on the mare's right side, preventing him from going straight to the comforting udder. The mare nuzzled her child's stubbly mane, as Zoe untied her and led them both across the corral to Rafe. "I thought he'd never quit!"

"The smart ones know when to give in."

She bristled, but he was looking off toward a scrap of flaming cloud in the west, with Venus setting below it. Perhaps that remark had not been aimed her way. *The smart ones learn what to ignore.*

He opened the gate, and she led mare and foal to the gate of the home pasture, where the other mares and foals grazed. She unclipped the colt, stroked him one last time, then sent him hurrying after his mother. He was already nursing greedily as she turned away.

By the time Rafe had tended to his mount, she'd washed up and was messing around the kitchen. They'd have one of the frozen casseroles that Mrs. Higgins had left them. Zoe set out a slab of cheddar, some bread and fruit to round out their meal, then collapsed on the sofa till her father came downstairs again, hair wet from his shower.

While they ate, they talked of ranch matters, her success with the foals today, a story Willy had told her at lunchtime about a rattlesnake and a rooster. Zoe picked chunks of chicken from her portion and passed them by turns to Woofle and Trey, who crouched under the table to either side of her chair, the only two guys at Suntop Ranch who didn't disapprove of her vegetarian stance.

At last Rafe set his plate aside and looked up.

Here it comes. To forestall him, Zoe said, "Mrs. Kershaw called at lunch."

"Did she?" The grim line of his mouth eased for a moment.

"I told her I'd be happy if she'd drive me to the doctor," Zoe reported dutifully. "Though really, Daddy, if you'd let me drive myself—"

"We've already been through that."

"But this is *so* embarrassing. If you'd just—"

"But I won't, and that is *that.*"

"Fine!" She clashed the utensils on her plate, stood and slammed it into the sink. "Whatever."

"Did you give some thought to what I asked? If you're dead set on the adoption route, then we have to start looking for an agency, or possibly a lawyer. Maybe the doctor will…" Rafe trailed off, as Zoe crossed her arms and leaned back against the counter.

"I have thought about it. I've thought about it a lot. And, of course, it's still adoption. But I have one more condition,

Daddy, besides what Sean and I said yesterday, about visitation rights and all.''

How the devil had she done it—reversed their positions so she was the one dictating conditions and he the one scrambling to fulfill them? A muscle fluttered somewhere below Rafe's eye, but he said with outward calm, "Oh?"

"I've been thinking—and Mrs. Kershaw completely agrees with us—with this. She says it's absolutely critical that a baby have *two* parents, not just a mother. So if Sean and I are going to give our baby up, it's got to be to a couple—not to a single mom or a single anybody. And, of course, the couple needs to be happily married, I guess— or at least happy. That's maybe the most important of—''

"Mrs. Kershaw put this notion into your head?" Rafe threw his napkin down on the table and stood. Damn the woman—she was crossing him at every turn! How the blue blazes was he supposed to produce not just one, but *two* loving adoptive parents who'd be thrilled and delighted to have the real mother wandering in and out of their lives at will? "You're asking for the moon, Zoe."

She shook her head, reminding him of the colt fighting the halter. "I'm asking for what my baby needs. If that's impossible to arrange, then I guess I'll just have to raise her myself. Sean says he'll stick it out with me—help me whenever he can right now, then marry me when he's eighteen.''

"You're…just…*kids!*" Rafe exploded. "There's no way you can do that! No way I want you to try to do that—''

"But—''

"No buts! Not another damn but, not one word.'' He stomped into his office, snatched up the phone and dialed.

"Hello?" Dana sounded breathless and harried. The hiccuping sobs of a baby sounded in the background.

Just what she deserved. "Did you tell my daughter that

a baby needs two parents? That she shouldn't give up her child if it's not to a couple?''

''*What?* Oh…well, not precisely, but I suppose I did—''

''You did a truckload of damage is what you did, and I'll thank you to keep your opinions to yourself from now on! What gives *you* the—''

''Rafe, I've got eight hungry dudes in my dining room, I'm in the midst of a Chinese stir-fry, Petra seems to be teething. This is *not* a good time to talk.''

''I'm not talking. I'm telling you—''

''Then tell me later!'' *Click!*

He snatched the phone away from his ear, swore at it, smashed it down onto its base—and it rang under his hand. He drew in a shaking breath, blew it out, lifted it and said evenly, ''We have to talk about this.''

''Rafe? That's got to be ESP!'' a woman cried happily.

Not Dana Kershaw with her velvety alto. A higher, chirpier voice—*oh, no!* ''Mitzy?'' he said stupidly.

''Who else? You were just picking up the phone to call me?''

CHAPTER TEN

"I'M SO GLAD you gave us a second chance!" Beaming at Rafe above the candle flame, Mitzy Barlow impulsively stretched a hand across the restaurant table.

Rafe swallowed and took it reluctantly. *Us.* That was the same song she'd sung on their last date. "It's you giving me a second chance," he said gallantly and all too truthfully.

She squeezed his fingers and widened her eyes at him. "But Rafe, it was all such a silly misunderstanding! I guess I came on like Suzy Homemaker, inviting you over to my place, but really, that was just so we could be more...comfortable. That's all it was, truly." Her fingers stroked his palm with soft insistence. "Why, when it comes to independence, I bet I treasure mine more than you do yours! A girl just wants to have fun, know what I mean?"

If he hadn't, she was more than willing to show him. Rafe sighed inwardly and nodded toward the dance floor, where several couples drifted to the slow music of the house's Friday-night band. "Dance?" Conversation was exhausting him.

"I'd love to."

She melted into his arms the way she had the last time they'd danced—had that been only two weeks ago? But though her body was as warm and willing as before, its effect on him wasn't the same. When she pressed her breasts to his chest, he felt a reflexive stirring, but that was all it was. Reflex. He might have left his heart back at the table along with his hat. *This isn't the one.* The words rose up unbidden, as if someone spoke from the bottom of a well. He frowned and pulled her closer.

She was the only one going. He'd thought, when Mitzy phoned him on Wednesday, that it must be Fate nudging him toward the obvious solution. If Dana Kershaw wouldn't take Zoe's baby at any price, and with Zoe insisting anyway that she'd give up her baby only to a two-parent family—a family that would grant her unlimited visitation rights!—then it was up to Rafe to find such an openminded, generous couple. *Local family,* he reminded himself ironically. Or if he couldn't find one—

Mitzy tipped back her head and wriggled against him, as he guided her in a slow turn. "What are you thinking?"

About babies. If he said that, she'd probably jump him here on the floor. "Thinking that lead guitar man has some nice moves." She smiled wickedly and bumped her hip against him, and he added, "But then, so do you." Which made her giggle.

I can't do this. That same voice, his but not his, welled up in his mind again. She was a fine-looking woman, but she came on too strong, or too eager, or just plain wrong for him. She smiled too much, showing too many teeth, and she laughed in all the wrong places. Always would.

Face it, he'd seen someone who *would* do, too recently, and the contrast was brutal. *But she's not available.*

And this one was too available. A man wanted to hunt his woman, as he would an elk out on the mountain, savoring the crisp blue day, the shivering gold of the aspen leaves, his own competence in the stalking, the quickening pulse as a form finally took shape through the bushes, the hammering heart as you drew down on the target. But Mitzy—Mitzy was a trout in a barrel, ready to leap into his arms.

Two weeks ago he'd been lonesome enough that he'd

thought he wanted that, if only for a few hot nights, but now... "Thank you," he said automatically as the dance ended. She tipped up her face and strained closer, and he realized she wanted a kiss. "Thanks for the dance," he repeated gently as he eased her out of his arms.

He walked her back to their booth with a hand on her back, her shooting him wounded and puzzled glances, then said, "If you'd excuse me a minute?" He fled to the men's room. *How long till I can decently take her home?* He'd been a fool to think this might work. A jerk to raise her hopes all over again.

But the men's room made a lousy refuge. Rafe knew from rueful experience that two women could swish off to the ladies' and stay gone for fifteen minutes or more, presumably while they dissected their dates or traded lipsticks. He'd always imagined a pink, frilly couch in there, crammed at any one time with three pairs of whispering, giggling women, while more waited their turn. Contrast that with the men's, where users went strictly one by one, and any man lurking there for more than the requisite two minutes was viewed with universal alarm.

So he used up his two minutes, then decided to kill a couple more on the phone. He could call Zoe and ask how her appointment had gone. And how she and Dana had hit it off on their own. Propping one shoulder against the wall, he had to smile as he pictured his tall redheaded daughter walking beside small, dark Dana. But his smile faded when no one picked up the phone back at Suntop. Zoe had estimated this morning, that Dana would have her back at the ranch by six-thirty at the latest. And now it was nine.

Took her telescope outside to look at the moon, he told himself. She'd been on an astronomy kick all last summer. Or perhaps she'd been shook by something Dr. Hancock had handed her this afternoon, and she was out walking and thinking. Give her twenty minutes, he decided, then try again. If she wasn't in by then, he'd call Dana. He hadn't spoken to her since Wednesday, when he'd yelled at her. After she'd sabotaged his plans that way, he'd been too angry to trust himself to be civil. *If you'd just see sense, Dana, I wouldn't be here courting a woman I don't even like.*

He was nearly to the booth when he realized they had company. A couple had joined Mitzy—the man's back blocked most of his view. Rafe smiled with relief. Four wasn't a crowd tonight; it was a welcome distraction. He reached the table, and smiled down at—Sean Kershaw and his missing daughter!

"Look who joined us!" Mitzy cried gaily. "You'd told me Zoe was a beauty, but I had no idea! And Sean, I'm so happy to meet you. What fun—a double date!"

"And what a surprise," Rafe said between his teeth, as Mitzy slid over to make room for him. He fixed his daughter with a stare that promised hellfire and brimstone when he got her alone. She'd broken every last edict he'd given her—Sean, off the ranch without permission, no doubt used the phone to set this up. Zoe tipped up her chin, giving him look for look, while she laid her hand over Sean's on the table. Rafe felt a reluctant flash of admiration beyond his outrage. She was no longer a child to be sent to her room, she was telling him. *Not my little girl anymore.*

"Where's Dana?" he asked, and felt another ripple of rage. Dana must have taken Sean along to the appointment, throwing the kids together even though she knew how Rafe felt about that.

"I told her you were meeting me here in town for supper, and that you'd drive me home."

"Dana's another of your little friends?" Mitzy cooed, not to be left out.

Zoe nodded, her gaze still locked on her father's. "And

I hope you'll drive Sean home, as well, since he rode down here on his bike.''

Rafe opened his mouth to say the kid could ride home thirty miles in the dark or sleep in a ditch, for all he cared—but there was Dana, who hadn't flouted his wishes, after all. Who probably this minute was worrying and wondering about her stepson's whereabouts. "I reckon I'll have to." Tied to his front fender like a trophy buck.

"So what brings you two to town?" Mitzy chirped. "A movie? Or a dance or…?"

"Actually, we came to meet *you*," Zoe said, and Sean nodded solemn agreement.

The devil they had! Rafe aimed a judicious kick under the table, but he bumped Mitzy's outstretched leg, instead. She twined it instantly around his calf and shot him a look that would have sizzled a snowman.

"I was wondering how you feel about children?" Zoe continued, studiously avoiding Rafe's evil eye. "Do you want a family?"

"Well, I—" Mitzy brought a hand to her low-cut neckline and giggled. "What is this, a job interview?"

"Zo-e." Rafe growled a warning. "Pay no attention, Mitzy. She's kidding." He glanced up to find their waitress standing at his elbow.

"Can I get you guys anything else?" She nodded at the newcomers.

"No!" snapped Rafe. "They're just leaving."

"Yes." Sean spoke up for the first time. "My date will have the spinach salad and I'll have a cheeseburger with fries. Ice tea for both of us." He looked Rafe straight in the eye. "And I'll pay for it."

You've got guts, kid, I'll give you that! The bruise on Sean's chin had faded to yellow-green. He'd put on a tie for this invasion. Rafe turned back to the murmuring women—to find Mitzy confiding, "Honey, I think family's the most important thing in the whole wide world!'' She nudged Rafe's leg with hers for emphasis.

"But do you want children of your own?'' Zoe persisted.

Mitzy shot Rafe a warily flirtatious look. "Eventually. Sure. Doesn't everybody?'' She rubbed an open hand down the top of his thigh.

He captured it and brought it up onto the table. "Could we change the subject, Zoe?''

"How about adoption?'' Sean chimed in. "Have you ever thought about that?''

"Do you mean Zoe?'' Mitzy reached across the table to capture Zoe's hands. "That's what all this is about? Honey, I would be so…so honored and *thrilled* to have you as my adopted daughter, if it ever came to that! Why, I— I can't tell you how—''

"Mitzy, let's dance!'' Rafe almost dragged her from the booth, then hustled her out to the floor.

"Oh, Rafe—'' Regardless of the surrounding dancers, she threw her arms around his neck and kissed him. "I had no idea!''

"Neither did I, Mitzy, believe me.''

He managed to calm her down during the dance, though since he had no intention of explaining his daughter's antics, Mitzy ended up more bewildered than enlightened. He kept an arm anchored around her as they returned to the booth, to find that the kids had been served.

"I'm taking Mitzy home,'' he announced, "and I'll be back here in twenty minutes. Don't budge from this booth. Not an inch.''

"I don't understand,'' Mitzy murmured, looking back over her shoulder and twiddling her fingers in farewell, as he marched her away. "Did I do something wrong?''

"Mitzy, you're the only one here who did everything right.''

THE THREE OF THEM maintained an edgy silence most of the way to the Ribbon River. Rafe had exiled Sean to the rear seat of the cab, resisting the temptation to let him ride out back with his bike.

"Mr. Montana," Sean blurted suddenly, "I don't want you blaming Zoe for tonight. This was my idea."

"Was it?" Rafe knew his own daughter better than that.

"No, it was me, Daddy, you know it was me! But you said the other night you were serious about Mitzy, so we wanted to meet her. See how she felt about babies. See if we liked her."

"Just because I'm seriously seeing a woman doesn't mean I'm thinking about adopting your baby!"

"Doesn't it?" Zoe demanded, turning to face him and hooking an elbow over the backseat.

The problem was, she could read him like a book. When they sat down with the hands for a round of penny poker, she was the one he never could bluff. Rafe tried anyway. "It doesn't. Besides which, I'll thank you not to meddle in my..." *Private affairs* sounded too stuffy. "In my—"

"Love life?" Zoe suggested with a smirk. "But you can meddle in mine?"

"Till you're eighteen, you're damn right I can—and I will." He turned off the highway onto the unpaved road that led to the dude ranch.

Sean leaned forward. "You can let me out here, Mr. Montana. Uh, please?"

"Not a chance. I'm handing you over to your stepmother. She's probably been worrying herself sick wondering where you are." It was past ten-thirty.

"I'm not hers to worry about." He gripped the back of the seat with both hands. "Please, sir? You'll only wake her up if you drive up to the house. I can bike from here."

But if you don't want to see her, I do, Rafe realized. He could picture Dana roused from her bed, her soft hair tousled like a child's, her long lashes drooping over her big, dark eyes. *Bedroom eyes,* they used to call eyes like that. He stomped on the brake. "Fine. Out with you, then. And Sean?" Halfway out the door, the boy halted and swung back. "Zoe is grounded, and from now on I expect you to respect that."

"Mr. Montana?" Sean looked down, then up—straight into his eyes. "I'll see your daughter whenever I can. Thanks for the ride." He closed the door and walked around back to lift out his bike.

Swearing heartily under his breath, Rafe reversed all the way out to the highway. Zoe sat forward in her seat, arms crossed, a tiny, private smile on her face, her gaze fixed on her friend, who stood by his bike in the headlights' glare, one arm uplifted in farewell.

"So…" Rafe growled after he'd driven a mile. "You, young lady, are in trouble." Though how he was going to ground her when she was already…

"That's what the doctor tells me," she agreed calmly.

The truck swerved, and he brought it back in line. "You really are?" Deep down, he'd cherished the notion that maybe this was all a Chinese fire drill, one of those—what did they call 'em?—hysterical pregnancies. Had told himself that if he entertained the notion of marrying Mitzy, it would not be necessary. So much for sacrifices.

"'Fraid so." Zoe crossed her forearms on the dash, leaned her head on them and sighed.

"So…" No mercy from the gods. Now he would have to do something. Find a way. "You went to all that trouble to meet Mitzy Barlow. What did you think of her?"

"Umm." Zoe sighed again. "You know that drugstore in Cortez that still has the old soda fountain? We stopped there once years ago, and you bought me a cherry Coke? With all that cherry syrup?"

Unable to gag it down, she'd offended the ancient proprietor who had made it special for her. Rafe grimaced. *You think Mitzy is syrupy?* So did he.

"She's really very nice," Zoe added hastily. "And if you like her, that's all that matters…I guess." The last words faded forlornly away.

She was picturing Mitzy raising Zoe's daughter in her own syrupy image. *Not gonna happen, sweetheart. I'll figure out something else.* He'd have to. No way could he see himself enduring eighteen years of pot roast and peas with Mitzy Barlow.

But he had to work something out, and soon. What had Dana said the other day—that no matter what choice was made, there was bound to be some heartache?

More and more, it looked like the trade-off would be Zoe's freedom—or his.

CHAPTER ELEVEN

From: RedColumbine@Westbest.com
To: SanDiegan@Pipeline.net
Sean Diego! Sorry I haven't written, but Dad has been
a GRIZZLY all weekend and he kept me on the run.
We rode up to the line camp Saturday to take the guys
some supplies, then looked over the cows and the
grazing. Took our bedrolls and slept outside the cabin.
You should have seen the stars. And I heard a cougar
scream near dawn—Harvard wouldn't have anything
to compare with that, not really. Sunday we came
back, then hung around the house all day. He's up to
something—making lists, talking to himself, growling
at the dogs and me. Locking the lists in his desk, so
I can't peek. Then this morning he called our banker
for an appointment and went into town. I've got a
NASTY suspicion that he's working out some sort of
prenuptial agreement for him and Mitzy—gagme-
withahoneyjar—Barlow. (Does she have something
I'm missing, or is Dad just too sex-starved to notice
she's a dweeb?) Uh-oh, he's driving up now. Gotta
go!! ZZZZoe+(?)

TUESDAY AFTERNOON, Dana had just put Petra down for
her afternoon nap, when she heard a car mounting the last
slope to the house. Drop-in tourists who'd seen her sign
out on the highway, she hoped as she went to the bedroom
window. Her cabins were only half filled this week.

Parting the sheer curtains, she saw, instead, Rafe Montana's black pickup truck dragging a horse trailer behind it. As the truck passed the house headed for the parking in the rear, Rafe looked up at her window, and their eyes met. He touched a finger to his Stetson and smiled.

What now, Rafe? They'd had no contact since that phone call last week, when he'd told her to keep her opinions to herself, and she'd hung up on him. She should have enjoyed being left in peace, she supposed, but instead it had been a week of surprisingly painful suspense—wondering what he meant to do about Zoe. Wondering how his ultimate solution would affect Sean's life—and hers. Wondering about that woman he'd said he was seeing seriously. *Wondering how I could have been so vain, feeling he might be attracted to me, just because he touched me once or twice...the way he looked at me.*

Still, she paused at the dresser mirror to brush the bangs back from her forehead. Petra had spit up on her shoulder, she noticed, so she hurried to her bedroom for a fresh blouse.

By the time she reached her kitchen, Rafe was knocking on her screen door.

"Coming!" *On his manners today,* she thought, since he'd waited outside. "Hello, Rafe." She smiled up at him briskly, to hide her embarrassment. An odd little jolt of pleasure went through her, seeing him standing there. Pleasure and surprise—he was always a little bigger and more vivid than she remembered.

"Dana." He lifted the brim of his hat an inch and lowered it again.

His very best manners. So he'd forgiven her. "You've brought horses," she noted, seeing a black tail switching within the nearest stall of the trailer and a cream-colored rump in the far one. And seeing Sean, who was just now retrieving his fly rod from the bed of the truck. Rafe must have collared him down at his favorite fishing hole by the bridge.

"I didn't know if you had any spare mounts, so I brought my own," Rafe explained. "Could I tempt you out for a ride?"

"Oh." His timing was perfect—Petra's afternoon nap time. No accident, she realized. Still. "I'd love to, Rafe." It had been months since she'd ridden. "But I can't leave Petra alone."

"Which is why I found you a baby-sitter." Rafe nodded at her stepson, who was glowering as he trudged up the steps. "I figure if Sean plans to be a daddy he could use all the practice he can get."

It wasn't fair, Dana told herself, that Rafe could demand cooperation from Sean that she only dreamed of. But why quibble with a gift horse? "Give me five minutes to change."

"This is Concha," he said a short while later, stroking the nose of a dainty buckskin. "She's gentle, and Zoe named her for her paces—she's smooth as a shell."

"She's lovely!" Her creamy coat contrasted dramatically with her black mane and tail and stockings.

Rafe held the mare's head while Dana gathered the reins and mounted, then he moved to her side. "Your stirrups are short." He caught her ankle and lifted her foot from the iron. "Let your leg hang."

She did so, her skin shivering at the feel of his hand encircling her. *He has a woman,* she reminded herself, staring straight ahead through the mare's black-tipped ears. He'd do this for Sean or for Zoe. It was only her panicked imagination that made the gesture seem significant, oddly possessive, as if he meant to stand there clasping her ankle forever.

He let her go and rebuckled the strap. "Two notches. I knew your legs were long, but I didn't..." He moved to the other side, extended that one, then mounted his big blood bay, his leg swinging up and over in an effortless arc as the gelding snorted and pranced in place. Settling his hat down over his dark hair, he said, "Which way?"

"Up!" She laughed. "I haven't been up on the mountain in *forever*." Not in more than a year, since her fifth month when she'd stopped riding.

Rafe kept the conversation strictly on horses as they made their way through the lower pastures; then the big wildflower meadows stairstepping toward the sky, slashed by forests of pale aspen and dark pine, outcroppings of raw red granite; then higher, silk-green meadows starred with columbine and Indian paintbrushes, a tapestry of crimson and blue and yellow. Once he'd satisfied himself that she could control her mount, he picked up their pace. They loped easily side by side, his ramping bay and her floating mare, smooth as a ride on a merry-go-round.

Finally Rafe lifted his hand, signaling a halt. Dana reined in beside him, and, as one, they turned their horses back toward the view. Far down the valley, she could make out one corner of her roof, a glint of the Ribbon River. "Beautiful," she murmured, stroking Concha's hot, sleek neck.

He nodded. "Almost as pretty as my land."

My land, said with such fierce, possessive pride that she wanted to smile, but didn't. *I bet he grew up poor.* She glanced at him sideways. He had an essential toughness, a harder edge than the men she'd grown up with, back in green, gentle Vermont—an upper-middle-class world filled with men who worked in offices and classrooms. *Nothing came easy to you,* she guessed. *No one handed you anything or smoothed the way.* Hence the pride in what he'd done by himself.

Still, she had her own pride. "I'd like to see anything prettier than this." She nodded toward the valley.

"Then sometime I'll show you." He smiled, but the

smile didn't reach his blue eyes as they roved over her face. "I'm glad you ride."

What's it to you? Suddenly she'd had all she could take of his scrutiny. She swung Concha uphill. Rafe followed, jogging knee to knee with her. "What did you want to say to me?" He hadn't brought her up here just to entertain her. He'd brought her to his home ground, atop a horse, because here he was most at ease—he wanted an edge, an advantage. *Wants my help again, but how this time?*

"I…" He gave her a sidelong, enigmatic glance. "I have a proposal for you."

She flinched inwardly at the word, then smiled at herself. He didn't mean *that.* "About Zoe's baby?" When he nodded, she said, "I meant what I said before, Rafe. I know it would be convenient for you, but I just can't do it. I'm sorry."

"That was just an idea off the top of my head, but now I've thought it through and I want you to hear me out."

She shook her head. "It's no good, Rafe."

"It could be very good," he disagreed, "for you and Sean as well as Zoe, and here's how it would work. First— and you can blame yourself for this part, Dana—we'd marry."

"What?" The mare stopped dead as her hand jerked on the reins. "You're—"

"I'm not crazy. You've convinced Zoe that her baby needs two parents, not one—so here I am. Not exactly what I had planned for myself, either, by the way."

Married to you. She couldn't look him in the eye, couldn't look away. Her gaze snagged on his mouth—that carved, full bottom lip curving ruefully…the breadth of his shoulders…those capable, knowing hands. There was too much of him—more man than any woman could use. And she needed none. Certainly not this one. "No." She sent Concha surging ahead.

Might as well try to outrun a centaur. He was beside her again in a moment, their knees only inches apart. "We'd marry and adopt Zoe's baby at birth," he continued, as if she hadn't spoken. "I'll live on my side of the mountain most of the time, and you'll live on yours."

And the other times? Or was she reading her own urges into this, turning a business proposition into something more?

"Whoa." Reaching over, Rafe caught her left wrist and pulled backward; at the same time, he reined in Tobasco, bringing them both to a halt. "Listen to me. I'll guarantee that you won't be overwhelmed, Dana."

With his big hand on her wrist, he'd guarantee. He must outweigh her by seventy pounds, and most of that muscle.

"You'll have all the child care you need or want, for Petra as well as Zoe's baby. A nanny or whatever you like, as long as the kids stay at home."

She had to smile in spite of herself. No, he wasn't exactly Mr. Day Care—not that Trueheart offered much in that line, anyway.

"As I said before, I'll assume all financial responsibility for Zoe's—and Sean's—baby." Reminding her that this mess wasn't all of Zoe's making. "Medical, living expenses, college when it comes time."

No small chunk of change he was talking there; still, that wasn't the point.

"Besides that, I'll bail you out, too." He let her go at last, as if his words alone could hold her.

"What?" She twisted in the saddle to stare up at him.

"You're not doing so well wrangling dudes, Dana. I understand you're two months behind on your mortgage payments."

"Who told you that?" Not even Sean knew that, so there was no way Rafe could have learned it through Zoe, which meant— "You talked to my banker?"

Rafe shrugged. "Doesn't matter. I made it my business to find out. What matters is that I'll pay off your debts and keep you out of debt."

"You did talk to the bank! Of all the arrogant, over-bearing—" She spun Concha back the way they'd come. "From now on, you can mind your own business, Rafe Montana!"

"Like you've been minding yours, Ms. Two-Parents-Are-Better-Than-One?" He trotted after her.

"Well, it's true!"

"Maybe, maybe not, but now we're stuck with it. So I want your help and I'm willing to pay for it."

"Eighteen years of mothering might come pretty high." Not that she'd even consider his proposition. She pulled down her hat, shutting him out.

"Then make it five years, if you prefer." He bent to peer under her brim. "Five would be enough to launch the kid. That would give Zoe time to make it through Harvard. After that, I could work something else out."

"Buy some other financially distressed mother?" she suggested dryly.

"Whatever. So what about five years? We'd draw up a contract—I mean to do that, anyway. At the end, you'd be free. I'd have your ranch running smoothly by then. There're lots of improvements that would make it pay."

She just bet he was itching to put his hand to her ranch. She'd seen the way he'd scowled at her corral, with its rotting rails, when they rode past. *Mr. High-handed, stomping across my land.* "Five years," she repeated, shaking her head. Not five years, not five minutes. *And I thought life had me overwhelmed?* A tornado didn't need five minutes to turn your life topsy-turvy, nor did a tidal wave, let alone Rafe Montana.

"Or less, if you found somebody you wanted to marry during that time."

She halted again and looked up at him. *So I can stop flattering myself. It's not me you want—not in that way.* "You'd release me—divorce me—if I met somebody?"

"As long as I approved him as a father for Zoe's baby, why not? She specified two loving parents. He steps in— that leaves me free to go." What he'd wanted in the first place. She felt a flicker of hurt, then a rising tide of anger, an impulse to lean over and shove him right off his horse. "How *convenient!*"

He nodded complacently. "As I said, works for everybody. Almost everybody."

She laughed—it was that or burst into angry tears. He was impossible! *Oh, yes, that works all right—for you!* But ridiculous as his proposal was, she found herself fascinated. He'd thought of everything. "What about Zoe, Rafe? If I adopted her child, it would be mine. I don't rent my heart out, not at any price. So what will happen if Zoe wants her baby back after she's made it through college?" She reined in, imagining the pain. *I've had enough pain to last me a lifetime.* "I couldn't bear that."

"And I wouldn't let that happen." Reaching across, he set a fingertip to the bridge of her nose and drew it slowly down to the tip. She sucked in a startled breath and her lashes shivered. "I promise. If you take the baby, it's yours forever." His finger moved on, down to her lips where it lingered. "And that's the kind of mother I want for my grandchild," he added huskily. "Somebody who cares like that."

She tossed her head, freeing herself of that touch, but it echoed along her nerve endings, sending tremors out to her fingertips. Her thighs tensed, setting Concha downhill at a flowing walk.

"So you're considering it," he said with satisfaction.

"No, I'm not." *You want somebody—not me, but somebody. Any mother would do. What about that woman you're seeing seriously—or did you try her and she's already turned you down?*

"Another thing I'd want. You have the best grazing on this side of the range, summer or winter, and it's all going to waste. Part of the deal would be that I can run cattle here. We'd work out some split, a way to share the profits on that. Sean could start earning his keep—he rides, doesn't he?—and learn a useful trade."

So now she understood why he hadn't gone to the woman he was seeing seriously and pitched his proposal to her. *She might make a mother for Zoe's child, but I bet she doesn't have land. While with me, he gets a two-fer—a double whammy.* His face almost glowed as he laid out his plans for her ranch. "You've thought of everything," she murmured ironically.

"I have. I'd want a long-term agreement on the grazing rights, by the way. They'd continue for eighteen years, with an option to renew, even if you go for the five-year plan, or if you remarry."

"Really," she said evenly.

"You see what that would do for your own operation, don't you? You'd have a lot more to offer, a much better draw. Dudes want to see cattle worked nowadays. They want to tag along on cattle drives, help out at the brandings, not just poke around the mountains on trail rides. So I'd put my steadiest, most easygoing cowhands over here, men who can put up with that nonsense and still do their jobs. You could start charging what the fancy guest ranches do. I figure we could double your take."

Which he probably knew to the penny! She urged Concha into a trot.

"So what do you think?" he asked, after they'd covered half a meadow and reached another stretch of forest.

"I think I'm a bit late—should be starting supper about now. I only have five dudes tonight—nothing compared

with the *fancy* guest ranches—but they still like to eat.''
She touched her heels to the mare, and she and Rafe flew
through the trees in single file, then down the next meadow
to the gate of the home pasture.

Rafe opened the gate without dismounting, let her
through, then reclosed it. ''We walk from here. I don't want
to load them up hot.''

No way Dana could argue with that. She nodded tensely.

''Well, what do you think?'' he repeated, a hint of ex-
asperation creeping into his voice.

''I think...'' Financial salvation. That was what he was
offering her—bribing her with. And the sense of relief, as
she imagined it, was startling. As if Rafe had lifted a half-
ton pack off her shoulders that she hadn't realized she was
carrying—till she was freed. But still. She shook her head.

''Whoa,'' he said, as they passed under the tallest tree
in the pasture, a massive, spreading oak that the horses
always favored for its pool of deep shade. ''Let's have this
out before we get back to the house.''

And Sean's big ears. ''All right.'' She reined in, and her
eyes fell on the wooden treads hammered into the gnarly
old trunk. Her eyes climbed them rung by rung to the
weathered plank platform some twenty feet above, and the
hutch perched on top of that. The tree house Peter and Sean
had built, two summers ago. She'd almost forgotten it; she
came this way so seldom. *Oh, Peter...how could I consider
anything less than love for even a heartbeat?* ''You said
that you'd spend most of the time on your side of the mountain, and I'd stay on mine. What about the rest of the
time?''

Dropping his reins on the neck of his gelding, Rafe took
off his hat, examined its band with a faint frown, then
dropped it over the saddle horn. ''You're talking about
sex...''

No, I'm talking about love. She held his blue gaze and felt her blood rising within like a boiling tide.

"What I'm trying to do here, Dana, is set up the most minimal marriage I can arrange. One that's fair to you, that doesn't clip my wings, but that satisfies Zoe's requirements. That saves her future."

"A marriage in name only, you mean." That would be more lonely—infinitely more lonely—than what she had now. A travesty of what she'd had before. But even worse, it would be an obliteration. Because when a house burns down to its foundations, and you build again on the same spot, somehow it erases the original structure. You no longer can picture the way it once was. *No, thank you. At least now I have memories to warm me.*

"Maybe a sham marriage for a while, if you wanted," Rafe agreed slowly. "But do you think it would stay that way? There's something between us, Dana. I feel it. You feel it, too."

"I *don't.*" Her heart was hammering in her chest, her adrenaline pumping her blood toward rage at his hint of a smile. "Don't flatter yourself."

"Oh?" Though he hadn't picked up the reins, his big bay sidestepped toward her little mare, edging Concha in against the tree trunk. "That's what I'm doing?" He lifted her hat off her head and dropped it over his on the saddle horn. His hand reached to cover hers on the reins, holding her horse in check. "Did you ever watch a cat, Dana, when she spots a mouse?"

Leaning back in the saddle, she felt her hair graze the tree trunk, and stopped. His face was a handsbreadth from hers, no more. She couldn't breathe with him this close. Half hypnotized, she shook her head.

"Her pupils expand—the eyes go from green to black in a second. Like *this.*" He brought the back of his knuckles to her eyebrow, brushed them slowly down her cheek, across her trembling mouth. "Like yours go all dark whenever I get this close to you. Excitement is what that is."

"Or fear." Crowding her like this. Their legs were pressed together from knee to ankle. The blood thrummed through her veins like the bass notes of the Ribbon River in springtime, when the snow melted.

Laughing under his breath, Rafe shook his head. "You're not afraid of me. If anybody should be shaking in his boots, it's me."

"I don't know what you mean." Still, the words gave her courage. She reached for her Stetson, dropped it back on her head.

"No?" Taking her hat by the brim, Rafe adjusted its tilt to his own satisfaction. Then, obedient to some invisible signal, Tobasco sidestepped away. Concha snorted and tossed her head, as if she, too, felt the sudden easing of tension. "Just as well, maybe."

At least, that was what Dana thought he'd said, the soft words echoing like an unsolved riddle rattling around her mind, all the way to the house. *Just as well, just as well.* But was it?

"Well?" Rafe asked again, as they dismounted by his trailer.

She didn't have to think. "No, Rafe. Find some other way, but leave me out of it." She was up on her back porch and nearly to the safety of her kitchen door before she turned back. "But thank you for the ride."

AFTER THE HORSES had clopped on down the hill, Sean lifted his dozing half sister off his chest and sat up. She yawned hugely, opened her big brown eyes and blinked at him. "Wow!" he told her reverently. "Did you *hear* that?" Staring over the edge of the tree house platform, he could just see the riders rounding the corner of the barn—Dana and Zoe's old man, all right. He hadn't been dreaming. Who would have believed? ''Some witness you are, Pet.''

From: SanDiegan@Pipeline.net
To: RedColumbine@Westbest.com
Scoop of the century, Red! You are NOT gonna believe this. Do you know where your old man went today with those oat-burners, or what he was up to? Starts out with me fishing on the bridge. I'd just hooked into this rainbow, two pounds at least, when I look up and see…

CHAPTER TWELVE

RAFE UNLOADED TOBASCO first and led him over to the watering trough, then into the barn. It was drawing on toward suppertime; Zoe was probably up at the house, defrosting another of Mrs. Higgins's casseroles. *Wonder what Dana's feeding her dudes tonight?* Something better than frozen macaroni and cheese, he bet. His stomach grumbled at the thought.

Damn the woman, anyway. Too stubborn to see her own good. He'd offered her a sweet deal. The feel of her lips, trembling against his fingers, moved across his skin. The memory of her big eyes going dark at his touch. He'd wanted to lift her off her saddle and onto his, taste her sweetness right then and there under the oak, seal their bargain with a kiss. *A sweet deal for all of us, it could have been.* The best solution he could imagine to a nasty problem. And now what?

The sun gilded Suntop to the west, but the rest of the valley lay in shadow. He pulled the string hanging down from the barn rafters, switching on an overhead light, then looped Tobasco's reins over the rail and turned back for Concha.

"Daddy?" Zoe called from down the aisle.

"What are you doing out here in the dark?" He went to prop his forearms on the half door to Miel's stall. The palomino had gashed herself somehow out in the pasture. Always a greedy feeder, she'd probably leaned on the barbed wire fence in quest of a greener mouthful on its far side.

Zoe had discovered the wound on her upper leg yesterday, and Willy had stitched and salved it. She'd stay penned inside for a few days to limit her use of it.

"Just hanging out with my baby." Zoe lifted the curry comb she held. "With Miel."

Not a statement that would have needed qualifying a month ago, when Miel had been her only baby. A beloved horse was all the baby his daughter needed, or should have, at sixteen. Woofle rose from the straw in the back of the stall and came to rear against the door, stump tail wagging, with Trey right behind.

Rafe scratched behind Woofle's grizzled ears as he asked, "How's it look?"

"Beautiful. No swelling. Willy says it'll barely scar."

"He's the best." Rafe eyed the brush. When she was troubled, she often groomed Miel while she thought things out. "What about you? You all right?"

"Mmmph." She drifted out after him, stood watching him unsaddle Tobasco, then wandered out into the dark. He frowned, then relaxed when he heard the sound of hooves on metal as she backed Concha down the trailer ramp. She led the mare into the barn, tied her far enough from Tobasco that they both could work, then unstrapped the horse's cinch. "How was your ride with Mrs. Kershaw?"

Arms full of saddle and blanket, Rafe paused in the door to the tack room, looking back. "How'd you know that?"

A flash of mischief broke through her pensive mood. "Elementary, my dear Watson. Concha is a lady's ride. By my count, you know exactly two ladies right now. Mitzy Barlow has fingernails out to *here,* and reins would spoil them. And what do you bet she's scared of horses?"

A bet he wouldn't take. Still, Rafe smelled a bluff somewhere. "Have you been using the phone, by any chance?" If she'd talked to Sean in the past two hours... He'd stopped in Trueheart for some tractor parts on his way home, then a coffee, when he encountered a neighbor.

Zoe's red-gold brows shot skyward. "You said no phone. Or have you changed your mind?"

"In your dreams—and would you please answer the question?" He hadn't been a father for sixteen-plus years for nothing.

"I have not." She stomped off with Concha's saddle, then came back and snatched up her curry comb. They groomed the horses in silence for a while, Rafe wondering how she could possibly be indignant after the stunt she'd pulled last Friday, but go figure. A teenage girl's reasoning was a mystery to him. *And then they grow up to be women.*

Zoe ducked under Concha's neck and started on her other side. "I don't want you to do this."

Crouched at Tobasco's feet, Rafe looked up. "Do what?"

"I don't want you wrecking your life to fix mine. I won't let you do that, Daddy. It's not fair." Her hands flew over the creamy coat, her voice squeaked, perilously close to sobs.

"What are you talking about?" He finished the front legs and stood, staring at her hunched shoulders. How the hell had she guessed?

"I won't let you marry Mrs. Kershaw just to make a home for my baby!"

"You think that's what I was—" He forced a laugh that sounded fake even to him. "Don't be ridiculous."

"You were thinking about Mitzy Barlow, but when you saw how I felt about her, you changed your mind. So now you're hitting on Mrs. Kershaw, and I think it's rotten. Stupid!"

"You don't like Mrs. Kershaw?" How could she not?

"I don't like you cleaning up my mess for me. It's bad

enough I screwed up my own life. I'm not going to screw up yours.''

''Zoe, don't worry about it. I'm taking care of things.''

''By marrying somebody you don't even know? There's only one reason to marry, and that's for love.''

Ah, teenagers. Life was so black and white, so simple. *And that's how I want to keep yours for a few more years.* Give her a baby at seventeen, and she'd learn about life's compromises and limitations all too soon, as Pilar had. *So leave it to me, Zoe.* He wasn't looking to mess up his life— far from it. But if he did, it would only be fair—the debt he owed her mother. *Your happiness is how I clear the slate.*

''So just forget it,'' Zoe continued, when he didn't speak. ''You don't have to marry anybody. I'm keeping my baby.''

No. You aren't. Rafe clenched his jaw while he brushed down Tobasco's hind legs, then his tail. ''What makes you so sure I'm not attracted to Mrs. Kershaw—to Dana?'' he asked finally. *If I have to marry for love, here goes...*

''You just met her,'' Zoe pointed out.

''You never heard about love at first sight?'' A good case of old-fashioned lust, anyway.

''That's what you said about Mitzy Barlow last week.''

Had he? Well, something like that. ''But this time I mean it. Dana's really something.''

Zoe turned around, leaned back against Concha's shoulder and cocked her head. ''Really?''

Rafe crossed himself. ''Cross my heart and hope to choke. She's very—'' *Sexy.* Each time he saw her, he got this irresistible urge to put his hands around her waist. His fingertips wouldn't quite touch, but they'd come close. He needed to find out how close. ''Very pretty,'' he translated, for a female-teenage audience.

Zoe's mouth curled in her *gotcha* grin, the same smirk

she wore when she stomped him at chess. "So you'd marry her, anyway, even if I wasn't having a baby?"

Well…no. He wasn't in the market and didn't plan to be. But he'd still be thinking about taking her to bed. "Sure," he lied.

Zoe snorted. "Yeah, right!"

"I would." She was backing him into a corner, the way she did sometimes on the chessboard, harrying his king with an army of niggling pawns and a wayward knight.

She crossed her arms and grinned. "All right. So prove it. If you really mean that, Daddy, then go right ahead. Court Dana and marry her for love—not for me. Then, if you're still happily married when I deliver my baby…" Her smile wavered; her voice wobbled. "Then I'd be honored and very…very grateful for you to adopt it. But that's the bargain. You have to marry for love."

How do you court a woman who doesn't want a man? Rafe had never even considered the problem before. Either the lady was willing, in which case the man tap-danced and showered her with little gallantries till she allowed him to win her—or she wasn't, in which case he tipped his hat and moved on. Since Pilar, he'd left his heart safely at home when he went calling, so the mating process had generally been pleasant, the risks not great, the rewards not enormous. Just pleasant. Sufficient unto his needs.

But now Zoe had changed everything. Rafe couldn't simply shrug off a loss this time and move on. He had six months in which to marry for love—at least, convince Zoe he'd married for love. And if he had to stick his head in the noose, he couldn't imagine that in six months of searching he'd find any local woman who'd do half as well as Dana Kershaw. A sexy, single woman with the best grazing in forty miles? A woman who rang his chimes every time he laid eyes on her? All his instincts cried that he should stop here, roll up his sleeves and make it happen.

But how?

All he could figure to do was skip over the courtship, since Dana wasn't having any, and start acting like a husband. Sooner or later, she'd get used to the idea—or he'd have to think of a better one. Rafe decided to start with her corral.

WHOK!

Dana opened her eyes to morning sunlight and blinked up at the ceiling.

Whok-whok. Crash!

Not a dream—but then what in heavens? She rolled out of bed and went to her window. Up by the barn, a familiar black pickup was parked, its bed filled with lumber. Beyond the rails of the corral, a tall figure moved, swung an arm back—whok! One end of a top rail flew out from its post. Rafe moved to the next post, applied sledgehammer again, and rail hit ground with a crash. *I don't believe it!* Rafe Montana, taking her corral apart.

Whok—crash!

He was demolishing her corral at—she glanced toward the clock on her bedside table—at seven a.m...? *I'll kill him!* She leaned out the window to scream at him, then thought better. Petra, still sleeping. Her dudes, probably wide awake by now. But at least she didn't have to add to the din.

Five minutes later she was storming up the hill, dressed and with teeth brushed, though she hadn't stopped to comb her hair. "Stop that!" she called. "Stop it now!" But Rafe was working on the far side of the pen—lumber crashing, hammer resounding—and he didn't turn.

He knocked out another rail, and she jabbed him between the shoulder blades. "What do you think you're doing?"

He swung around—just a little bigger and more vivid than she'd remembered—and smiled. "There you are." A rivulet of sweat darkened the front of his shirt. He swiped a bare forearm up his brow and grinned at her, like a small boy delighting in destruction.

"Here I am," she agreed, "asking what the *hell* do you think you're doing, wrecking my corral?" She crossed her arms and glared.

"I'm fixing it. We had some extra planks left from re-building our weaning pen. And I noticed last week this needed doing, so..." He turned away and walloped the fence.

"Will you *stop* it! You're waking my guests!" She swept an arm toward the far side of the meadow, where the cabins followed the course of the river.

"Oh." He looked, then shrugged. "Well, they should be up now. Missing the best part of the day."

"They're on *vacation,* Rafe. They can sleep as late as they like. So stop that."

"I can't stop here." He hooked a thumb at the fallen planks. "Corral's useless like this."

It was indeed. This was where her wrangler gave her dudes their riding lessons, when he deigned to do so. Where the horses were gathered for saddling each morning before the trail rides. "You'll have to fix it."

"What I intended to do." Frowning, he brushed a knuckle under her lashes. "Hey, it's nothing to cry about."

"I just...I just..." *I don't need this, Rafe! Don't need you here, larger than life, joggling my emotions.* She walked such a tightrope of calm nowadays. It was so easy to push her off.

"So I'll stop till you say it's okay to make noise. All right?" He caught her shoulder and walked her downhill toward her house. "But if I have to wait, could I fix myself a cup of coffee?"

WHEN SHE CAME downstairs again a half-hour later, with Petra yawning on her shoulder, the kitchen smelled of coffee. And baking bread. Rafe stood tall at the table, chopping onions on a block, while Sean worked at the counter, cracking eggs into a bowl.

"Coffee?" Rafe crossed to the stove and poured a cup. "Sean tells me that you make breakfast every morning for your wrangler," he said, handing it over. "So we figured we'd get a jump on the job."

We—right. Sean shot her a smoldering look, and kept on cracking. Dana didn't know whether to join her stepson in resenting this invasion, or rejoice in his discomfiture. "I see." She retreated to the table and sat. Miracles didn't happen every morning; might as well relax and observe this one. She sugared her coffee one handed, then sipped and wrinkled her nose—cowboy coffee, strong enough to peel paint. Hastily she added some cream from the carton he'd set out on the table. "What's in the oven?"

"Biscuits." His big hands wielded the knife deftly, whacking the onion into cubes. "Breakfast is my specialty. Mrs. Higgins and Zoe handle suppers."

He turned up the heat under a cast-iron skillet, added olive oil, then the onions, checked the biscuits, and said to Sean, "Five more minutes. Where's the damn wrangler?"

"He wanders in any time between now and nine," Dana volunteered. Depending on the state of his hangover. This was a Saturday, after all.

"That won't do. How the heck do you schedule his chores or your own if you don't know when he'll show?" He swung back to Sean. "Go get him. Tell him if he's not here *pronto,* we'll feed his share to the dogs."

"Don't have a dog," Sean growled, nevertheless heading for the deck.

"You ought to. How do you know when somebody's coming?"

"They knock on the door," Dana said dryly. *Or barge into the kitchen, like some people we won't mention.*

Rafe shook his head, disapproving, but willing to forgive. "City slicker. And I guess when you find the wrong person standing on your doorstep you call the police. But out here…"

He was right; the vast distances meant that a quick response was impossible.

"You ought to have a big, capable dog around the house if you don't have a man. I gave Zoe an Airedale when she was ten to keep an eye on her when I wasn't there."

She smiled, imagining little Zoe with an indomitable father on one side and a capable Airedale on the other. Safe as houses… It was a different world out here. *His world more than mine.* She shouldn't scorn his advice.

He stirred the sizzling onions, then brought the coffeepot over to pour her a refill. "What are you doing here, Rafe?" *I told you the other day, your idea won't work.*

His blue eyes moved over her face. "Being neighborly. That's another thing we do out here. We take care of ourselves, and we take care of our neighbors when they need help, because sooner or later we'll be the ones in need. Your corral needed mending, and I had the time and the lumber. That's all."

She doubted it, but how to challenge him without calling him a liar? "How's Zoe?" This all came back to her in the end. There'd be no tall, dark cowboy in her kitchen without Zoe.

"Still queasy most mornings, but the doctor said that's natural." He looked over from the stove for her confirmation. "I remember Pilar threw up every morning for the first three months."

"That must have been hard."

He grimaced. "You could say that." The back door opened, and Sean and Tim pushed through. "Just in time for breakfast," Rafe noted, holding out his hand. "You must be Tim."

They ate well, but in silence. Sean was sullen, Tim morose and wary, Dana veering between wry amusement at the way Rafe dominated the table and dismay at the odd little riffles of delight that shot through her at unexpected intervals. It was so good simply to be allowed to sit back and relax. She didn't have to seize the day, because Rafe had seized it for her—by the throat—and was energetically shaking the dickens out of it on her behalf.

The moment Tim put down his fork, Rafe said, "You take the dudes for a trail ride at noon?" Information he must have extracted from Sean.

"Was thinking about it," Tim allowed, erring on the side of caution.

Rafe's eyes narrowed as he put down his mug. "Yes...or no?"

"Uh, yeah. I reckon. If any of 'em want to go." Which was nonsense. The deal was that the guests were given a ride every morning, and that a picnic with a longer outing was supplied on Saturdays. Tim shoved back his chair and stood. "So I reckon I'll, uh...go look to the tack."

Rafe conveyed incredulity with one lifted eyebrow. "It's not cleaned and mended and ready to go?"

"Um, most of it. Few things might need lookin' after."

"So does your corral. When you're done with the tack, meet me there. You can put in a few hours digging postholes before you ride." Rafe gazed after the retreating wrangler for a thoughtful moment, then asked, "You're paying him full-time wages?"

"Just barely. Plus room and board. He's got one side of the shotgun cabin."

"Full-time wages for half a day's work, if you're lucky," Rafe observed. "Life's too short to try to ride herd on a layabout. You'd be better off without him."

Neighborliness didn't extend to hiring and firing her staff for her. "Not quite." Not unless she wanted to lead the trail rides herself.

He shrugged and dropped the matter—and turned to her stepson, who'd sat silent through this exchange. "Who washes the dishes around here?"

Sean's look of dawning alarm reminded Dana of a rabbit pinned in the headlights of an oncoming truck. "Uh, she does." He stood hastily and collected his plate.

"While you do what, instead?" Rafe inquired pleasantly.

"Um…" The red crept up Sean's throat, and he shuffled from foot to foot.

"What I figured. Well, today you can do them. Then come up to the corral and give me a hand." And now it was her turn. "A last cup of coffee out on the porch?" Rafe suggested.

He'd just knocked an hour's worth of chores out of her day. She opened her mouth to say that she could get used to this, then thought better and said, "Sounds lovely!"

CHAPTER THIRTEEN

SATURDAY RAFE FIXED her corral. The following Thursday he reappeared at her kitchen door, an hour after breakfast. Dana had just turned out a batch of bread on her pastry slab and her hands were sticky with dough, when he knocked on the screen door.

"Come in—oh, Rafe!" A little shiver of pleasure moved up her bare arms and across her shoulders. "What are you doing here?"

"Come begging a cup of coffee to start with." He nodded at the pot on her stove. "Mind if I do?"

After the effort he'd put into her corral last week—four new posts and a dozen planks or more? She was indebted much deeper than a cup of coffee. "Of course not. I'd take one, too, if you'd fix it for me."

That done, he settled across the table from her to watch, sipping slowly. How did he do it? One moment her kitchen was a prison, a place of lonely, endless drudgery. Now it felt as if the sun had swung around to this side of the house. As if life had a purpose once more, rather than simply a trudging sense of surviving each day, only to be faced with the next, then the next. A man around the house beat an Airedale any day.

Outside, a whinny sounded nearer than the pasture. "Yours?" she asked, cocking her head.

"Tobasco. And I brought Concha along."

Her heart lifted at the prospect of a ride, but she made a teasing face. "You just happened to have a couple of extra horses, so you thought you'd bring them over? Right neighborly, pardner.''

"It is, isn't it?'' His blue eyes locked on hers—then moved deeper, as if their foreheads, the tips of their noses, touched, mind speaking directly to mind. *You know what I'm doing and why,* his eyes said.

And you know my answer. She tore her gaze away and dropped it to her hands, kneading mechanically. He knew it, and yet still he sat here sipping her coffee. Well, he couldn't say she hadn't warned him.

"I thought we'd ride your fence in the home pasture,'' he said finally. "I noticed several posts rotted off at the base the other day. One good push, and it would all come down.''

"Maybe I like it that way,'' she muttered defiantly. She couldn't let him do this; he had his own ranch to tend.

"Yeah, you'll like it when one of your horses tries to step across the wire and tangles his feet and falls. It isn't pretty when he starts struggling. And it's dangerous cutting him out. Do you even own a pair of wire cutters?''

"There might be some up at the barn.''

He blew out a breath, not quite a snort, but merely said, "I'll check.'' He swallowed some more coffee. "Sean should carry a pair everywhere he rides. I'll see he has some.'' He went back to her coffeepot to refill his cup, then put it back on the stove. "Where is Sean, anyway? If he doesn't know how to mend fence, it's high time he learned.''

Her mouth tightened. "He's out and about someplace.'' Hands on the spiraling dough, she could feel his eyes on her face.

"He gave you trouble this morning?''

She aimed a breath upward, blowing bangs back from her eyebrows. "No more than the usual. We have this continuing battle about the computer.'' She tipped her head toward a table pushed against the far wall, next to the ancient pie safe, where Sean's computer lived. "Peter gave it to him, but he was very clear on the way he wanted it to be used. He'd seen too many of his students turn into virtual recluses, holed up in their rooms, cruising the Internet for hours on end, visiting Web sites they shouldn't, playing too many games, chatting with questionable strangers. He said the best way to prevent that was to put the computer in the family room, so you knew what your kid was doing. It should be a tool for research, not a substitute for a social life."

"Makes sense to me."

"And to me, but not to Sean. And I do feel guilty limiting his time, when he's stuck out here in the middle of nowhere. When I first pitched our moving to Colorado to Peter, I imagined it…differently." *I imagined Peter alive, for one thing, with time to give to Sean.* Imagined Sean adjusting well to his new school, making friends in the neighborhood. "The distances out here—I don't guess there's another boy his age within ten miles. And I don't know that he's tried very hard to fit in. The only friend I know for certain that he's made is Zoe."

She watched Rafe's face cool and harden, then he looked away. His eyes lit on Petra, who sat in the corner on a raft of towels. Absorbed in the plastic containers Dana had given her, she was pouring water from a quart container into a butter tub. "Now, *she* knows how to amuse herself," he noted with approval. "Not such a hellraiser as Zoe was."

"Peter and I are—" She swallowed. *Were.* "Quiet, patient types. She comes by it honestly."

The water overflowed the smaller container. Petra shrieked with startled laughter, put the quart down and waved her hand at her achievement, glancing up to be sure Dana had seen. "Wa!"

"More water than you planned on," Dana agreed, grateful for the interruption. "Why don't you show Rafe how you can pour it back."

Rafe stood, went over and hunkered down on his boot heels. "Show me, sweetheart. What have you got there?"

Even crouching, he must seem enormous to her daughter. Petra studied him earnestly, arrived at some decision and smiled. "Nuh-wa!" She picked up the butter tub and offered it to him.

"Mighty nice. Suppose we poured some of it in here…and some here?" Rafe poured half the water back into the quart container, the other half into a third tub. Petra stared, thunderstruck at this new concept. Rafe laughed, rubbed his palm lightly across her head and returned to Dana. "You're not drinking your coffee."

"Hands too sticky. I'll do it in a minute."

"Here." He picked up her mug and held it to her mouth.

"There's no need," she protested, drawing in a breath, as his hand fell on her shoulder.

"But who likes cold coffee?" Nudging her lower lip with the rim of the cup, he tilted it slowly. Eyes meeting his through the rising steam, she gave up and drank. Her heart must have been pounding all along, but suddenly she could hear it, a big, purposeful striding in her ears—taking her where? "Thank you," she whispered, as the cup drew back.

"My pleasure." Brushing a knuckle under her lip, he caught a drop.

It shouldn't be this way. She shouldn't be feeling what she was feeling.

"Ma-ma-ma-*ma!*" Petra called, demanding her attention. Peter's child. Dana slapped the dough into a ball and went to see.

ONCE SHE'D SET THE DOUGH on the warming shelf above the stove for its first rising, then taken Petra upstairs for a diaper change, she had a little time to spare. "Come with me," Rafe urged. "We're wasting daylight."

"I can't leave her, Rafe, and she won't be ready for a nap for hours."

"So bring her along."

"On horseback?" Dana shook her head. "If I fell with her…"

"Then let me carry her." His hands closed around the baby's fat waist. "Go change."

Not a good idea, she told herself as she returned upstairs, but the chance to be out in the mountain air, out in sunlight and flowers… *He knows how to tempt me.*

She found Rafe and Petra out back inspecting the horses. Rafe held the baby facing forward in the crook of his left arm while he showed her how to stroke Concha's velvety nose. Petra patted the mare and squealed. "A born horse-woman," Rafe declared, giving her back to Dana. He swung up on Tobasco. "Now, let me have her."

Dana bit her lip. "Rafe, I really don't think—"

His hands didn't fall. "I started Zoe at six months, Dana. I won't drop her."

This is his world and he knows it, she reminded herself, looking up at him. He wouldn't drop Petra, wouldn't let his horse run away, she knew that, but still… *I want her safe with me. He wants to show her his world and he's saying he can protect her.* She let out a slow, shaking breath and relinquished her daughter.

Petra's mouth formed into a pink *O* of astonishment, as Rafe settled her onto his lap, one hand curled around her stomach. She patted the saddle horn, reached beyond it to grab a swath of Tobasco's black mane. Giggling delightedly, she looked down at her mother to make sure she shared this moment.

A moment Rafe had given her, overriding her mother's

fear on Petra's behalf. *Thank you, Rafe.* The look on Petra's face was a gift surpassing six miles of new fence. Dana swung up on Concha and brought her side by side with the bay, as Rafe moved him out at an easy walk.

"Okay now?" Rafe asked huskily.

Eyes on her daughter's rapturous face, Dana nodded. "Very okay."

They rode most of the fence line, Rafe holding Petra while he instructed Dana to wiggle each fence post without dismounting. When she found a rotten or loose one, he gave her orange surveyor's tape, and she tied a bit of it to the wire. As they rode they talked of little things: Petra's first adventure with solid food—pureed carrots, which ended up on the ceiling; Sean's love of fly-fishing and photography; the spectacular crimson columbine Zoe had hybridized, which had bloomed for the first time last week. They talked a bit about their pasts; Dana's years teaching high school English in Vermont, then her two years with the Peace Corps in Pakistan; Rafe's early years as a cowboy after Pilar died, back when he lived in ranch bunkhouses, while Zoe stayed with Pilar's parents and he could visit her only on weekends.

How could you bear it? To be separated like that. To find each week that she'd grown, that you'd missed out on some crucial little triumph—her first bicycle ride, her first lost tooth? Dana wanted to touch his shoulder, as if touch could soothe the long-ago pain that echoed behind his matter-of-fact words. Unable to do that, she leaned, instead, to stroke her daughter's silky head. She glanced up at Rafe, and found their faces only inches apart—saw his pupils expand, his eyes changing from blue skies to storm clouds. *Excitement whenever we come close...* Who knew what her own eyes were revealing? She straightened abruptly.

"She's getting sleepy," Rafe said after a pause, rubbing her daughter's stomach. "In fact..." He shifted her so that she lay cradled in the crook of his right arm. "Gone, I'd say. Riding's as good as a car."

"You're not tired of holding her?"

"Not at all." He nodded ahead. "Now, there's a beauty."

While she leaned to tie ribbon to the sagging post, he said, "I've been meaning to say something…about Suntop."

She turned, surprised at how serious he sounded, then her eyes focused beyond him. "Will you look at that!" Sean, climbing down from the tree house in the oak tree at the center of the pasture. "So that's where he goes! I thought he'd outgrown it."

"Aha!" Rafe's eyes gleamed with satisfaction. "Think I will hand you Miss Sleepyhead for a minute."

"Then let me get down." Dana dismounted, accepted her daughter and watched Rafe lope purposefully in pursuit of Sean, who'd set off downhill, giving no sign that he'd seen them. Horse and rider came to a sliding halt in front of the boy, as if they were heading a stray calf. Observing the ensuing exchange, even at this distance Dana could see Sean stiffen, every angle of his body expressing outrage, while every line of Rafe's conveyed calm implacability. Her stepson threw up his hands abruptly and changed direction, trudging off toward the barn, shoulders slumped, kicking weeds as he went.

Dana bit her lip and looked down at her sleeping daughter. *Peter, am I doing wrong letting Rafe boss him around? But he's been so lost without you. Maybe a man in his life is what he needs.*

She waited, but no answer came, only the song of a mockingbird, far-off, trill upon triumphant trill. What had Sean himself said the other day when she was talking about the needs of a boy-child to have a man to follow?

I had that once, he'd said so wistfully that it had almost roken her heart.

Should I try to find that for him again, Peter? Or am I etraying you? Betraying his love for you?

No answer but the bird, spangling the day with notes of adiant joy.

The shadow of a horse and rider fell over her. "Looks ke I've found my help, Dana. I've sent him for the post-ole diggers."

She glanced at her watch. "And I should get back to my read. But thank you for my ride. For Petra's first ride."

Rafe touched a finger to his hat and his slow smile crin-led his eyes. "Anytime."

From: SanDiegan@Pipeline.net
To: RedColumbine@Westbest.com
Zoe, your old man is driving me CRAZY!!!!!!!!!!! What's he trying to prove, anyway? The Ribbon R was doing fine without him. I've got blisters on top of my blisters. I guess he's trying to punish me for getting you pregnant, and this is the only way he can find to do it—death by posthole digger. From now on, how about warning me when he's headed this way? Anyway, I REALLY miss you. Saw a pretty columbine yesterday and I felt like breaking some-thing. This SUCKS deluxe. What are we gonna do? Love you, Sean

From: RedColumbine@Westbest.com
To: SanDiegan@Pipeline.net
Hey, Seanster, don't take it personally. I think it's just his demented way of hitting on your stepmom. By the way, is she interested? I think he's a studmuffin my-self, but maybe I'm prejudiced. Sorry about those blisters, but mending fence is a handy skill. I can do

it myself. Gotta run now. I've got five foals to exercise today. (He's working my butt off, too.) BIIIIG HUG, Zoe+(?)

IT TOOK FOUR DAYS, spread over two weeks, to complete the repairs to the home pasture fence line. Tim and Sean did much of the work, but Rafe was the driving force behind everyone's labor. Each day Dana found herself falling deeper and deeper into his debt, found herself both grateful and dismayed by her growing obligation. Needing to balance the equation, she cooked hearty lunches for him and his crew, but that hardly moved the scales, compared with hours of backbreaking labor, setting posts and stringing wire. Besides, she was fairly certain that Rafe didn't own an endless supply of spare fence posts. She suspected he was buying them somewhere, but when she demanded that he let her pay for the materials, he laughingly brushed her aside.

The least she could do was invite him to supper, but most days he turned her down, citing a need to go home to Zoe. The day they completed the job, however, he worked til almost dark. Then, after he'd packed his truck, he appeared at her kitchen door.

"It's done," he said briefly, looming tall against a red-lavender glow—the sun had set. A cool wind blew, carrying the smell of clean sweat and leaf mold and bruised grass from him to her. He flexed his shoulders beneath his damp shirt, easing sore muscles.

"Rafe, I don't know how to thank you."

"Step out here and see the moonrise. That would be thanks enough."

"Hardly." Still, she slipped out for a moment to see an amber moon creeping above the eastern peaks, chasing one silver planet up the purpling sky. "*Beautiful*'s not a big

nough word," she murmured, after they'd stood shoulder
o shoulder in mute fascination till it cleared the mountain-
op.

He nodded. "In Spanish, the word for heaven and for
ky is the same. *Cielo.*"

See-EH-loh, she repeated silently. The word was liquid,
ensual on the tongue. Pilar taught him that, she realized
vith the oddest twinge of—not quite pain, not quite re-
entment. She put it briskly aside. "It's gorgeous, but we're
ust minutes from sitting down." Her guests were gathering
n the living room, enjoying their hors d'oeuvres around
he fire she'd kindled against the evening chill. "I've tried
efore, but I'll say it again. You're welcome to stay for
upper. You must be starving."

"This time I reckon I'll take you up on it, if you really
nean it. That lunch you made us seems about a hundred
ears gone."

"Of course I mean it." Though she half regretted the
nvitation as soon as it left her mouth. He needed a change
f clothes and a shower. Water was no problem, but she
ad no clothes to lend him. Peter's were up in the attic,
acked away in boxes scented with sprigs of lavender and
ose petals from her garden, against the day when she found
he courage to give them away. She'd sooner Rafe come to
er table in his birthday suit than in Peter's clothes. Not
hat they'd fit him anyway, she realized, looking up at him.
Ie was taller, broader, longer of leg.

"I don't suppose Sean would have a T-shirt that would
t you."

He laughed under his breath. "No need. I always carry
 change of clothes in my truck. Is there a hose out here I
ould use?"

"You know where the bathroom is upstairs," she re-
ninded him. How long ago that seemed, and how he'd
cared her that night! *If you'd just said, "Hey, it's me, Rafe,*

stomping into your life,'' Somehow she felt she would have known that here was a friend, not trouble. "Supper's in ten minutes, so you'd better hurry."

She introduced him to her dudes that night as a neighbor—then gritted her teeth at the arch looks passing among some of the women. It didn't help that Rafe—by accident or inclination, she didn't know which—had chosen the seat at the opposite end of the table from her own. Not that he tried to pose as the host, but he had a natural authority to which people instantly responded. Before the soup course was done, the women were plying him with questions about Indians and rodeos; the men, about ranching and hunting. He didn't try to dominate the talk—far from it. His answers were delivered with a cowboy's dry humor and modesty, brief and straight to the point. Still, the conversation flowed around him. *I could hire him for the nightly entertainment,* she thought, watching him over the candles.

The only one who wasn't charmed by Rafe was Sean. Her stepson sat glowering, grimly shoveling food into his mouth till he'd cleaned his plate. Then, rather than waiting for his usual second helping of everything, he mumbled his excuses and retreated upstairs.

After supper, Rafe assisted in clearing away, then offered to help with the dishes. "Going for sainthood?" she teased him, and shook her head.

"*Cielo,* maybe, but not sainthood," he murmured, lounging against the counter next to the sink.

Dana kept her eyes fixed on her rubber-gloved hands. *What are you trying to do to me, Rafe?* He hadn't mentioned Zoe's problem in weeks, except to report that the morning sickness seemed to be easing at last. *So then, why are you here?*

You feel it, too, he'd told her weeks ago up on the mountain. And there was no denying it. Blindfolded, she'd still have felt his presence, as if the air had changed to warm velvet brushing against her skin, her nerves crisping with his nearness, the blood sliding through her veins like molten honey.

But even though I feel it, Rafe, it's no good. Even if you were offering me love, not sex, I'm still a coward. A chance of love didn't come without risk—and to risk losing again? She'd already had enough pain in her life. No. Whatever he was offering, she didn't need it. She kept her ambitions small and realistic these days. She'd settle for peace.

Rafe cocked his head. "Nice tune." He went to the swinging door and propped it open a few inches with the doorstop. In the living room, someone had found the CD player. The velvety tones of a Tony Bennett song drifted through the night. Dana glanced automatically at the playpen, but Petra slept on, bottom high under her blanket, sweet face a dreaming blank.

"I should be going," Rafe said regretfully, "but first I wanted to ask you something. Got a minute to come out front?"

"Sure." She drew off her gloves and followed him through the dining room, then paused in the archway to the living room. A new song had just started, and three couples were shuffling around the room.

"There you are, Dana!" Leo Shultz cried gaily. He was the most sociable guest of her current set. "Come dance with me." He drew her, protesting, out on the floor—she'd danced with no man since Peter, and didn't want to now. She glanced back helplessly at Rafe, mouthing a "Sorry," and found that he was scowling. Somehow that eased her own reluctance.

And Leo was the perfect partner with whom to break her long fast. His own cheery wife, Martha, was paired with Ira Kravitz from Aspen cabin, and Leo chortled and bumped hips with her every time they danced past. If Peter had been sitting on the couch watching them, he'd have been smiling. ''Marvelous dance, marvelous dinner, most marvelous vacation I've had in years!'' Leo declared at the end of the song, as he escorted her back to Rafe—as if she were a wheelbarrow he'd borrowed from a next-door neighbor.

''Sorry,'' Dana apologized, when he'd departed. ''What did you want to show me?''

''A question about paint, but it can wait.'' A new song had begun—''Till There Was You.'' Rafe settled a hand on her waist and drew her close. ''One of my favorites,'' he noted, clasping her hand and lifting it to his chest, just a hand span above his heart.

Not with you, Rafe, I can't do it! But how could she refuse, after she'd humored Leo? And she was already past the point of refusal, following his strong but simple lead, her body instinctively answering his. ''Is it?'' she said on a scrap of breath. Her heart had mysteriously ballooned to fill up her chest—all thuds, no oxygen. She felt dizzy, stunned sightless by his body heat and his nearness; all she could do was give herself to his hands and the music. Tremors filled her as if she were the guitar string quivering, as if the horn blew its shivering notes across her skin.

Rafe dipped his mouth to her temple. ''All right?'' he murmured huskily. His fingers slid around her waist to her back, splayed against her spine. Fanned upward in an absent caress, then down again.

I should be. It was only a song. Only a dance. It shouldn't shatter her. Shouldn't.

It ended before she could find an answer. His lips brushed across her hair. His fingertips followed her spine upward, exploring the shape and size of her, then dropped away when she stepped back. ''Thank you,'' she whispered, her throat aching too much for louder words.

They'd ended at the foot of the staircase. She reached out, needing to go, unable to do so without...something.

Some gesture. She fingered a button on his shirt. "Thanks, Rafe. And...good night." Avoiding his eyes—she knew they'd be dark, the pupils wide with her nearness, as hers were with his—she turned and fled up the stairs.

CHAPTER FOURTEEN

From: SanDiegan@Pipeline.net
To: RedColumbine@Westbest.com

So now your old man's REALLY messed us up. Our wrangler quit a few minutes ago. Dana's gonna have a COW when she gets back from the grocery store. What happened was your dad showed up this morning and announced we were going to paint the house. (Is he always this hyper?) Tim said he was a wrangler, not a house painter. Your dad said "Tough," that while he was taking Dana's money, he could work for it or walk. So the three of us scraped paint all day—front of the house is more bare wood than paint now. And megalousy work in the heat—the paint chips and dust stick to your sweat and your arms want to fall off. Tim finally threw down his scraper and walked away about an hour before sundown. I figured your dad would tear a strip off him, but he just sort of smiled to himself and kept scraping. Then tonight, I'm sitting here in the kitchen, hanging out with the Pet-beast while Dana goes shopping, and Tim stops by to drop off the key to his cabin. Tells me to tell Dana to find some other slave—he's outta here. I know just how he feels, too. If I had someplace to go, I'd be gone for sure. Except for you, you, you. You're the only reason I'm still here, Zoe. I don't know what I'd do if my mom finally decided to take me, like I've been bugging her to. (Want to run away

with me to San Diego? It beats this dump four ways
from Sunday, I'm telling you.) WHUH oh, the
BEAST is crawling this way—wants to know what
I'm up to. Wants to help me play with the keyboard.
Wants to sit in my lap—not with THAT diaper you
don't, babe! Better sign off quick. I
LOOOOOOOOOOOOOOVE YOU, RED.
Your Sean Diegan
P.S. Like I told you last week, day after tomorrow is
my birthday, the big 1-5. Is there a chance in the
world he'd let you come to my party? Dana always
makes this stupid fuss. It's way beyond embarrassing,
with the dudes and all, but at least there's cake and
ice cream. Think you could ask him? I REALLY miss
you and I want to pat your freckled tummy. (Now
that would be a birthday present.)

"TIM QUIT," Dana said flatly as she opened the back
door to admit Rafe. She'd returned home too late from town
the night before to call him then, and perhaps it was just
as well. Overnight, her fury had cooled to manageable pro-
portions, or nearly. "I knew he wasn't going to stand still
for that!"

"For some honest hard work? No, I reckon that was too
much to expect."

And you didn't expect it, did you? she thought, seeing
the satisfied curl of his mouth. *I wouldn't let you fire him,
so you persuaded him to walk.* The man's arrogance was
boundless. "What do I do now? Some new guests checked
in yesterday, and they're hot for their first trail ride." She
wanted to bite her tongue as soon as she'd said it. Asking
for Rafe's advice, she was playing right into his hands.

"You loan me your phone." He brushed the back of his
wrist against her bare arm, nudging her aside.

Crossing her arms, she retreated to the far side of the

kitchen. Stood, stewing, while he punched in a number. She shrugged and went back to making pancakes. *All right. You got me into this mess. Let's see how you get me out.*

"Zoe?" Rafe murmured behind her. "I need to talk to Willy. Could you run get him?" He swung around to lean against the counter, tapping one boot.

Across the room, Petra looked up from the beach ball she was trying to chew. She flopped over onto hands and knees and made a scuttling beeline for Rafe. He dropped down on his heels. "How's my girl?"

Dana stiffened. *Not yours, Rafe. None of us is. You can't just annex a family, or a ranch, because you feel like it.* Still, she stole a glance every so often, watching him draw a clean red bandanna from his back pocket and tie it around her daughter's neck. Petra chortled and proceeded to pull herself up the leg of his jeans till she stood swaying against his knee, holding up her new adornment for his admiration. "Would you look at this?" Rafe called on a note of laughter.

"She's been doing that off and on all week," Dana told him, softening in spite of herself. How could you resist a man who thought your daughter was adorable?

"Be toddling before you know it—oh, Willy?" A few brisk words and the conversation was done. Rafe put down the phone, scooped Petra up and sauntered over to where Dana was whipping batter. "You've got a wrangler for the rest of this week. If you suit each other, maybe he'll stay."

WILLY PROVED TO BE a seventy-something cowboy with a shrewd-comical face and a salt-and-pepper beard that could have served as an industrial dust mop. Battered black hat in his hand, he stopped by the kitchen to introduce himself and ask her desires for the day. With that understood, he chucked Petra under her chin, then drove his truck and horse trailer—he'd brought his own mount—up to the barn.

"Ha!" Petra declared, watching as he backed a big, rangy chestnut down the ramp.

"That is a horse," Dana agreed. "Or did you mean Willy was funny?" And to be relied on, she admitted, hearing her own deep sigh of relief. If Rafe had chosen him, then Willy would do. "Blast the man, anyway, trying to run our lives for us, Pet."

But by lunchtime she'd forgiven him. Hard not to, when the whole house echoed to the sound of scrapers dragging across brittle paint. A job Dana had always hated herself. *I shouldn't be letting him do this.*

But just how did you stop an irresistible force? And if you only half wanted him to stop? *That's the real problem.* She wasn't wholehearted in her resistance, and Rafe knew it. *He manipulates me as easily as he maneuvered Tim into quitting.* But to what end? His original purpose? Or did he, too, find his original feelings subtly changing as the days passed, like the Ribbon River wearing rough stones to pearly smoothness? *I don't know. Don't think I want to know.*

She'd just completed the potato salad that would go with the chicken sandwiches for her paint crew, when Sean scratched at the back door. "Getting hungry?" she asked, coming to meet him, glad that he'd remembered the rule she'd made yesterday; Petra was not to be exposed to paint dust, since there was no way to be sure it was lead-free.

"Yeah, but I wanted to ask you something."

"Sure, what is it?" Anything. He'd been so sullen these past few weeks, with Rafe pushing him. Sometimes Dana felt as if their relationship had taken a giant step backward.

"I know what I want for my birthday present." He raised his gaze from his toes to her face.

Peter's brown eyes. "What's that?" she asked, though she'd already knocked the bottom out of her monthly budget, buying him a lens for the Nikon that his father had given him.

"I want Zoe to come to my party tomorrow night. Do you think Mr. Montana would let her if *you* asked?"

"Oh, Sean." *Ask me for the moon, why don't you?* Rafe seemed determined to keep them apart.

"Please?" He flattened a hand to the screen between them. "Will you, Dana?"

"Of course I'll try. But promise me you won't get your hopes up?"

Leaving Sean to eat his lunch on the back porch, with one ear cocked for Petra, who was dozing in her kitchen playpen, Dana brought a tray around the house to the front. Rafe stood up on the porch roof, dragging a two-handed scraper along the flaking clapboards between the dormers. The muscles clenched in his sweat-soaked shirt, then lengthened, clenched again. Muscles in her stomach, and lower, pulled tight at the sight of him. She stiffened her shoulders and called, "Lunchtime!"

They ate it down by the river, talking lazily of possible paint schemes for the house, and then of Willy. He was Rafe's oldest cowboy, his steadiest, hands down his funniest—just wait till she heard his yarns about the old days. "But he's getting a bit creaky for range work, though he's too mule-stubborn to admit it. If I could find him a soft spot where he still felt useful…" Somehow Rafe implied she'd be doing him a favor if she took Willy on.

"We'll see how he likes dudes," Dana promised. And now, if she was helping him out, then… "Rafe, did Sean tell you that tomorrow's his birthday?" Swiftly she made her plea. She couldn't take time off from the Ribbon R to give Sean any sort of celebration in town, not to mention the problem of money. So the affair would be simple—just an extraspecial supper, then cake and ice cream. "But he hasn't any friends that I know of to invite to the party. Except...Zoe.''

Rafe's brows shot together. ''And whose fault is that? You said he doesn't make much effort to fit in.''

''I don't think he knows how. He's a fish out of water out here. Half the kids in his class are ranch kids, so he's at a disadvantage being a city slicker. And the others are jocks, and he's not that, either.''

''That's one of the hard lessons a man needs to learn in life—how to find his feet wherever he goes. How to make friends.''

''I think, behind all his cockiness, he's fairly shy, Rafe.''

''I reckon you're right, but still, he needs to learn.''

It's not your place to teach my son, Rafe! Though she didn't doubt he meant it kindly. ''But about Zoe?''

''I'm sorry, Dana. I want her heart-free and ready to go as soon as her baby's born. Zoe needs to get on with her life, not always be looking back over her shoulder.''

''But Sean—'' She stopped as he shook his head. The man was a rock.

''Your first concern is Sean, Dana. But mine has to be Zoe. The answer's no.''

There was no use in fighting; she'd never win this one. And if he wouldn't oblige her in this, still, he had in every other way. *I tried, Sean.* One more time she'd failed him was the way he'd see it. She sighed and said, ''How is Zoe, anyway? Is she showing yet?''

''She's taken to wearing baggy sweatshirts, so it's hard to be sure, but yes, I'd say so.''

She watched the muscles quiver in his jaw, but pressed on. ''What about adoption agencies? Have you looked into those yet?'' *This is a test,* she realized suddenly. If he'd given up on her as the solution to his problem, then he must be addressing that. And she wanted to believe he'd given up. Wanted to believe that whatever Rafe was doing here, whatever kept bringing him back to the Ribbon R, it had nothing to do with Zoe.

His expression went a bit darker. "I spoke to a couple of agencies, but they say with Zoe's restrictions... Doesn't look promising."

"Maybe a private placement?"

"Maybe," he said shortly. "I've talked to my lawyer."

He had nothing further to volunteer on the subject, so Dana gave up prying. She stacked their plates on the tray and started to rise, but he put a hand on her knee. She subsided and cocked her head.

"I've been meaning to say something, and now I've got to," Rafe said. As if he'd forgotten it, his hand stayed in place. "It's about Suntop. I don't own all of the ranch— or even much of it."

"Oh?" *Why are you telling me this, Rafe?*

"I'm the ranch manager. Old man Tankersly owns Suntop. It has been in his family for a hundred-something years. But he had only daughters, three of 'em, and they all ran off to the city. He needed somebody to run the place for him—he moved down to San Antonio ten years ago, and he only stays up here for half of each summer, which is why I'm telling you this."

"Rafe, you don't have to tell me anything." Though apparently he felt he had to. His face was set, the muscles ticking faintly beneath his suntanned skin.

"I didn't want any...misunderstandings...false pretenses, is why. I own fifteen percent of Suntop, Dana, which is enough to bring me a very good living and always will be. Ben Tankersly thought the best way to keep me, and keep me working for his best interests, was to make them the same as my own. So once he'd decided I'd do, he paid me partly in land and partly in money, till I'd reached fifteen percent."

"I see." She nodded, not understanding the pain in his face.

"But that's all of Suntop I'll ever own, Dana. He'll never sell out to me at any price. He wants the ranch to stay in his family, and he wants it intact. His daughters don't care about the place, but they have two young sons among them so far. Tankersly's hoping that when his grandsons grow up..." He shrugged. "It's years before I'll have to deal with that, but I thought you should know."

"I see." Rafe was warning her that if she'd thought he was a rich man, she was mistaken. If anything, she liked him more for that, not less. Still, she felt a shadow creeping across her heart, a high, thin layer of ice-filled gray swallowing the sun. "Thanks for telling me. There was no need."

He grimaced. "Not the way I saw it. Besides, old man Tankersly took a notion to visit early this year. He phoned last night. He'll be flying in Thursday, which means I won't be able to finish painting the front of your house this week. Fact is, I won't be able to be around much at all, for the next month while he's visiting."

"Rafe, please, don't worry about it. But shouldn't you be over at your place getting ready for his visit?"

He stiffened as if she'd slapped him. "A well-run ranch is ready for an inspection at any time."

"Of course." She put a placating hand over his. "I imagine Suntop runs like a clock."

"As much as a ranch ever does." He'd stopped bristling. His eyes flicked down to their stacked hands, then rose to hers with a question stirring in their depths.

Hastily she gathered up the tray and stood. "I've stuck poor Sean with Petra."

AFTER SHE'D DISMISSED Sean, Dana took Petra upstairs to nurse and to nap. Lying in bed with the dozing baby cradled against her, eyes closed, she realized that her somber mood still lingered. Something Rafe had said? Picturing his face, hearing his scraper attacking the paint on the far side of the house, she felt a shiver start low in her stomach and rise to her breasts, her nipples hardening as if Petra still suckled. There was no denying her attraction. Was that the root of this sadness?

Something to do with what he told me... His chagrin at not owning all of Suntop Ranch...

That was it—land. He'd made it plain from the start that he'd like to lay his hands on the Ribbon R, but now she was beginning to grasp the extent of his desire. Fifteen percent of the county's largest ranch wasn't enough land for Rafe. He wanted more.

She had it.

When you're thinking—hoping?—that maybe his feelings are changing as yours are, just keep that in mind.

ONCE RAFE HAD LEFT for the day, she told Sean of her failure to move him regarding Zoe. He took it as she'd expected—slamming out of the kitchen and disappearing for the rest of the night. Not even supper lured him down from his room. At least she had plenty of privacy to bake a German chocolate cake—his favorite—and ice it.

THE NEXT MORNING her stepson's mood held steady—in the basement. When she wished him a happy birthday at the breakfast table, he grunted and shrugged. "Big wonderful deal."

As he was finishing his meal, Rafe's truck pulled into the yard. "Oh, *crap!* He thinks I'm gonna work on my birthday?"

He did indeed. "Best present a man could give himself" was Rafe's response. "Putting his own house in order. You own a quarter share in this ranch, Dana tells me."

Sean shrugged. "So what? I'd sell it in a heartbeat."

Standing in front of the stove, Rafe swung deliberately around, coffeepot suspended, one eyebrow raised. "Really? I'd like to buy it."

Dana sucked in a breath, as Sean rocked back on his heels. But before she could open her mouth, he'd recovered. "Sure, we could talk about that—if you'll let me see Zoe."

The hungry light in Rafe's face flickered and died. "Forget it." He smacked down his mug without refilling it. "Let's get to work. I want a coat of primer on the front by the end of the day."

"Whatever." Sean stalked out the door.

"And you can forget about cutting a deal with a minor," Dana said dryly, after he'd gone. "The terms of Peter's will say he can't sell without consent of his guardian, and that's me." *And I don't see you as my partner, Rafe.* Not if all he cared about was business.

CHAPTER FIFTEEN

WHEN SHE CALLED THEM to lunch out on the deck—pain
chips still being forbidden in her kitchen—Dana found tha
the mood hadn't lightened. Sean was still mutely sullen
Rafe briskly ignored the boy's sulking, which was probably
the best way to deal with it.

While they ate, Dana filled the edgy silence with a repor
on Willy's first day as a wrangler. Last night at supper, th
guests had praised him to the skies. His stories were fas
cinating, his humor droll. He was a fount of natural histor
and cowboy lore. And apparently he liked to teach. He wa
currently up in the home pasture, showing some of th
dudes how to rope a horse.

"If he wants to stay on after this week, we'd love t
have him," she said.

"Up to him," Rafe reminded her. "Suntop has been hi
home for thirty years or more, so..."

"He said he'd rather continue living in your bunkhous
than move into the wrangler's cabin here," Dana said
"But maybe that will keep him from feeling homesick."

Sean stood abruptly. "Can I use the truck?"

"Didn't your mother ground you after your brush wit
the state police?" Rafe asked quietly. He knew she had.

"Yeah, but I want to go get the mail—all right? I coul
do it on my bike—I'd be glad to—but it'd take me an hour
I thought you wanted help painting."

"It's you who needs help painting," Rafe reminded hin
with measured calm.

"So, yes, but you should get back quick as you can," Dana cut in. "The keys are on the dashboard."

After the truck had rumbled away down the hill, Rafe said, "Not sticking to your guns. That's no way to straighten him out."

"Normally I'd agree with you, but today's his birthday. And there's one person he hasn't heard from."

Rafe scowled. "You mean Zoe?"

"Make that two, then. But I meant his mother. Margot."

Rafe blew out a breath. "That's nice. Damned if people should have kids if they don't want them." He stood abruptly and held out his hand.

"Well, I want him." She let him lift her to her feet. "He was the sweetest kid when I first knew him, Rafe." Now only Zoe, and sometimes Petra, saw that side of him. But Sean needed an outlet for his best instincts—if they were to live on.

"If you don't mind my saying so..." Rafe's thumb fanned across the back of her hand. "Sometimes he really seems to..."

"To hate me?" She nodded unhappily. "He thinks it's all my fault, Rafe. I'm the one who persuaded Peter to give up teaching and move here. And I'm the one who wanted a romantic anniversary weekend and insisted Sean stay home, so that he wasn't there to help." She pulled her hand away and hugged herself. "Plus, I'm the witch who taught Peter how to cross-country ski—he'd never tried it before we moved to Colorado. And then, after the avalanche—" She shivered as if she still stood knee-deep in powdery snow. "I had to choose between staying and searching by myself, or going for help. I looked—I really did—I don't know for how long..." She'd been half hysterical, in shock. "But there was just *nothing*." Nothing but white, white, a ball of choking white, burying all hopes and dreams beneath it. "Sean thinks I made the wrong choice."

Rafe drew her in, wrapped his arms tight around her. She buried her face against his warmth, and stood shuddering. "In an avalanche, sweetheart—" his lips brushed across her hair "—there usually isn't a right choice."

She nodded blindly against him. "I keep telling myself that. Peter would say that. But Sean—"

"Sean thinks life should have been otherwise, and you're the only one he can find to blame."

"Something like that." She lifted her head at the sound of her pickup wheezing up the hill, then stepped out of Rafe's arms. This wasn't the day to add to her stepson's bad mood.

"Any mail?" she asked hopefully, as Sean slammed the truck's door.

"Nothing." Sean headed around the side of the house, back to work.

Usually there was something, if only bills. "You sure it's come yet?" she called after him.

"The mailbox flag was down. We got zip. *Nada.* Crap all!"

Rafe grimaced. "Happy birthday." He started to turn away—swung back and drew his fingertips down her cheek. "Hey, thanks for lunch."

THE MEMORY of Rafe's arms around her was like a wall between Dana and the blues for the rest of the afternoon. Things would work out, she told herself. They were bound to. If this wasn't Sean's happiest birthday, well, there would be other and better ones.

She came downstairs from putting Petra down and stepped out onto the front porch. The first-floor clapboards were primed a smooth, flat white. "Hey, this looks wonderful!" She went down the steps to check the porch roof. Sean was busily painting, with only a third of the second floor left to cover. "You guys are heroes!" She glanced around. "Rafe left?"

"Yeah," Sean said, his eyes on his brush. "Said he had to do something in town, but he might stop by later."

"Later," meaning the party? Had he taken pity on Sean, possibly changed his mind about Zoe? Dana didn't dare ask. "Terrific." She bustled into the house. Whatever Rafe's plans, she had supper and a party to put together.

From: RedColumbine@Westbest.com
To: SanDiegan@Pipeline.net
Happy birthday to you, Happy birthday to you! HAPPY BIRTHDAY DEAREST SE-AN, haaaaaaappy birthday to you!!!!!!!!!! I wish I could be there at your party, Sean. (I tried, I really did try.) But I and the whatzit will be THINKING about you all day, sending the most excellent vibes. And whatever you wish tonight, WISH BIG! I've gotta feeling it's gonna come true. So eat some cake for us, too. HUGS AND KISSES, Zoe+(?)

From: SanDiegan@Pipeline.net
To: RedColumbine@Westbest.com
Zoe, I don't know if your dad is stopping by Suntop before he comes back here tonight. But if he does, MAKE HIM BRING YOU. Or hide in the back of his truck? I'm so lonesome I could die. Your Sad Diegan. P.S. Thanks for my birthday card, but I want to TALK to you.

DANA HAD MEANT to give Sean his gift before the party, but she hadn't found the moment. Though he'd prowled in and out of the kitchen all afternoon once he finished painting, he'd been so glumly absorbed in his computer that she'd decided to wait. Perhaps a slice of cake would bump him into a receptive mood, if not a festive one.

At least the guests were in a mood to celebrate. Those who had stayed on the ranch for the day were boasting about their new roping and riding skills, thanks to Willy. The ones who'd gone into Durango had come back with glowing accounts of the steam train excursion up to the old mining town of Silverton. "Panoramas to die for!" proclaimed Suzie Shurman, one of their New York City dudes. "I bought the most beautiful postcards—oh!" She clapped a hand to her mouth. "Your mail!"

Everyone looked up politely.

"The postman was just putting it in the box when we reached the highway this morning. So we picked it up to save you a trip. It's still in the car." She turned to her husband. "Eric, would you run get it?"

Dana glanced at Sean's face and looked away. *Margot, if you haven't sent him at least a card, I will never forgive you.*

By the time she had cleared the salad plates, Eric was back. He presented a pile, mostly of bills, with a flourish and a panted "Sorry about that."

"Not a problem at all," she murmured absently, thumbing through them. *Come on, Margot. Come on—ah! Bless you!* "One for you," she noted casually, handing a large square envelope to Sean. The oversize, ornately self-conscious script on the return address was definitely his mother's.

He sat, turning it over and over in his hands.

"Love letter?" Suzie suggested slyly.

Sean growled something wordless and ripped it open.

"Oooh, a birthday card!" Suzie crowed, seeing the blazing birthday cake on its cover. "Is it your birthday, Sean?"

"It is," Dana said, covering for him. She'd meant to announce that anyway, to prepare them for dessert. Sean was sitting utterly motionless, except for his eyes. He'd opened them to their utmost width, as if trying to read in a dark room. Then he blinked, too deliberately, widened them again and closed the card. Folded it once, twice and jammed it into a pants pocket. *He's trying not to cry,* she realized. *Oh, Sean, I wish you'd waited to read that.* She stood. "Well, I trust everyone likes lasagna?" One of Sean's favorite foods.

During the meal she fielded most of the friendly questions aimed at Sean, until the guests gave up and the conversation turned to other topics. Her stepson ate mechanically, his eyes lifting from his plate only to focus on the window that overlooked the driveway, then dropping back to his food.

"More garlic bread?" Dana waved the basket under his nose.

"Um—uh, no. Thanks." Sean put down his fork. "Do you think he's coming back?"

"Who?" Then she realized. *He's waiting for Rafe.* Hoping for Zoe. She reached out for his cheek, then stopped herself. Too often he'd made it plain that he didn't like her to touch him. "I don't know, Sean. He didn't promise, did he?" Because if Rafe had, then sooner or later he'd be here. She'd learned that much about the man.

He brought a sigh up from his toes. "Guess not."

But as Dana rose to clear the main course, Sean jerked upright. "It's him!" A faint rumble of a big pickup truck climbing the hill sounded beyond the walls. He started to rise, but Dana shook her head. "If it is Rafe, he's probably just dropping off more house paint." *Don't get your hopes up, Sean.* He was building too much on so little.

Hands filled with her tray, she pushed through the swinging door—to find Rafe coming in the back one. The sleeves of his work shirt were rolled to his elbows; his hands and forearms, smudged with grease. "Sorry to be dropping by so late.'' He strode over to her sink and reached for the soap. ''I was down in Durango. Would have been here an hour ago, but I made the mistake of stopping to help an old gal with her car—flat tire. Then it turned out her spare was flat, so I had to—'' He shrugged. ''Anyway, here I am.''

With no Zoe in sight. Clearly, he hadn't even stopped by Suntop if he'd been down in Durango. She buried her disappointment. ''Well, you're just in time for cake and ice cream and coffee.''

''Was hoping I'd be.''

Carrying in the coffeepot, with Rafe following with the ice cream and bowls, Dana tried to prepare Sean with a rueful grimace and a little shake of her head. He didn't get the message. His eager eyes shot past her to take in Rafe, then swung beyond him—to a door that stayed closed. ''I'm afraid not,'' she murmured, drawing up an extra chair beside her own.

''Oh.'' Sean slumped back in his seat, his lips clamped and quivering.

He desperately needed a hug. If she'd offered one, he would have exploded. Dana stood, irresolute. *Will he feel worse if I bring in the cake, or neglected if I don't?* And meantime her guests expected a dessert and assumed it would come with candles. *Play it through to the bitter end,* she decided, and went back with a heavy heart to fetch it.

At first she thought they'd all carry it off. At the sight of the blazing birthday cake, the guests and Rafe broke into a hearty, off-key rendition of ''Happy Birthday,'' and somehow Sean mustered a shaky smile, then enough wind to blow out the candles. But while the slices were served out, he stared blankly down at his own portion, not eating.

Would his gift cheer him up or only sink him further in gloom? But Dana desperately wanted him to know she cared. Even though, in spite of all her efforts, everything had gone wrong, she cared. She drew the gift-wrapped parcel from its hiding place in the sideboard and set it before him. "Happy birthday, Sean!" she whispered under cover of the guests' cheerful chatter.

His mouth twisted, then stilled. "Thanks." He touched the bright paper, but made no move to open it.

Okay. At least she'd made the gesture. Perhaps opening it later was a better idea.

But her presentation had cued Rafe. His arm stretched past her, bearing a small, oblong package, also gift wrapped. "Happy birthday, Sean."

This one cut through Sean's daze. Mouth ajar, he stared at Rafe for a moment, then ripped into the gift.

Thinks it's from Zoe, Dana realized, her heart sinking, just as he drew the small object from its wrapping. A tool of some sort, like a big, multipurpose pocketknife, only larger. The gift one man would choose for another.

"It's got about everything you'll need," Rafe said beside her. "Wire cutters, a screwdriver. I carry one myself."

"Just what I'd want—if I wanted to be a dumb-ass cowboy!" Sean shoved back his chair and stood. "Thanks, but no, thanks!" He spun away, knocking his chair over, and slammed out through the kitchen door.

"Oops!" murmured one of the guests, breaking the pin-drop silence.

"Yeah, puberty," agreed another with a nervous chuckle. "If you could just lock 'em in a safety deposit box for five years or so, take 'em out when they reach twenty-one…"

The conversation turned determinedly general, everyone filling in the awkwardness in a rush, careful not to look at Dana or Rafe.

Dana put a hand over his fingers and squeezed. His face was red, but utterly expressionless. "I'm sorry, Rafe. Come out to the kitchen with me?" Sean would be long gone by now. Out to the tree house he and Peter had built, she supposed.

"I'm so sorry," she said as soon as the door had swung shut behind them. "You didn't deserve that." After a hard day's physical labor—labor that was a gift to Sean as well as her—Rafe had driven seventy miles round trip to buy a birthday present, one he'd chosen with obvious care. "He's had a rotten day."

"What the hell got into him?" Rafe moved past her to toss his gift on the kitchen table. He set her own, the un-opened lens, carefully beside it.

While she washed the dishes, she tried to explain—the arrival of his mother's card, with its unknown, apparently disappointing message…his hope that he'd see Zoe…

"I gave him no reason to think that," Rafe objected.

"I know you didn't. Hoping against hope, I guess you'd call it. He's very lonely, Rafe, and somehow your daughter cut through that."

"Yeah, and look what it cost her."

"I know. I'm sorry." She was too heartsick to argue who'd done what to whom, who would pay for it most dearly.

Rafe reached past her to turn off the taps. "Speaking of which, I better be getting on home to her. Walk me to my truck?"

"Of course." She followed him out and across the deck. Crisp black upon gray, their shadows danced at their feet across the boards. She turned to look up at a silver-dollar moon riding high in a velvety sky. "Oh, wow!"

She felt his warmth at her back, then his arms came around her, snugging around her waist. "Beautiful," he agreed, his voice husky in her ear.

His jaw was bristly with a day's growth of beard; it rasped against her temple, and she shivered. Letting out a long, slow sigh, she allowed herself to relax and lean back against him—safe at last. And happy. Happiness blossoming like a moonflower in the dark. *Oh, Rafe... * Could anything that felt this natural and right be wrong? Reaching up, she cupped his rough cheek with her palm and whispered, "Rafe, I'm so sorry about tonight." He'd intended nothing but kindness.

"I'm not." His arms flexed, molding her tighter against him as he lipped her ear. "Not now I'm not." His heart was thundering against her shoulder blade. Shuddering, she arched her neck, and he kissed the corner of her mouth. Molten heat cascaded down her body, raising her nipples, roiling her stomach. Her hips rocked instinctively—he groaned and dipped his head to kiss the side of her throat. She drew in her breath in a stuttering gasp, sipping moonlight, then Rafe was turning her in his arms, clasping her waist, lifting her up on tiptoe.

"Yeah, *right!* " a bitter voice sneered from the near distance.

Gently, Rafe lowered her feet to the deck. "Sean," he said wryly, turning his head toward the yard.

Not good, not good, tonight of all nights! Dana tried to step back from Rafe's embrace, but his arms hardened around her, holding her there. He rested his chin on top of her head, as she turned to look at Sean. *Mine,* the gesture said simply.

"You are so *dumb,* Dana!" growled Sean, advancing up the steps from the yard. His hands were jammed deep in his pockets. "You think he really likes you?"

"That's enough, Sean!" Rafe snapped.

"He's doing this for *Zoe!* They made a deal—a bargain! She said she'd let him adopt our baby, but only if he fell in love and married you! So that's what he's pretending to do. But all he wants is what he wanted all along. A mommy for Zoe's baby!"

"Shut up, Sean!" Rafe brought his hands to Dana's

arms, pushed her away, but she grabbed his shirt with both hands.

"*No,* Rafe. Don't you dare touch him!"

"Sucker!" Sean jeered, ducking past them to the kitchen door. "Why would he want *you?*" The door banged, and he was gone.

Dana's fingers had gone numb. All of her was numbing, as if she'd wandered into a deep freeze and lost her way. Her hands slipped away from his shirt, and she shook her head.

"Dana…" Rafe said uncertainly.

"Is it true, Rafe? Was that the bargain?"

His hesitation was as good as a confession.

"I see." She spun out of his loosened grasp. "You'd better go."

"Dana, look, let me explain."

"I've heard enough, thanks!" For Zoe—he'd done it all for Zoe. "Please get out of here and *please* don't come back." She walked into the house—and locked the door behind her.

CHAPTER SIXTEEN

From: RedColumbine@Westbest.com
To: SanDiegan@Pipeline.net
Sean, whatever you said last night—how could you?
Dad landed on me like a ton of bricks. He thinks
we've been talking on the phone, which means he
thinks I'm a liar, which means now I AM a liar, since
I let him keep on thinking that. Thanks so much!
What happened over there, anyway? He came home
mad, woke up madder and drove off maddest to pick
up Mr. Tankersly at the airport. Did he fight with
Dana, too, or just you? Tell me quick. I've gotta
know. Zoe+((??))

From: SanDiegan@Pipeline.net
To: RedColumbine@Westbest.com
Zoe, I blew it. I saw them kissing and something
snapped and I shot my big mouth off. What happened
was this...

From: RedColumbine@Westbest.com
To: SanDiegan@Pipeline.net
Wow, gee, I don't know what to say. I'm sitting here
crying, with stupid Woofle trying to lick off my tears.
I guess you wrecked about everything, didn't you?
And I thought I had it all worked out. He was going
to fall for your stepmom, they were going to adopt
our baby and give it a wonderful home, you and my

dad were going to be best friends and I'd go off to Harvard only a year late and I could visit my baby whenever I wanted. Stupid me. I guess that's what I get for messing around with a dorky sophomore. I'd like to shake you within an inch of your dorkish life! So what now, smart guy? Got any better ideas? Z+((!!))

WAITING AT THE local airfield for old man Tankersly's chartered plane to arrive, Rafe stood in a phone booth near the window, punching numbers. "Dana," he said quickly when she answered. "It's me. We have to talk."

"No, Rafe, that's not necessary." Petra was crying in the background, water running. Her voice wasn't so much cold as flat. Tired. Drained of all warmth and emotion.

I did this to you. "Dana, please, if you'd just give me five—"

"No! There's nothing that needs explaining. Look, I can't talk now, so—"

"Then could I speak to Sean, please?" Any connection was better than none.

"Um." She made a humming sound of uncertainty, then called, "Sean?"

Intertwined with the baby's sobs, he heard the rise and fall of question and answer. So the kid was there in the kitchen. Rafe marshaled his words and his anger. *If not for you, Sean.* None of this would have happened. He'd never have hurt Dana.

Nor met her. He squinted as, beyond the end of the runway, a dark, insect-like shape banked into the final approach. Tankersly.

"Uh?" Sean grunted warily in his ear.

"What are you going to do about the house?"

"Huh?"

Rafe ground his teeth. "We've got the front of your

house prepped and primed, and now I can't help you. So what are you going to do, Sean?''

''Um...''

If he could have reached through the phone and grabbed the kid by the throat... ''What would your father do? Didn't he teach you to finish what you start?''

''Yeah,'' the kid said, so low Rafe barely could hear it, then added in a rush, ''Mr. Montana, I'm really sorry.'' *Click!*

Rafe held the disconnected phone out from his ear and glared at it. Then cradled it viciously. ''Not half as sorry as I am, kid.'' Yanking his hat down over his nose, he stalked out to greet the old man.

NO MORE SADNESS in her life. It was a promise she'd made to herself, made to Peter, months ago, and Dana meant to stick to it. She had to be cheerful for Petra, for Sean. It was the most important gift you could give a child, the habit of happiness. The expectation of goodness to come.

So now, just when she'd made it to a resting place on the climb back to contentment, to be thrown back to the base of the cliff! And to have humiliation heaped on top of sorrow. *How could I have been such a conceited fool, thinking Rafe was starting to...well, to like me a little? Me as a person. Me as a woman.* When all the time it was Zoe.

Worse than the stinging humiliation was the loneliness. He'd not been gone for a day, and already Dana missed him. Missed the happy, fizzing expectation that any minute he'd be knocking at her door, walking into her kitchen, bringing strength and laughter and vitality. That was over now. It had never really existed outside of her mind. He wasn't there for her; all along he was there for Zoe.

So now...how to get back to happy?

At this point, she should be qualified as an expert. *Take*

it one day at a time, she reminded herself wearily. Pretend she was recovering from a nasty case of the flu, not a wound of the spirit. Simply pace herself, focus outward on the most essential chores, not inward. Don't think, don't feel, just do. Start with the laundry, she decided, once the dishes were done.

UP IN SEAN'S BEDROOM, turning out the pockets of his jeans, stacking interesting pebbles, a bit of elk horn, a case of fish lures, a stub of pencil onto his desk, she came at last to a piece of card stock, folded to a tight, tiny square. Unfolding it, she saw the blazing birthday cake and drew in her breath. Margot's card. *Not yours to read,* she chided herself, unfolding it a final time. And if it hadn't hurt Sean, she would have left it alone.

Dearest darling Sean,
I know it's been months and months and months since I've written, but I've been having such a marvelous, mystical time at the spa, I'm sure you'll forgive me. I've been studying aromatherapy, and I've come to realize that—at last!—this is my Path in Life. (Much more on this later.) And I've found a lovely, lovable, clever man to share my life, who adores me and whom I'm sure you'll adore when you meet him. Which brings me to your question: I would *love* you to come and live with me. We belong together. But my house is so tiny, only two bedrooms, and I need one of those for my office and my extra clothes. So could you be patient just a little while longer, sweetheart? As soon as Ivan finds a job, and I start my aromatherapy boutique, we'll be moving to a larger house. Something charming on the beach, I think. Then I'll definitely send for you, my dearest darling, I promise. Meantime, have a happy, HAPPY, spiritual Birthday.
Your loving Margot

"You silly, stupid, heartless woman." Dana sank onto the bed. So this was why Sean had lashed out at her and Rafe last night. *The person who should love you most in the world clearly can't be bothered with you. Rafe deprived you of Zoe's affection. And then you stumbled on us, looking as if we'd found our way to love.*

For one foolish minute, that was just how she'd felt— loved. Safe. Her heart on its nest at last. *Dream on.* As Sean said, how dumb could you be? Squaring her shoulders, she sighed and refolded the note, then tucked it back into the pocket where she'd found it. Returned all his other treasures to the rest of his jeans. Dumped everything back on the closet floor where she'd found it. She'd do her laundry today, then ask Sean to bring his own dirty clothes down to the washer tomorrow.

BEN TANKERSLY WAS—how would Zoe put it?—a high-maintenance owner. One who required all Rafe's time and most of his attention.

Hadn't always been that way. In the years when Rafe first rode for Tankersly's brand, the old man had been tough—tough as an old cedar stump—but easygoing. You knew your job and you did it without him looking over your shoulder, or you were gone yesterday. And that was the basis on which he'd eventually made Rafe his manager—*Handle it, man, then tell me later what you did and why.*

But since Tankersly had moved down to San Antonio to live with his eldest daughter ten years ago, he'd changed. Misses Suntop, Rafe told himself, and had only six weeks each year to renew the love affair. Only six weeks to ride every inch of his land, see every cow, boss every hand, check every barn and outbuilding and hen coop. That was

how the days went, and he wanted Rafe at his side, like a
general wanted his aide-de-camp at his elbow while inspecting the troops.

That was how they spent their days. Evenings, after supper, were for sitting around in Rafe's den, drinking the
finest whiskey money could buy—Tankersly flew in a case
every year—and munching fried pork rinds (a treat the old
man's daughter forbade him at home), while they went over
bloodlines and breeding charts, last year's feed costs, next
year's forecasts for the price of beef, maintenance sched-
ules and water rights. And once they'd exhausted all that,
he wanted to talk about the good old days.

Or sometimes the new.

LATE IN THE THIRD WEEK of his visit, the boss had invited
himself to supper. Though he had his own professional
"chef" up at the big house, who looked like an aging
showgirl—Rena appeared mysteriously each summer, then
vanished till the next—Tankersly often preferred Montana
cooking. After Zoe had fed them a meal of macaroni and
cheese, then retreated upstairs with astrophysicist Stephen
Hawkins's *A Brief History of Time* under one arm, they'd
settled with drinks before the fire, dogs snoring and twitch-
ing at their feet.

Tankersly took a considering sip of his whiskey, held the
glass up to the firelight and gruffly observed, "Somebody
knocked up your princess." *Princess* was a synonym for
daughter, in the old man's vocabulary. He'd first come to
fatherhood in his fifties and sired three of his own.

Rafe grunted and took a swallow. *Let's not talk about
this.*

"One of your hands?" At eighty-two, Tankersly felt, if
not entitled to pry, then entirely safe in doing so.

Rafe snorted. "I don't hire crazies or suicides."

"Damn sure hope not. Played doctor with a school chum, then? She always said she'd grow up to be a doctor."

"Hmm." Rafe rose, went over to the fire and added a log.

"If you want a name for the brat, I guess I could propose, but I don't reckon she'd have me."

Rafe turned and met the old man's eyes, as dark and inscrutable as a turtle's. He had wondered for the first years of his employment if he was perhaps Tankersly's bastard, the way he'd been singled out and brought along. Not that he hadn't worked his butt off to earn the bossman's respect. But selling Rafe a portion of his land, making him a partner in Suntop—that had been a gesture of either princely generosity…or implicit acknowledgment. Rafe had never dared ask him which, and it was too late to ask his own mother.

With the passing years, though, his first conviction had gradually faded. The old man dropped hints and allusions Rafe took to mean that they were not, after all, father and son. Now here was another. Tankersly would never offer to marry his own granddaughter, even in jest.

He smiled, resigning himself to the conversation. "Zoe would probably have you, but I expect Rena would snatch her bald."

The old man chuckled. "Or if not her, Luisa." Apparently confirming a rumor Rafe had heard years ago from Tankersly's middle daughter. That the old man had spent every Christmas for the past dozen years in Guadalajara. That there might be an entire shadow family down in Mexico.

"So what are you going to do with her?" Tankersly insisted, breaking Rafe's reverie.

What he'd been wondering every spare minute for the past three weeks, when he wasn't worrying about Dana. He should be making other arrangements for Zoe's baby if his original plan was a bust. As it seemed to be. He'd tried calling Dana every morning for the first week, till finally she'd stopped answering. Either Sean picked up the phone or—more embarrassing—Willy, who'd quickly discovered that breakfast at the Ribbon R beat bunkhouse chow any day.

I need to go see her.

But she'd told him to stay away, and she'd meant it. *She trusted me, and now she doesn't.* He felt that loss as if he'd been plundered, as if he'd reached into his pockets and found the bottoms sliced out, the floor fallen away below his feet. Something to stand on—to build on—that now was lost.

Trust was such a fragile emotion. And if by some unforgivable clumsiness or cruelty you forfeited trust, how did you ever regain it? Was it even possible?

If the answer was no, then that was Rafe's loss—his and Zoe's. But what kept him staring up at his ceiling night after night were Dana's losses.

Once upon a time, Dana had trusted love—then seen it snatched away in a torrent of snow. Then he had come, offering the shape of love, if not its substance—until Sean had declared it a fake, a pretense. And in all honesty, Rafe hadn't been able to deny the boy's accusation.

What had that second loss done to her sense of trust? Because something told him that unlike a man, a woman *needed* to trust love—was sorely crippled if she couldn't. *God, Dana, if I hurt you…*

And maybe what he'd done had cut even deeper than that. *Thanks to Sean—and thanks to me—maybe now she doesn't even trust her own desirability. She thinks I was courting her for Zoe's sake, not because she's a lovable, sexy woman.*

And worse, if she thought that, she thought right. Well, half right. When he'd started the courtship, it *had* all been for Zoe.

The memory of the pain dawning in Dana's big eyes as Sean's words hit home was enough to make Rafe leap up from his chair and walk out of the house. He couldn't sit still, when he remembered.

And he couldn't forget.

But neither could he figure how to make amends.

"If you're worried about folks talking," Tankersly said, "you could send her to me and Risa till she drops. She'd like San Antone."

"Thank you, Ben. I'll keep that in mind." People talking had never worried him much. But then, this was Zoe they'd be talking about. *Got to do something and soon.*

The only solution he wanted was Dana Kershaw.

WILLY LOOKED UP from the bowl of batter he was stirring, as Dana walked into the kitchen. "Mornin', Missus. Mornin', chipmunk." His name for Petra.

"Good morning, Willy." She'd given up asking him to call her Dana the first week of their acquaintanceship. Willy was of the old school, which meant she was Missus or Ma'am, or Missus Kershaw when he was feeling formal or disapproving. "Pancakes today?" If she was late coming down, he started without her. She set Petra in her high chair and poured herself half a cup of coffee.

"Yup. Banana-blueberry." He scowled down at the batter, stirring, stirring, then finally said, "You got a phone call, while back."

"I thought I heard it ring. Dudes?"

"Maybe." He stirred some more. "Sorta hard to say. The...um, woman was...tipsy, I reckon."

She'd known Willy nearly six weeks now, and this was the first time Dana had heard him refer to a member of her sex as anything but "girl" or "lady," "ma'am" or "missus."

"Really. A wrong number maybe?"

"She asked for Sean."

Oh. *Margot*. Dana walked over to the refrigerator, opened it and stood staring blindly into its depths. Margot, drinking at eight in the morning. So much for her latest spa cure. She sighed and reached for the bacon. "Did she get him?" *Tell me no*.

"Nope. He whipped through here on his way down to the river 'bout a minute before she called. Snagged a sandwich and said he'd be back 'bout noon."

Thank God for that, anyway. "Did she say what she wanted?" Margot had called a few times, raging and weeping and drunk after Peter's death, but not once in the past year.

"Well, she wanted Sean in the worst kinda way, and once I convinced her she wasn't gonna get him, no matter how ugly she cussed, she started askin' for you."

Margot never called except when she wanted something, even if it was only to vent. "Did you tell her I'd be down soon?" She reached for her cup and gulped; she'd need caffeine to face Margot.

"Told her I thought you mighta gone to town. Couldn't say when you'd be back." He grimaced. "Got a right earful for that."

"I'm sorry. That's Sean's real mother, and she isn't always…reasonable." Dana blew out a breath. "Would you do me a favor, Willy?"

"Yup."

"Don't tell him she called." *Whimsical* was Margot's middle name. By the time she'd sobered up, quite likely she'd have forgotten what she wanted, or whom she'd phoned.

No such luck. The phone rang again that night after supper, and when Dana picked up, the caller said briskly, "Dana? This is Margot Kershaw. I want my son."

THE LAWYER Dr. Hancock recommended to Dana, Durango's expert on custody cases, gave her a free fifteen-minute consultation the following afternoon—then suggested she post a thousand-dollar retainer so he could contact Margot's lawyer immediately. "Nothing like a preemptive strike in cases like this," he assured her.

"I...I'll have to think about this, then get back to you in a day or two," she said slowly, rising to go. *If I had a thousand dollars to spare, I wouldn't be two months behind on my mortgage.* "But thank you. You've been very kind."

She'd meant to shop for groceries after the appointment, combining errands as she always did, but when next Dana noticed her surroundings, she was speeding down the highway for home. Just as well, she told herself, and turned inward again. A thousand dollars...and that was just to get him started. *Willy could help me sell the horses.* They were easily worth twice that. But what was a dude ranch that couldn't offer trail rides?

Bankrupt. Not that they weren't headed that way anyhow. But sell the horses and they'd slip even faster down the long, slippery slope to insolvency.

There was no way the bank would give her a second mortgage when she couldn't quite keep up with the first. Neither could she borrow from her parents—schoolteachers who'd retired last year and were now touring Europe on bicycles. They'd earned their financial freedom through thrift and hard work, and they'd saved a modest margin for their pleasures. That was precisely what she'd be usurping if she asked for a loan—face it, a gift, since she didn't see how she'd ever repay it—the extras that made their retirement years worth living. And Sean might be Dana's son, but he wasn't their grandson.

So what do I do, Peter?

No answer, but a bird flew across the road, drawing her eyes. Toward a wide valley opening out to the north, a road winding up it. She was coming to the fork in the road, the right hand of which led past the Suntop Ranch. Sean had pointed it out to her more than a month ago. She had never passed this fork since without a pang. *Rafe*. He hadn't tried to contact her in weeks. Doubtless he'd made some other arrangement for Zoe by now.

But if he hadn't?

She pulled over to the shoulder of the highway and sat, hands clasping the top of the steering wheel, forehead resting on wrists, for a very long time. Then she straightened, started the pickup and chose the north fork.

CHAPTER SEVENTEEN

"COMPANY COMING," observed Anse Kirby from his higher vantage point, where he straddled the ridgepole of the barn. He and Rafe had commenced reroofing a week ago, partly because the building needed it, mostly because it was one of the few places old man Tankersly would leave them in peace. Now that they'd stripped the shingles off, they were committed to the job, even though the boss had flown off to Texas yesterday.

Halfway up the long ladder, with a load of shingles balanced on his shoulder, Rafe didn't look around. "Miguel?" The farrier should have arrived this morning, though his promises weren't worth a sack of cold cow chips. He did the best shoeing in a hundred miles, and knew it. He'd come when he pleased.

"In a cute little skirt and legs a man could die for? I sure hope not. Must be one of Zoe's friends."

Zoe was still grounded, forbidden company. Rafe heaved his bundle over the ends of the ladder and onto the footing board, then looked around. Dana Kershaw stood beside her old pickup, peering up, one hand shading her eyes against the sun. His heart lurched in his chest as if he'd missed a rung on the ladder.

"Dana," he croaked, and started down. He caught a glimpse of Anse's wide, white conspirator's grin, then the overhang of the eaves cut off his view. Dana. He'd been wondering what to do for six weeks now, telling himself he'd have to do something as soon as the old man headed south.

She made any and all alternatives he'd considered seem shabby. He'd never seen her in town-going clothes before—a white tailored shirt, a short, slim navy skirt and—his pulse ticked up a few beats—high heels. "Welcome to Suntop," he said huskily, halting before her. He'd forgotten how small she was. He had an impulse to walk right into her—simply duck his head till their mouths connected, while he shaped his hands to her trim bottom and pulled her up close and personal. *Reckon I missed you.*

"Rafe," she said simply. But there was no light to match his in her eyes.

Down boy. He eyed his palms ruefully—too tarry to even shake her hand—and said, "Let me clean up, okay?" He strode over to the horse trough, wishing she'd called ahead so he could have showered and changed.

Whatever had brought her to him, Rafe wanted to hear it in private, not out here in the barnyard with Anse leering down from the roof, or up at the house, where he'd have to share her with Zoe. "I was about to go check the yearlings. Come with me?"

Her skirt was a little tight for scrambling into a high truck. He opened her door, then, when she hesitated, sizing up the climb, he simply caught her by the waist and lifted her up. His heart was knocking as he walked around the truck to his side. *I want her.* One touch had reminded him how much.

They talked of this and that as he drove. She seemed a bit daunted to learn that the whole width of the valley and on up into the mountains to the west and north was Suntop. He felt a certain satisfaction that she was seeing his land at last. He might own only fifteen percent, but that was a small slice of a very large pie. *I didn't come to you as a beggar.*

The truck rumbled across a cowcatcher at an open gate and into the horse pasture. He honked the horn, three short beeps, then stopped the truck—as the yearlings burst over the hilltop, ears pricked, tails streaming, coats gleaming. Bucking and romping and full of themselves. Eager for oats.

"Oh!" Dana sat upright. "Oh, they're beautiful!"

"Sit here, while I feed them." He walked around back, scooped up a bucket of oats from the bin and strolled into the roistering herd. "Easy, there." A dip of a silken muzzle into the bucket. A pair of ears pinned back as another shook his head and shoved for position. "You, behave." He smacked a third on the shoulder. "Wait your turn, bub." They teased and jostled one another like kids in a cafeteria chow line, but they knew better than to shove the teacher. Five minutes, and everyone had had his treat.

Holding the bucket for a filly with a muzzle dainty enough to drink from a teacup, he looked up and saw that Dana was leaning halfway out her window, eyes aglow. *We feel the same about so many things.* He couldn't see why it wouldn't work. Hooking a hand under the filly's throat, he walked her back to the truck; she was as docile as if he held her halter. Zoe had trained her well last year. "Zoe named this one Arriba. Half Arabian, and it shows, doesn't it?"

Dana nodded, rubbing the little mare's dished face, the mobile tip of her velvety muzzle. "She's beautiful." Tears gathered in her gray-green eyes, and she blinked them away.

Something wrong here. Or maybe just too many emotions jostling for position at once, like the colts? He let the filly go back to her mates and waited for it.

"How *is* Zoe?" she asked, her eyes following the herd.

"Okay. Moody as all get-out," he added truthfully, "but

I reckon that's natural." Worried, as he was. Something had to be decided, and soon. "Not happy to be getting fat."

Dana nodded. "That is hard. Especially if you don't…" She shut her mouth abruptly.

"Don't…?" he prompted, clenching his hands at his sides to keep them to himself. All his responses to her seemed to begin and end with touching.

"Don't have anyone telling you how beautiful you look pregnant, even when it isn't the truth." Her voice quivered with swallowed tears.

It was odd to feel liking for a dead man, especially when you were also glad he was out of the way. *Because I want your woman, Peter Kershaw, even if you were a good man.* A man who wouldn't begrudge him now, Rafe suspected. He'd want her cherished.

"I try," he assured her. "We all try. Too hard, maybe. She says the next cowboy who pats her stomach is going to have his hat jammed down around his jug ears. Getting a bit crabby, as I said."

"Have you found someone to…adopt her baby yet?" Her eyes flicked up to his and shot away, off toward the mountains.

His pulse quickened. She had a reason for asking, a reason for all this welling emotion. *Tell me, Dana.* "No," he said indifferently. "Tankersly left yesterday, and we've been pretty busy around here, what with haying and all, so… No. Not yet. But soon."

"I see…" Her hands crept toward each other along the windowsill; they connected, comforted each other. "Do you—" She heaved a long sigh. "You remember that…proposition you made, that day we went riding up on the mountain?"

Goose bumps rose across his arms and shoulders; his blood surged. He kept his mouth even, his face relaxed, holding his excitement inside the way you did in poker when you drew a third ace. "The proposal I made?" he corrected her casually.

"That…yes." She let out another wavering sigh. "I was…thinking about it."

Were you, by God! Have you been lying in bed nights, thinking what I've been thinking? If so, she was hiding it well today, but women were hard to read. And it would be hard for her—he was glad it would be hard—to go from one man to another. She was that kind of woman. Nothing would come easily or be taken lightly. "What's changed?" he asked bluntly. *Tell me you missed me.*

"I…got a phone call. From Sean's mother, Margot."

Not what he'd hoped, but still. Rafe crossed his forearms on the edge of the window—her fingers retreated to safety—and said simply, "Tell me."

Half an hour later, he figured he had it all. Sean's mother had fallen off the wagon for the umpteenth time and lost her new boyfriend in the tumble. Apparently she'd looked to this Ivan to finance some new venture having to do with smells and how they made you feel—aromatherapy? Some sort of shop to sell these scents. So now Margot wanted Sean to comfort her, and since apparently Dana had had the foresight to tie up his college money in an untouchable trust, Margot wanted Dana to buy out Sean's quarter share of the ranch. Sean could be her partner in an aromatherapy boutique in San Diego, instead of a landowner in Colorado.

So he supposed Dana hadn't exaggerated—this wasn't just a tiff between a first and second wife. This Margot was clearly a nutcase, if she thought exchanging prime grazing land for a smelly little shop in the city was any kind of a reasonable trade.

On the other hand, bad as that would be for Sean, it wouldn't be bad for Rafe. He could buy a chunk of the Ribbon R free and clear, whether Dana wanted him as partner or not.

And if all he wanted was land…Rafe drummed his fingers on the steering wheel—he'd long since climbed into the truck to hear her out. *But I don't.* He wanted it all—Dana Kershaw in his bed, a mother for Zoe's baby, a prime chunk of land. *So throw for it all.*

But what he didn't much want was Sean, like a burr under the saddle blanket. Mooning over Zoe, making Dana unhappy no matter how she tried to win him over. "You know," he said, when he was sure she'd finished, "she is the kid's mother. And the lawyer has told you square that he can't guarantee you'll keep custody, no matter how hard you fight. Would it maybe be simplest to…hand him over?" Rafe didn't like himself as he said it. The kid was a sulky little son of a gun, but he had guts. He'd done his best to stand by Zoe.

Dana shook her head emphatically. "No. And if you'd heard her, Rafe… She doesn't want Sean, doesn't even ask about him—it's all *me, me, me.* What *she* needs, how lonely *she* is now that her boyfriend's gone, how Sean will be a help and a comfort to *her.* You see what I mean? She doesn't want her son so that she can love and protect him. Doesn't want him so that she can make sure he'll grow up true to himself and strong, then she'll launch him out into the world like some beautiful bird she's set free…"

He smiled to himself at the image. *We do think alike.*

"She wants a caretaker, a parent, a—a teddy bear to squash in her arms when it's dark outside, because she's lonely and afraid. And she wants his money, because she's too much of a child to try to earn her own. She wants to *use* Sean, not mother him! Peter would never forgive me, if I let her have him. It's just—no! Whatever it takes, I'm keeping him."

It could take more than she had. *On the other hand, you throw me into the mix.* There'd be money enough for the best lawyer. And the custody battle would be here, where

Rafe had...influence. You didn't run the biggest ranch in the county without making powerful friends. Tankersly had taught him that. Judge Baxter had hunting rights in perpetuity at Suntop. He'd brought down a bull with a twelve-point rack on Rafe's land last fall; its head hung in his courthouse chambers to remind him who his friends were. And they'd be going into court a married couple, able to prove that they could provide Sean with a stable home, against a single mom who couldn't, wouldn't, stay sober, who'd discarded all her custody rights once before when it suited her.

We could give it a damn good try. Even if Margot won in the end, delaying her for a year or two would give Sean a better chance to grow into himself. He'd be formed by seventeen if Rafe had anything to do with him—tough enough and old enough and strong enough by then to survive a bad year. But let a weepy, neurotic drunk get a stranglehold on the kid at fifteen, before he'd found his own way... "Okay," he agreed. "What else do you want?" *Let's get the terms on the table.*

"I..." She didn't like it that blunt. Dana hugged her elbows and stared through the windshield, a delicate pink creeping up her throat. "You...talked about giving me a divorce in five years if I wanted it. I think that would be best for both of us."

Why do you think that? And why should that gall him like a stone in his boot, when it was what he'd wanted, too?

"You wouldn't be giving up too much of your freedom that way, and who knows, by then maybe I'd want to remarry."

You'd be married. To me. Though he'd offered this, hadn't he?

"I'd keep the child, of course. That's got to be understood. But you and Zoe would be welcome to visit whenever you liked.''

I wanted a good mother—I've found one, he thought wryly. ''Zoe wanted two parents for her baby, not one,'' he reminded her.

''I know, and the baby *would* have two parents for the first five years—the formative years. I…suppose if you insisted, we could split custody after that. If you had to do it that way…'' Her voice trailed away unhappily. ''I know that's not precisely what Zoe specified, but I have to consider myself—and you, too.''

Thanks, but I can take care of myself. ''There are also the grazing rights I wanted,'' he added, since they were bargaining. ''A lifetime lock, as long as you own the Ribbon R. A split of profits on the cattle I'll run there. I'll have to work that out, show you some figures.''

''Whatever. I think you're right. If the Ribbon R were a working ranch, I could attract twice the dude business that I'm doing now.''

He nodded. *So do we have a deal?* He felt both excited and oddly…flat, as if there should have been something more to this. *It's a good deal,* he told himself. *Works for everybody.*

''Just one more thing,'' Dana said in a tiny voice. ''Since…'' She clasped her hands in her lap till the knuckles showed white. ''Since we're agreed that we're doing this for Zoe, not for any other reason…there's no reason for this to be anything but a…marriage in name only.''

No *way.* He was giving up his freedom to chase other women—without getting Dana? What kind of a fool's bargain was that? Right up there with trading prime land for an aroma-thingummy shop! ''That doesn't sound very—'' *Fun.* ''Practical,'' he finished, voice carefully neutral. *Not a chance I could keep my hands off you.*

She bristled, reminding him of Zoe's little half-Siamese

cat puffed up to dog-chasing size. "Perfectly practical. You wanted a business arrangement, Rafe, and that's what I'm offering. You help me save Sean—I help you save Zoe."

What about the fact that every time we come within kissing range, sparks fly? How long do you think we'll keep a lid on that? He was half tempted to reach for her and prove his point, then and there. But she was stretched so tight at the moment, if he stroked her once, she might fly to pieces, blowing their bargain to kingdom come.

Still, he couldn't let it go. "Zoe's main requirement—thanks to you, by the way—is a two-parent, loving family. She's very clear on that. I don't see how I could sell her on a make-believe marriage."

"You seemed to think you could before," Dana observed in a bitter, brittle little voice, looking off again toward the mountains.

Putting a finger to her chin, he brought her head around. Her soft lips parted at his touch. "I meant to wed you and bed you and make the best of the deal while we were together," he said fiercely. "I don't call that a sham."

Eyes flashing, she jerked her chin out of his grip. "Whatever you care to call it, I don't want it! I'm offering a merger of interests—a business alliance, not a marriage of…hearts."

Marriage. To Dana. Rings and lace and driving off with tin cans clattering behind, hands clasped. *With my body, I thee worship.* He didn't know about his heart, but his body was ready and willing to worship hers. Too ready. He shifted uncomfortably in his seat.

"Well?" she demanded. "Take it or leave it."

She was in no position to demand anything. But with a five-month pregnant daughter, was he? *Begin in the way you mean to continue,* his mother used to tell him. He should never agree to something he couldn't hold to, didn't mean to hold to.

Bottom line is, if I can't change her mind, can I live with the bargain?

If he had to, he could, but damned if he liked it.

So the key here was to change her mind. Or persuade her to *know* her own mind. He leaned close—and her eyes widened and darkened, her lips parted slightly. His heart leaped in glad response. He wasn't alone in this feeling, whatever she said. *So bargain for what you want.* "Marriage in name only, as long as it looks like the real thing to Zoe. That means same bedroom."

"Separate beds," she countered instantly.

It was a start. *Patience,* he reminded himself. You didn't saddle a filly the first time you showed her the halter. "You've got yourself a deal," he said huskily. "When?"

THERE WAS NO REASON to delay and plenty of reasons to clinch the deal *pronto*. Rafe hadn't much interest in the ceremony itself; he found himself looking beyond it—frankly, to the wedding night. And Dana seemed inclined to something cold and quick and businesslike—a justice of the peace, she suggested, afternoon appointment, so she could get back in time to cook for her dudes.

Zoe had grander plans. "You *have* to be married in church!" she cried, when Rafe told her about the J.P. The tears sprang to her eyes the way they did so often nowadays. "What will my baby think if you're not?"

How could someone who'd yet to even show his face run the show this way? Rafe remembered reading somewhere that you could see a hurricane was coming for days before it arrived by the ripples it sent ahead. "I doubt if he'll care one way or another." Somehow he'd convinced himself that his grandchild was a "he," though no one had a clue. Zoe had refused to be notified when she went for her ultrasound.

"She'll care immensely! She'll think you didn't love each other if you don't do it right."

What Rafe didn't want was *Zoe* thinking that. So far he'd avoided a quiz on just when and how he and Dana had fallen in love, how far they'd fallen and so on. Rafe hoped to keep on finessing the details. "Fine, if you think that's important, find us a church." Zoe attended sometimes with Mrs. Higgins or a town friend; Rafe, practically never. He had no need for a church while he had God's mountains to ride, or for a minister to tell him what any man could know if he opened his ears outdoors and used his eyes. But some people liked it formal on Sunday—and to each his own.

Zoe already had a church in mind, down in Trueheart. A girlfriend's father was minister, and a few phone calls determined he'd be delighted to perform the ceremony— Saturday after next happened to be free.

When Rafe presented Zoe's plan over the phone, Dana sounded taken aback, but after a long silence, she sighed and agreed. "If that's what Zoe wants, why not. It's all the same to me."

Rafe winced. She was going to take some thawing, but that would have to wait. "Good, I'll tell her." He gave his daughter a thumbs-up through the office door, then, as Zoe pantomimed her desire, said, "Um, I think she wants to talk with you."

"Mrs. Kershaw?" Zoe stroked her stomach nervously and looked up at her father. "I don't have a thing to wear, and I haven't a clue what I—" Her face shifted from worry to delight. "Really? I'd like that! Let me ask Daddy." She put a hand over the phone. "May I go shopping with Mrs. Kershaw in Durango?"

COMPARED WITH her last wedding, simple but heartfelt, this one might be a travesty, but Dana didn't have the heart to say so to Zoe. *I'm her proxy in this,* she realized, just

as Rafe stood for Sean. She could fight that all the way—
or she could give in and accept it with grace and good
humor. Somebody ought to enjoy the event anyway. So
Dana went with the flow.

Once she'd resolved not to spoil the day for Zoe, she
decided to make the most of it. Poor kid hadn't been off
the ranch all summer, aside from a few trips to the doctor.
Dana made an appointment for them both at the best salon
in town, prescribing a cut and a new style for Zoe—the
stylist took off six inches and layered the back, creating
bounce and fullness instead of straggling curls. Zoe walked
in a little girl—and walked out a sleek sophisticate.

For herself, she settled on a trim, along with some suggestions for the wedding day—how to make the most of
her own short and simple style with a circlet of silk flowers,
and subtle eye shadow to emphasize her eyes' natural color.

Once beautified, they went on to lunch at the fanciest
restaurant in town, per Rafe's recommendation, where
Dana ordered a Shirley Temple for Zoe and a glass of
champagne for herself. Somehow on the fumes of that single glass, they both managed to get giggly and girlish and
confidential. Rafe had reared himself a charming daughter—fierce and funny and passionately committed to a
dozen causes, from Save the Black Rhinos to Doctors Without Borders. She was brimful of plans and interests—everything from hybridizing wildflowers to Indian archae-
ology to piloting airplanes. *I can see why Rafe wanted her
free to fly.* Dana could also see why Sean had hitched his
wagon to Zoe's shooting star; the girl's enthusiasm was
catching.

But if lunch was a rousing success, choosing a dress for
the bride was not so easy. Zoe had set her sights on floor-
length white—lace, veils, all the trimmings. The fairy-tale
gown every young bride imagines.

"But I've been married before," Dana tried to point out. "It isn't appropriate the second time to—"

"This is the first time you've married my father," Zoe countered with a stubborn tilt of the chin. "And who cares about appropriate? You'd look gorgeous in white. Dad will be wearing black."

"How about this?" Dana suggested, holding up a simple amber silk, knee-length, dressy enough for cocktails.

Zoe wrinkled her freckled nose. "Too short, too...*uh-uh.*"

It was almost three-thirty, and Dana couldn't see how she could spare another day from her dudes for shopping. "Then what about this one?" A flowered print in pinks and burgundies—which earned itself another disdainful grimace. "Or this?" A pale-blue gown, too slinky for a wedding. She put it back on the rack before Zoe could veto it.

"What about a change of shop?" Zoe suggested.

This was the biggest department store in town, with far and away the best selection. But perhaps Zoe knew some boutique. It was really her wedding, after all. "Lead me to it."

Zoe led her to a hole-in-the-wall place on a street filled with used bookstores and consignment antique shops. A vintage-clothing boutique, where last year, Zoe confided, she'd found a fabulous black leather motorcycle jacket. Five minutes of rummaging the racks, and Zoe cried, *"Yes!"* She held her find up, and its pale satin reflected a rosy glow from her fire-engine curls.

Perhaps the dress had been white once and simply gone creamy-gold with age. It was simple, elegant, floor-length, a custom gown from the thirties, superbly cut on the bias so it hugged Dana's curves when she stood still and swirled when she walked. Zoe loved it, and, in truth, so did Dana. "We'll take it," they told the clerk.

"And so now that we've got that settled, what will my

bridesmaid wear?'' Dana demanded as she dove back into the racks. "And *don't* tell me a motorcycle jacket." Somewhere along the way, the day had tipped from a rueful chore into delight.

CHAPTER EIGHTEEN

THE CHAPEL THAT ZOE had chosen for the wedding might have been drawn by an artistic eight-year-old. Perched at the top of a smooth green hill above the town of Trueheart, it was a tiny white clapboard box, with a graceful steeple pointing to the blue-blue late-August sky. There was a simple stained-glass window of Easter lilies to either side of the arched and varnished outer doors, presently thrown open to welcome all comers, and stone steps leading up to those doors.

Dana hardly could have accounted for how she had come to these steps, the shadowy threshold she must cross. The last two weeks had passed in such a blur. All that frantic activity, the endless, niggling decisions required for even the most modest of ceremonies—leading to this moment of doubt and stillness, with not a soul in sight but her and Sean.

No one to see if she decided to turn and go.

"Dana, we're *late*," Sean muttered, tugging at her elbow. "Come on!"

She gulped, nodded, counted the steps going up—*five, six, seven, eight*—then four paces across the darkened foyer to the inner doors and—

Here comes the bride, here comes the bride, insisted a wheezy little organ at the front of the chapel. A grinning cowboy usher held each door wide. And all eyes on both sides of the aisle turned toward the rear to see if it was truly so.

Couldn't be, Dana told herself, staring back at all those smiling, expectant faces. This *had* to be an incredibly vivid dream, complete with everyone she knew in Colorado. Willy, with his beard fanned out over a multihued patchwork vest. Most of her present dudes, in their vacation finest. Dr. Cassandra Hancock holding Petra, who was dressed in a blue frilly pinafore. Also Michele Minot, another friend from Trueheart. And a host of strangers—all Rafe's cowboys and most of his neighbors—tanned faces and white grins under a hovering flock of cowboy hats. His housekeeper, Mrs. Higgins, and Zoe's best friends, Lisa Harding and Vickie Carter. Each and every one of them expecting her to walk down this aisle to where a tall man in a dark suit stood waiting at an altar ablaze with wildflowers.

"Dana, you gotta move," Sean begged at her side, tugging on her elbow. "Let's go!"

Sean, who'd dragged her into this dream, who now anxiously stared at her with his father's brown eyes. *Peter, what am I doing here?*

Taking care of his son the only way she knew how. No dream, this; she'd made a bargain.

Come on! Zoe mouthed silently from the front of the church. Looking like a blushing bride herself in a pale-pink empire gown, vintage 1960s, she stood next to Rafe's best man and top hand, Anse Kirby.

Zoe looked frantic; Rafe looked...dangerous. He was wondering if she was going to chicken out on him now, at the last, most humiliating moment possible.

Petra had been staring at her, thunderstruck, rosebud mouth ajar, from the vantage of Cass Hancock's arms, and suddenly it must have hit her—who this vision in creamy satin must be. She pointed a chubby arm and yelled, "*Mama!*"

Dana burst into startled laughter, Rafe broke into a wide, rueful grin, the whole church joined in with relief, and seizing the moment, the organist pumped the organ into the bridal march again. Suddenly movement was possible. Dana drifted down the aisle, homing in on her daughter, whose eyes widened to black-fringed astonished flowers as she neared. Coming even with her, Dana touched her petal-soft cheek and floated past. And now it was Rafe she steered by, his blue eyes like a beacon drawing her to port.

Blue eyes that swept her from head to toe and back again as she neared—this was the first he'd seen of her gown. And then she was standing by his side, amazed as always to find him a little taller, more vivid than her memory served. Or perhaps that was only the heels on his western dress boots.

He offered his forearm, and she curled her fingers around it—hard and warm and solid—the first time she'd ever taken his arm. *We've never even really kissed!* With second, third and fourth thoughts about the bargain they'd struck, she'd done her best to avoid him these two weeks, burying herself in the details of the wedding, thanks to Zoe's constant suggestions and proddings. But here he was at last, this stranger who was about to become her husband.

And do you, Dana Kershaw, take this man to have and to hold... The familiar words twined in and out of her mind, a golden thread sewing other ceremonies, other faces in her past, to the present dreamy moment. There came an expectant pause, and Rafe nudged her and muttered, "You do."

"I..." He placed his other hand on top of her fingers and stroked them once, and she sucked in a long shivery breath, and said, "I do." His fingers settled down over hers, warm, comforting...possessive.

"I do," Rafe said clearly, when his time came.

"Then you may now kiss the bride," prompted the beaming minister.

She stood frozen, staring up at the man. This was it, the

moment when past intersected the present and ricocheted off into an unknowable future. *This* was the defining moment, not the rings, or the words, but the kiss—a gesture of pure emotion to seal a strictly business arrangement. *Can't do it. Not for the first time. Not with everyone watching!* Rafe's hands slid across the buttery satin at her waist, clasping her firmly. He drew her in, but for a moment she couldn't move her feet—she bent like a willow at the waist, though her face lifted imploringly to his. She bit her bottom lip, and from only inches above her, he smiled, his eyes crinkling.

"It'll be all right," he whispered, and rubbed his nose along hers.

"Oh, will it?" she whispered back, aching to believe him.

For answer, his mouth settled softly over hers. "Yes." He spoke into her. "Oh, yes." His tongue touched hers for an instant—she shuddered and instinctively moved closer— and he lifted his head and smiled down at her. "It sure will be."

Dimly, beyond his words, she heard the congregation cheering, saw from the corner of her eye Zoe, all freckles and tears, and Sean, caught between a smile and a frown.

Then, to the triumphal strains of "The Wedding March," they paraded back down the aisle, man and wife, Rafe's arm around her waist. They came even with Petra, and she held out both arms and demanded, "Mama!" in a tone that brooked no denial.

"That's my name," Dana laughed as she lifted her out of Cass's hold. And that was how they walked out of the chapel—a threesome, with Zoe and Sean arm in arm at their heels. A *family,* Dana told herself, as confetti and glitter showered down upon them.

THE REST OF THE AFTERNOON whirled past in a happy blur—photographs on the steps of the chapel, cake and champagne at Michele's restaurant down in the town. Dana was introduced to a flood of congratulatory strangers and kissed by too many cowboys to count. She met Zoe's great-aunt Emilia, who'd come all the way from Phoenix; the local veterinarian; Sheriff Noonan; an Indian archaeologist who was excavating a site on Suntop land; one of the Tankersly daughters. Finally, late that afternoon Rafe put a hand to her back and said, "They won't leave till we do, so what do you think? Shall we go?"

I can't. Her heart rose into her throat.

Because if Zoe had shaped their wedding, Rafe had crafted its finale. He'd put his boot down when Dana had proposed going back to the Ribbon R for the first night. "You've been running around like maniacs, you and Zoe, all week. This is *your* night to relax. The dudes can do without you for once," he'd pointed out, insisting she find someone—Cassandra, as it turned out—to stay over and keep Petra.

Since her baby had been born, Dana had never slept farther from her than the next room. Though Petra was essentially weaned now, apparently her mother was not. The thought of a night apart made Dana feel so helplessly homesick, she wanted to cry. And layer that emotion on top of all her fears and her shyness... *I've married a man I don't know, not really.* They'd made a bargain, but what about tonight? Trapped with him in a strange hotel, far from all she knew and held dear?

At the expression on her face, he smiled and brushed a slow knuckle across the underside of her mouth. "Trust me?"

His touch went through her from lips to toes, and she trembled. For all that she didn't know about him, everything she *did* know was straight and true. And it was much too late to turn back now. Wide-eyed and solemn, she nodded.

His eyes crinkled. "Then, Mrs. Montana, that's a good start."

RAFE HAD RACKED his brains about how to do this—their honeymoon night. Had it been his choice, if this had been a normal marriage, he'd have proposed they ride up into the mountains to one of the line cabins, his favorite one by an alpine lake. They'd spend half a week up there, loving and lying in bed till noon, then rising to cook simple meals on a wood-burning stove, fly-fish or ride or walk a little, then back to a bearskin by the fire. Flowery meadows to roll in by day, stars by the millions to wish on at night, and no one for miles and miles around. That was his idea of a honeymoon.

Maybe next year, he consoled himself.

This year, he'd figured Dana needed something less…threatening. All that time to fill, with nothing but each other? Rough way to start a marriage in name only— he almost snorted at the phrase. And she was doubly frazzled, putting a wedding together in two short weeks and leaving her baby overnight for the first time. *Patience,* he reminded himself.

"You're sure you reserved a room with two beds?" Dana dithered as they walked down the hotel corridor. This was the third time she'd asked since they'd left their reception.

"It has two beds." Only one of which would need making in the morning, he sincerely hoped.

"Oh! Where's our luggage?" She'd hurried off to the telephone to call the Ribbon R, while he checked them into this hotel, the oldest and grandest in Durango.

"I sent it on ahead." With a hefty tip for the bellboy, and the request that he be sure the champagne Rafe had ordered was on ice, then make himself scarce. Because of one of the groom's prerogatives, Rafe had determined he wouldn't be cheated. And he didn't want an audience.

"This is it," he said, stopping before a numbered door on the top floor—a suite, but not *the* bridal suite, with all that heart-shaped foofaraw to spook her. Luxurious but understated, he'd specified. He fished the room key out of his coat pocket and handed it over, and she looked up at him, startled.

"Need both hands for—this." He scooped her up, smiling as she squeaked and threw an arm around his neck for fear of falling.

No fear of that; she didn't go a hundred and ten; he could have carried her to Paradise and back without breaking a sweat—at least, not that kind of a sweat. Her legs kicked over his arm; her lips were parted in startlement and dawning outrage. *"Rafe!"*

"Mrs. Montana, this might be a marriage in name only—" reminding her that he hadn't forgotten "—but all the same, it's a marriage." He hoisted her a little higher in his arms. Every muscle in his body was flexed, standing to attention, ready and eager to pounce. His heart was stretched out in a dead run, headed for the barn. "And since every last man in Trueheart got to kiss you today—what the heck—what's one more, and that one your husband?"

"Rafe…" she said on a note of warning, shaken with laughter.

"Open the door, Dana." He almost sang it.

She shook her head, her hair brushing his arm. "I…don't think so. Maybe we need to review our terms here."

"You promised to love and obey, Mrs. Montana."

"Not obey," she pointed out, trying not to smile. "They took that out years ago. And as far as—"

He didn't want to hear she didn't love him. He pretended to drop her, and she yelped in alarm. "The *door,* Dana, before my arms break.'' An out-and-out lie, that, but it got her attention. She clucked her concern and jammed the key in the lock, then opened it.

He maneuvered her over the threshold, careful of those slender legs, so long for her height, then nudged the door shut behind them. Leaned back against it. ''Well...'' He looked around approvingly. If it had to be a city hotel, this one would do. And there was a fireplace, with a fire laid ready for lighting.

''So now you can put me down,'' Dana prompted, tossing the key onto one of the two king-size beds.

''There's the matter of that kiss,'' he reminded her huskily, dipping his head.

Her eyes were huge; her lips, half curved into a smile. She was scared nonetheless. ''Rafe, we had a bargain.''

''Sure did, surely do. But I don't recall one clause that said no kissing.'' He touched her lips with his own, the lightest of teasing contacts, then backed off a hairsbreadth, hovering. She shivered in his arms and sucked in a shaky breath. Made no further protest. *Good.* He closed that tiny gap and brushed his mouth across hers, as light as a butterfly landing on a flower that trembled in the wind. Then just as slowly back again, soft as silk, his heart thundering. *Oh, Dana, let me in.*

She made a murmurous sound deep in her throat, and the tip of her tongue crept into view—flicked nervously along the tremulous gap, then vanished.

Taking that for the shyest of invitations, he closed his lips over her bottom lip, plump and dark as a berry—he'd been aching to do this for months. She moaned something wordless, seemed to lengthen and soften in his hold, while her arm tightened around his neck, drawing her up and him down.

He slid his tongue into her—wet, warm...delicious. *Gently, gently,* he reminded himself, even as he hardened below. He was shaking with the effort not to plunge into her, all his instincts crying that he should plunder and sack and make her his own, and do it *now*.

Dana was shaking, too. She pulled away and stared up at him. "Put me *down*, Rafe."

He set her on her feet immediately, but couldn't make himself let her go. His hands smoothed up her arms, restlessly down again. Her eyes were pools of darkness to drown a man. "Dana?"

She shook her head and backed away. "Remember why we're doing this?"

Because I'll die if I don't have you this minute?

"For Zoe," she reminded him, when he didn't speak. "And for Sean."

Still punishing him for the way he'd deceived her. He got it. "You're a hard, hard woman, Dana Montana."

Slowly she relaxed into a smile. At least his forbearance had earned him a little more trust. "You're just finding that out?" She turned her back on him—at the sight of her trim hips, he almost groaned aloud—and said, "Have I got time for a bath before supper?"

"You've got all night, if you want it." And one hell of a honeymoon night it was looking to be. "Save some cold water for me."

HE PROWLED THE ROOM blindly for a while, ears tuned to the thunder of water in the bathroom. With the taste of her on his lips, it was impossible to control his imagination. He saw himself stripping off his clothes and joining her in the tub, picking up that bar of soap… *Down, boy.*

He halted before the fireplace, stared at it till it took meaningful form, replacing the inner visions, then knelt and lit the fire—saw them loving before it, Dana kneeling astride him, all wet, sliding silk…rising and sinking in exquisite slow motion. *Stop,* he told himself desperately. Yes, he'd had his hopes for tonight, but he'd sworn to be a gentleman, come what may. Hadn't realized he'd catch fire this way. That it would be so damn hard. He glanced down at himself and grimaced.

Once he had the flames leaping, he realized it had been a while since the water stopped. She was soaking, he supposed, and his mind conjured up a mound of foamy bubbles with treasure below. Whatever she needed, *he* needed a drink.

A moment later he gripped the stems of two crystal flutes in one hand and knocked on the bathroom door. "May I come in?"

He heard a squeak of alarm and a startled splash. "No!"

She must have meant "Go." He opened the door. "Champagne, Mrs. Montana?" He got one heart-stopping glimpse of her sitting upright, yanking frantically at the shower curtain—then the show was over.

"Sorry," he said, unrepenting. "Champagne?" He pushed his hand and one glass through the curtain's gap, waggled it invitingly.

She sighed and took it. "Thanks."

"What shall we toast?"

"Privacy," she growled.

"Back rubs," he suggested. If she'd just let him get his hands on her, he could make her sing.

"Not a chance. Um…five years of fruitful friendship?"

Five years like this would kill him. He finished his champagne in a gulp. "So…are we ordering in or going out?"

Her sigh sounded as if it came up from the bottom of the ocean. "I'm so tired, Rafe."

"Fine. Come to bed."

"Just what I'm planning to do. Which one did you choose, the one near the windows or near the fire?"

Yours. He'd hoped—somehow convinced himself these past few days—that, womanlike, she meant to punish him for hurting her pride, then graciously relent after he'd wooed her humbly and long. Now he was beginning to wonder.

When she came out of the bathroom, he had his answer. Dana wore a terry-cloth bathrobe, supplied by the hotel, over her own pajamas. He closed his dropped mouth with a *snap*. A pair of flannel pajamas with a pattern of blue teddy bears! She looked maybe twelve—adorably jailbait twelve—but her message was crystal clear. No real bride would have been caught dead in such an outfit. If she'd meant to let him win her in the end, she would have come gift-wrapped in silk and lace for their wedding night. This package said, in mile-high letters, Keep Off!

She'd meant what she said—marriage in name only.

He sat down on his own bed with a frustrated *thump*. "You want to order pizza or burgers?"

SLOWLY HE ROLLED OVER on top of her—a living roof of hard, warm muscle, encircling arms—sheltering her from the cold, empty world. He filled her, and she arched her back and murmured with the shattering sweetness, rocked her hips, begged for more of him, *more, please more...*

A faint *rattle* sounded nearby. Warm, red light probed her closed eyelids. They were loving in the morning then, though it had been night only a moment ago.

Her breathing steadied and slowed as the sensation of his solid weight faded...spun away to nothingness, like dust motes spinning in sunlight... Her loins throbbed, empty and unfulfilled. *A dream,* she realized at last, eyes closed.

A dream—and the man hadn't been Peter; it had been...Rafe. Rafe Montana. She shuddered—a long throbbing release of pent-up tension. Rafe...she'd married him yesterday; *that* had been no dream. Dana lay motionless, pictures of yesterday taking on color and form behind her eyelids—the church, the ceremony, Zoe and Sean waving and smiling as she and Rafe drove away. *No dream; it really happened!*

But loving him? She drew a forearm over her eyes, shutting out the light. *Did we?* She could remember he'd wanted to—he'd made that very clear—but after champagne and pizza, she'd gone to bed alone.

But sometime in the night? Had he joined her? Her hand drifted in slow exploration down her chest, down her stomach, skimming over her pubis—her flesh leaped alive at her touch, meltingly eager for more…

No loving in the night, she realized with a long sigh. Only incredibly vivid dreams of loving. But she had none of that satisfied heaviness; those delicious aches; no lingering, irrepressible smile. Her body walked a brittle razor edge of desire this morning. Tears of frustration hovered behind her lashes. *Oh, what have I done?*

And where was Rafe? She opened her eyes—to sunlight. Someone—Rafe—must have pulled back the curtains to welcome the day. Water was running in the bathroom. Her husband…readying himself for the morning. She grabbed a pillow and pulled it over her face.

So…*what do we do today?* Somehow she'd never envisioned the day-to-day reality of marriage to Rafe when she made her bargain. How would they fill the time today, on this honeymoon that wasn't a honeymoon? *Do we act like tourists, go see all the sights?* Sit down and have a marathon heart-to-heart? There was so much she didn't know about him.

She wanted neither tourism nor talk—wanted to go back to the Ribbon R, go back to Petra, go back and pretend this wedding had never happened.

Because there had been no unknowns or uneasiness in that life before Rafe, if no real happiness. Better that than this feeling of being utterly lost and alone…trapped between her old life and an unworkable new.

The phone rang at her bedside—she winced and hugged the pillow closer. Who? Then realized—Cass had the name of their hotel! *Petra!* She threw off her pillow as the phone rang again—and Rafe sat down on the edge of her bed, lifted the receiver.

"Yes?" he said curtly.

She half sat up. He was dressed in a pair of new jeans and nothing else, his chest hair curly and damp, his face half shaved, half covered with foam. He glanced down at her and his scowl faded. "That's all right, Cass. What's the problem?"

Dana grabbed for the receiver, but he shook his head and leaned away, so she scrambled up and knelt beside him, her temple almost touching his. "Uh-huh," he said, absently hooking an arm around her waist to steady her there.

At his touch, her body reacted instantly—throbbing within, ready and eager to resume what she'd only dreamed. She felt her nipples rise to brush painfully against the flannel of her pajama top. She could hear Cass's voice, but not the words. "Is Petra all right?" she whispered frantically.

"When?" he snapped. "Does it look like he slept in his bed?" He put a hand over the mouthpiece. "Sean took off sometime in the night—took your truck."

CHAPTER NINETEEN

"THAT KID is nothing but trouble!" Rafe swore, not for the first time, as they drove under the rising sun name board of the Suntop Ranch. He'd tried to phone ahead, but at eight-thirty in the morning he'd reached no one at his own house; and not one of his hired hands, who should all be outdoors.

"I don't know what got into him," Dana fretted. "He seemed all right yesterday—not exactly happy, but..." Not entirely sullen, either, she'd thought, when he'd solemnly kissed her and wished her happiness outside the church. "If he's run off to Margot..." The lawyer had told her that possession was nine-tenths of the law and that a sympathetic judge was the rest of it. If they had to battle for Sean's custody in San Diego...

"This is where he'll be," Rafe said grimly, "and when I get my hands on him—"

"You'll leave him to me."

"Don't count on it. This isn't a mistake. It's willful disobedience."

"If you'd arranged for someone to spend the night with Zoe..." In the flurry of all the preparations, she hadn't thought to ask, had never *dreamed* he would leave his daughter alone after the wedding.

"She's almost seventeen, Dana. Has gone camping out in the hills by herself, with her dog, since she was twelve. There were eight Suntop men within calling range if she needed help—any one of 'em would stand between her and a bear—and it wasn't my choice, anyway. Her great-aunt Emilia decided to visit friends while she was here in town, and Mrs. Higgins flew out to her daughter's in Oklahoma after the party.''

But even if Zoe had been safe by herself, still, last night of all nights she must have been lonely. Rafe and Dana had celebrated the wedding that should have been hers, and, as far as Zoe knew, had been joyfully consummating that union last night. Had she and Sean decided to celebrate their own reunion?

"I don't see my pickup," she said worriedly, as they roared up to the backyard of the ranch house.

"Anse would check on any strange trucks around the place, and Zoe knows it. If Sean's here, he'll have parked out of sight. In the barn, probably.''

He stomped into the house with Dana scurrying at his heels, through a mudroom, on into a large kitchen—where Zoe stood scrambling eggs at the stove, a radiant smile on her face.

"Hi, you guys! You're just in time for breakfast.''

Sean sat across the room, straddling a chair backward, his Nikon, propped on its backrest, aimed at Zoe. The camera shutter clicked, then he looked around at them with an odd mixture of a child's wary defiance and a young man's serenity. "'Morning, Dana. Rafe.''

Dana pulled out a chair beside him and sat down with a sigh. He was growing up before her eyes, and there wasn't a darn thing she could do about it. She and Rafe had climbed aboard the roller coaster ride and there was no stepping off. But at least Sean was still *here* to be mothered, however badly she did it.

"Breakfast sounds wonderful.'' She didn't dare ruffle his hair as she wanted to, but when she touched his shoulder, he didn't withdraw.

AT LEAST THE PROBLEM of how to fill her first married day had been solved. After a breakfast during which Rafe sat glowering while Zoe prattled on and on about the wedding and Sean prudently kept his eyes on his plate, Dana had driven her stepson back to the Ribbon R. Rafe would see her sometime later, he'd said, not specifying when, or even which day. Had some issues to discuss with his daughter, he'd growled; he meant to settle this once and for all.

Short of leg irons, she couldn't imagine how. "That wasn't a very good idea," she murmured to Sean, as they drove away. "You know he wants you two to…" How to tactfully put it—break up? Drift apart? Go back to being children? But his willful Pandora had opened the box and now… "Whose idea was this, anyway?" Zoe's, she'd bet.

"Mine. I wanted photos, Dana." He touched the camera on the seat between them. "I want to remember it. How she looked, carrying *my* baby. She's so *beautiful.*"

"Yes, but you broke the law driving over there without a license."

"I don't give a *damn* about the law!" His voice cracked, and he glared at her as if this were her fault along with everything else. "I *love* her. You gotta clue what that means?"

"Yes," she murmured, eyes on the road, "I do, Sean. Hurts like a bear sometimes, doesn't it." *No punishment,* she decided, because how did you punish love? But perhaps there was some way to disable the truck so he couldn't do this again. She'd have to ask Rafe.

Whenever I see him. The road blurred for a moment before her, as a feeling like homesickness swept through her. And it wasn't the Ribbon R or Petra she was missing.

BUT ONCE HOME, the Ribbon R swept her up in her usual round of chores and demands—a baby who had sorely missed her and now, in compensation, whined to be carried around all day as if she were six months old instead of ten. Dudes to be waited upon—one bunch checking out and their cabin to clean, then a new bunch checking in. A flurry of phone calls from hunters for the fall season. She turned them all down—no hunting on *her* land—and found herself grateful that now, with Rafe's financial backing, she could afford to follow her conscience on that. She baked for the week, cooked and served supper and ate it with her guests, her ears tuned all the while for sounds of a truck mounting the hill.

They hadn't discussed yet how they were going to blend households, though he'd insisted on their sharing a bedroom. But maybe he'd meant only when he felt like it—a few nights a week?

Or maybe less—maybe he'd changed his mind entirely—now that she'd made it clear that she meant to stick to the terms of their bargain.

By bedtime, she was exhausted and trembling, on the edge of tears. If Rafe hadn't come by now, he wasn't coming. She bathed, changed to her oldest, most comforting nightgown, soft as chamois, sheer as silk from years of washing, and climbed into bed. Lay there with the lights out, staring up at the ceiling, as lonely as she'd ever been in her life. Missing him—could it be? Not Peter this time, but Rafe…

Oh, Peter, what have I done?

No answer…as if somehow her bed was a boat and she'd gone adrift from the shore, floating out into dark, uncharted waters. Tears trickled; she brushed them angrily aside. Who'd made this bargain, anyway?

And what did you really want from it? So far he'd given her everything she'd asked for. Taken nothing she wasn't willing to give in return. So why these blues? Exhaustion, she told herself—and sleep answered.

THUMP.

Through her lashes she saw a golden light, a tall, stumbling shadow. Rafe, across the room. He'd switched on the lamp by the daybed and now stood awkwardly at its foot, hanging on to the brass bedstead. *Thump.* His second boot hit the floor.

"Rafe," she murmured, turning on her side to watch, smiling drowsily. *You came.*

"Sorry to wake you. First thing I'll need around here is a bootjack."

He meant to stay—to move in. His hat rested upside down on her bureau. Her eyes blurred and her smile widened. "We'll get you one tomorrow. What time is it, anyway?"

He padded over and sat on the edge of her bed. "Past twelve. I've been down in Durango at the airport, seeing Zoe and Emilia off to Phoenix."

"You sent her away!"

"For a few months. Seemed like the best I could do. She's bored, she's lonely, she ought to have a woman around. But I can't bring her to you, with Sean living here. And she won't promise me that she'll never see him again—we banged heads half the morning on that one. Don't know if they had sex last night or not—she says it's none of my business—but either way, that's not how to break off their attachment. So…" He shrugged. "Bye-bye, Zoe."

She covered his hand on the bedspread with her own. "I'm sorry, Rafe."

"Me, too. I'd rather airmail Sean to Patagonia. No return address."

No use arguing that one. She smoothed her hand up his wrist, marveling at the rugged size of it compared with her own, and its warmth, the crisp, curling hairs. "Did you eat?" At least she could feed him.

"I did. Down in Durango. Figured I'd get in too late to bother you."

"Would have been no bother at all." She found herself wanting to take care of his needs. Most of his needs. Those that didn't conflict with her own.

His other hand moved to cover hers. "I'm ready for bed is what I want. So where do I sleep?"

"Here." She sat up and took back her hand.

He leaned closer and cupped her cheek. "You mean—"

She shook her head. "I mean the daybed's too short for you. If I'd known you were coming…"

"This is crazy, Dana, you know it?"

I know it. She didn't speak. But how else could she protect herself?

Warm and gentle, his hand smoothed down her face. His palm shaped to the curve of her neck and drifted lower, raising goose bumps. "I like this better than your teddy bear pajamas." His eyes roamed over her body with shameless approval. "Seems a little more—" Reaching her collarbone, he drew the flat of his fingers slowly, deliberately across the soft, clinging fabric—the tops of her breasts beneath it—and smiled as her body responded, her nipples rising for his touch. "More welcoming?" His eyes rose to hers with the question.

"It isn't." She slid out the far side of the bed, and his hand fell away. "Shall I change the sheets for you?"

"Don't you dare." His fingers moved to the placket on his western shirt, and he watched her steadily as, snap by snap, he bared his chest.

She retreated to the daybed and sat, weak-kneed. He was too beautiful.

He hung his shirt over a bedpost, then reached for his belt buckle, his eyes locked on hers.

"No…um, pajamas?" She'd fallen asleep last night when her head hit the pillow. Hadn't seen.

"Not since I left my mama's house at seventeen, no, ma'am." The zipper of his Wranglers was coming down, its sound a sexy snarl in the late-night stillness.

"Oh." She flipped back the covers on the daybed and slid in, primly turned her back—and watched the enchanting shadows moving across her wall, then his silhouette growing taller…wider…heroic or monstrous or both, climbing up to the ceiling as he advanced. She sucked in a breath and held it. If he kissed her…

The light on the table behind her flicked off. "'Night, Mrs. Montana."

She blinked and let out her breath. "Sweet dreams, Rafe."

He snorted; the bed creaked; she smiled, closed her eyes…and slept.

From: RedColumbine@Westbest.com
To: SanDiegan@Pipeline.net
Hey, Sean-*de-mi-corazón*, here I am at last, writing you on a Phoenix Public Library computer. Aunt Emilia doesn't have one, and had a hissy-fit when I asked if I could set up a local server through her phone line for my laptop. *Invención del diablo*, computers, and that's that. So I won't be able to write you every night, as you've probably noticed, but hey, you know how I chop through the books. Should get here a couple of times a week, anyway.

I cried for two days straight after Dad put me on the plane, but that's no good for Ms. Ariel Bliss (I'm SOOOOO glad you like that)/Mr. Peter Rafael (tho that ain't gonna happen—she kicks like a girl). (Oh, yeah, she kicked for the first time on the plane, with glee, it felt like. Gonna be a pilot like her momma someday, you bet.) So I decided to stop whining and, as Dad always says, make the most of it.

Emilia and I've spent the past few days down in Tucson with my grandparents, the Cavazos. I told you they retired out here, didn't I? Lots of love and LOTS of clucking disapproval at my tummy—*¡qué lástima! ¡qué vergüenza, niña!*—my grandfather wanted me to go to Harvard even more than Daddy did, since that's where my mother meant to go.

They lightened up a bit when I explained that I still mean to go, that the dean sent me the book list for all the classes I would have been taking and that I'm doing the reading on my own. (Plan to ace 'em next year.) And Abuelo Paco suggested that since I have all this time on my hands, I should look into auditing some classes at the junior college near Emilia's house. Brilliant idea. I mean to do it.

Meantime, how'z it feel to be a mighty junior? Did you get Hendricks for English? What about your other courses? And how about Yearbook—you are going to sign up again, aren't you?

OOOPS, look at the time! Emilia will be picking me up any minute, and I haven't checked out a single book. So write me and tell me EVERYTHING— school; if you're happy or sad; how are Daddy and Dana? (Does my dad seem happy with her? That's REALLY important—a deal breaker, far as I'm concerned, if he isn't. He calls me a couple of times a week, but it's like trying to quiz a clam, and I can't tell what he's thinking if I can't see his face.) Meantime, *muchos abrazos* (we speak only Spanish at Emilia's and I'm trying to think in it), Zoe+((Ariel Bliss)).

From: SanDiegan@Pipeline.net
To: RedColumbine@Westbest.com

Red, don't you EVER do that to me again! I was giving you one more day to write, then I was going to hitch out there and find you, though I didn't remember your aunt's last name, and your dad gave me the Evil Eye the one time I tried to ask him. (What is her last name and what's your address, just in case?)

School's a bummer, just like I figured. Didn't get Hendricks, got Franz, and she's snooze-city. Or would be, except she alphabetized me into a seat in the middle of a nest of goat-ropers (sorry, cowboys), who have a thing about city slickers like you-know-who, so I'm too busy ducking spitballs and Copenhagen juice to doze off.

Did sign up for Yearbook and the newspaper. Shooting pix is the only worthwhile thing I do around here.

About your dad and Dana, dunno, it's sorta weird. He's sleeping here every night, though he leaves way early and comes back late, except the days he works over here. At first they laughed a lot, but lately it seems sort of tense. You know how you can feel the lightning coming on top of a mountain? Like that—prickly air whenever one of 'em walks into the room. And he can't take his eyes off her, the same way I watch you. But I don't hear anything late at night, which is a relief, but sort of strange. Maybe grownups do it quieter, or only in the day when I'm gone? YUK! Turns my stomach to think of it. Meanwhile, here comes Dana to start supper, so I guess I'll split before she asks me what I'm doing. (Why do women DO that?) I wish to God I'd been there with you, Zoe, when our baby first kicked. I miss you so much I can't even talk about it. Everybody here has somebody but me—Willy's got his horse, the Pet's got Dana, Dana and Rafe have each other—and here I sit, without you.

Please, please, PLEASE try to take some photos of yourself, even if it's just one of those throwaway cameras. I'm missing everything—MISSING YOU. Your, Sean

RAFE LEFT THE HOUSE most mornings at seven to make the forty-five minute drive to Suntop. What he'd do when the cold weather closed in Dana couldn't imagine, didn't want to think about. But meantime, she'd taken to rising with him, sending him off with a hot, hearty breakfast, though he insisted he could cook his own.

So he could; still, she liked doing for him. Liked sitting across from him at the table, sleepily sipping her first cup of coffee while he ate, asking him what his plans for the day might be. She didn't get to talk with him as much as she might have wanted to these days, four weeks into their marriage. The lazy pace of summer was picking up as September drew to a close. Each morning Rafe stood out on the deck with his face turned to the sky, studying clouds, sniffing the cool breeze. Soon it would be time for fall roundup—a crucial matter of timing, he'd explained. Bring the herds down from the mountains too early and they'd cut into the winter's grazing in the home pastures. Bring them down too late, and Rafe risked doing it in the snow, losing cattle or even men.

A hard life, ranching, she mused, as she washed their breakfast dishes, but Rafe seemed to love every part of it—working outdoors, making his own decisions, something new to do every day. He never slacked off and he never complained. When he wasn't working at Suntop, he was slowly whipping the Ribbon R into shape—meant to have it ready for cattle by the spring.

She jumped, as he loomed up behind her smelling freshly of toothpaste, his hat settled in place for the day. "I'm gone now.'' His hands landed on the edge of the sink, either side of her waist.

He was standing too close for her to turn around, so instead she turned her head. "Back for supper tonight?" Usually she fed him later.

"I'll try to make it, but don't hold it for me." Bending, he kissed her nape.

Heat starred out from the warmth of his mouth—searing down her spine to tighten her hips in a reflexive curl, rushing out her arms in a flurry of goose bumps. His lips brushed back and forth in a hot, leisurely caress, then roamed up to her earlobe—lava pooled in her stomach.

"Hey," she protested weakly. He didn't do this often.

For just a second, the zipper of his jeans nudged her hips—an electrifying touch—then he edged away. "Hey yourself, lady." He caught one end of her apron bow and pulled it free, stood fingering the string as she turned and leaned against the sink, at bay, looking up at him.

Oh, Rafe, don't do this to me.

"When?" he demanded huskily.

On the day I believe you're here for me—not because you need a substitute mommy for Zoe. And not because you need a woman, and I'm the closest available. Her pride wouldn't let her say that. Love had been no part of their bargain; it was too late to demand it now. She shrugged. "When the cows come home?"

Amusement and frustration warred in his tanned face. He tugged her apron string once more, and when she didn't budge, he draped it over her shoulder. Laid one fingertip to the corner of her mouth. "Might be sooner than you think, Mrs. Montana. Wind's blowing from the northwest." He traced the line of her lips to the far corner and turned away.

Whatever that means, she thought, retracing his caress

with one fingertip as he banged out the door without a goodbye. She turned back to the sink and the dishes.

It was getting harder to resist him every day. But to simply give in? She thought she knew where that would lead.

Straight to bed—and straight to heartache. Let Rafe love her, and she'd end up loving *him*. She had no doubt of that anymore. Something in him spoke to her, touched her. Had from the very start. Let him all the way in, and he'd own her, body and soul.

While he remained unowned, untouched. With the freedom he'd always said he wanted intact, unsurrendered.

Dana couldn't imagine a lonelier fate than to go down love's road alone. She brought the back of her hand to lips that still tingled. *Touches me, wants me, oh, yes. But doesn't love me.* She'd come to realize, these past few weeks, that when she'd made that bargain with him, she'd inadvertently set him a test.

And Rafe had failed it.

Because if he loved me, he'd never have agreed to divorce me in five years. Never have agreed to let me go. Love didn't come on a five-year plan.

Neither would he have agreed to the condition she'd set; that this be a marriage in name only. Dana grimaced. Not that he wasn't doing his best to wiggle out of *that* clause!

But without giving what she needed in return. He was kind to her always, passionate often.

He'd spoken not one word of love.

SOMETIMES RAFE THOUGHT he'd made a mistake opting for patience. If he'd kissed her past resistance that first night, seducing her in a hot rush as he damn sure could have done, then he'd have gotten them over this hump, to put it bluntly. By now they'd be easy with each other, smugly confident, lost in all the wonderful ways that man could please woman, or woman enslave man.

Instead, he'd held back on their wedding night—and a simple difference of opinion had grown as high as the San Juan Mountains, with no pass in sight.

Maybe I could have, maybe I should have, he told himself, scowling at the highway unreeling before him, leading him east to Suntop, *but I didn't.*

Because he'd been afraid. Worried that if he rushed Dana off her feet and into loving, but couldn't carry her past regret—where would they be then? What if she woke up the next morning feeling that she'd betrayed her love for her late husband?

Not a good start, he'd figured. Much better to take it slow and patient. He wanted Dana to come to him in her own sweet time, and to mean it when she came.

Sound arguments, he'd thought at the moment, but now Rafe wondered if he'd simply been a coward. And giving in to fear was always such a damn mistake. Not just that it belittled a man, but that tactically it never worked. Bold paid off, where timid went wanting.

And he was wanting bad nowadays. With no end in sight.

CHAPTER TWENTY

From: RedColumbine@Westbest.com
To: SanDiegan@Pipeline.net

Sean Diego, that last letter was a real whiner. I know you think you've got it bad, but THINK about it. Who got to stay home with his family in Colorado, and WHO GOT EXILED? Here I am without my dad or my dog or my horse, and anyway I'm getting too fat and ugly to ride. Oh, yeah, I got my first STRETCH MARK this week, and my face and hands and feet look all puffy—and you think YOU'VE got problems? I'm sorry, I'm sorry, I'm a raving grump tonight, a mopey wreck. For once it's raining, and Aunt Emilia won't let me drive across town to the bio class I'm auditing Tuesdays and Thursdays. The old girl's going deaf, so she turns up her game shows full blast, and I can't even THINK, much less study. I finally snuck out the back door and squelched off to the library (for which she'll give me grief later) and got your latest. I'm sorry to hear the creeps at school are bugging you. Somehow you've gotta learn to laugh it off and joke back, Seanster, or you've got to warp into some parallel dimension where the trogs can't touch you, like I used to do. Your prob is that they think you think you're better than they are. (And you are, but don't EVER let 'em know you think so.) And also, they're scared that the girls are going to realize what a hottie you are (which they will, if you ever talk to 'em), so they're trying to whittle you down to size before you steal all the women. So don't despair. I know it seems like FOREVER, but the year will be over before you know it—here it's October already!!!!—and then you'll be a senior. (And a father, sort of.) You know, nobody has discussed that—at least not with me, WHO SHOULD BE IN ON ALL THIS, BUT WHO SOMEHOW GOT DUMPED OUT IN LEFT FIELD—but what are Dana and Dad and you and me going to tell Ariel Bliss? You think it will confuse her if we tell her the truth? Would she be happier and more secure thinking she's my half sister and your stepsister? Whoops, my time on the computer is up; they only give you half an hour here. Gotta go. Anyway, cheer up, Seanster, and look at it this way—you could always be SEVEN MONTHS PREGNANT!

Biiiiiig Hug, Zoe+((A.B.))

P.S. Yeah, I'm taking pix, though trust me on this, pink-freckled watermelons are not particularly scenic.

FOR ONCE HE'D BE on time—early, even—for supper, Rafe thought, turning in at the sign for the Ribbon R. He'd spent the afternoon, he and half his hands, helping his neighbor Tripp McGraw round up a herd that had gone astray after a border fence came down. They'd scattered up and down the state highway, a danger to traffic and themselves. Rafe and his men had taken the south end of the problem, while McGraw and his brother took the north. Except for a nasty fall Rafe and Tobasco had suffered as they scrambled to head a panicked calf off the road while an eighteen-wheeler bore down on it, blasting its airhorn like an idiot, the drive had gone smooth as butter. After the last straggler had been eased back through the gap and onto McGraw land, Rafe had called it a day. His left side, where he'd landed on it, was stiffening up. Home early and a hot shower, he'd promised himself, and here he was.

Home... His eyes swept past the low concrete bridge over the river to the white ranch house tucked into a bench in the rising hills. Not his home, this place—he still didn't feel that—much preferred Suntop. But the woman *inside* that house... That was where this feeling centered, this feeling of homing. Where he was taking his battered body and the memory of that evil wind that had sucked at him and Tobasco as they crashed down on the edge of the pavement and the truck had thundered past not three feet beyond Rafe's outstretched arm. *A close one.* Too close to tell her about it in any detail, but all the same he needed her smile to wipe out that moment of blank acceptance when he'd thought he was a goner. When you were shook and bruised and a little bit rattled, you went home for comfort—wherever, whoever, home was.

Gunning his truck for the last rise, he saw Sean working up on the scaffolding he'd helped him set up last week. Second side of the house coming along nicely to match the front, which Sean had finished all by himself before the wedding. Had to hand it to the kid; he had grit and persistence when he put his mind to a goal. Rafe grimaced. *Which is why it's just as well I sent Zoe away, much as I miss her.* "Looking good," he called as he drove past. The kid's shoulders jerked, but he didn't turn—just kept on scraping paint.

Rafe frowned as he parked the truck and trailer. The boy was generally polite these days, though he had his moods. Walking around back to unload Tobasco, he changed his mind and strolled on till he stood looking up at Sean. "When do you figure to paint this side?" *Talk to me, boy.* He kept too much inside.

"Sunday," Sean muttered without turning.

"Want some help when you get to it?" Last thing Rafe

felt like doing, but he'd bullied Sean into this chore. "What?" he demanded when the kid growled something over his shoulder.

Sean turned around. "I said I can do it my*self!*"

Rafe let out a grunt of surprise. The kid had a shiner— a beaut. His left eye was half closed and purpling fast. "*Nice one.* Where'd you get it?"

The boy shrugged. "School, where else."

Rafe stifled a sigh. So much for his long, hot shower, then a cup of coffee at the kitchen table while he watched Dana cook. "Get down here, son."

WHEN SEAN DIDN'T COME to set the supper table, Dana went looking for him. He wasn't out on the scaffolding— wasn't anywhere in sight. But Rafe's pickup, with trailer attached, was parked out back, hours before his usual arrival. She had twenty minutes to spare till the roast chicken came out of the oven. So…up in the barn or down by the river? Since he'd brought a horse along, Dana guessed uphill. A few feet from the open door of the barn, she heard Rafe's voice.

"Good, good, carry it through. Punch *through* it, Sean, like you're nailing something a foot behind your target. *Yeah,* like that."

Bared to the waist, her two males shuffled around each other, fists upraised, heads weaving. Dana crossed her arms and stared. On the far side of the barn, Willy slouched on a bale of hay, a chaw of tobacco bulging one bushy cheek. "That a way, *yeah,* clean his clock for him, boy!"

Sean advanced on his opponent. Rafe retreated, flicking lazy jabs at his head. Blocking a punch with his forearms, he taunted, "That the best you can do?"

"*Uhh!*" Sean lunged for him.

Rafe slipped inside Sean's fist to tap the boy's chin. "Knockout," he announced, then grabbed his shoulders.

"Let me tell you *again*. If you open yourself up like that—"

Sean had swung around in his hold—the last of the daylight touched his face. One eye was swollen shut, turning eggplant purple.

"*Rafe!*" she exploded. "How could you?" He glanced around, surprised, then pleased, to see her. Not for long he wouldn't be. She dug an elbow into his ribs, shoving him back from her stepson. "How *dare* you?" She cupped Sean's jaw in her fingers, sucked in a breath.

Sean laughed delightedly. "He didn't do it, Dana. Honest!"

"Then who?" She swung around, her eyes lighting on her husband's magnificent torso, then rising till she met his amused blue eyes.

"Not me," Rafe assured her, hands held palm up in surrender. "We've just been sparring."

Her eyes focused on his left shoulder, and the thundercloud bruise that stretched from elbow to biceps. "You call this sparring? You lunatics!" She put fingers to it, and he winced.

"And Sean didn't do that. Fell today is all that is."

"It's cut, too—abraded," she said accusingly, cradling his arm with both hands as she studied it.

"Nothing to speak of. Just a concrete burn."

"Utterly certifiable, the both of you." She hooked her fingers over the front of his belt and tugged him toward the door. "Let's get this cleaned up—*now*. And you, Sean, are due for an ice pack. Sorry, Willy, the show's over, but stay for supper?"

LATE THAT NIGHT, after Rafe had soaked in the tub, then padded into their bedroom in his old flannel bathrobe, Dana checked his arm again. "You've definitely had a tetanus booster in the past five years?" He was seated on the bed, near the lamp, and she'd peeled his robe off his shoulder. He smelled deliciously of soap and warm man.

"Mmm," he agreed in a sleepy growl.

She moved the light closer, making sure she was seeing only scabs, not embedded gravel. "What happened?"

"Fell."

She smiled in spite of herself. An easterner would have given her a ten-minute report, a Californian a half-hour saga, including every emotion he'd felt throughout the experience, climaxing with a life-altering epiphany—but a Colorado cowboy? "Fell *how?*" She ran a fingertip up an unabraded patch of skin, taut over swelling muscle, and he shifted restlessly.

Word by word, she dragged the story out of him, till she knew enough to guarantee herself a good nightmare—the truck thundering past within inches of the flailing horse and trapped rider. Also, "If Tobasco fell on his left side, then—" she reached for the hem of his bathrobe "—what about this leg?" Lifting it above his knee, she cried, "Oh, Rafe!"

"Just bruised," he protested, putting a restraining hand over hers. "I was wearing chaps."

"Let me look at it." She pulled the hem out of his hold and rucked it up nearly to his lap—then realized that the contours beneath had changed radically—substantially. She bit her lip to stop a laugh, but it shook her voice, anyway. "Show me."

"Be glad to." His voice had gone all husky. "But it might be more than you can handle."

Do not giggle, she warned herself. "Oh-h-h, I doubt it. When I was in the Peace Corps, I took several courses in first aid."

"That's just what this needs—first aid...last aid...all the aid in between you can possibly give it."

If only I dared. She cocked her head, then said with quick relief, "Petra's crying. I'll have to go see." She ran a hand lightly up his thigh, glanced up questioningly as he groaned, then realized and smiled. "It does look okay." The leather chaps had protected him from the concrete, though not a thousand pounds or more of struggling horse. "As long as you're sure it's not broken..."

"Got the full use of it, as I could show you."

I bet you could. Still, the thought of the oncoming truck, how close she'd come to never seeing him again—a wave of raw emotion swept through her. *This arrangement may be an emotional disaster, but I like you sitting on my bed, Rafe Montana. Thank God you came back to me!* She pressed her lips to his thigh, then rose hastily and stepped back. His hand that had been reaching for her hair was left hovering midair.

She returned from soothing Petra—with a glass of water, two aspirin and a renewed resolve. Giving in to Rafe would be a joy now—and certain heartbreak later on. And she'd promised herself no more heartache in her life. Her growing attraction didn't change that one essential fact of her existence.

So she gave him his painkillers and backed off from the bed. She'd stayed away long enough that he'd lost his man-on-the-prowl look, gotten sleepy. Also naked, she noted, seeing the bathrobe hung on his bedpost. "I think you should stay in bed for a day or two," she said, while he swallowed his pills.

"Keep me company?" Smiling, she shook her head, but he didn't smile back as he set his glass aside. "Then, no. I've got a ranch to run. Roundup starts this Saturday if the weather holds."

She moved across to the daybed and sat. "Wish I could go with you." To ride high into the mountains with Rafe... The late-autumn flowers, the crystalline air, the elk bugling their mating calls... Maybe she could ride above all her worries and fears up there, simply be a woman with her man.

He let out a long breath. "Maybe next year."

Will we have a next year? By then, surely, he would have lost interest if she still wouldn't share his bed. He'd have found some other, less cowardly, woman by then, someone willing to risk her heart and damn the consequences. While she… *I'll be here, keeping my half of the bargain.* "By next year I'll have my hands full with Zoe's baby."

He grunted—though whether it was agreement or dissent she couldn't tell—and eased himself down under the covers. She switched on her own lamp, then rose to switch off his. If he was too stubborn to take a day to recover, then he needed his sleep.

He turned carefully onto his side to watch her. "While we're talking about it, I've been thinking…I mean to take Sean along."

"On roundup? But he wouldn't be back on Monday for school, would he?"

"Nope. But school's where he got that shiner."

She ran a hand up through her hair, tousling it distractedly. "I know, I know. I don't know how to help him, Rafe. He's not making friends."

"Doesn't know how. Kids are devils always—and at this age? I imagine they're riding him pretty rough. But he takes it too much to heart. He's got to learn to take his knocks and come up laughing, then hassle 'em back."

"That's what you were teaching him out there in the barn? Advanced social skills?"

"That's part of it, yeah. A week out on the mountain with my hands, and he'll learn more. More than he would in a year of schooling. He's got to learn to get along with men, Dana. Somehow he's missed out on that."

He'd had Peter, until nineteen months ago. But Peter had

been a schoolteacher, a man who moved easily through a kinder, gentler world than this. "Maybe for your world, he does. But it's just as likely that he'll go back to the coast when he's grown. Work in computers, or some such. He needs to learn to get along with *people*."

Rafe yawned and stretched mightily under the covers, trapping her eyes, drawing them down the long, rugged length of him, then shook his head against his pillow. "If he's lucky, he'll live among men and come home to women. A woman."

"That's how you see the world, men and women apart?" Married to Rafe, sometimes she felt like a captive dropped into a savage Indian tribe.

"No, ma'am," he murmured. "By no means. But men— real men—can't live in a woman's world and be happy. Though we sure like to visit." Their eyes held, speaking when there were no words left to say, till she broke first and turned away. After a moment, he switched off the light.

RAFE WAS PREOCCUPIED and busy over the next few days, preparing for roundup. Dana hardly saw him, but his words lingered on in her mind. *We sure like to visit.* So there he was, condemned by his own words. That was what he wanted to be in her world—a visitor.

Fine for him. But this time she wanted someone who'd stay. Who wouldn't allow himself to be called away, not on any account. Not by death. Nor by that mindless male urge for unencumbered freedom that had broken so many hearts—most of them female. Dana didn't need it—didn't need Rafe, if that's what he was. But, oh, she could miss him.

RAFE HAD ALWAYS rated himself pretty high in the patience department—he bowed to no man when it came to breaking horses and breaking them kindly—but now he was beginning to worry. Maybe Dana would outlast him.

Usually the easiest of men, he was starting to notice his own temper. It was fraying around the edges, tightening his muscles when he moved, putting an edge to his voice when he spoke. Hard to say if that was really temper—he had no one to blame but himself for this fix, so how could he justify anger?—or sheer, untapped testosterone looking for release.

Whichever, he didn't feel like a gentle man, much less a gentleman, nowadays. So till he'd mastered this mood, he did his best to avoid Dana. No more smiles or sexy teasing in the bedroom. No more kisses stolen in the kitchen on his way out the door to work. Because he couldn't guarantee anymore that once started, he could stop if she asked him to. Couldn't guarantee that if he *could* stop, he could without words he'd later regret.

A few days apart would do them both a world of good, he told himself. He always did his best thinking up in the mountains.

From: SanDiegan@Pipeline.net
To: RedColumbine@Westbest.com
Hey, Red, guess what? Your old man is taking me on roundup! We leave in the morning from Suntop. I'm sleeping over here tonight, since I had to go to school today, but he's spending the night over at your place—last-minute prep, I guess. Then Dana's driving me over at dawn. So Yippie-yi-etc and it's me and the little dogies. I'm REALLY stoked. Beats school any ol' day. And how, by the way, is your dogie? Taken any pix this week? I've got the one of your bellybutton that you asked Lisa to pass on to me in my wallet. I kiss it nightly—in case you feel any tickling, that's me, not A.B./P.R. So gotta run. Still

haven't packed my saddlebags yet, and Dana's fussing about if I have enough clean Jockey shorts (wimmin). But please, please remember this. I LLLLLLLLLLLL-OOOOOOOOOO VVVVVVVVV EEEEEEE You, Zoe Montana! Your Colorado Cowman, Sean.

THEY WERE RUNNING LATE on this day of all days—very late.

Racing to get ready, his arms piled with clean clothes from the dryer, Sean had stumbled over Petra—she'd taken a nasty tumble, bumping her head and bruising her feelings. She was fine now, but the fall plus the change in their usual routine had left her tearful and grumpy, demanding to be held, throwing tantrums, then furiously determined not to be bundled into her coat and shoes when they were ready to go.

Then, on top of Petra's toddler tactics, Dana's old pickup chose this frosty morning not to start—perhaps the battery needed replacing? Sean had coasted it down the hill, trying to pop the clutch, and had succeeded for a minute—then it wheezed and died again. Luckily the mountain bikers in Cottonwood Cabin had already been up and about. They'd jumped her battery from their sports ute, and that had done the trick.

So here they were at last, an hour late, wheeling under the Suntop name board. "What if he left?" Sean dithered, his nose nearly touching the windshield.

"He wouldn't do that." Dana wasn't as certain as she sounded. Rafe had been awfully brief these past few days—worrying about something, the drive perhaps. And he didn't suffer fools when it came to his ranch work. He'd told Sean to be here at dawn, and they'd blown it. *Please, please Rafe.* She hadn't seen Sean so happy or excited in months.

The truck roared around the last curve, over a creek lined with aspens, then the manager's house and the barns rose up before them. The yard was filled with neighbors' trucks hitched to trailers, saddled horses, men mounting up. And the still center to all this swirl of activity, Rafe, sitting his blood bay, Tobasco.

His eyes nailed them as she parked the truck and slid out. No smile of greeting, though she hadn't seen him for more than a day. Leaving Sean to gather his gear, Dana hurried across the yard, as he swung down and tied his horse.

"You're late," he noted, as she halted awkwardly before him, fighting her urge to not stop until she hit his chest.

"My fault," she said immediately, "I'm so sorry." *But please don't blame Sean.* Don't let him start out on this adventure scolded. In the privacy of her kitchen, she would have touched his arm and explained the events of the morning. But not out here with half a dozen hands standing around, watching the boss with his new wife.

His face colder than she'd ever seen it, Rafe shrugged and looked away, to where Anse Kirby was helping Sean tie on his saddlebags and his blanket roll. Some silent message was passing among the gathered men. Spurred boots stepped up into stirrups—they were cowboying up, as Willy would put it. Dana spotted her wrangler, as she thought of him, seated on the top rail of the corral, chewing furiously to hide his wistfulness at being left behind.

Anse had mounted. Sean swung up on Concha—good, Rafe had assigned him a gentle but lively mare. Rafe turned and tightened Tobasco's cinch, then untethered the gelding's reins and swung back to face her. "Well..."

She was missing him already, more than she could say, especially here, among strangers. "Take care of Sean for me," she begged in a low voice, laying a hand on Rafe's arm. She felt his muscles flex at her touch.

He nodded curtly, a muscle fluttering in his cheek below his eye.

"And of yourself." She was beginning to realize that it would look strange if she just waved goodbye. Would feel awkward and hypocritical if she offered to kiss him, something she'd never done before. It was Rafe who'd initiated all kissing till now.

"Don't worry about me."

But she would; so many things could happen up there. "Of course not. Well…"

His face hardened and he jerked away, gathered the reins. *Don't go like this, mad at me.* Dana slid a hand to the top of his shoulder. "See you in a few days, then?" She stood on tiptoe to kiss his cheek.

His free arm snagged around her, hauling her close. She gasped in surprise at the suddenness of his response, its latent violence. His mouth came down on hers with none of the gentleness he'd always shown her before—demanding this time, arrogantly taking what she'd offered, then more. His tongue swept roughly into her; his heart was slamming against her breast; he'd bent her so far backward that she had to grab for his shoulders. Dimly, she heard someone whistle, then he brought her upright, dropped her flatfooted and swung away.

Shock gave way to hurt, then furious humiliation. *Why was he so mad at her?* Just for being late or— But this was no time to demand an explanation. His boot was already swinging over Tobasco's rump. He found his stirrup, straightened his hat and called loudly, "Let's move on out!"

She stood glaring up at him—ignoring the grinning cowboys that filed past—daring him to meet her eyes.

"'Bye, Dana!" Sean called, and trotted after Anse Kirby, who touched his hat in farewell.

Rafe's eyes swung down to hers, and they were nearly

black with emotion. Tobasco pranced in place, and she stepped back.

"What was that about?" she demanded in a quivering undertone.

He laughed aloud, one harsh incredulous bark, then brought Tobasco sidestepping alongside her. "See you in a few days." Reaching down, he touched her trembling mouth, and for just a moment he softened. Then he was past her, loping away after his men.

He didn't look back, even once.

CHAPTER TWENTY-ONE

IT WOULD HAVE BEEN bad enough if they'd parted in perfect amiability. She still would have missed him. But to have Rafe leave her like that, in anger—an anger she couldn't explain—was far worse. Dana drifted around her empty house all weekend, restless and blue and confused.

Forget it, she tried to tell herself. She'd simply crossed him at the worst possible instant—when he had a roundup to organize, a dozen urgent issues competing for his attention—and he'd lashed out. The first time he'd ever really lost his temper with her; that's why it cut so deep.

When he returned, all would be forgotten, forgiven. They'd be just the same as before, warily tender and always aware of each other, but most of all—most precious of all—*liking* each other.

She'd come to depend on that more than she'd realized; the contentment of having a friend around the house. Someone to listen to how her day had gone and to tell her of his. Someone to share a laughing glance when Petra did something marvelously silly, like the time she played dress-up with his Stetson and her brother's sunglasses. Someone to share her concerns about Sean.

If I lost that… Emptiness all over again, even deeper and darker than before.

But don't be silly, she'd tell herself, shying away from the abyss. She was exaggerating one moment's petty irritation into something permanent and awful. In a few days Rafe would return, and life would be as before.

Somehow it didn't feel that way. That bruising kiss felt like some sort of...divide. *He's angry at me, and not because I was late.* But for what, then? Because she refused to share his bed?

When she wondered about that, Dana grew angry herself. They'd made their bargain, and sex had been no part of it. If now Rafe was blaming her for that, he was being unfair.

She didn't think of Margot till her letter came on the Tuesday.

ADDRESSED TO SEAN, of course. Sitting in her pickup, which she'd pulled over just beyond the highway mailbox, Dana held it up to the light, but the envelope was opaque. She studied its childish, disturbingly erratic script for a moment, then grimaced and tossed it back on the pile of mail. Trouble, whatever it was, she told herself, and fought the temptation to not deliver it. But much as her instinct told her to shield Sean, there were some things one couldn't do. He had a right to mail from his own mother.

Margot...Dana had been waiting for her next move. Expecting it for weeks now. The custody expert she and Rafe had hired—Rafe had paid the thousand-dollar retainer with barely a grimace—had contacted Margot's San Diego attorney the week before the wedding. There had been some preliminary legal posturing and declarations, both sides claiming swift and certain victory in any eventual encounter; then each had withdrawn to his respective corner. Papers would doubtless be filed and soon, Dana's lawyer had assured her, then the real fireworks would start.

Instead, there had been a resounding silence until now, this letter.

It wasn't until Dana placed it on Sean's desk that the thought occurred to her. It was Margot who had pushed her into this marriage, who'd sent her running to Rafe to save Sean.

But for seven weeks now, Sean hadn't needed saving. *I must look like the little boy who cried wolf!* Rafe had rescued her from…precisely nothing. At least, nothing so far.

Could he possibly think—no, surely not—that she'd invented the whole Margot threat out of thin air? Dana sank down on Sean's bed, starting to feel like a fool. Could this be the source of Rafe's bad temper? He was beginning to wonder if she'd tricked him into this marriage, using Margot as her excuse?

Don't be ridiculous, she chided herself. It was Rafe who'd first proposed their arrangement, for Zoe's sake.

But two months later, it was she who'd finally set the deal in motion, citing Margot's threat as her reason.

I wonder what arrangement he'd have made for Zoe if I hadn't come begging his help? Had she perhaps barged in unknowingly on other plans he'd been making? Plans of some sort that Rafe now regretted he hadn't completed?

Maybe, happy as she had been with this arrangement, she was starting to seem a bad bargain to Rafe. That could account for his temper.

HE'D BEHAVED BADLY, very badly, taking out his temper in a kiss.

He *wanted* to behave badly with Dana Montana—his own wife, damn it!—for a good nonstop week or more. Maybe that would shut off his mind, let him sleep again at night. A sound sleep—not like the ones he was having these days, where he woke from torrid dreams, unsatisfied, on the sweaty point of explosion. *I signed on for five years of this?* He must have been out of his mind!

Still, Rafe was missing her, his thoughts moving faster than the damn cattle down the mountainside. Going to have to work something out when he got home.

Home… There the thought was again, and that was the problem. How did you give an ultimatum—insist on a revision of terms—when she held all the aces? What was the use in threatening to walk out, when he wanted her and she didn't want him? Where was his leverage?

Or his pride if he stayed?

From: RedColumbine@Westbest.com
To: SanDiegan@Pipeline.net
Seanster, You probably won't get this before you go, but I'm SO GLAD Dad took you on roundup. I'm sitting here with tears dripping down my silly nose, thinking of how beautiful it is up there, and how I'm missing it, Miel and Woofle and the guys, the campfires at night, the frosty mornings, the aspens all shivery golden. Not that I'm not having a good time here, too. Finally meeting a few kids over at the college. I borrowed some study notes from a guy, that night I missed. He's pre-med, too, hoping to transfer to Stanford next year, so we had a lot to talk about. Kinda neat to meet someone who shares your dreams. Ouch!—now THAT was a kick, Ariel Bliss, you beast. Guess she's telling me it's time to check out a book and go, soooo… Hey, one last half-a-thought, Seanster. About the L word? I don't think we should use that anymore. It was never really part of the plan, you know. This was just s'posed to be some friendly scientific inquiry, till the big OOOPS! You know how I feel about you—you'll always be my very, very, very BEST FRIEND. But I think we should remember, that's just what we are—amigos. (Besides, now that Dana and Dad have married, it's practically incest, isn't it?) So anyway, that's all. I love you, too, but with a little l. Talk to you soon, Cowboy. Your pear-shaped pal, Zoe+(((((((AB))))))

HE DIDN'T KNOW what he wanted anymore from this bargain. Take the long view had always been his approach, but with Dana filling up his whole horizon, that wasn't working. Hard enough to look past tomorrow when all his thoughts circled around tonight, Rafe admitted as his truck closed the final few miles to the Ribbon R.

"Do I *have* to go to school tomorrow?" Sean shifted restlessly on the seat beside him. "I'm awful tired."

Rafe smiled to himself. First whine he'd heard from the kid all week. Sean had done well for a tenderfoot. Had taken to heart Rafe's advice to keep his mouth shut and his eyes wide open. He'd tried hard to pull his weight without getting in the way, and mostly he'd succeeded. The men had accepted him, not because he was the boss's stepson, but because he'd made it plain that he wanted to learn and that he knew nothing. That they had something valuable to give him. The older men in particular couldn't resist that attitude, and the young ones followed their elders' leads.

"Sure you do. Have to pay for your pleasures."

How could he pay for his own? What coin would Dana accept? Six days up on the mountain had calmed his temper, but the separation had only whetted his desire. And for once, the high country had granted him no clarity. He knew how he'd gotten himself into this mess—all for Zoe—but where was he now? Where did he want to go with it, beyond Dana herself? An image of himself lying between her slender thighs, her long legs wrapped around him, made him clench the wheel. His eyes whipped guiltily toward the boy, then back to the road. *Yes, oh, yes—but beyond that?*

He didn't know what he wanted anymore, only what he'd wanted before—his freedom. Only knew now that somehow this had changed.

But wherever it is we're going, sex has to be one of the stops along the way. One of the necessary steps toward...whatever. Dana had to trust him, had to accept him, if they had any prayer for any kind of a future.

Maybe, if she'd missed him as much as he'd missed her, she was seeing that now.

DANA WAS HALFWAY THROUGH the supper dishes, when the back door burst open letting in an icy draft—and her two cowboys, tall and rumpled, Sean carrying his saddlebags slung over his arm as Rafe did, his hat tipped to precisely the same angle.

"You should have called," she cried, whipping off her rubber gloves. "I'd have held supper."

They were sunburned and looked as if they'd slept in their clothes for a week. Sean wore a jaunty grin on his face that she hadn't seen in a year or more. *It was a success,* she rejoiced.

"Rafe didn't want us to barge in in the middle." Sean dumped his bags by the washing machine. "So we stopped at Moe's."

"I could have fed you a real meal if you'd come home. You probably haven't had a vegetable all week, not counting ketchup."

Sean shot Rafe a triumphant smirk. "What'd I tell you she'd say?"

"He had a double order of onion rings, along with his three cheeseburgers, so reckon that's vegetables enough for tonight," Rafe assured her.

"Reckon it is," Sean declared with satisfaction, heading for the front of the house.

"Son, take your bags with you," Rafe called. "You unpack your own dirty laundry."

"Right." Sean scooped them up and went.

Without a sour look or an argument! "Thank you, Rafe," she said softly. He'd given her stepson something precious, a gift beyond her own giving. "But how did he get so dirty?"

"Green hands always ride drag in a cattle drive. He's been eating dust for three days."

"And loving it, it looks like."

"He got along fine." Rafe wandered over to the coffee-pot. "Any left here?"

She joined him at the stove. "Let me make you a fresh pot."

"Nope. Just want a swallow to wash Moe's cooking out of my mouth."

"You should have come home," she told him. *Let me take care of you.* They were standing very close, and his eyes were more dark than blue.

"Well, here I am," he said gruffly.

"Yes." *Here you are, and I missed you so.* But nothing had changed, really. Her head still said one thing—stick to the bargain and stay safe—and her heart quite another. She touched a snap on his shirt and turned away for a clean cup. "How was it up there? Did you have snow?"

He sat down at the table and told her, while she finished the dishes. Upstairs, she could hear the water in the pipes—Sean showering. Down here, Rafe was painting her pictures—lowing cattle, a night of shooting stars, a bear that might have been a grizzly he'd spotted across a valley, though they'd not been seen in these hills for a generation. "And what about here?" he asked after a while.

So she told him, knowing that her bits of news and gossip didn't really matter; it was the unspoken message under her words and his that counted. *We still care about each other.* Whatever his reason had been for anger, it seemed to be gone now, and he was saying he was sorry. Saying also that he still wanted her, the way his eyes followed her around the kitchen.

And still, I don't know what I want. Or didn't know how to take it and be safe. The tension was building in the room, his eyes speaking one question—the big one she couldn't answer. She snatched up a folded stack of towels from the top of the dryer. "I'll take these up for you. He's finished now."

Passing the open door to Sean's bedroom, she saw him seated on his bed, dressed already in his pajamas, his face bent low over an unfolded sheet of paper. Margot's letter. Damn, she'd forgotten it! Biting her lip, Dana stacked the towels in the bathroom linen closet, set out a fresh, fluffy one for Rafe on the towel rack, then returned, stealing a glance as she passed. Sean sat as before—and this time she saw his face. All traces of his earlier happiness had vanished.

Oh, damn you, Margot. And on tonight of all nights! She slipped into Petra's room to check on her, and stood watching her sleep. *I will never, ever hurt you,* she swore fiercely to her daughter, reaching down to brush a soft, dark curl off her cheek. Not a promise she'd keep, she knew, thinking of her own mother, their rows and blowups over the years. Love and hurt seemed to be two sides of the same golden coin—open yourself to one and you made yourself vulnerable to the other. *But if I ever hurt you, sweetheart, they'll be little hurts. Hurts meant kindly, with your best good in mind and with the best of my intentions.* Not hurts delivered blithely, obliviously, by a mother who could see only her own needs and wants, no matter how they might damage her child.

She raised her head as booted feet passed the door— Rafe, heading for the bathroom. *And how do we hurt each other, you and I, while we're guarding our hearts?* Rafe, who had taken her stepson under his wing, who'd offered her his protection. *And for all that generosity, what have I given him in return?* The comforts of a home, yes, but not what he really wanted.

My body. She stood in the dark, very aware of it—a feeling like hot honey flowing through her veins, sweet and heavy and golden, amplifying the endless stride of her pulse.

He wanted her body and she'd have given it gladly, except that it came attached to her heart. *Oh, Rafe, if you'd say one word about loving me...*

WHEN HE ENTERED their bedroom at last, she sat on her daybed, dressed in a nightgown that telegraphed her ambivalence. Simple, almost virginal white, but so soft it clung to her every curve. She ran a hairbrush through her short hair, the stroke of the bristles a comfort and a torment. She needed to be touched, maybe as much as he did.

"Margot wrote him a letter," she said, when he paused at the foot of his bed to study her.

"Oh?" He sat down and frowned. "What did it say?"

"I have no idea. He's just read it. Looked miserable when I peeked in his door."

"Blast the woman," Rafe said quietly. "Damn and blast her."

"Maybe I should go talk to him?" Already she was accepting him as her authority on Sean.

"I wouldn't. Don't want to crowd him. I'll see if I can get him to talk in a day or two." Rafe blew out a long breath. "There was a message for me back at Suntop on the answering machine. Kelton called. Said to drop in to his office any day this week."

Their lawyer, down in Durango. "So he's had news?"

"S'pose. I'll go down there tomorrow. Need some ointments, anyway. Want to come along?"

She shook her head regretfully. "I have two cabins checking in, a hiking club from Denver."

"Then I'll take care of it."

A wave of warmth moved through her. To have someone else to rely on, taking care of the things she couldn't get to or handle. More and more he felt like her partner, her...husband. Her hand dragged the brush again. "I've been thinking, Rafe."

"Mmm?"

"It's time you brought Zoe home. She's coming into her eighth month—and she's living with an elderly old maid. That's not right. She should be here where I can keep an eye on her. Where she can see Cass Hancock if any problems arise." She watched Rafe's smile fade and his face harden.

"I agree, but what about Sean? He's stopped mooning around, or at least he's hiding it better—but to throw them together again?"

"I know, but—"

"And there's the problem of space. I'm sure Sean would be delighted to share his bedroom, but—"

"But she *has* to come home, Rafe. She could be starting Braxton-Hicks contractions any day now. They're terrifying if you don't know what they are, and—"

"So what about this—?" Restlessly he stood, walked over to the bureau, reached for his hat. Stood fingering it and frowning. "Sean lives here for the next few months with Willy. And I'm sure Mrs. Higgins would be happy to come in a few days a week to beat back the bachelor dust, cook for 'em. You and Petra and Zoe and I move back to Suntop. I've been meaning to speak to you about that, anyway. Once the heavy snows start, I have to be on the ranch to feed the stock. Can't depend on getting through from here if there's a blizzard."

She couldn't see leaving Sean. She'd promised to love him, guide him. Might as well send him back to Margot if she couldn't do the job. She ran the brush through her hair thoughtfully. "Or I suppose Petra and Sean and I could stay here." *Like before.* The old desolation crept through her at the thought. The house would feel empty, no one coming home to her in the evenings. "And you and Zoe could go back to Suntop.'' She looked up and met his eyes. *This is a test, Rafe Montana. If you love me, you'll never consent to our parting.*

He scowled and shook his head. ''What's the use in having Zoe home if she doesn't have a woman to look out for her these final months? I'll need you at Suntop.''

For *Zoe.* Not because he loved her, needed her by his side, couldn't bear to let her go—but for the safety and comfort of his precious daughter. *Nothing's changed but my stupid, gullible heart!* Imagining that what she needed and wanted was so.

But it wasn't.

She smacked her brush down on the bedside table, snapped out the light. ''Guess we'll have to think about it.'' Though no way would she abandon Sean. That was where her loyalty belonged.

''What's the matter?'' Rafe padded closer in the dark— became a tall, looming blackness over her bed, smudged by her trickling tears.

She wiped her eyes angrily. Didn't trust herself to speak.

He sat down on the edge of her bed. ''Dana?''

If only you wanted me. Me—not a mother for your grandchild, a woman when you needed one. ''Nothing,'' she muttered. ''G'night, Rafe.''

A big hand dropped down out of the dark, fumbled for the top of her head, stroked her hair. His fingertips rotated in tiny circles against her aching skull. ''Nothing...'' he repeated with husky disbelief. ''Your time of month?''

She let out a *hiss* of outrage and jerked her head away from his caress. ''That's none of your business!''

''It's the business of any man who lives with a woman to know when to get his head down and lie low,'' he disagreed, laughing under his breath. ''Is it?''

''No! Go to bed.''

Hot and callused, his fingers slid around to her nape,

massaged her gently. She could feel the faintest tremor below his strength. "I'd like to."

Like, not love. That was all he was offering. That—and a night she'd never forget. Might never recover from. To open her heart would be to let in a pain that might kill her this time. His invisible fingertips played across her cheek, found her lips, sought the dampness within. She shook her head—*no, Rafe*—even as her hips rocked upward, the rustle of covers belying her thoughts.

His fingers found her chin, traced a lingering line down the arch of her neck. She'd have to refuse him in words, but they snagged in her throat. Then his hand lifted away, and she sucked in a breath of relief.

His fingers alighted again—on the swell of her breast. Her skin came alive, roughened, electrified—it was now or never. "*No*, Rafe." She sat up abruptly, just as he cupped his palm to her—she filled his hand to overflowing. He groaned aloud and buried his face in her neck.

"I said *no!*" She twisted away, pushed herself over against the wall, since he blocked the route to the floor. "I mean it!"

"I heard you." The bed bounced as he stood. "You don't have to yell, believe me."

She was panting with emotion, her hands cupping her own aching breasts, her tears scalding. *Rafe*... It wasn't that she didn't want to give to him, but if he wouldn't take— didn't want—what she was really offering... "I'm sorry," she said miserably, wiping her eyes.

"Me, too," he said from somewhere above her. "You know, one of these days I'll stop asking."

Stop asking and simply take? She'd almost—*almost*—be relieved if he robbed her of the choice she couldn't make. Should not make. Though she'd never forgive him.

Across the room, his bed creaked, covers rustled. Her

tears wouldn't stop streaming, her heart galloping. Slowly she sank back to stare up miserably into the darkness.

Someday I'll stop asking.

She blinked as it hit her, what he meant. He meant something far worse than that someday he'd insist. He meant that someday he'd stop wanting her. The thought cut like a dull knife, pressing down on her heart. She couldn't bear for Rafe to stop wanting her.

But, then, what does that make me? A tease?

SOMETIME AFTER MIDNIGHT, Dana accepted defeat. There was no way she'd sleep tonight, at least not in this room. A glass of warm milk, perhaps, then she'd try the living room couch. The first few months after she'd lost Peter, that was where she'd bedded down. Something about its mushy softness, or the fact it held no associations, often did the trick when all else failed.

Rafe didn't stir as she crept from the room. She tiptoed past Sean's room, then Petra's, then on down the stairs. But as she passed through the dining room, she paused. A crack of light showed under the swinging door. Surely she'd switched off the lights.

Some sense of caution made her open the door an inch, then peek through its gap. Across the kitchen, Sean sat at his computer, typing furiously. The desk lamp beside him traced a glistening line of moisture down his cheek.

Oh, Sean. And what would Rafe tell her to do?

She could hear him as clearly as if he stood beside her, one comforting hand on her shoulder. *Mind your own business.* Letting the door fall back into place, she padded back to the couch—and finally slept.

From: SanDiegan@Pipeline.net
To: RedColumbine@Westbest.com
What the HELL do you mean, don't use the L word?

I LOVE you, LOVE you, LOVE YOU with the biggest L in all the world! You know it, I know it. I've never tried to hide how I felt. You never stopped me till now. What's changed, Zoe? Dana and your dad marrying means nothing to us. It doesn't count and you know it. Are you just being blue and crabby tonight, or do you really mean it? If you do, I don't see how I can live without you, or why I'd want to. We aren't just best friends—you're my ONLY friend. The only woman I'll ever want or love. I think I should come out there and we should talk about this. If you don't write me soon, I guess that's just what I'll do. Mom is asking me anyway to hitch home to San Diego. Saves her the money it would cost her to use a lawyer, to fight for my custody. (At least somebody, somewhere out there, wants me.) And Phoenix is right on my way. So write me—or plan to find me knocking at your door sometime soon! Your LOVER—never your brother—Sean.

CHAPTER TWENTY-TWO

WHEN DANA WOKE on the couch in the morning, Rafe was gone. He'd somehow walked past without rousing her, then out of the house. His words hung like a pall over her heart. *Someday I'll stop asking.* Was this that day already? He hadn't even asked her for his breakfast.

Sean, too, was gone, she found, though there was evidence on the counter that at least he'd made himself a peanut butter sandwich. Must have ridden his mountain bike down to the bus stop on the highway per his usual routine.

They'll both be back tonight, Dana told herself. *Please, God.*

The weight on her heart said they would not. That happiness had fled forever.

But premonitions didn't clean cabins or make beds or change dirty diapers. She tucked her heartache away and went to work.

She'd just checked in her hiking club and sent them to Willy to sign up for trail rides, when the phone rang. *Rafe!* Her heart gave a joyous leap.

No. Mr. Haggerty, principal of Trueheart High School. "Mrs. Montana? I'm afraid we've had a problem down here with Sean. Could you come in and see me?"

"AFTER HE'D KICKED IN his own gym locker and half a dozen more, he went down to Mrs. Lindstrom's class and called Mike Andersen and Joe Petit out into the hall," said Mr. Haggerty.

"The two boys who Super-Glued his locker closed with all his clothes inside while he was in the shower," Dana summarized, determined to keep the facts straight, in the principal's mind more than in her own. The man seemed determined to blame Sean entirely for the brawl. "Mrs. Lindstrom didn't stop them?"

Mr. Haggerty drummed his meaty fingers on his desktop and fixed her with the glare he must use on rebellious students. "Mrs. Lindstrom is a student teacher," he growled finally. "And Andersen and Petit are 'backs on our football team."

"Not inclined to obey a woman's orders, plus they're both bigger than Sean, then," Dana guessed. "Also older?"

"They're seniors, but that's entirely beside the point. Sean bloodied Andersen's nose and he loosened a few of Petit's teeth. What the dental bill will be is anybody's guess."

"And Sean?"

"Sean has a black eye and a ripped shirt."

"Did they black the same eye they did last week, or were they kind enough to alternate?" she asked icily.

"We don't know that last week's fight was with the same students as this week's. Your boy seems to have quite a chip on his shoulder."

"I presume, if someone locked *your* clothes away, Mr. Haggerty, you wouldn't take it kindly, either? Or would you?"

He reddened and shoved his chair back from his desk. "Maybe I should discuss this with his father. Where's Rafe? Is he reachable?"

"He's down in Durango this afternoon." She'd tried to call him at Suntop herself, before she left the Ribbon R, but Anse Kirby had answered the phone. "I'm not sure when he'll return. May I see my son now?"

Haggerty assumed an expression of smug righteousness. "That wouldn't be advisable for discipline, Mrs. Montana. He has been suspended—in house, of course. I don't hold with rewarding misbehavior with a vacation. And he's upset, you know. A good cooling down period—"

"I'm very upset, too, that you're unable to protect my son from bullies." *Shut up, Dana, shut up,* she advised herself. She'd taught in public schools long enough to recognize this breed of petty disciplinarian. Once his mind was set, it was set in concrete. She'd do her stepson no favors by demanding special treatment on his behalf. *Calm down.* Maybe sending Rafe to bat for Sean was the smart thing to do. Quite likely the two men had known each other since grade school. And to be brutally honest, Rafe could walk into this office and command a level of attention and respect that a five-foot-three indignant mother would never be accorded.

"All right," she said levelly. "When *may* I see him?"

SEAN WAS TO BE DELIVERED into her custody in the principal's office at three-fifteen, it was decided, a few minutes after school let out for the day. Which would give Haggerty a chance to dress Sean down in her presence, Dana suspected, then gloat over his sentence—five weeks in-house suspension.

That gave her three hours to drive in to Durango and back again. With any luck, she would find Rafe at their lawyer's office and bring him back to help her deal with Haggerty. Gritting her teeth at the thought of her stepson sitting forlornly alone in some windowless room with torn shirt and blackened eye, she marched off to her truck.

RAFE PICKED UP the pinkeye ointment, an antibiotic salve that Willy swore by, and some parts for the tractor. He encountered his banker at lunchtime, and took him along to a better restaurant than he'd have chosen alone. But while his boots carried him about the town on his errands, his thoughts were elsewhere, back at the Ribbon R, back with Dana.

Coming home to her last night had been so sweet. There'd been those few moments she'd endured his loving—his hand still tingled as if he held her, his groin muscles jerked tight at the memory—and then it had turned so bitter. *This has got to stop.* His own needs shamed him. *You don't keep on offering what the other doesn't want.* He was acting like a schoolboy, like Sean mooning after Zoe—not like a man who knew the ways of the world. There were some things that wanting could never change.

After a lunch he hardly tasted, he dropped by the lawyer's. Because whatever he decided for himself, it didn't alter his obligations. He'd told Dana he'd help her fight for Sean's custody, and so he would. Besides, the kid had shown himself sensible enough to grasp the value of what Rafe and his men had offered him up in the mountains. The life of a free man. Sean deserved a helping hand.

At least the news at the lawyer's was good. "You've got yourself a kook, there," Kelton announced, his three-thousand-dollar lizard skin boots propped on his half-acre desktop, his hands clasped behind his head. "A pure, prime, California kook. We ever get her in court, we'll eat her alive."

But it looked as if Kelton wouldn't have the pleasure. He'd finally pinned down Margot's lawyer by phone and gotten the story off the cuff. The woman had pulled a tantrum in her lawyer's office two weeks ago, demanding that he work for her on spec, his eventual legal bills to be paid out of Sean's inheritance—once Margot had been granted custody and Sean's portion of the Ribbon R had been sold.

When her attorney had suggested that no reasonable man would work on such a basis, that some cash up-front would be an excellent spur to his progress, she'd flipped out, as Kelton put it. Had accused her own man of a gross lack of compassion, creativity, comprehension of the finer points of the law, to say nothing of justice. Had called him a sexist, a fascist, a money-grubbing shyster and a left-brainer, to boot. Then informed him that his office had lousy *feng shui,* whatever that was. In short, Margot's lawyer had suggested she take her business elsewhere, and she'd flounced out of his office in tears.

"And my guess is that's the last you'll hear of her in an official capacity." Kelton swung his boots down to his silk oriental carpet.

"Unofficially, that type has more lives than a slasher in the last reel," Kelton continued. "She'll pop up and scare you every six months or so, but she's strictly short attention span. Wait three weeks and she'll wander away again." He lifted a file off his desk. "Did put a P.I. on her as you asked me to do, and there's plenty of ammunition if we ever do need it—which we won't. As of Saturday night, she's shacked up with a new boyfriend, bar pickup, and he's a beaut. Want the particulars?"

Rafe grimaced and shook his head. "File it in case of need and take your man off her tail." He himself was in need of fresh air.

Coming down the stairs from Kelton's office, he was already considering how much he'd tell Dana. Enough to ease her mind, but not enough to pain her. He knew her well enough by now to be sure she didn't wish Margot Kershaw any harm. Wouldn't be happy to hear that the woman was self-destructing. He hadn't told Dana he'd played hardball, setting a private investigator on Sean's mother, and there was no reason to tell her now. He shoved through the downstairs back doors—and stopped short.

"Why, Rafe Montana!" Mitzy Barlow stood beaming at him, one long-nailed hand pressed to her heart. "How *are* you? It's been months since—'' She tossed her hair and smiled. "Well, it's been too long!"

He let out his sigh slowly between his teeth, hoping it looked like a normal breath, and offered his hand. Sending a message. "Mitzy, it's good to see you." Any other day he wouldn't have minded. She was always easy on the eyes, and how could you dislike a woman who tried so hard? Here she was doing it again, turning his handshake into something that would have caused one man to punch another.

Still, he stood patiently, courteously, hoping his eyes weren't glazing over as she rattled on. A chatterer compared with Dana's quietness. A magpie compared with a mourning dove. How he ever could have seen himself bedding her... But back then he hadn't known there was someone like Dana Kershaw in the world, waiting around the next corner.

But not waiting for me—missing her husband. That was his whole problem, Rafe was starting to think. He'd rushed in when he should have waited. Had only himself to blame for his sorrows.

"...So when she told me you were married, I almost swallowed my ice cube!" Mitzy declared, regaining his wandering attention. "And I know it's late to be wishing you all the happiness in the world, but Rafe—" She fluttered her eyelashes as she stood up on tiptoe. "Do I still get to kiss the groom?"

THE PARKING LOT behind Kelton's office was almost full. Pulling into a slot in the last row, Dana looked around. No sign of Rafe's truck. Either she'd missed him or he'd yet to arrive. She could ask Kelton's secretary, she decided, and reached for the door handle—then paused. A tall, familiar shape stood in the shadows outside the back entrance—Rafe. Facing a smaller, curvier figure—a woman dressed in a mauve business suit that hugged her like a second skin. High heels that propped her bottom up at a preposterous angle. *Woman on the prowl,* shrieked that outfit, and right now her body language was announcing the prey.

Dana's husband.

But Dana hadn't claimed him, made him her own. And now, watching this huntress fling her arms around Rafe's neck and do her best to dive down his throat, Dana sat frozen, the first shards of ice piercing her heart. *Too late,* said a bleak little voice inside her. *You waited too long to know what you really want, and now it's too late.*

Rafe had stopped asking. Asking *her,* anyway.

Long after he'd straightened, patted Ms. Mauve on the shoulder and strode off toward the street with a silly grin plastered all over his face, Dana sat motionless, blinking back her tears. She had nobody in the world to blame but herself.

AND BAD AS IT HAD STARTED, this miserable day wasn't quite done with her yet. When Dana walked back into Mr. Haggerty's office at precisely 3:10 p.m., he fixed her with an accusing eye. "Where's your son, Mrs. Montana?"

SEAN HAD WALKED OUT of in-house detention at precisely 3 p.m., with orders to wait for his mother in the principal's office. That was the last anyone had seen of him.

Dana drove home, assuming he'd caught the bus, would be sulking somewhere around the Ribbon R. But a search of his room showed his fly rod propped in its usual corner, his camera on the desk. He wasn't in the barn, his tree house or down along the river.

By dusk she was starting to worry. By nine, she was frantic. She'd searched all of Trueheart, plus the little airport between the ranch and town, and she'd done it alone. Because Rafe was missing, too.

Please, God, let them be together. They'd bumped into each other someplace near the school, she told herself, and Rafe was listening to Sean's troubles—had taken him out for a male-bonding supper of junk food somewhere down in Durango.

When Rafe's truck finally rumbled up the hill at eleven that night, she flew out of Petra's bedroom, down the stairs, to meet him at the back door. "You have Sean, don't you?"

His face, which had just started to lighten to a wary smile, went back to somber. "He isn't here?"

IT WAS PAST 1:00 A.M. by the time they'd searched Trueheart again, then all the ranch buildings at Suntop, then spoken with Sheriff Noonan. Past two by the time Mrs. Higgins arrived to care for Petra and cook for the dudes, until their return. A starless night of lowering clouds, as they drove southwest bound for Phoenix.

"Maybe we should call Zoe," Dana suggested, not for the first time, but again Rafe disagreed.

"He's got eleven hours' head start, but the road's rough and it isn't direct. And drivers don't pick up hitchers late at night. She won't have him yet, even if Phoenix is where he's headed."

"It is—has to be." The more she thought of it, the more certain she grew. Whatever was paining him, the fight or something else, Sean had taken his woes to the one person he really loved. His wise woman and lucky charm, Zoe Montana.

And this time, Dana wished he'd borrowed her truck. God, let him be all right! He was only fifteen, and not half as tough as he thought. To hitchhike some four hundred miles, through harsh high desert, mountain passes, across the Navajo reservation, with the threat of an oncoming blizzard for most of the way?

"All Zoe could do is sit there and worry. That wouldn't do her any good. With any luck we'll find him shivering beside the road between here and Flagstaff."

They didn't—though they drove with agonizing care, gritty eyes sweeping each side of the road, stopping in each dusty little town they passed to speak with the local law, asking them to keep a watch, then halting at every truck stop to question the sleepy waitresses. Each time Rafe passed a patrol car, he pulled over and walked back to talk. "Snow's coming," he said grimly, the third time he returned to the truck.

Sean had worn only a light jacket to school that morning. No proof against a blizzard. *Please, please,* she prayed, but said only, "Shall I drive for a while?"

West of the state line at Four Corners, the blizzard socked in. The snowplows had yet to turn out, and Rafe slowed the truck to a crawl, windshield wipers frantically sweeping. Rafe reached out and took hold of Dana's hand for a while, but the road was too dangerous for that. Instead, he drew her over beside him, and they drove like that, pressed together for comfort.

THE FIRST RIDE he'd caught had been the best. A battered old pickup with a tarp-covered bed. He'd untied the cover and crawled beneath it while the truck was parked outside Moe's Truckstop. That ride carried him through most of the freezing night, all the way through the reservation and out the far side. Too far. In spite of his shivering, Sean had fallen asleep after Flagstaff, and when he woke near dawn, the pickup was pulling into a gas station halfway to Kingman, fifty miles out of his way.

He'd scrambled out and taken half the morning to retrace his route east to Flagstaff, then south. By the time he reached Phoenix and figured out the bus routes, it was ten in the morning. He was grubby and exhausted and hungry enough to eat a horse, but any time now he'd see Zoe, and everything would be fine.

"SHE'S NOT HERE," said the tiny old woman with the black, snapping eyes, who opened the door to his knock. "Who are you? You're that boy she keeps talking about?"

He had to smile. "Yes, ma'am, I guess I am."

She sniffed. "You look too young to be studying to be a doctor, but what do I know? Everybody's too young, and their manners—*huh!*"

It wasn't him she meant—and suddenly Sean wanted to sit down and cry. "Could you tell me where I could find Zoe, Miss Cavazos—please, ma'am?"

Aunt Emilia directed him to a junior college halfway across town. Zoe should be sitting in on some science class there, or maybe in the student union. Who knew, with that girl? Like her mother, Pilar, who wouldn't settle down, head always off in some book.

An hour later, Sean stood in the doorway to the student union, scanning the crowded tables. She'd be here. Had to be here, when he needed her so. *Zoe, I love you with a big L. If you love me...*

His eyes focused like his zoom lens—on a head of blazing red hair across the room. He let out a cry of relief, then stopped short as he realized. That was his Zoe, all right, but she sat huddled over a table, her temple pressed to the cheek of the boy sitting beside her. Except he was too big, too old, to be called a boy—years older than Sean. Zoe sat with a young *man,* whose arm was draped comfortably around her shoulders while they read a book that lay open on the table.

As Sean stood paralyzed, Zoe turned to say something.

The man listened, nodded gravely, then kissed the tip of her freckled nose.

"Hey, why don't you just stand in the doorway?" Somebody bumped into Sean from behind.

Ready and eager for a fight, he whirled to shove back, but the kid had already passed by. *Love* had passed him by—just like that. The only woman he'd ever love in his whole life loved somebody else now. Sitting there, radiantly beautiful and ripe as a pear, with his unborn baby in her lap, she was loving somebody else.

Sean didn't look back. Blind, numb, his heart just starting to break, he walked.

IN FLAGSTAFF, the Navajo police directed them to the hospital. A young, unidentified man had been struck by a hit-and-run driver sometime the previous night and taken there. They lost nearly two hours gaining permission to see him, and when they did—*thank you, oh, thank you!*—it wasn't Sean lying there with a hangover and two broken legs. Dana's heart went out to the boy's mother, wherever she was, waiting and worrying.

Grateful and subdued they drove on, to reach Phoenix at last at eight that night.

ONCE ZOE HAD STOPPED laughing and crying and hugging them, the news was not good. She hadn't seen Sean, she reported with a startled, stricken face.

Her great aunt Emilia might have done so. A young man with manners better than most young men nowadays had come asking for Zoe sometime that morning—or was it perhaps the morning before? No, no, no, this one, because she'd been watching *General Hospital* when he'd come to the door. She couldn't say quite what he looked like, and as for age, well, they were all young these days, weren't they? But she'd sent him on to the college where Zoe wasted her time most days.

"I didn't see him," Zoe repeated, wringing her hands. "But if he missed me there, he'd try back here, wouldn't he?"

Aunt Emilia made them sit down while they waited and eat a meal of meat loaf with green salsa and instant mashed potatoes. By ten that night, they all had to admit, if that really had been Sean at the door earlier, he should have returned by now.

"Unless he hitched on to his mother in San Diego," Zoe said worriedly. "She'd been begging him to run away to her, he said."

"Said?" Rafe repeated ominously.

"E-MAIL!" HE GROWLED an hour later, as they drove east across the desert. "They've been talking all this time by e-mail?"

Dana kept her smile to herself. Rafe was so superbly competent in his own hands-on world, he tended to dismiss technology—till it reared up and bit him.

"Did you know that?" he demanded.

"No. Oh, no." Though she'd had her suspicions once or twice, and when she'd seen Sean typing so furiously at the keyboard the night before last...*I should have guessed trouble was coming.*

Rafe snorted, then let it go. Drove for a few miles in silence, then said, "I still think you should have stayed back there at Emilia's, in case he shows up in the morning. Gotten a good night's sleep. Let me go on to Margot's by myself."

"No." *You've stood by me all this way. I'll stand by you.* It was another four hundred miles to San Diego. "If he shows up, Zoe will sit on him." They'd told her they'd check back by phone every few hours in the morning.

Meanwhile, it was crucial that they head off Sean before he reached Margot, persuade him to come home. Possession was nine-tenths of the law, Kelton had warned them. Let him reach San Diego, and they might never get him back.

"At least we don't have to worry about him out in the snow now." Rafe was following his own thoughts. "And clearly he's road smart. He made good time to Phoenix, given the conditions."

"Yes." Her earlier frantic anguish had settled to a grinding worry, but Rafe was right. Sean had passed through the most dangerous terrain in his first leg of the journey. Not that there weren't a hundred other dangers still to fear, but she put them all doggedly from her mind. Sean was clever and determined, and he had her and Zoe's and Emilia's prayers—and Rafe's tireless energy—working on his behalf. *We'll find him. I promise you, Peter, we'll find him.*

Rafe rubbed her shoulder with his free hand. "Why don't you try to sleep. If we take it in turns and stay fresh, we'll have a better chance of spotting him."

So she lay on her back, with knees bent and, gladly giving in to Rafe's suggestion, pillowed her head on his thigh. Lay that way for a long while, infinitely comforted by his warmth and the vibrations of the road rising up through the seat. After a while, his right hand came down from the wheel to cradle her forehead, and her eyes swam with tears. He'd backed her so completely in this ordeal, without question or complaint. *Oh, Rafe, what would I do without you?* Reaching up and back, she found his wrist, brought his hand down to her lips and kissed it. "Thank you!" she whispered.

"My pleasure." Heavy and warm, his hand lay in her hold, not demanding anything, but not retreating.

She kissed it again, then brought it down and tucked it beneath her chin, smiled once—and fell fast asleep.

SUCH A BITTERSWEET sensation, having her rest her head in his lap. Rafe's muscles were jammed tight with her nearness, his hand almost trembling with the need to smooth on down over her breasts, exploring and claiming and worshiping every inch of her he could reach. His heart was heavy and full, just that she trusted him this far. *Oh, Dana.* His woman, even if she didn't know it.

Not long after they'd crossed the Colorado River, the border between Arizona and California, he glanced down to find her eyes wide open, pools of gleaming darkness in the truck's dimness. He moved his hand slightly, and she let it go. He was brave enough to bring it up to her mouth. To draw a fingertip across her softness, which curved at his touch to a smile, then replace it below her chin in a paradise of neutrality. "Can't sleep?" he murmured.

"Off and on. Was lying here thinking…" Her fingers twined about his, and she sighed. "You've never told me about Pilar, Rafe. What was she like?"

CHAPTER TWENTY-THREE

MILES PASSED under the truck's wheels, till she was sure he wouldn't speak—then suddenly he did. "They don't look a bit alike. Zoe's hair comes from my mama, and her height from me, I reckon, while Pilar was tiny like Emilia, and dark. But their...intensity, that's the same. The quickness. And the curiosity—Pilar was interested in a thousand different things. She'd plow through the books, researching this or that. She was so smart she was scary, and she was smart in the right way. Not just knowing facts and figures—she put facts and figures *together* to come up with ideas about the way things or people worked. Wasn't one of those types who memorize the world tree by tree—she saw the forests. Would have *planted* forests someday if she'd had the chance."

You admired her. That came through in every word he spoke. *But what about love?* Perhaps he'd loved Pilar so much that he could never love again, not all the way, not the way she needed. "So that's Pilar," she said softly, rubbing his hand with her thumb. "What about you and Pilar?"

"Us together?" Rafe shifted beneath her, then stilled. More miles passed. "There's not much to tell," he said abruptly. "I wrecked her life."

The offhand pain in his voice brought her rushing to his defense. "Who said so? Pilar said that?"

"Often." One bleak little word, barely audible above the hum of the tires.

"But what did she mean by that?" How could having a man like Rafe Montana in her life ever be anything but a blessing?

He laughed under his breath without humor. "She meant I was the cheap young cowboy who bought the economy-price condom that burst at the wrong moment and changed her whole life. Wrecked it."

"How could she blame *you* for that?" No one had forced Pilar to risk teenage sex.

Rafe laughed that bitterly unhappy laugh again. "Easily. Whenever it hit her that there she was, living in a shabby little trailer with a baby crawling around her feet and a no-account husband who could hardly put food on the table, no matter how hard he worked. When, instead, she could have been off at Harvard, studying to become Dr. Cavazos, the way her father had hoped and planned for her. She didn't just feel a failure, Dana—she felt she'd failed her whole family. And family was big to Pilar."

Reaching back, she rubbed her knuckles along the top of his thigh, desperately needing to comfort. To heal a wound she couldn't touch. "But you didn't do it to her. I mean, not by yourself."

He shrugged. "Pilar didn't see it that way. Guess I did want sex more than she did. She never let me forget that I'd promised—sworn to her—that nothing would go wrong if we loved each other."

"But even so, Rafe, even if you did—and what eighteen-year-old boy doesn't, in the heat of the moment?—afterward, she had a choice. She could have gotten an abortion."

"Pilar didn't see it that way," he repeated so softly it sounded as if he spoke to himself. And so they'd married, and now it was hitting Rafe that his first marriage had been very much like his second.

He'd always been able to satisfy Pilar, make her sing

like a little mockingbird and then beg him for more. And
Dana—somehow he knew, if she'd only let him, that she'd
answer him like music. Like rock to river or moon to sun.
They'd be good in bed together—so much better than good.

But no matter how he'd tried with Pilar, he'd never been
able to make her losses up to her. She'd never forgiven
him, and in never forgiving, had never given him her love.
Not love as he thought of love—a mating of bodies and
souls.

And now, a dozen years later, here was Dana—the same
way—holding back the one part of her that really mattered.
That she wouldn't let him into her bed signified something
much deeper—that she wouldn't—couldn't?—make room
for him in her heart.

Maybe it's something in me. Because Dana, at least, had
loved before. Time and time again, she'd made that clear.

Up ahead, the lights of a truck stop pierced his inner
blackness. Rafe sighed with relief and slowed the truck.
"Maybe he'll be here."

BUT ONCE AGAIN they came up empty, and when they
drove on, Dana insisted on spelling him at the wheel. Rafe
folded his coat to a pillow, leaned back in the angle of seat
and door and stretched out his cramped legs. "Wake me
the minute you get sleepy," he warned her.

"I will, but tell me one more thing before you nap."
Dana tipped up her chin as she did when she was facing
something hard. "Tell me what happened. How she died."

You're not asking much. But it was Dana who asked.
Rafe stared at the lines in the highway sweeping under
them and away. "One night…in our sixth year together, I
came home dog-tired and Pilar showed me a letter from
the dean of admissions at Harvard. Without telling me anything, she'd reapplied to go there. She had grades and test
scores off the charts. And she was a minority, which they

like to recruit. They'd said sure, we still want you, and here's full financing to boot.''

''What about you?'' Dana asked quietly.

''She said I could do what I liked. I could go with her or I could stay, but we both knew what that really meant. There was no job that I'd take in Boston. I couldn't live riding subways instead of horses, working inside a concrete box, breathing canned air. Fluorescent lights instead of the open sky? It wasn't possible. I asked her why she couldn't study in Denver or Boulder, someplace closer where maybe we could have held it together.''

''But she wanted her old dream back.''

''That's right. Like our years together had never happened. Just erase the nightmare and get back to reality— like that. So I told her fine, if that's what you want, go on. But I'm not waiting back here with my hat in my hand, hoping, for five years or eight years or however long she stayed away. I said I'd want a divorce.''

Dana nodded to herself. ''And how did she take that?''

Why the hell are we talking about this? He shifted angrily. ''She burst into tears. Not that the discussion had been exactly calm till then—our fights never were. We were both shouting and swearing, and poor Zoe was hiding in the bedroom. She hated it when we fought. Well, Pilar saw my ante and raised. She said fine, she'd take that divorce, but she wanted her daughter.''

''Oh,'' Dana said on a note of quiet pity.

''And I said I'd see her in hell first. I said there was no way she was getting Zoe, no way she could care for her properly if she did—not and be a full-time med student. And Pilar kept insisting that she *had* to have her daughter, that she'd work things out, she could put Zoe in day care. And I'm yelling that no child of mine is going to be raised by strangers, cooped up in some lousy city, when she could live in Colorado with her own pony and dog, free to ride a hundred miles in any direction. No way! I'd fight her for custody every inch of the way, and by God, I'd win. She could go if she wanted, but Zoe was staying.''

He was speaking in almost a shout, he realized, the old passions echoing down through the years, with the power still to stampede his heart and his breathing. He rolled down the window and leaned his head out into the icy slipstream till his lungs ached, then he rolled it up. *Let's drop this, can we?*

"And so?" Dana prodded. She'd removed a splinter from his palm a few weeks back with this same grave-faced determination.

"So she smashed a dish against the wall and screamed she hated me and out the door she flew. And I...never saw her again. Her car hit a bridge abutment out on the highway, not five miles from our trailer.''

"Oh, Rafe!'' Dana reached for his hand.

But to his mind, he deserved no comfort, wouldn't take it now. He pulled away. "I figure maybe she was crying so hard she didn't see it.'' He let out a long, slow breath between his teeth. "Or maybe...maybe she did.'' Pulling his hat down over his eyes, he slouched lower in the seat. "I need some sleep.''

She had to be careful her own tears didn't blind her. Dana wiped her lashes and drove on. *And now I know why you're so determined for Zoe to fly free and high. To live to her full potential. You're paying Zoe the debt you think you owe her mother.* Oh, yes, love was a two-faced coin.

"HE'LL BE HERE,'' Dana said the following day with passionate conviction, as they drove down a street in a San Diego suburb. "Oh, let him be here!''

If he wasn't, Dana was going to fall apart, Rafe realized, as he scanned the address of each bungalow they drove slowly past. She hadn't had a real sleep in—what?—two days now? This must be Sunday, he calculated, his mind sluggish with exhaustion.

"There it is!" Dana pointed at a bungalow no different from the rest, except that nobody had picked up the wind-blown trash. Bits of bright plastic and wadded paper were snagged in the rock garden that was its front yard. Crushed beer cans were tossed helter-skelter on the gravel.

He parked the car, then caught Dana's wrist as she tried to leap out. "I'll do this, Dana." From everything Kelton had told him, he figured Margot was a flake.

An absent flake, ten minutes of hard knocking proved. Rafe knocked so hard that finally the next-door neighbor popped his head over his bleached cedar fence. An older, white-haired man, with wire-rimmed glasses and a pinched mouth. "She's gone, as anybody could see," he snapped, and bobbed down again.

Rafe walked to the fence and looked over. Old Crabby was rearranging his own rock garden—potted cacti, a spade and a bag of soil set out beside him as he knelt in the gravel. "Know when she'll be back?"

The old man sat up on his heels. "You better believe I do! Same time she always comes home—two hours after every sane person on this block has gone to sleep. And now she's taken up with that biker trash? Last week the thug chained his Harley to my car's back bumper. When I complained to Margot, she laughed and said he was afraid somebody would rip him off. What about me, I said, who can't use his own car? If that isn't ripping—"

"Actually, we're looking for Margot Kershaw's son," Rafe broke in. He glanced aside, as Dana took his arm and leaned over the fence.

"He's only fifteen," she said, voice quivering. "Have you seen him?"

Mr. Crabby pushed his glasses up his nose and sniffed. "Young Sean? Well, of course, I have. He sat there like a stray pup on her front steps last night, till finally I came out and told him she wouldn't be home till long after midnight.''

"Where did he go then?'' Dana cried.

Mr. Crabby gave her a look of exasperated contempt. "Why, here, of course. He ate an entire pound of my hot dogs and all my potato chips, thanked me kindly, then went back to sitting on her steps. I guess she let him in when she came home at two. I always look at my clock when she wakes me.''

BUT AS TO WHERE Sean was now, Mr. Albert Hinkley wouldn't hazard a guess. Margot and her sleazy boyfriend had rumbled off a couple of hours ago in the company of several other bikers—all of them three sheets to the wind in her neighbor's humble opinion, though who asked him? But the old man insisted, with increasing indignation in the face of Dana's pleading to be sure, that they hadn't taken the boy along.

So perhaps the kid, still exhausted after 800 miles of hitching, was sacked out inside his mother's cottage. While Dana sat, near tears, in the truck, Rafe walked around the bungalow, peering through the curtainless windows. The place was a pigsty, but he saw no sign of Sean.

"Wait here?'' Dana said faintly, when he returned.

"Let's think this through,'' Rafe suggested. "If he was expecting any kind of warm welcome from his mother, doesn't sound like he got it. And there's not a lot of space for a guest in there.'' And how would the kid feel, sharing his mother with a drunken biker? Or the biker feel, sharing Margot with her son?

"And she didn't make time for him today,'' Dana murmured thoughtfully. "Went off with her friends, instead. Oh, Rafe—after he went to such trouble to get here. What he must be feeling!''

"Yes," Rafe agreed, taking her hand. "So he's blue and tired and nobody loves him, is how he sees it. Is there anybody else Sean might turn to, feeling that way? An old school buddy or—"

Dana let out a laugh that was halfway to a sob. "There's Margot's father!"

A retired plastic surgeon, living north of the city in San Clemente. Dana had never met him. Knew almost nothing about him, except that he'd divorced Margot's actress mother when Margot was five. Every year he sent Sean a birthday card with a handsome check, and another check for Christmas. Not once since she'd married into the family had he asked to visit his grandson. But it was her best guess.

Rafe consulted a map, and they drove.

THE SUN WAS SINKING into a blue, blue Pacific when finally they stood on the doorstep of a pink stucco, Spanish-style house that was two-thirds of the way to mansion, in a neighborhood where every second dwelling seemed to have a pool out back or a Mercedes coupe in the garage. A neighborhood where nobody tended his own lush garden, Rafe was sure.

"*Be* here," Dana murmured as she jabbed the doorbell.

A tall, lean, bald man in his late sixties opened the door and regarded them without enthusiasm. "If this is a solicitation, then please don't—"

"Dr. Swenson?" Dana cut in eagerly. "My name is Dana Kershaw…Montana. I'm—"

"Sean's stepmother!" Swenson warmed rapidly. "I've been trying to reach you all afternoon."

"He's here?" Dana cried, as he swung the door wide.

"Out back with my dachshund. Please come in."

THE TWO MEN STOOD at a picture window looking out over a flowery, terraced backyard. Sean sat on the grass at the far end, slump-shouldered, head drooping, rolling a tennis ball for a fat red dachshund, which waddled after it.

Dana came into view walking toward the boy, who didn't see her yet. "She wants him?" murmured the surgeon, eyes fixed on the scene.

"We both want him."

Sean's grandfather let out a long sigh and nodded. "Then that's a load off my mind. I've been sitting here telling myself that it's never too late to be a father. Since I botched it so badly with Margot—was too engrossed with my career to be there for her when she needed me—I told myself this would be my last chance to get it right. But frankly, Rafe, it's a young man's job."

"A job I want," Rafe said softly. "He's a good kid."

Dana had come to a halt some twenty feet behind the boy. The dachshund, trotting back with the ball, spotted her first, dropped his prize and barked. Sean turned, and Rafe watched his head jerk up in surprise.

Rafe didn't think Dana spoke as she closed the gap between them. When the two stood eye to eye, she hesitated for an endless, agonizing moment, then she reached out— and folded the boy into a fierce hug. Sean stood frozen, his face working, then slowly at first, then faster, his arms rose till he hugged Dana back.

They were still standing that way, arms locked around each other, foreheads touching, when Rafe and the doctor finally turned away. Dr. Swenson let out another long sigh, then gave Rafe a broad smile.

"Well…that seems to be settled. So come have a beer and tell me where he got those black eyes and why he ran."

"DO YOU KNOW what he said to me?" Dana murmured, waving as they drove away. Sean stood on the front porch under the arm of his grandfather, waving back with a tired, shy grin. "He said, 'You guys came all this way just for me?'"

Rafe caught her hand and squeezed. "And you said?"

"Oh, something about 'of course! Where do you think you belong, you silly goose, but with us? Will you please, please come home?'" She sighed contentedly and sagged against him, her head coming to rest on his shoulder. "So...thank you, Rafe, for finding him for me."

"For us." *If there is an us.* Tonight, with her head on his shoulder, they felt a couple, really married.

"You think we did right letting him stay?"

"Absolutely." Dr. Swenson had asked to keep Sean for a visit now that the boy was there. Had promised to fly Sean home in his private plane the following weekend. The way Sean's face had lit up at that, Rafe figured that was worth a month of makeup homework. "Sends the right message—that he's welcome home, not that we're dragging him home by his collar."

"And you don't think we have to worry about Margot?"

"Sean's no fool. I think he's learned his lesson there, for good and all." And Margot's father had privately promised Rafe that if Margot ever changed her mind again and decided she wanted her son back after all, he'd cut off her monthly allowance till she reconsidered.

"If all the therapy I'm paying for ever takes effect and she suddenly grows up, now that would be a different story," Swenson had added sternly. "But I'm afraid it's a little late for that."

In return, he'd asked that they allow Sean to visit him once or twice a year, and he would serve as the safe bridge to Margot, so that some sort of emotional connection between mother and son was maintained.

Swenson, seeing their exhaustion, had also offered to put Rafe and Dana up for as long as they liked, but Rafe had thanked him and asked for a recommendation to a nearby hotel, instead. A single room with his own wife beat a palace with company any day, to his mind. *Whether we share a bed or not.*

THE HOTEL WAS A LOW, Spanish-looking affair, built on craggy cliffs above the ocean. Would have made a nice spot for a honeymoon, Rafe found himself wistfully thinking. They took a room with a balcony overlooking the water. Rafe ordered sandwiches sent up, while Dana showered. Then he opened the sliding glass door and let the sound of the waves fill the room.

Then it was his turn for the bathroom, and when he came out, clean and shaved for the first time in days, he found Dana fast asleep under the covers of the bed nearest the balcony. He stood longing to join her. Imagining himself pulling her close and curving to fit her warm backside, kissing her nape, then sinking into delicious sleep, the sweetest of dreams, with his face buried in her fragrant hair.

But not without an invitation. Somehow the inviting was more important than the party. He sighed, pulled back the covers of the other bed, crawled in, fell asleep before his head hit the pillow.

SHE WOKE—somehow knowing it was near dawn—to the sound of waves combing up a beach. Dana stretched luxuriously and turned her head. Rafe was a long, dark, motionless shape on the other bed.

Shouldn't be over there when I'm here. They'd been so close these past few days. *Why are we apart?* At 4:00 a.m., she could find no logic to it. Trying to live her life avoiding pain—what kind of a life was that?

A rotten one if it kept her apart from Rafe Montana.

And if she'd thought to protect herself from pain, she could see now her resolution had been foolish, utterly useless. He hadn't needed her body to claim her heart. Rafe had it now, and there was no going back. She loved him—would love him always, whether she let him into her bed, or slept cold and lonely forever.

And in loving him, yes, she'd suffer heartache. When her man hurt, she'd hurt, too. If he ever left her, by choice or as Peter had gone, well, she might not survive it this time.

But still...*he's here now and so am I and I love him.* However much time she was granted, it wouldn't be enough, so why was she wasting it? The night was full of a rushing peace, the certainty of waves, time out of mind, caressing the shore. Dana slid her legs out of bed before she could second-guess herself, stood paralyzed with fear for a hundred heartbeats or more—then an especially large wave hit the sands with a shuddering roar.

She slipped back the covers and slid softly in beside her husband.

RAFE CAME HALF-AWAKE to the feel of kisses on his chin, his cheek, his shoulder. He'd dreamed this too many times. Grumbling, he turned away onto his side and relaxed again.

Soft and warm and deliciously damp, the invisible lips returned to kiss his nape...between his shoulder blades—he was suddenly wide-awake and hard as a rock. He sucked in a startled breath.

"Just me," she murmured at his back, and brushed her nose across his skin.

"Dana?" Couldn't be, he was dreaming.

"Who else?" she laughed in a husky whisper. "No—please don't answer that."

His body was revving like a tractor engine, testosterone raising his goose bumps and all else, his head not getting enough blood to comprehend just what had inspired this miracle. He didn't dare move. "Couldn't...um...sleep?"

She kissed his nape again—driving a ragged shudder

down his spine to curl his toes. "I just...wanted to thank you. For everything, Rafe. Not just these past few days with Sean, but...everything you've done for us...for me."

If he turned, she could reach other parts of him.

But he might scare her off. An agonizing dilemma, but bold paid off where timid went wanting. He turned, bending one knee up discreetly to tent the covers. His heart was racing. She kissed his shoulder, and he sucked in his breath, held it while her lips brushed delicately down the line of his jaw. "That's...all you wanted?" he asked casually—except his voice was shaking.

"No-o-o," she admitted in a sassy purr he'd never heard before.

It brought an incredulous smile to his lips. No dream. This was happening. *At last...*

She rose up on one elbow to lean down over him in the dusk, and found his nose. Kissed the tip of it. "I want *you.*"

The miracle was not his to question. Not right now, anyway. Rafe shifted around to face her and cupped the side of her warm face, thumbed her moist, smiling mouth and laughed shakily as he kissed it. "Mrs. Montana, you've had me since the first time I walked into your kitchen."

AFTER THEY'D LOVED, she fell asleep to his kisses—tiny skimming kisses covering every inch of her sweat-slick, quivering skin. She stretched and purred, and exhaustion sucked her down into a smiling dream. She woke only when Rafe entered her for the second, or was it the third, time? They didn't keep count here in Paradise.

He covered her like a hunk of sheltering sky, kissing her eyelids, her smile. Filling her to trembling ecstasy, he remained ruthlessly, rigidly, motionless, pinning her hips to the bed as wave after wave rumbled up the shore, till she was shuddering with need, begging for release, fighting his control.

Then he moved one inch deeper and the universe shattered, and she could hold it inside no longer. "I love you!" she panted—cried it again as his mouth came down over hers—*I love you*—in a moan that he swallowed with a victorious growl. He moved faster, harder, deeper, and she wrapped herself around him and wept it. *"I love you!"*

WHEN HE HAD TAKEN IT ALL—everything she had to give— every emotion, every last arch and thrust and heart-slamming convulsion, Rafe lay atop her, his weight on his elbows, his big hands framing her face, heart speaking softly to heart. He kissed her eyelashes, the tip of her nose. She smiled blindly.

"Did you mean that?" he whispered above her. "Really mean it, or was that just—"

She reached up and put a hand over his mouth. Looked deep into his eyes. "Truly." Forever and ever.

Within and without her, she felt his satisfied sigh, and he nodded.

Do I get to hear it back? Though somehow she knew it already. What he'd shown her tonight, what he'd been showing her all along if her fear hadn't blinded her, was all about loving. He was a man of deeds more than words.

"Then I reckon that means I can renegotiate a few terms of this bargain," he said with rich satisfaction.

She arched her back and stretched—then smiled, as he gasped and his hands tightened on her. "Marriage in name only? I'm afraid we've already broken contract on that one," she said.

"I was talking about that five-year clause. *No* divorce, Mrs. Montana. Not in five years. Not in fifty."

She brushed a hand up through his thick hair, then cupped his cheek and said with solemn mockery, though the tears trembled on her lashes, "Oh-h-h, I think I can live with that."

THEY STAYED THERE for two days, leaving their room only to walk hand in hand on the beach, speaking only to Zoe and Mrs. Higgins by phone and to the smirking bellboys who dropped the breakfast, lunch and supper trays off at their door. Finally, on the third morning, while Dana was scrubbing Rafe's back in the shower, she said, "It's time to go home. And why don't we pick up Zoe on our way?"

CHAPTER TWENTY-FOUR

ZOE GAVE BIRTH on the twelfth of December, three days after she turned seventeen. For a first delivery via natural childbirth, it went better than most. Dr. Cass Hancock expressed the opinion that horsewomen were tougher and more flexible than their city sisters.

At the height of the pain, the mother did express some rather heated opinions about the young father, who'd gotten all the fun and none of the work...her know-it-all stepmother, whom she'd chosen to assist her in this birthing...and her own shamefully neglectful father, who really should have warned her about boys—or at least locked her away till she turned twenty-one. Also lambasted was the physicist Stephen Hawkings, who, now that Zoe thought about it, didn't know piffle about the nature of time. *"Try childbirth, Stevo, then come back and tell me!"*

But all was tearfully, laughingly, totally forgiven and forgotten when eight-pound Peter Raphael Montana finally made his debut nine hours after the first real contraction. Zoe shut up and stared with rapturous wonder at the squalling baby they'd placed on her freckled stomach. She ran a timid fingertip over his downy, dark skull, smiled broadly—then burst into tears. Looked up at Dana and cried piteously, "But what am I going to *do?*"

"Sleep on it, sweetie," Dana advised, and kissed her cheek. "Sleep and then think."

IN SPITE OF ALL RAFE'S protests and tirades, Zoe demanded that she be allowed to nurse her son on the first night of his birth, and Dr. Hancock backed her up. She was nursing him again the next morning, when Sean tapped on her door and came in alone.

"Hi." He kissed her cheek, inhaling the scent that to him would always be Zoe. Then he stroked his son's head, sat staring at him spellbound for several minutes. Drawing a deep breath, he said, "Mind if I take a family portrait?" He'd left his Nikon and tripod out in the hall.

Her blue eyes glistened, though she smiled. "Family, Sean?"

"Whatever you decide, yeah. We were—are—a family." He hadn't meant to sound so fierce. He patted her hand, and when finally she nodded, he went for his gear, began setting up his tripod at the foot of the bed.

"Remember how we started all this?" she said softly behind him. "You were doing me a favor…just a bit of friendly, scientific inquiry into human sexuality. Helping me smooth out the rough spots before I went off to college. You can't take this so hard, Sean. It was just an accident."

"Penicillin was an accidental discovery, wasn't it?" he said gruffly, and wiped his nose.

"Yeah, it was. And maybe we've made something even better. But Sean Diego?—you've got to promise me one thing."

"I don't have to promise you anything, Red." He fixed the camera to the tripod, hooked up the shutter cord, wiped his eyes and turned.

"But would you?" she coaxed. "If you love me, would you promise?"

"You know I do." His eyes wouldn't stop. He dropped down on his knees beside her and buried his face against her arm. "You know how I feel!"

She ruffled a hand through his hair, back and forth, back and forth. "Then *promise* me you'll get over me. Get on with your life. I'd just die, Sean—really die—if I thought my stupid experiment messed you up. Don't you *dare* do that to me. You're my best friend in all the world.''

''I don't *want* to get over—'' She smacked the back of his head, and he shut up, groped for her hand and kissed it.

Zoe pulled gently away and ruffled his hair again. ''You know what Lisa Harding told me last week?'' she murmured after a while. ''She said she saw you and Karen Peabody sitting together in the library, laughing like a couple of hounds.''

''Lisa's a lying, nosy, run-off-at-the-mouth little—'' He winced as she smacked him again, then he lifted his head and snarled at her. ''Hey! Cut that out!''

Zoe's grin was wide and triumphant. ''So it's true!''

He shrugged sullenly. ''She likes me, I couldn't care less about her.''

''So try harder, best friend.'' Her eyes filled again. ''You *better* be happy, Sean Kershaw, or I'll never, ever forgive you.'' She jerked her chin at the camera. ''So are we going to do this or what?''

THEY'D COLLECTED their mail on their way into town, and now Dana sat reading it while Rafe paced up and down the waiting room. ''By God, Dana, if this falls apart now!''

She glanced up from her letter and smiled. Touched his hand, as he stomped past her. ''Then we'll love her anyway, and we'll work it out.''

He swore and paced on, and after a few minutes she folded her letter and tucked it back into its envelope with the colorful foreign stamps. ''Cat got word from the institute, and it's exactly as she predicted, given Zoe's grades. As long as we pay her way, they'd be delighted to take her through the summer.''

Catherine Danner, a fellow schoolteacher who'd worked

with Dana in the Peace Corps, was now a biology instructor on the tall ship *Peregrine,* an education and research vessel for the Winslow Institute of Oceanographic Studies. The ship carried a crew of some thirty college students and instructors on voyages around the world. For the next few months they'd be stationed in the Caribbean, while they did a census of humpback whales. Then they'd head on through the Panama Canal for the South Pacific.

Rafe had insisted that if Zoe was to relinquish her baby, she couldn't be near little Peter for the first year. And quite probably he was right. Send her to Cat, had been his wife's suggestion. Distract her with a lifetime adventure under the nurturing wing of a warm, wise woman before Zoe went on to Harvard in the fall.

"Great. Good. That's in place, anyway." Rafe stopped, thumbs hooked over his belt, frowning back at her. "Now all we have to do is sell her on the idea. You shouldn't have let her nurse."

"Not my choice to make, love." Setting her papers aside, Dana stood and went to her husband; she slid her hands around his lean waist to lock them behind his back.

Rafe resisted her embrace, then, glancing toward the doorway, which remained empty, gradually relaxed. He dropped his head, to rest his chin on top of her hair. Let out a long, deep sigh. "I know," he muttered. "But still…"

"Just remember, whatever happens, I love you. We love her. We'll work it out."

RAFE KNOCKED ON THE DOORJAMB, then pushed through the half-open door to find Zoe, sitting up in bed, cradling her son. She glanced up at him, and her smile faded. The baby let out a startled grunt as her arms tightened around it.

"How's he doing?" Rafe asked, hating that hunted expression in her eyes. He sat down beside her on the edge of the bed.

"He's doing everything perfectly. He's…he's perfection, Daddy. Look at his fingernails! And his eyes."

The baby blinked in Rafe's direction, then yawned hugely with an admirable tongue. Rafe laughed and held out his hands. Zoe bit her lip, then handed him over— giggled tearfully when her father cradled the baby on one forearm and offered a fingertip, which was immediately clutched in a tiny red fist. "Hi there, stranger." He didn't resemble Zoe at that age, though Sean insisted he did. Rafe thought possibly he looked like Sean; Dana had been reminded of the baby's namesake, Peter Kershaw. *You're your own self entire, hotshot, but you'll learn to love horses if I get any say in the matter.*

Peter Raphael yawned mightily again, looking like nothing so much as a wrinkled pink bullfrog, and fell fast asleep. They admired him in silence awhile, both of them scared to speak, till finally Rafe said, "So what do you figure?" He looked up in time to see the first teardrop fall, then too many more. *Damn it. Do I ever get to stop hurting the people I love?* "What do you want, sweetheart?" He reached with his free hand to wipe a tear off her freckly nose.

"I don't *know,* Daddy, I don't, I don't, I just—" She shrugged helplessly and the tears dripped faster. "He's *so* beautiful, but…"

That one little word gave him the courage to go on. "You used to trust me once upon a time," he reminded her. "I realize a lot has changed…but I'm still the man you used to listen to. Want to hear what I think?"

She sniffed, reached for some tissues on the bedside table, held them to her nose, then nodded over them. "Uh-huh."

He met her woeful eyes, then gazed down at her son,

nestled in his arm. "I think you did the right thing at the wrong time, baby. I know I did, and I've never regretted you—not for one single, solitary moment. But it was *hard,* sweetheart, so hard." Harder than he could ever make her understand, he feared. "I'd like life to be easier for you. Easier for this little guy, too."

"But it *hurts!*" She grabbed the whole box of tissues and hauled it into her lap.

"I know, I know, sweetheart, I know it does. But think, when was the last time it hurt this bad?"

She considered, balling a tissue in her fist. "You mean...yesterday?"

Nodding, he smoothed a palm over the baby's velvety, fragile skull. "Pain's about gone now, though, isn't it? And see what you've got to show for it."

"It's not the same!"

"No? Then what about when we wean the foals? You'd swear their hearts would break, theirs and their mamas, when we move them apart." His tenderhearted daughter practically lived in the weanlings' pen, consoling the frantic babies for the first few days. "But within a week or two, you know how it always is. The colts are off in their own herd, romping and kicking up their heels together, having the time of their lives. The mares are off grazing, not a worry in the world."

"You think it'd be that easy?" she whispered bitterly.

No lies between us. He shook his head. "I think it'd be the toughest thing you've done yet in your life. But I think it's the right thing."

"I don't *know!*" she wailed, then held out her arms. "Give him to me!" Hugging the baby to her breast, she covered his fuzzy head with kisses.

Rafe wished desperately that he could call Dana for help, but she'd steadfastly insisted she had to stay out of this.

Cheek pressed to her baby's head, Zoe stared off into

time and space. "If I...gave Peter to you and Dana—I'm *not* saying I will—but...if I did...what would you tell him about me?"

Rafe felt the first faint stirring of hope. "How 'bout the truth? That you're his mama, and you loved him more than life itself, but you were too young to do right by him. So you chose the very best parents for him you could find."

"And when I come home to visit?"

"He'll know you're his mama and that we're his grandparents, Rafe and Dana, who love you both."

She sniffed and knuckled her nose. "You really... think...it would work?"

"I know it would. Peter would have more folks who love him than most kids, that's all."

Letting out a long, shivering sigh, she looked down at her son. "I just don't *know*."

Rafe stroked her baby's hot cheek, her damp one, then rose. "Don't reckon deciding will get any easier the longer you wait." Zoe closed her eyes and bobbed her head in agreement.

"And there's one thing more you need to think about while you're deciding," he said finally, dreading it. "One thing you have to promise me if we do this, and that's that you won't go back on your decision, Zoe, later on. Once you've given him to us, Peter stays with us. I won't have you breaking Dana's heart someday or taking your son from the only home he's ever known. This is a once-and-for-all decision. Understand?"

"Yeah," she murmured bleakly. "Sure, I do. I understand."

There wasn't much more to say. *Time to pray.* "Want to think some more?"

Zoe shook her head emphatically. "No. I've decided."

THEIR PLANE WAS LATE touching down on the Caribbean island of Martinique. *Peregrine* was scheduled to sail at three o'clock, and Rafe feared they'd miss it.

"Maybe it's fate," said Zoe, half hopeful, half dismayed, while she sat tensely beside him in the back of the cab that raced past cane fields, then shantytowns, then stone city streets, toward the harbor at Fort de France. But for the first time in six grim weeks, her eyes were alive with interest— taking in the vivid tropical flowers, the lush jungly greens, the laughing people in every shade from ebony to coffee- with-cream. The cab came to a screeching halt at the base of the stone quay, and she let out an audible gasp. "That's *her?*"

At the end of the pier, two masts raked the sky above a long, low white hull. Rafe realized the ship's scale when he noticed the tiny figures up in the rigging. "I reckon so." Definitely the school ship—a steel brigantine of 135 feet. He'd been studying boats this winter for his own peace of mind.

"Hurry!" Zoe shoved her door open, grabbed her back- pack and camera and slipped out—to stand jittering beside the cab.

Rafe smiled as he paid the driver. For six long weeks he'd worried that he might be doing the wrong thing. Won- dered if he was breaking her heart for all the wrong reasons. Six weeks while he'd lived alone with his daughter at Sun- top, making sure she'd recovered in body, if not entirely in spirit. While Dana had cared for young Peter at the Ribbon R with the full-time help of Mrs. Higgins. A cold and bit- terly lonely and doubt-filled winter for them all. But now...maybe...

"Daddy, look!" Zoe pointed overhead. Far up in the impossibly blue tropic sky soared an enormous bird like none Rafe had ever seen. Pure white, trailing a long, grace- ful scissor tail. "And—*oh*—there! Could it be Mont Pe- lée?"

Far off beyond the old colonial town, their bases shrouded by clouds, reared razor-toothed mountains—one of them a volcano, he'd been told.

Hoisting her duffel bag to his shoulder, he walked beside her. She moved like the old Zoe he feared he'd lost forever—long, jaunty strides, at almost a run. She seemed as taken as he was by the fantastic colors, the strange smells of bananas and seaweed and flowers and fish and diesel fuel. *Peregrine*'s engine was already idling, he realized, hearing its muffled vibrations as they neared. People—kids of both sexes, and adults—bustled around its decks or bounded up the shrouds into the rigging.

"She's so big!" Zoe muttered. "I never thought..."

He dropped his free hand on her shoulder and bent his mouth to her ear. "Remember, sweetheart, I want you to give it a try for a month. Then, if for any reason you can't stomach it, call us from wherever you are, and we'll send you a ticket home. Or if you want, I'll come get you."

"Okay, Daddy," she agreed absently, her head tipped back as her gaze followed a young man moving along the foremast yard, some sixty feet above deck.

Glancing down at them, the sailor must have caught her eye, because he grinned and waved. Zoe smiled shyly and lifted a hand. Rafe narrowed his eyes at the kid in warning—and was blithely ignored. *That's one lesson she's already learned,* he told himself, crossing his fingers.

"Zoe?" called a woman hurrying down the gangplank. A honey-blonde matching Dana's description of her friend Catherine Danner. "Zoe Montana? You are? Thank heavens—we're about to sail! Come on board. And you must be Rafe—Dana's husband." Her handshake was firm as a man's; her green eyes, kind and ruefully laughing. "I meant to invite you aboard for a tour of the ship and to see Zoe's cabin, but as you can see, we're sailing, so..."

Two tanned and T-shirted young men bounded down to

the quay to untie the ends of the gangway, then stood waiting—and eyeing his daughter. *She's grown, she's grown,* Rafe reminded himself. "Well..." He shrugged. Maybe it was better this way. He hated goodbyes. "Then good to meet you, Cat, and take care of her for me. For us."

"You bet I will!" She lifted the strap of Zoe's duffel bag off his shoulder and onto her own. Gave him a warm, wide smile. "She'll be fine, Rafe, I promise you." Cat turned and walked up the gangway, then hopped down to the deck.

"Well, Zoe?"

And then she was in his arms, tears streaming, mouth tremulous and widely smiling. Hugging him so hard he thought she'd crack a rib.

"Bye, Daddy! Tell Dana thank you for—for everything. And...and kiss my baby for me?"

"Every night!" he promised huskily, his throat aching. "And remember—"

"Hey, Montana, come aboard!" bellowed a bearded man of Rafe's own age, hooking a thumb toward the deck.

"G'bye!" One last kiss on his cheek, and she was running lightly up the gangplank. Hands were casting off the dock lines, then jumping aboard. Rafe watched the gap between ship and shore gradually widen from one he could have leaped...to one he couldn't. Watching Zoe's pale, freckled face...her wide, tearful, shining blue eyes... growing smaller, ever smaller, below her frantic wave—till she was a tiny, gawky, frantically waving figure topped with a patch of fire-engine red.

In the outer harbor, a quarter-mile out, the boat seemed to pause. To raise sails, Rafe realized. Great wings of white, rising and opening one after another from the stern toward the bow. Then the two yards on the foremast rising—clouds of billowing white spreading slowly to the warm trade-winds. Wings to carry her off to sea, right over the edge of the curving world. He stared, almost grudging to blink, as the ship gathered way and moved off. Soaring on and on and on...

"Fly away, Zoe," he whispered. "Fly..." He blinked once more—and she was gone.

He stood for a moment more, squinting against the hard, hard tropic blue—then let out a long, deep breath and turned for shore.

Back toward the plane that would take him home. To a woman who waited. A family that needed him. *Some fly free, some fly home to the nest.* And that was another kind of freedom.

A smile crossed Rafe's face. His steps lengthened, then lengthened again—till he was as close to running as a grown man could justify.

Your Romantic Books—find them at

www.eHarlequin.com

Visit the *Author's Alcove*

➤ Find the most complete information anywhere on your favorite author.

➤ Try your hand in the Writing Round Robin—contribute a chapter to an online book in the making.

Enter the *Reading Room*

➤ Experience an interactive novel—help determine the fate of a story being created now by one of your favorite authors.

➤ Join one of our reading groups and discuss your favorite book.

Drop into *Shop eHarlequin*

➤ Find the latest releases—read an excerpt or write a review for this month's Harlequin top sellers.

➤ Try out our amazing search feature—tell us your favorite theme, setting or time period and we'll find a book that's perfect for you.

All this and more available at

www.eHarlequin.com
on Women.com Networks

Daddy's little girl... **THAT'S MY BABY!** by

Vicki Lewis Thompson

Nat Grady is finally home—older and wiser. When the woman he'd loved had hinted at commitment, Nat had run far and fast. But now he knows he can't live without her. But Jessica's nowhere to be found.

Jessica Franklin is living a nightmare. She'd thought things were rough when the man she loved ran out on her, leaving her to give birth to their child alone. But when she realizes she has a stalker on her trail, she has to run—and the only man who can help her is Nat Grady.

THAT'S MY BABY!

On sale September 2000 at your favorite retail outlet.

HARLEQUIN®
Makes any time special ™

HARLEQUIN

SUPERROMANCE®

You are now entering

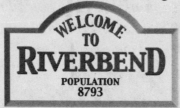

WELCOME TO
RIVERBEND
POPULATION
8793

Riverbend...the kind of place where everyone knows your name—and your business. Riverbend...home of the River Rats—a group of small-town sons and daughters who've been friends since high school.

The Rats are all grown up now. Living their lives and learning that some days are good and some days aren't—and that you can get through anything as long as you have your friends.

Starting in July 2000, Harlequin Superromance brings you Riverbend—six books about the River Rats and the Midwest town they live in.

BIRTHRIGHT by **Judith Arnold** (July 2000)
THAT SUMMER THING by **Pamela Bauer** (August 2000)
HOMECOMING by **Laura Abbot** (September 2000)
LAST-MINUTE MARRIAGE by **Marisa Carroll** (October 2000)
A CHRISTMAS LEGACY by **Kathryn Shay** (November 2000)

Available wherever Harlequin books are sold.

HARLEQUIN®
Makes any time special ™

Visit us at www.eHarlequin.com

HSRIVER

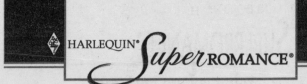

HARLEQUIN
Duets™

Pick up a Harlequin Duets™
from August–October 2000
and receive $1.00 off the
original cover price. *

Experience the "lighter side of love"
in a Harlequin Duets™.
This unbeatable value just became
irresistible with our special introductory
price of $4.99 U.S./$5.99 CAN. for
2 Brand-New, Full-Length
Romantic Comedies.

HARLEQUIN

SUPERROMANCE

COMING NEXT MONTH